JILL WILLIAMSON

BY DARKNESS HID

BLOOD OF KINGS BOOK I

MARCHER LORD PRESS

By Darkness Hid by Jill Williamson
Published by Marcher Lord Press
8345 Pepperridge Drive
Colorado Springs, CO 80920
www.marcherlordpress.com

Cover Designer: Kirk DouPonce, Dog-Eared Design, www.dogeareddesign.com
Cover Photo By: Kirk DouPonce
Creative Team: Jeff Gerke, Kristine Pratt

Library of Congress Cataloging-in-Publication Data
An application to register this book for cataloging has been filed with the Library of Congress.
International Standard Book Number: 978-0-9821049-5-8

Errata corrections: 6/30/10

To my sweet husband, Brad,
for all his patience, love, and support.

To my parents, Jule and Marlene Peterson,
who told me so many wonderful stories.

And to Pastor Joe Torosian, for encouraging a newbie writer.
The time for my power to eclipse yours has come.
I am the master.

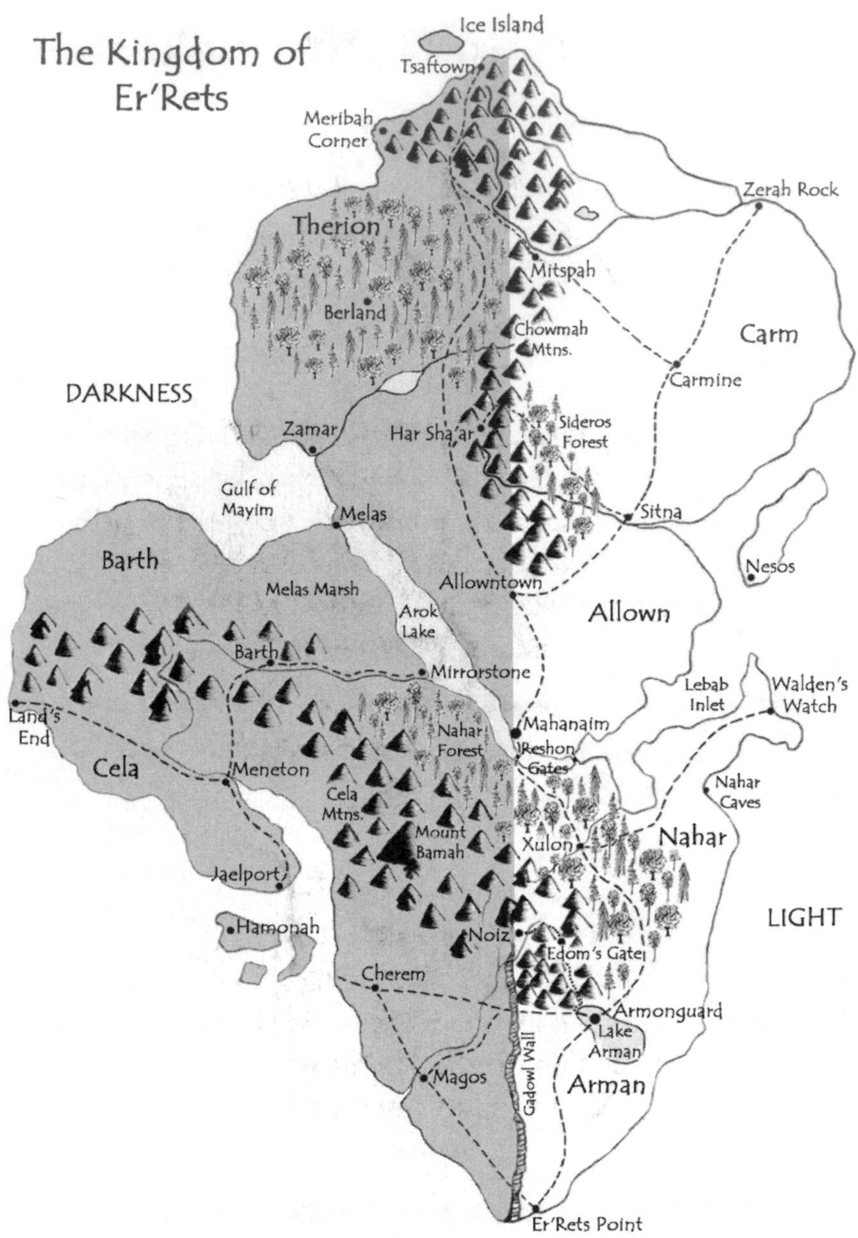
The Kingdom of Er'Rets
Ice Island
Tsaftown
Meribah Corner
Zerah Rock
Therion
Mitspah
Berland
Chowmah Mtns.
Carm
Carmine
DARKNESS
Zamar
Har Sha'ar
Sideros Forest
Gulf of Mayim
Melas
Sitna
Barth
Nesos
Melas Marsh
Allowntown
Allown
Arok Lake
Barth
Mirrorstone
Lebab Inlet
Walden's Watch
Land's End
Mahanaim
Nahar Forest
Reshon Gates
Cela
Meneton
Nahar Caves
Cela Mtns.
Mount Bamah
Xulon
Nahar
Jaelport
LIGHT
Hamonah
Noiz
Edom's Gate
Cherem
Armonguard
Lake Arman
Gadowl Wall
Magos
Arman
Er'Rets Point

Advance Praise for *By Darkness Hid*

"This thoroughly entertaining and smart tale will appeal to fans of Donita K. Paul and J.R.R. Tolkien. Highly recommended for CF and fantasy collections."

Library Journal

"I love a good fantasy, and *By Darkness Hid* more than fills the bill. With an unpredictable plot, twists of supernatural ability, and finely crafted tension between the forces of good and evil, Jill Williamson's book had me captivated. I jumped into the skin of the heroine and enjoyed her journey as if it were my own."

Donita K. Paul, author of the Dragon Keeper Chronicles: *DragonSpell, DragonQuest, DragonKnight, DragonFire,* and *DragonLight*

"Jill Williamson is a major arrival. She presents characters full of mystery and leaves room for plenty of further exploration. *By Darkness Hid* is a fast-paced addition to the world of swords and sorcery, using a backdrop of political and spiritual intrigue to heighten the tension. When readers begin lining up for the sequel, you'll find me at the front of the line."

Eric Wilson, author of *Field of Blood* and *Haunt of Jackals*

"*By Darkness Hid* is a compelling debut fantasy novel that beautifully illustrates the battle between good and evil. For someone who is not normally a fantasy reader, this story not only kept me riveted to the pages but anxious about the outcome as well. Ms. Williamson really knows how to keep a reader's attention by putting her characters into impossible situations. I am anxiously awaiting the next installment in this series."

Michelle Sutton, author of the YA novel, *It's Not About Me,*
Editor-in-Chief of *Christian Fiction Online Magazine*

"Wow . . . what a great start! Author Jill Williamson pulls the reader into this saga so completely that waiting for the rest of the series to be published will be agony indeed. Witty. Snappy. Humorous. *By Darkness Hid* is definitely a jewel in the crown of Marcher Lord Press. Be sure to pick up this title for a great read."

Michelle Griep, author of *Gallimore*

"Reminiscent of Shakespeare's romantic method of hiding his heroine in the guise of a man, Jill Williamson has taken her fantasy, *By Darkness Hid*, and filled it with twists and turns. Both hero and heroine are characters that will remain in my heart for a long time. Having swordplay, mental powers, romance, and a thrilling new take on the term 'royal blood,' I completely enjoyed this book."

M. C. Pearson, Director of FIRST (Fiction in Rather Short Takes), Wild Card Tours Blog Alliance

"I just may have a new favorite fantasy series. *By Darkness Hid* is captivating and unpredictable, with numerous well-foreshadowed twists. This is my kind of story. For those who are drawn to epic fantasy or classic fantasy, this is a must-read. For everyone else, I highly recommend *By Darkness Hid*."

Rebecca LuElla Miller, Administrator,
Christian Science Fiction and Fantasy Blog Tour

"*By Darkness Hid* had me arguing with my mom as I wanted to stay up all night to read it. Now anytime I think about knights, Jill's book comes to mind. I enjoyed reading it so much, and I cannot wait to read the next one!"

Keegan Pearson, age 13

"No! That can't be it! You'd better make a sequel. I was so into it. I loved it all! I didn't think you could just end it right there. Please write more! This was a great read."

Querida, age 16

"*By Darkness Hid* is not fine—it's great! I loved it. And not once did it bore me. It's full of adventure and romance, with unique characters you sympathize for. It makes you wish you could go back in time and live through a culture full of danger and mysteries. I just wanted to keep reading more and more."

Cosette Luque, age 17

"An imaginative fantasy—different from everything you've read before. You'll cheer for strong, independent Vrell and wince each time poor Achan is mistreated and misunderstood. I'm anxiously awaiting the next installment!"

Debbie Maxwell Allen

PART I

ACHAN

I

Achan stumbled through the darkness toward the barn. The morning cold sent shivers through his threadbare orange tunic. He clutched a wooden milking pail at his side and held a flickering torch in front to light his way.

He wove between dark cottages in the outer bailey of the castle, mindful to keep his torch clear of the thatched roofs. Most of the residents of Sitna still slept. Only a few of the twenty-some peasants, slaves, and strays serving Lord Nathak and Prince Gidon stirred at this hour.

Sitna Manor sat on the north side of the Sideros River. A brownstone curtain wall, four levels high, enclosed the stronghold. A second wall sectioned off the outer bailey from the inner bailey, temple, and keep. Achan wasn't allowed to enter the inner bailey but occasionally snuck inside when he felt compelled to leave an offering at Cetheria's temple.

The barn loomed ahead of him in the darkness. It was one of the largest structures in Sitna Manor. It was long and narrow, with a high, thatched gable roof. Achan shifted the pail to his torch hand and tugged the heavy door open. It scraped over the frosty dirt. He darted inside and pulled it closed.

The scent of hay and manure drifted on the chilled air. He walked to the center and slid the torch into an iron ring on a load-bearing post. The timber walls stymied the bitter wind, and Achan's shivering lessened.

The torch cast a golden glow over the hay pile, posts, and rafters and made Achan's orange tunic look brown. A long path stretched the length of the barn with stalls on each side penning chickens, geese, pigs, and goats. Two empty stalls in the center housed hay and feed. He approached the goat stall.

"Morning, Dilly, Peg. How are my girls? Got lots of milk for me?"

The goats bleated their greetings. Achan rubbed his hands together until they were warm enough to avoid getting him kicked. He perched on the icy stool to milk Dilly and begin his tedious routine. He could have worse jobs, though, and he liked the goats.

By the time Achan had finished with Dilly, the stool under his backside had thawed, though his breath still clouded in the torch's dull glow. He lifted the pail to get a better look. Dilly had filled it a third. Achan set it between his feet, slapped Dilly on the rear, and called Peg. When he had finished milking her he moved his stool outside and set the pail on top of it. He grabbed a pitchfork off the wall.

"Anyone hungry?"

Dilly and Peg danced around as Achan dumped fresh hay into the trough. The goats' excitement faded to munching. The other animals stirred, but they were not his responsibility. Mox, the scrawny barn boy, had arrived a few minutes ago and now shuffled from stall to stall at the other end of the barn.

As Achan leaned the pitchfork against the wall, he had to pause. A chill ran through him that had nothing to do with the temperature. He felt the familiar pressure in his head. It wasn't painful, but it brought a sense of a looming, sinister shadow. Someone was coming.

"Lo, Mox!" a familiar voice called from near the barn's entrance.

"Moxy poxy hoggy face, we know you're in here."

Achan sucked in an icy breath and slid back into the goat stall. The voices belonged to Riga Hoff and Harnu Poe, Sitna Manor's resident browbeaters.

Mox's young voice cried out. "Stop it! Don't do that! Ow!"

Achan set his jaw and thunked his head against the wall of the stall, earning a reprimanding look from Dilly. Poril would flay him if he returned late. And there was no guarantee he could beat both boys. He should mind his own business. Regular beatings had made him tough—they could do likewise for Mox.

Or they could cripple him for life. An image flooded his mind: a young slave being dragged through the linen field by Riga and Harnu. They'd crushed his hands so badly that all the boy could do now was pull a cart like a mule. Achan sighed.

He edged to the other end of the barn, stepping softly over the scattered hay. Two piglets scurried past his feet. He clenched his jaw. If the animals got out, Mox would be punished by his master too. Riga and Harnu knew that, of course.

Achan spotted them in a pig stall at the end of the barn. Harnu was holding Mox's face in a trough of slop. The mere thought of the smell turned Achan's empty stomach. Riga leaned over Harnu's shoulder laughing, his ample rear blocking the stall's entrance. Fine linen stretched over Riga's girth and rode up his back in wrinkles, baring more skin than Achan cared to see.

He sent a quick prayer up to the gods and cleared his throat. "Can I help you boys with something?"

Riga spun around, his mess of short, golden curls sticking out in all directions. His face was so pudgy Achan could never tell if his eyes were open or closed. "Stay out of this, dog!"

Harnu released Mox and pushed past Riga out of the stall. The torch's beam illuminated his pockmarked face, a hazard from working too close to the forge. "Moxy poxy piglet got out of his pen. He needs to learn his place." Harnu stood a foot taller than Riga and was the real threat in the barn. He stepped toward Achan. "Looks like you need to learn yours too."

Achan held his ground. "Let him go."

Harnu's gaze flitted to a pitchfork propped against the wall. He grabbed it and swung. Achan jumped back, but the tines snagged his tunic, ripping a hole in the front and scratching his stomach. Achan squeezed his fists and blew out a long breath.

Harnu jabbed the pitchfork forward. Achan lunged to the side and grabbed the shaft. He wrenched the weapon away and spun it around, prongs facing Harnu. He waved it slightly back and forth, hoping to scare the brute into flight.

"The barn is off limits to your instruction. Anything else I can do for you boys? A little hay? Some oats, perhaps? Drag you to the moat, tie a millstone to your ankles, see how well you swim?"

Like a dog being teased with a bone, Harnu lunged.

Achan stepped back and raised the pitchfork above his head the way he'd seen knights do in the longsword tournaments. With nothing to stop his hurtling bulk, Harnu stumbled. Achan swung the tines flat against Harnu's backside, and the bully knocked head first into the chicken pen. The birds squawked and fluttered, sending a cloud of dust over Harnu.

Riga slipped past the stall and made toward the milk pail. Achan darted forward and stuck the pitchfork in the clay earth to snag Riga's foot. The big louse tripped and sprawled into the dirt and hay.

Footsteps behind Achan sent him wheeling around just in time to lift the pitchfork to Harnu's chest. Over Harnu's shoulder, Achan could see Mox climbing out of the geese pen with a squirming piglet under one arm.

Harnu raised his hands and stepped back, a thin scratch swelling across his reddened cheek. "Lord Nathak will hear 'bout this, stray. You'll hang."

Achan knew he wouldn't hang for a tussle like this, but he might be whipped. And Lord Nathak's guards were merciless. But Achan doubted Lord Nathak's servants would bother their master with such a trivial matter. He shrugged. "Not much to tell. You fell into the chicken pen."

"You attacked me with a pitchfork when I caught you trying to steal a horse."

A tremor snaked down Achan's arms. Stealing a horse was cause for a hanging. And no one—especially Lord Nathak—would take the word of a stray over a peasant, even one like Harnu. Achan jabbed the pitchfork out. "If Lord Nathak hears a breath of that tripe, I know where you lay your head."

Harnu snorted and beat his chest with a clenched fist. "You dare threaten me?"

Achan glanced around for Riga, but the swine had vanished. He backed toward the hay pile, feeling cornered. Achan took another step back, keeping the pitchfork aimed at Harnu. His boot knocked against something.

Harnu cackled and pointed behind Achan's feet. Achan looked down. The stool and pail lay on their sides, milk seeping into the clay soil.

Pig snout!

Riga charged out of the hay stall with a roar. Achan turned, but Riga jerked the pitchfork away. Harnu rushed forward and battered Achan to the ground.

The pitchfork dug into Achan's back. He gritted his teeth, not wanting to give the brutes the satisfaction of hearing him scream. He was more upset over the spilled milk than the pain.

Pain, he was used to.

Mox pointed at Achan from the end of the barn, his face gooey with slop. "Ha ha!"

The ungrateful scab was on his own next time.

Dilly and Peg kicked against the wall of their stall, agitated by Achan's distress.

Harnu crouched in front of him, grabbed the back of his head, and pushed his face toward the puddle seeping into the dirt floor. "Lick it up, dog!"

Achan thrashed in the hay but lost his battle with Harnu's hand. He turned his head just as his cheek splashed into the milky muck. The liquid steamed around his face. Harnu released Achan's head and sat back on his haunches, his wide lips twisting in a triumphant sneer.

Riga chortled, a dopey sound. "I'd like a new rug, Harnu. What say we skin the stray?" He dragged the pitchfork down Achan's back.

They never learned.

Achan pushed up with his arms. The prongs dug deeper, but he was able to slide his right arm and leg underneath his body and twist free. He grabbed the handle of the pail and swung it at Harnu's face. Harnu fell onto his backside, clutching his nose.

Achan scrambled to his feet. He grabbed another pitchfork off the wall and squared off with Riga.

The portly boy waddled nearer and lifted his weapon. Achan faked an upswing.

When Riga heaved the pitchfork up to block, Achan swung the shaft of his weapon into Riga's leg.

The boy went down like a slaughtered pig.

Harnu approached, pinching his nose with one hand and wiping a fistful of hay across his upper lip with the other.

"This does grow old," Achan said. "How many times do I have to trounce you both?"

"I'm telling Lord Nathak." Harnu sounded like he had a cold.

"You've no right to attack us," Riga mumbled from the dirt floor.

Achan wanted to argue, *And what of Mox?* but he'd sacrificed enough for that thankless whelp. He grabbed both pitchforks and fled from the barn.

Pale dawn light blanketed Sitna Manor. Achan jogged toward the drawbridge, glancing at the sentry walk of the outer gatehouse. The squared parapet was black against the grey sky. A lone guard stood on the wall above like a shadow.

Achan ran through the gate and over the drawbridge. As usual, the guards ignored him. Few people in the manor acknowledged anyone wearing an orange tunic. One small advantage of being a stray. He sank to his knees at the edge of the moat to wash the blood off the pitchforks.

Riga and Harnu wouldn't let this go easily.

Achan sighed. His fingers stiffened in the rank, icy water. One of these days he'd accept pretty Gren Fenny's offer to weave him a brown tunic, and he'd run away. He was almost of age—maybe no one would question his heritage. He could tell people his mother was a mistress and his father was on Ice Island. Sired by a criminal and almost sixteen, people wouldn't ask too many questions.

But could Achan convince Gren to come with him? He scrubbed the pitchfork prongs with renewed vigor to combat the dread in his heart. Any day now, Gren had said. Any day her father might announce her betrothal and crush Achan's hopes. He'd hinted at running away together, but Gren hadn't seemed keen on the idea. She loved her family. Achan tried to understand, but as a stray, the concept of family was as foreign as a cham bear. He could only dream of it.

When the pitchforks were clean, Achan returned to the barn. His attackers had left and, thankfully, had not done any damage they could blame him for. He shuddered to think of what their feeble minds hadn't. The torch still burned in the ring on the post. They could have burned the barn to ashes. They were truly the thickest heads in Sitna, maybe even in all Er'Rets.

Not that Achan was much brighter, sacrificing himself for an ingrate who was probably out chasing piglets.

Achan hung one pitchfork on the wall and used the other to clean up the hay. When the ground was tidy, he grabbed the empty pail and sat on the stool to catch his breath.

The consequences of his heroism were suddenly laid before him. The scratches on his back throbbed. The goat's milk had completely soaked into the ground, the front of his tunic, and his face. Only the latter had dried, making the skin tight on his left cheek. His nose tingled from the cold. He shivered violently, now that he'd stopped moving. He scowled and pitched the pail across the barn. It smacked the goat stall, and the girls scurried around inside, frightened by the sound.

But Achan didn't want a beating. So he picked the pail up again, dragged the stool into the stall, and managed to squeeze another two inches of milk from the goats. It was all they had. Poril would be furious.

Achan jogged out of the barn, around the cottages, and across the inner bailey. By now, more people were stirring—it was almost breakfast time. He wove around a peddler pushing a cart full of linens and a squire leading a horse from the stables. A piglet scurried past, just avoiding the wheels of a trader's wagon. Achan ignored it. Mox could hang for all he cared.

Pressure filled his head again.

This time the insight that followed was not dread but kinship and hope. Achan paused at the entrance to the kitchens and turned, seeking out the source of the sensation. His gaze was drawn to the armory.

There, Harnu slouched on a stool clutching a bloody rag to his nose. His father stood over him, hands on hips. The warm glow of the forge behind their menacing forms brought to mind the Lowerworld song that Achan had heard Minstrel Harp sing in the Corner last night:

When Arman turns away, Shamayim denied
　　To Lowerword your soul will flee.
At the fiery gates meet your new lord, Gâzar
　　And forever in Darkness you'll be.

Achan shuddered. The sensation of kinship was definitely not coming from them.

He spotted someone else. A knight stood leaning against the crude structure of the armory, watching Achan with a pensive stare. He wore the uniform of the Old Kingsguard—a red, hooded cloak that draped over both arms and hung to a triangular point in the center front and back. The crest of the city of Armonguard, embroidered in gold thread, glimmered over his chest. The knight pulled his hood back to reveal white hair, tied back on top and hanging past his shoulders. A white beard dangled in a single braid that extended to his chest.

Achan recognized him immediately. It was Sir Gavin Lukos, the knight who had come to train Prince Gidon for his presentation to the Council.

For what purpose did the knight stare? Achan had never met anyone above his station who hadn't wished him harm or hard work. Yet his instincts had never been wrong. Sir Gavin harbored no ill will. Achan gave the old man a half smile before entering the kitchens to face Poril's wrath.

Achan settled onto a stool by the chest-high table that was worn by years of knives and kneading. The kitchens were two large rooms under one roof. One was filled with water basins, tables, and supplies for mixing. The other held six chest-high tables and three hearth ovens that left the room sweltering nearly all day.

Poril, a burly old man with sagging posture, poured batter into stone cups and carried them to one of the hearth ovens. Serving women scurried about filling trays with food and gossiping about Lord Nathak's latest rejection from the Duchess of Carm.

Achan's stomach growled at the smell of fried bacon and ginger cake. He wouldn't be able to eat until after the nobility were served, and then he would be allowed only one bowl of porridge. Poril had a knack of knowing if Achan had eaten something he shouldn't have. Achan suspected the serving women's tongues flapped for extra slices of Poril's pies.

The scratches on his back burned. He was in no mood for Poril's daily lecture, nor could he stomach the cook's nagging voice and the queer way he spoke about himself using his own name. Especially not when he was hungry and had a beating coming. He only hoped Harnu would keep his accusations of thieving to himself. Maybe it was time to talk to Gren about that brown tunic.

Poril scurried back to the table with a linen sack of potatoes. His downy white hair floated over his freckled scalp. Sometimes Achan wanted to laugh when he watched Poril. The man looked more like he should be wielding a sword than a wooden spoon. Some of the serving women said Poril was part giant. Achan wasn't convinced. The cook might be tall and thick, but his sagging posture and thinning hair just made him look old.

"It's what comes from giving a stray responsibility, that's what. But Poril's a kind soul, he is. Mother was a stray and no kinder woman there ever was, boy, I'll tell yeh that. Worked hard so Poril could have better, she did."

Poril dumped the potatoes onto the table. Several rolled onto the dirt floor, and Achan scrambled to pick them up. He spotted a crumbled wedge of ginger cake on the floor and stuffed the spicy sweetness into his mouth. It was even a bit warm still. Achan took his time setting the potatoes back on the table and pressed the lump of cake into the roof of his mouth to savor it, hoping Poril wouldn't see. Then he grabbed a knife and hacked at the peel of the biggest potato.

Poril pointed a crooked finger in Achan's face. "It's only 'cause Poril's the best cook in Er'Rets that Lord Nathak won't be aware of yer blunder with the milk today, boy. 'Tis my responsibility to beat some sense into yeh, not his. Poril's a fair man, and yeh deserve to be punished, that's certain. But turning yeh over to the likes of the master is cruel. And cruel, Poril's not."

Achan set the peeled potato aside and picked up another. Poril always threatened to tell Lord Nathak of Achan's every misstep, but the man was all talk. He was more scared of Lord Nathak than Achan was. True, Poril was not as cruel as some, but he was of the opinion that beatings with the belt were kinder than beatings with a fist. Achan grew tired of both.

Poril clunked a mug of red tonic onto the table beside Achan's potato peelings. Achan glanced at it.

The old man's grey eyes dared him to refuse. "Drink up, then. Poril's waiting."

Achan sucked in a long breath and guzzled the gooey, bitter liquid. The taste killed the lingering ginger cake flavor on his tongue. He'd been fed the tonic every morning his whole life, and every morning Poril insisted on watching him drink.

The thick mixture always churned in his gut, begging to come back up. Achan sat still a moment, breathing through his nose to calm his nerves. Then he rose to settle his stomach with a few mentha leaves from the spice baskets. Achan might not have free range of the kitchens, but Poril had learned long ago to allow Achan as much mentha as he needed.

Poril always claimed that Lord Nathak had insisted Achan drink the tonic to keep away illness—that strays were full of disease. But the tonic hadn't prevented Achan from being ill several times in his life. Plus no other stray he knew had to take it. The one time he'd refused, he'd received a personal summons from Lord Nathak.

Achan shuddered at the memory and chewed on the leaves. Their fresh taste dissolved the tonic's bitterness and tingled his tongue.

Poril wiped his hands on his grease-stained apron and sprinkled a bit of sugar over the prince's ginger cake. Hopefully he'd forget to clean the crumbs off the table when he left to deliver it.

"Never wanted yeh, Poril didn't. But the master brought yeh to Poril to raise, and that's what Poril's done. Yeh brought none but trouble to the kitchens, the gods know. None but trouble. 'Tis why I named yeh so."

As if an orange tunic wasn't humiliation enough, *achan* meant trouble in the ancient language. Achan returned to his stool and raked the knife against another potato, trying to block out Poril's braying voice. His pitchfork wounds stung, but it would be at least an hour before he could tend to them.

" . . . and Poril will teach yeh right from wrong too. That's Poril's duty to the gods."

If that was true, Achan would like to have a little talk with the gods. Not that the all-powerful Cetheria would be burdened by the prayers of a stray—despite all the pastry tarts Achan had offered up at the entrance to the temple gardens over the years.

Day-old tarts didn't compare to gold cups, jewels, or coins when you're trying to win a god's favor.

An hour later, Achan stood over the sink basin, washing dishes while Poril delivered Lord Nathak and Prince Gidon's breakfast. There were servants to do the task, but Poril insisted on being present when the first bites were taken.

Achan shifted his weight to his other leg. He hated cleaning dishes. Standing in one position for so long made his back ache, and today, with his pitchfork wounds, the pain doubled.

Though strays were lower even than slaves in most parts of Er'Rets, Achan had more freedom than most slaves. Poril kept him busy tending the goats, getting wood, and keeping the fireplaces hot and both kitchens clean, but at least there was variety. Some slaves worked fifteen hours a day at one task. Such tediousness would have driven Achan insane.

Achan dried the last pot and hung the towel on the line outside. When he came back in, Poril had returned. The cook wiggled his crooked fingers, beckoning Achan to follow him down the skinny stone steps to the cellar. Achan sighed, dreading the bite of Poril's belt buckle.

The cook lived in a cramped room off of the cellar, furnished with a straw mattress, a tiny oak table, and two chairs. Achan slept in the cellar itself, under the supports that held up the ale casks, although he barely fit anymore. He feared to be crushed in his sleep one night when he rolled against one of the supports and it finally gave way.

As per routine, Achan went to Poril's table, removed his tunic, and draped it over the back of one chair. He straddled the other chair in reverse and hugged it with his arms. His teeth fit into the grooves of bite marks he'd made over the years. He clenched down and waited.

Poril ran a finger down one of the scratches on Achan's back. "What's this?"

Achan quivered at the feel of crusty blood under Poril's touch.

"Well? Speak up, boy. Poril don't have all day to waste on yer silence."

"I met some peasants in the barn this morning."

"Spilled yer milk, did they?"

Not exactly, but Achan said, "Aye."

"Yeh cause trouble?"

Achan didn't answer. Poril always complained when Achan defended himself or anyone else. He said a stray should know his place and take his beatings like he'd deserved them.

"Ah, yer a fool, yeh are, boy. One of these days yeh'll be killed, and Poril will tell the tale of how he knew it would come to pass. The boy wouldn't listen to Poril. Had to smart off. Had to fight back. Not even Cetheria will have mercy on such idiocy."

Achan doubted it mattered if he stuck up for himself or not. If a stray was invisible to man, how much more so to the gods?

He heard the swoosh of Poril pulling his leather belt from the loops on his trousers. He hoped his pants fell down.

When Poril was done flogging Achan, he swabbed his back with soapy water, washed the blood from his tunic, and gave him an hour off to rest while it dried.

Good old Poril.

A kindly presence flooded his mind.

Achan was returning from the well carrying a heavy yoke over his shoulders with two full buckets of water. He rounded the edge of a cottage and found Sir Gavin Lukos heading toward him. Achan stepped aside, pressing up against the cottage and turning the yoke so the buckets wouldn't hinder the great knight's path. The buckets swung from his sharp movement, grinding the yoke into his shoulders.

Sir Gavin slowed. "What's your name, stray?"

Achan jumped, wincing as the yoke sent a sliver into the back of his neck. Sir Gavin's eyes bored into his. One was icy blue and the other was dark brown. The difference startled him. "Uh . . . Achan, sir."

The knight's weathered face wrinkled. "What kind of a name is that?"

Poril's voice nagged in Achan's mind, *'Tis trouble, that's what.* "Mine, sir."

"Surname?"

Achan lifted his chin and answered, "Cham," proud of the animal Poril had chosen to represent him. Chams breathed fire and had claws as long as his hand. Such virtues would tame Riga and Harnu for good.

Sir Gavin sniffed. "A fine choice." His braided beard bobbed as he spoke. "I saw a bit of that ruthless bear in the barn with those peasants."

Achan stared, shocked. He'd seen the fight? Would he tell Lord Nathak? "I . . . um . . . " Had Sir Gavin asked him a question? "I'm sorry?"

"I said, what's your aim, lad?'

"I should like to serve in Lord Nathak's kitchens . . . perhaps someday assist the stableman with the horses."

"Bah! Kitchens and stables are no place for a cham. That's a fierce beast. You need a goal fit for the animal."

What could the knight be skirting around? "But I . . . I don't have a . . . what choice have I?"

"Aw, now there's always a choice, lad. Kingsguard is the highest honor to be had by a stray. Why not choose that?"

Achan cut off a gasping laugh, afraid of offending the knight. "I cannot. Forgive me, but you're . . . I mean . . . a stray is not permitted to serve in the Kingsguard, sir."

"It wasn't always that way, you know. And despite any Council law, there are always exceptions."

Achan shifted the yoke a bit, uncomfortable with both the weight and the subject matter. He cared little for myths and legends. Council law was all that mattered anymore. Despite his fantasy of running away, he was Lord Nathak's property, nothing more. The brand on his shoulder proved that. "Even so, sir, one must serve as a page first, then squire, and no knight would wish a stray for either."

"Except, perhaps, a knight who's a stray himself." Sir Gavin winked his brown eye.

A tingle ran up Achan's arms. He'd known Sir Gavin was a stray because of his animal surname, but it had been years since strays had been permitted to serve. Surely he couldn't mean—

"Come to the stables an hour before sunrise tomorrow. Your training mustn't interfere with your duties to the manor. Tell no one of this for now. If I decide you're worthy, I'll talk to Lord Nathak about reassignment to me."

Achan's mouth hung open. "You're offering to train me?"

"If you're not interested, I'm sure another would be eager to accept my offer."

Achan shifted under the weight of the yoke. "No. No, sir. I'll be there tomorrow."

"Good. I'll show you a trick or two you don't yet know."

Achan grinned. "Yes, sir."

2

At the rooster's crow, Achan dressed and hurried out of the kitchens into the dark morning.

He stood for a moment to allow his eyes to adjust. He hadn't wanted to call the attention of Poril or anyone else by carrying a torch at this hour. The plump moon still hung low in the sky, and, with the torches lining the parapet wall above, the shapes of cottages slowly formed before him. He saw no sign of life but the sleeping guards on the parapet wall and the moths fluttering around the torches.

He started off at a silent jog, keeping on his toes. The frigid air stung his eyes. His mind raced. All his life he'd dreamed of being a knight: riding a horse and wielding a sword to protect the weak. Could the gods have finally taken notice of his measly offerings over the years? Could his station in life really change? If so, would Gren's father look at him differently?

A sour thought slowed his steps, and he slid on the frosty dirt. How would he find time to serve two masters? Achan had seen Prince Gidon's squires scurrying around the manor on various errands. How could Achan manage to serve Sir Gavin's needs *and* Poril's?

The stables sat between the gatehouse and the barn. The animal dwellings looked identical but for the stables being twice as wide. Most peasants felt the barn a waste of space, but the prince entertained often and needed the room to house his guests' mounts.

Achan found Sir Gavin leaning against the western entrance to the stables, a torch in one hand. The knight smiled, his teeth thin and wolfish in the orange glow. Someone had obvious reasons for bestowing the surname Lukos. Or perhaps the name had changed the man. Achan hoped over time he wouldn't grow to resemble a fire-breathing bear.

Sir Gavin's smile faded as he looked Achan over. "You're rail thin. Do you eat?"

"What I'm given."

Sir Gavin slid his torch into a groove beside the stable door. "What do you know?"

"Kitchens, mostly." Achan wrung his hands at his sides, his mind scrambling for words that might impress Sir Gavin. "I know about animals. I tend the goats, and I've helped Noam with the horses some."

Several horses inside the stables whinnied as if in agreement.

Sir Gavin looked inside, perhaps wondering what had spooked the animals. He turned back to Achan. "Do you ride?"

"Never, sir."

"Hmm. Can you read?"

"Some. Poril's recipes and lists of ingredients."

Sir Gavin held up a wooden practice sword, the sight of which warmed Achan's soul. "Ever use a waster?"

"No, sir, but I've sparred with poles." Servants gathered nightly to dance and play in the northeast corner of the outer bailey. Achan had grown up in the Corner, wrestling slave and peasant boys and fighting with sticks.

Sir Gavin grunted and looked slightly displeased. "How came you to Sitna?"

"Lived here all my life."

"Your father?"

"I don't know, sir."

Footsteps crunched over the frozen dirt. Noam, the stable boy, approached the entrance. Noam was tall and lanky and reminded Achan of Minstrel Harp's song of the stretched man. Noam's face was long and narrow and his thin frame seemed almost breakable. His gaze flicked between Achan and Sir Gavin. He met Achan's eyes with raised brows. Noam hadn't been at the Corner last night when Achan had told Gren about his opportunity with Sir Gavin. Noam pulled open the door and went inside, his torchlight spilling out the cracked-open door.

"What about your mother?" Sir Gavin asked.

Achan looked back to the knight and sighed. Some strays—like Noam—knew the identity of at least one parent, but Achan knew nothing of either. "I don't know, sir."

Sir Gavin raised a white bushy eyebrow, as if a stray not knowing the identity of his parents was some interesting fact. "How old are you?"

"Nearly sixteen."

Sir Gavin raised the other eyebrow and rubbed his chin, his eyes boring into Achan's. "You've not been a page, much less a squire—and most squires start at fourteen." He squeezed Achan's upper arm and sniffed long and hard like he was coming down with something. "You've got muscle, but you'll need to get stronger. If the cook won't give you enough, come to my quarters at mealtimes, and I'll see you better fed. Tell no one of our arrangement for now. Come. Let us begin your training."

Sir Gavin led Achan out of the stronghold and into a nearby wheat field. The sky was grey now, and the flat land stretched out in all directions. Frost painted glistening white stripes in the furrowed, dead fields.

Sir Gavin plunged the waster into the frozen earth and it listed to one side, not having gone very deep. He folded his arms. "First things first. Whenever you come against an attacker you need to study him in a glance. You've no time to dally in this, do you understand?"

Achan nodded. "What am I looking for, sir?"

"Weapons and armor, mostly. Different rules apply depending on whether your opponent is wearing armor, what kind of armor, and what kind of weapon you both have. There will be times when you see that you are outmatched. Every man wants to be brave, but sometimes it's best to run."

Achan had never heard of a knight running from anything.

Sir Gavin must have read his expression. "Aye, lad. We've all had to retreat at some point in life. Doesn't mean we can't keep fighting the next day. But you have to know when you're beat. My point is, sometimes you can tell if you're beat before you start fighting.

"Take a sword, for example," Sir Gavin said, toeing the waster. "There are all types. Those with a rounded tip are cutting swords and therefore useless against all types of armor. And since that sword can't cut through armor and doesn't have a sharp point to pierce it, if you're carrying a cutting sword and meet an armored opponent, you're beat. Until you've been fighting as long as I have and are willing to risk your skill against armor—which is a daft thing to do, but you might have reason—you'd best not take on an armored man with a cutting sword. Understood?"

"Aye," Achan said.

"Some will say that one should never fight without a shield. It's true that the shield is a formidable weapon. One you can barely live without if you have no armor. But shields are often forgotten, broken, or dropped. So until you learn to hold your own without one, I shall not give you that crutch."

Achan shifted and the frozen grass crunched beneath his feet. He struggled to grasp Sir Gavin's meanings. It was almost as if the man were speaking in a foreign tongue. The sky was a pale grey now. They were running out of time before Poril would be expecting the milk.

"All right, then." Sir Gavin yanked the waster from the grass and handed it to Achan, hilt first. "Let's see your grip."

Achan took the handle with both hands and spread his feet the way he'd seen knights do. He put his right foot forward and held the sword out in front, tipped slightly to his left.

Sir Gavin frowned and fingered his beard braid.

"Is something wrong?" Achan asked without moving. "Are my feet right?"

"You're fine," Sir Gavin said. "It's just . . . not many are left-handed."

Achan relaxed his posture and brought the sword down to his side. "Is that bad?"

The old knight's eyes twinkled. It was like looking into two versions of the world: one a blue sky under a bright sun and the other a dark sky filled with stars.

"Not bad at all," Sir Gavin said. "We will use this to your advantage. You will train right-handed as well as left-handed. A warrior is only as good as his biggest weakness. This way we will make you strong with both hands. It's not a big difference with a longsword. You'll notice it more with the short sword."

A thrill washed over Achan. He was going to learn the short sword, too? "What other weapons will I learn?"

"Once you've got a grasp on the longsword, I'll teach you the short sword and shield. Then the axe and the dagger. That should do to keep you alive."

Achan's eyebrows sank in puzzled humor. "Because so many are looking to kill me?"

"Riga and Harnu, to start."

Achan stiffened. "I can take care of them. What about the lance, sir? Will I learn to joust?"

"No. Jousting is a sport these days. The lance will only slow down your training on the other weapons."

"Are you in a hurry to teach me, sir?" Perhaps the knight would give him some important detail that would give him hope with Gren.

"Aye. I told you already: you're behind. Practice all you can and waste no time on thoughts of jousting."

The clip-clop of hooves turned Achan's head back to the stronghold. Noam led Prince Gidon's ebony courser over the drawbridge and into the field to exercise it. His curious gaze fixed on Achan and Sir Gavin.

The knight took the practice sword from Achan. "Keep this waster with you as much as possible, and whenever you can, practice guard positions. See here." He raised the weapon above his head. "High guard." He lowered it straight out in front. "Middle guard." He pointed it at the ground between his feet. "Low guard. Practice switching between positions quickly and smoothly." He swung the waster to the side of his right leg, then the left. "Back guards. Practice those too. You use an axe?"

Achan nodded. "Keeping the hearths hot is my responsibility."

"Good. An axe uses different muscles than a sword. If I'm to train you in the axe, I need you strong enough to handle it."

"But what about you?" Achan asked. "Shouldn't I see to your needs? Clean your armor, get your meals? I'm not sure which horse is yours. How will I—"

Sir Gavin raised a calloused hand. "Not necessary, lad. You'll be of little use to anyone a weakling. Get yourself strong first." He handed the waster to Achan.

Achan accepted the sword without meeting Sir Gavin's eyes. He was far from a weakling. His fight with Riga and Harnu was proof of that. Besides, the wooden sword was lighter than he expected.

But after practicing the guard positions over and over, Achan's arms ached desperately and the waster didn't seem so light anymore.

At sunrise, Sir Gavin dismissed him. Achan hid the waster under in his wool blanket and rushed through the milking with aching forearms.

When Poril left to deliver Lord Nathak and the prince's breakfast, Achan quickly washed the dishes and ran to Gren's cottage.

No one answered the door, so Achan jogged around to the back. He found Gren standing in a wooden tub, skirts hiked up to her knees, legs splattered with dark, smelly water. A long rack stretched creamy wool on tenterhooks behind her like a frame.

He stood watching her from the shaded wall of the cottage. Her chestnut hair hung long and silky to her elbows. As always, she wore her grass green dress that made her hair and skin look lustrous. Achan had once told Gren she looked pretty in green, and he'd never seen her wear another color since. He wished she'd wear a cloak, though. Outside in this cold with her feet in water like that . . . she was likely to catch a fever.

"Is it so terribly difficult to remember a cloak, Gren?"

She gasped and her wide, brown eyes found his. "You scared me!" She lowered her voice. "Well? How did it go?"

"He gave me a waster."

"Really? How exciting!"

"If I became a knight . . . " Achan inhaled deeply, still slightly out of breath. The rank smell of urine and dung from Gren's fulling water filled his nostrils. "Would that change your father's opinion of me?"

Gren's smile faded. She looked down to where her feet vanished into the smelly liquid and stomped on the fabric a bit. She didn't speak for so long it seemed she'd forgotten to answer. "More wool," she finally said. "We're to dye it red for Prince Gidon. You'd think he has enough red clothing by now. I wish I could work with the silk that Lord Nathak orders on bolts from Nesos."

Achan's joy fizzled. Gren's change of subject did not bode hopeful.

She must have read the disappointment on his face. "Oh, Achan," she said. "You know Father's been threatening to marry me off for two years."

Two long, torturous years. He faked a smile. "I thought he was only teasing."

She laughed, but it didn't ring true. "I'm fifteen. Girls marry as young as twelve."

Achan met Gren's eyes for a moment. They were sad eyes, filled with heartache.

She looked back to her wool. "I think he's settled on someone. I heard him and Mother talking about a . . . v-veil." She paused as if to recover from saying that word. "He hasn't told me yet, though . . . but . . . " She looked at him and sighed. "Doesn't it take years to become a knight?"

Achan nodded. Plus, Sir Gavin had asked him not to tell anyone, which meant he couldn't plead his case to Gren's father without going against Sir Gavin's wishes. Achan was going to have to scrounge the great hall for table scraps to take to the temple.

At this point, pleading to the gods was his only hope.

Achan sat on the ground in the Corner, leaning against the brownstone curtain wall. Gren sat on his right. Their shoulders touched, as if by accident, but their outside arms both reached behind their backs, where their fingers intertwined in secret.

Night had fallen, and Minstrel Harp stood on the back of a cart plucking his lute and singing a lament about a kinsman man who fell in love with an otherling woman. Such marriages were forbidden, but no law could dampen the affection they held for one another.

The song had transfixed the normally rowdy crowd. Even the small children were still as the bard sang. Achan wondered if the pie he'd taken from the kitchens to offer up to Cetheria would make a difference—and if Poril would notice it missing.

The Corner was literally the northeastern corner of the outer bailey. The space was too jagged and narrow to build another cottage in and far enough from the keep that the revelry did not disturb Prince Gidon. Most nights at least two dozen peasants, strays, and slaves came to socialize, dance, or hear stories. Children wrestled or played games. This was where Achan had learned to fend for himself.

Someone tapped his shoulder. He jumped and severed his contact with Gren.

"It's only me." Sir Gavin slid down the wall on Achan's left. He nodded toward a farmer, who stood glowering at the bard. "What do you see, lad? If he were your opponent?"

Achan straightened and glanced at the farmer. "Well, if I didn't know him—"

"Nay, what you know matters. Use it."

"Aye, sir. That's Marel Wepp. He works in the linen fields. The dark-haired girl he's staring at is his eldest, Mistal. She's—"

"Mist*el*," Gren whispered.

Achan pursed his lips at Gren and continued. "She's a singer, and Minstrel Harp always pays her lots of mind."

"A jealous man can be dangerous," Sir Gavin said. "What else do you see?"

Achan noticed that Marel's beefy arms were crossed. "Marel is strong. I've seen him strike men before. I see no weapon on him."

"Doesn't mean he doesn't have one. Some weapons are small."

"Well, he wears no armor."

Sir Gavin raised a bushy eyebrow. "Are you certain? Did you hear any? Chain coats can be hard to see."

"No, sir. But he's a farmer. He wouldn't own armor."

"So armor is only for the rich?"

"I suppose so."

Sir Gavin stood. "Go get your waster and meet me behind the barn."

"Aye, sir." Achan smiled at Gren and hurried away.

When he reached the barn, Sir Gavin was waiting with his own wooden sword. Only the moon lit the hay-strewn ground behind the barn. Achan could barely hear the music still playing at the Corner.

"I want to explain some things about parries," Sir Gavin said. "For a new swordsman, defense is your primary goal. Tell me, where do most knights strike first?"

Achan thought back to the tournaments he'd seen over the years. "The legs, sir?"

"Aye. A crippled man is a small threat. So that is where you need to be guarding first. Always parry with the flat of the blade, otherwise you chip or dull your cutting edge. Now, a cut most often comes at you from an angle. Why do you think that is?"

Achan shrugged.

Sir Gavin moved his waster in slow motion as he spoke, demonstrating his words. "If you come straight down, you risk chopping your blade into the dirt or your knee if you miss. If you strike level sideways, you risk throwing your weapon or throwing yourself off balance."

Achan could just see himself pitching his sword at his attacker as if skipping a stone.

Sir Gavin brought the waster to his center, with the hilt pointing out from his abdomen as if he were holding a yoke plow. "All parries can be made from the middle guard position. You aren't trying to strike with a parry. You're trying to ease their strike against you. Meet their blow by stepping up to it, or cushion the blow by stepping back."

Sir Gavin spent the next hour showing Achan the different ways to parry attacks. Achan took dozens of strikes to his forearms and shins from Sir Gavin's wooden blade. He was having the most trouble with the leg strikes.

Sir Gavin swung his sword at Achan's shins again. Achan dropped his waster to low guard and moved it over to block his left leg. The swords clacked together, but Sir Gavin's pushed Achan's back enough to touch his leg.

"Better, but a steel blade would've nicked you good. Make sure you move your blade out far enough so you won't be cut if it's knocked back." Sir Gavin took a long breath and blew it out in a cloud around his face. "You've done enough for today, lad. You'll be plenty sore tomorrow. Ease into the routine. The first week will be the hardest."

It was. Over the next few days, Achan never sat still. If he wasn't running an errand for Poril or crawling under the tables in the great hall collecting scraps to offer Cetheria, he was sneaking away to go through his sword exercises. Poril snapped at his absences with threats of the belt, so Achan did his best to be two places at once.

With the added activity, his appetite grew. Poril's portions didn't change, so Achan started joining Sir Gavin for meals.

He ate his fill like never before, always saving something nice and whole for Cetheria.

While they ate, Sir Gavin would talk about noble etiquette and table manners. Once Achan began eating with more grace, Sir Gavin moved on to speak of the other cities in Er'Rets and the nobles who lived there. He began with Sitna, where Achan lived. Sir Gavin said it was a tiny manor built for the sole purpose of raising the prince. He said that in most strongholds, the kitchens had at least three cooks who fed over two hundred people three meals a day.

Achan soaked it all up and spilled it out to Gren each night at the Corner.

By the second week, his arms ached less, his blisters had faded to calluses, and he felt more confident about his role as a squire. Although Sir Gavin would still not accept his service. Squires were required to bring their master meals, clean their armor, and care for their horses. Sir Gavin would have none of it.

Achan woke one morning to find a new orange tunic neatly folded on the floor by his pallet. He blinked his sleepy eyes until it dawned on him.

Today was his coming-of-age day. Or at least the day Poril celebrated it. He was sixteen now. A man.

He slipped the new tunic on. The linen was coarse and loose-weaved as ever, but at least it was new and clean.

The kitchens were deserted when Achan passed through the sweltering room. Poril must have set the tunic out the night before.

Achan met Sir Gavin in the wheat field for his daily practice.

"Is that a new tunic?" Sir Gavin asked.

"Aye," Achan said. "Ever-thoughtful Poril gives me a new one every year when my age changes."

Sir Gavin stroked his mustache. "What is your day of birth?"

Achan shrugged and moved his waster from middle guard to low guard and back. "No one knows for certain, so Poril always celebrates it on the first of spring. This is my sixteenth."

"Well, I should like to give you something as well. A day of birth is one thing, but you are a man now. And I feel you deserve a man's weapon. As soon as you finish your squire training, I shall give you a real sword."

Achan's lips parted. "Sir? Truly?"

"Aye. Truly."

Achan stared at the old knight, dumbstruck at the mere idea of owning his own blade. "Wait. Am I really that close to becoming a knight? I thought—"

"You're close enough to be publicly declared my *squire.* And, in case you didn't notice, most squires have a real sword."

Achan had noticed, but he also knew his situation was far from normal. He still couldn't fathom why Sir Gavin needed him as a squire. He wasn't doing squire's work, after all. He'd done nothing but learn from the knight since he'd been recruited. Not that he was complaining.

All day long, Achan walked tall. He hoped to see Gren—she always remembered Achan's day of birth in some way—but he didn't see her. When Poril went to bed that night, Achan snuck out to the Corner.

A piper was playing a merry tune from his wagon, and several couples were dancing and laughing. A dozen more stood around talking. Mox and a larger boy were wrestling. A grin came to Achan's face when he saw Mox was losing.

"Achan!"

Achan spotted Noam sitting on a stump behind the dancers. Achan wound his way through the crowd until he reached his friend.

"Look at you, all crisp and stain-free in your new tunic," Noam said, grinning.

"Aye, Poril never forgets my day of birth. And he hasn't beaten me since Sir Gavin came along. Perhaps the gods have noticed my offerings of late."

"Well, they're giving you new boots too, if you can get your feet in them." Noam held out a pair of brown leather boots. "My feet grow so fast I barely had time to wear these."

"Really?"

Noam nodded. "There's a hole here." Noam showed where the heel was separating from the sole. "But I figured Gren could fix it for you, if you ask her nicely."

Achan grinned and accepted the boots. His first pair of boots. They would make such a difference on cold mornings.

"You're really training to be Sir Gavin's squire?" Noam asked.

"Gren told you?"

"That, and I have eyes. You batting around that waster everywhere you go."

"He said he would give me a real sword soon."

"Will Lord Nathak give you up then?"

Achan frowned. He'd never heard of Lord Nathak giving up a servant. Could Sir Gavin convince him? "I don't—"

"Achan!" Small hands slid around his waist as Gren hugged his side.

Her action shocked him. She had never shown any affection in such a public place. He liked how she felt, tucked under his arm. She smelled faintly of fulling water and cinnamon, a strange combination that was very much Gren.

"Hello," he said. "I looked for you earlier today, but . . . "

She sighed. "More fancy fabrics for the prince. He could order every person in Sitna a new outfit and not make a dent in his stores."

"But that would be a kind thing to do, and so not in line with his character," Noam whispered.

"Well, he isn't the only one who can get fabric. I can weave." She took Achan's hand and tugged him between the curtain wall and the nearest cottage.

"Bye, then," Noam called.

Gren led Achan as she wove around the cottages until she came to her own. She stopped behind the frame that was stretching a new batch of wool. She lifted something off a hook on the back side of the frame.

"What are you doing?" Achan asked.

She shook out some fabric and held it up against his chest. It was so dark behind the frame, Achan could hardly see.

"What is it?"

She slapped his chest. "It's a shirt, silly, and a fine one. Brown, to match your skin. Happy coming-of-age day, Achan."

He looked down into her dark eyes and trembled. He had never felt so close to anyone. Her simple act of giving him something unique . . . and not another orange tunic or even hand-me-down boots. She treated him like an equal, though he was a stray and she the daughter of a craftsman.

A brown shirt to run away in and not be suspected of being a stray.

He gripped her shoulders. "You'll come with me?"

Her eyes glistened in the distant moonlight. Her breath grew ragged, and she looked down at her hands, which were still holding the shirt against his chest.

He moved his hands up her shoulders and took the sides of her face in his palms. "Gren?"

She lifted her gaze to his. Tears streaked down to her chin. He wiped them away with his thumbs. "I'll talk to your father soon. Sir Gavin promised me a real sword. Any day now he'll publicly declare me a squire. Then surely your father will at least—"

"Grendolyn? Are you out there?"

Gren stiffened at the sound of her mother's voice. "I have to go. Happy coming-of-age day, Achan." She bounced up to kiss his cheek and darted out from behind the frame, leaving Achan alone.

A vast allown tree grew outside Sitna Manor. The trunk was as thick as two grown men and its long upper branches splayed out against the blue sky. It loomed over the curve of the Sideros River at the edge of a field beside the stronghold.

In the summer, the tree made a shady haven that was Achan's favorite place to sit and watch the setting sun. Today, the tree looked lonely with its bare branches reaching up to the heavens as if pleading for Dendron to bring warmth sooner. No tree around compared to its glory. Achan felt drawn to it.

His stomach full from a second lunch with Sir Gavin, Achan set off toward the allown tree to meet Gren. It was less cold today than it had been. Spring had arrived. He trudged across the field, swinging his wooden sword to beat the tall, dead grass out of his path. The sword already felt light and familiar in his grip.

Gren leaned against the thick trunk. The barren branches bounced in the chill wind and cast dancing spider web shadows over her. The vast, brown Sideros River flowed past three paces from Gren's feet. Her chestnut hair blew to the other side of her head, baring her chapped and rosy cheeks. Why couldn't the weaver make his daughter something warmer for the winter cold? Her coarse linen cloak was too drafty and Gren too flighty to remember the hood.

If Achan had owned a cloak, he would've offered it.

He hid the sword behind him and approached, his trousers swishing in the grass. Gren turned, her eyes rimmed in red. She'd been crying. Achan wanted to say something to comfort her but didn't know what. Instead of words, he pulled the wooden sword from behind his back.

Her brown eyes widened and her lips parted in a slow smile. "Oh, Achan! You're really going to become a Kingsguard knight."

He knelt between the bumpy roots beside her and gasped a laugh. "I never thought my station could change. The gods have blessed me greatly, Gren."

She rose to her knees. "Well, show me how it's used . . . on that leaning poplar." Gren pointed at a frail tree right at the edge of the river. The wind had already bested the poor sapling. Its roots poked out from the soil on one side, and the flimsy trunk leaned over so far the barren branches swam lazily in the swift, brown current.

Achan shrugged, happy to please Gren. He trudged toward the cockeyed sapling and pressed the tip of the wooden sword against the flaky trunk. "Halt, you foul excuse for a tree! In the name of Dendron, god of nature, surrender! Or I shall cut you into tinder for my fire."

Gren's merry giggle floated on the wind.

Though Achan felt incredibly silly, he warmed to her smile, so he played along. He sucked in a sharp breath. "You dare speak that way in the presence of this fine lady? I shall run you through!" He whacked the blade against the tree again and again, more like chopping wood than Sir Gavin's swordplay. The pitiful sapling hunched lower, the trunk sinking into the yellow grass, the upper branches into the river.

The ground beneath Achan's feet shifted. A deep cracking sent him scuttling back from the river bank. The tree, dragging a clump of roots and soil, ripped from the turf and sagged into the river. The current swelled briefly, sending a surge of icy water up the bank and over Achan's ankles. He gasped as the freezing liquid seeped into his shoes and sent a violent shiver through his body. He turned to Gren, his mouth gaping, and uttered a small cry.

She giggled and jumped to her feet, clapping. "You've done it, my good knight. Look! Mine enemy retreats."

Achan turned back to the river to see the sapling floating downstream. One branch remained above water, flapping in the wind like a sad flag. He laughed and turned to Gren. She stood beaming, her hair blowing about her face.

He marched toward her, knelt, and offered her his wooden sword on the palms of his hands. "For you, my lady."

She hugged the waster to her heart, but her smile faded. Her eyes focused just over Achan's head and went wide with fright. "Riga, no!"

Achan reached for his sword, but someone pulled him away by the back of his tunic. The weary threads cracked under the pressure. He realized that it wasn't Riga pulling him—because his assailant dragged him past the potbellied peasant. Riga glared down over chubby cheeks. With his thick, sneering lips and squinty eyes, he looked to be suffering severe indigestion.

Achan's captor yanked him to his feet and twisted him around.

It was Harnu. The scar on his cheek had mottled and darkened in the cold air. His jaw clenched as if something in his mouth tasted bad.

Achan smirked. These two should take more care over what they ate if it affected their appearance so.

Harnu gripped both of Achan's wrists with one strong hand, squeezed his shoulder with the other, and pushed him back until his body leaned dangerously over the edge of the riverbank. Achan tried to get a decent foothold, but his frozen toes ignored his commands.

Riga spoke from the allown tree beside Gren. "Is this stray bothering you, my dear?" He draped a pudgy arm around Gren's shoulders.

Her expression steeled, but she didn't move away.

"Leave her be!" Achan yelled. "She's done nothing to you."

"It's *her* honor I seek to protect, dog!" Riga said. "No maiden should consort with a stray at all, much less . . . alone."

Achan fought against Harnu's grip, pedaling his wet feet on the muddy bank, hoping to get some anchorage. "What Gren does is not your business."

"On the contrary. She *is* my business, or hasn't she told you?" Riga leered at Gren. "But of course, my dear. Why would you waste your sweet breath sharing such intimacies with a stray?"

Achan didn't like Riga's tone or the flush in Gren's cheeks. "What are you on about?"

Riga straightened and sucked in a deep breath that brought his stomach in and his chest out. "Gren and I are betrothed."

Achan's gaze flickered to Gren. The fact that she wouldn't meet his eyes told him that Riga spoke truth. "Gren?"

Harnu squeezed Achan's wrists tighter, preventing his wiggling hands from escaping. Achan's mind clouded.

Gren suddenly looked up. Tears streaked down her chin. "My father has made arrangements with Vaasa Hoff."

Achan's face tingled as the blood drained away. Gods no. It couldn't be true.

Riga snatched the sword from Gren and held it up. "Pilfering a squire's practice sword is a wicked thing to do, even for a stray. Whose is this?"

Achan lifted his chin. "Mine."

Harnu leaned as close to Achan as possible without giving up his dominant position. "You'll never be a knight, goat boy. Or a squire or a page. And you'll never—"

"Marry a pretty girl," Riga said from Gren's side.

Harnu's breath smelled like soured milk. "The closest you'll ever get to the high table is to clean the scraps from the floor when everyone's gone." With that, Harnu shoved Achan backward.

Gren's scream silenced in Achan's ears when his body plunged beneath the icy surface.

Muted bubbling . . . a gulp of frigid water . . . a foot on something solid. Achan pushed off and kicked wildly toward the light. It had been Gren who had taught him to swim at age seven when none of the peasants would play with him.

His head burst through the surface. He gasped and twisted around. Gren, Riga, and Harnu stood on the bank, shrinking from sight. The forceful current swept him along. No matter how hard he tried, his efforts to swim for the shore seemed useless.

Like his life.

Gren and Riga? Why? Didn't Master Fenny know Riga was a selfish, lazy pig who couldn't deserve Gren in a million—

Achan saw a chance to escape the river. The poplar he had bested had gotten wedged into the entry channel of the moat that surrounded Sitna Manor. Achan reached for it and snagged the tip of a branch between his second and third fingers.

The branch held, and his body paused in the swift current. Water parted around his buoyed form. Hand over hand he pulled himself toward the side channel. Stiff brown branches snapped and scratched his face and hands. Finally he safely entered the murky current of the moat.

He let himself float along beneath the towering walls of the fortress. He shivered in the stinking water. The moat's current was weak and didn't flush the sewage from the manor's privies and kitchen as well as it was designed to. The brownstone walls of the manor loomed above. Two guards on the wall laughed and pointed down. Word spread on the sentry walk. By the time Achan sailed around the northwest corner, at least ten guards had congregated at the gatehouse.

Achan swam to the edge and hoisted himself up. Dirt from the bank muddied the front of his waterlogged tunic. His limbs shook with cold, and he stumbled under the portcullis, ignoring the jeers from above.

A figure stepped in his path. Sir Gavin.

Achan stood, soaked and stinking, trembling in the breeze. "I've l-lost my w-w-waster." And, he realized, his shoes. He was thankful Gren was still repairing Noam's hand-me-down boots. He would've hated to have lost those.

"In the moat?"

"R-Riga an 'ar-nu."

Sir Gavin nodded. "You'll have to make another."

Great. Now he had to learn carpentry or woodsmithing or whatever craft it took to make a wooden sword. At that point he didn't care. He had to get warm. He slouched past Sir Gavin toward the kitchens.

He squished down the stone steps to the cellar. He stripped off his wet clothes and crawled onto his pallet under the ale casks to warm himself. The image of Gren's tearful face was branded on his mind. Betrothed to Riga Hoff?

Pig snout!

"What about your sword?" Achan asked Sir Gavin as he filed the edge of his new wooden blade. White oak shavings peppered his feet with each stroke. "I've only seen you with your waster. You have a real one, don't you?"

Achan loved the smell of fresh sawdust and always enjoyed coming to the woodshed. Sir Gavin sat on a fat stump that was used as a chopping block. Rows upon rows of firewood were stacked up against the curtain wall. Achan had always wanted to see if he could climb it and reach the walkway above.

"Aye." Sir Gavin whittled a small block of pine. Achan had no idea what he was making. "But it would look mighty strange for me to tote around two swords everywhere I went, wouldn't it?"

Achan nodded. As he filed, he weighed matters with Gren. Strays were rarely permitted to marry anyway, so his hopes of a future with Gren had never been founded on reality. And, like Gren had said, her father had been looking for a husband for her for years. But Riga Hoff? Sure, Achan had expected *someone* to snatch up Gren. But not Riga. Someone older. Someone with life experience. Someone less like a swine. Someone mature and wealthy who could give her better clothes, provide for her. Young men rarely took a—

"If you're not careful, lad, the blade will be uneven. An uneven sword is difficult to learn on."

Sir Gavin's warning snapped Achan out of his lament. He quickly looked over his work and turned the wood to work a new spot. He clenched his teeth and returned to his thoughts. Never mind Gren—unless Achan could succeed as a knight and get out of Sitna, the best he could hope for was to end up like Poril. He shivered at the thought of a life serving Lord Nathak's meals and having to watch Gren and Riga's children chase the chickens around the outer bailey.

It took three days to finish the new waster. It wasn't as smooth as the last one, but Achan liked it better. It was his craftsmanship, after all. He set about his squire training with renewed vigor. The rest of the time he did his regular work for Poril, steering clear of Gren. He couldn't bear to face her just yet. Tired of walking around barefoot, he'd begged Noam to go and fetch the boots from her.

After one late-night practice, Achan asked, "Sir Gavin, can't I try a blunted blade? I'd like to at least hold one." The old knight had mentioned that blunts were used prior to real blades, and Achan was eager to get to the real thing.

Sir Gavin sniffed in a deep breath. "Aye, then. Tomorrow morning you can try it, but I think you'll see right away that you're not ready."

The next day, Achan met Sir Gavin in the wheat field before dawn, eager to prove himself worthy of knighthood and impress Master Fenny. As quickly as possible. Maybe a long engagement was planned. Maybe there was still a chance.

"Before we start," Sir Gavin said, stabbing one of the steel blades into the grassy soil, "we need to go over the basics."

Achan hid an impatient sigh. He recited: "Stay focused. Breathe deep. Mind your footwork. Look your attacker in the eye."

Sir Gavin cocked his head to the side. "Look him in the eye, but not just to stare him down. You want to watch all of him at once, see if you can anticipate his next move. Right?"

Achan nodded.

Sir Gavin handed him the blunt hilt first, then drew his own blade from the ground. "Now we'll see how you hold up against some real cuts. But I warn you, blunts are much more painful than wasters."

The fun was over. Sir Gavin knocked the blunt from Achan's hands six times before Achan could grip it tightly enough to hold on to it through a strike. Every hit rattled the bones in his arms all the way to his teeth.

He had trouble remembering everything at once. If he focused on following through with his arms so the strikes didn't sting, he forgot about his breathing. If he focused on his breathing, he forgot his footwork and stumbled. If he focused on his footwork, he forgot his arms and took a bruising blow or dropped his blade. And when he did get hit, the strikes hurt deeper than with the waster. He never once managed to look Sir Gavin in the eyes.

Sir Gavin paused for Achan to retrieve his blade from the ground yet again. "This is why we start with wasters. Tomorrow we go back to my way, but for today . . . " Sir Gavin grew ruthless. He nagged with each blunder and whacked Achan on the forehead with the flat of the sword.

Thwack! "Ow!"

"Pick it up! If I wanted to kill you, you'd be dead."

Thwack! "Ow!"

"Never parry with the edge. Always use the flat."

Thwack! "Raise your sword. Middle guard. Else I can run you through."

Thwack! "Don't attack from low guard. You're not good enough yet."

Thwack! "Stop whining and keep your grip tight . . . but not too tight."

That night, Achan slept like he'd been drugged.

He woke to tremendous aches. They were back to using the wooden wasters that morning, and Sir Gavin guided him through slow motion role-play lessons. This was a much easier way to learn.

By the time Sir Gavin brought back the blunts, Achan could actually keep up. Still, he went to bed each night with fresh bruises on his hands, forearms, and shins.

Little by little, with each passing day, Achan improved.

3

One morning, as Achan choked down his tonic under Poril's careful eye, Sir Gavin entered the kitchens.

The knight's presence sent Achan's heart racing. Had Sir Gavin convinced Lord Nathak to give him up already? Achan breathed deeply to calm his stomach.

The three serving women who were gathering meals for Prince Gidon's officials stopped what they were doing and stared at Sir Gavin.

Poril hovered around him like a fly. "How can Poril service yeh, my good sir knight? Do yeh desire bread? Some porridge?" Poril waved one of the women over. She carried a tray that was being readied for Chora, Prince Gidon's valet.

Sir Gavin ignored Poril's offerings and stared over the cook's shoulder, his expression curious. "What does the lad drink?"

Achan stumbled around the other two other serving women and headed toward the spice baskets in search of mentha leaves. He didn't want to miss a moment between Sir Gavin and Poril, but he also didn't want to lose his stomach on the kitchen floor.

"'Tis a tonic to keep the ills away," Poril said.

Sir Gavin's boots scuffed against the dirt floor as he moved to cut Achan off between two tables. Achan stepped back as the knight snatched the empty mug away and sniffed it. "If it's sour enough to turn his stomach, perhaps the recipe is wrong or the ingredients stale."

"I assure yeh, my good sir knight, the recipe is precise. Poril does not make errors in measurements or ingredients."

The smell of hardboiled eggs and sausages set Achan's stomach roiling. If only he could reach the mentha basket. "That's how it always tastes, sir."

Sir Gavin held out his empty hand to Poril, still clutching the mug in his other. "A crust of bread?"

Poril fluttered to the racks and handed the knight a chunk of flatbread. Sir Gavin ripped off a corner, wiped the inside of the mug, and popped it into his mouth.

Achan watched, cringing slightly, but knowing it couldn't taste as bad muted by bread. Nevertheless, Sir Gavin's face flushed. He spat the doughy lump into the mug and rounded on Poril. "You'd poison this boy?"

"Gods, no, my good sir knight! 'Tis not poison!"

"Nor is it given to 'keep the ills away.'" Sir Gavin spat again. "Why, then, do you give him this?"

Poril's eyes widened. His face flushed. "Because . . . Poril is sworn to . . . to keep him from . . . infecting the prince."

Sir Gavin turned to Achan. "Have you ever met the prince, lad?"

Achan couldn't speak. His tongue seemed to shrivel in his mouth. Poison? Who would want to poison him? Sir Gavin stared, waiting to be answered. Achan shook his head. He had seen the prince lots of times, but he had never been close enough to breathe on him.

"And you never thought to question before you drink?"

Achan didn't know what to say. He'd sensed the tonic was wrong, but what could he do? He was a stray, branded by his owner. "I—"

"'Tis not the boy's place to question orders," Poril snapped. "Lord Nathak demands the boy drink the tonic. Poril doesn't question His Lordship, nor should you."

Achan struggled to comprehend what was going on. Did Poril's answer mean Lord Nathak wanted to poison Achan? Why? He'd been drinking the tonic for years. It hadn't affected his health—had it?

Sir Gavin gripped Poril's shoulder. "Never give this to him again! Do you hear?"

But Poril stood his ground. "Poril does beg yer pardon, my good sir knight, but Poril does his *master's* bidding. If my good sir wishes the boy not take the tonic, then yeh must take the matter up with Lord Nathak hisself."

"I will." Sir Gavin released Poril, tossed the remaining bread into the mug, and banged it down on the bread table. "And I'm taking the lad with me for today. Don't expect him 'til morning."

Poril sputtered. "Well—what do yeh mean, my good sir knight?"

"I mean, *my good cook*, I'm in need of an assistant today, and I'm taking yours. Let's go, lad!"

Achan took one step forward, then stopped to keep the tonic down.

"Poril has much to prepare for tomorrow, he does. Prince Gidon's coming-of-age celebration. Over two hundred are expected. Could my good knight not find another assistant?"

"Could *you* not?"

Achan looked from Poril to Sir Gavin and back to Poril, unsure of which master to obey.

Finally Poril decided for him. "Yeh heard the good knight, boy. Be quick about it."

Achan started for the spice baskets to get mentha leaves, but Poril yelled, "Now! And Poril had better not hear any complaints from the good knight, or Poril will punish yeh good."

Achan scrambled around the table and out the door, his stomach churning. The morning air was cool but warmer than previous days. The sky was a bright, cloudless blue.

Sir Gavin paused for Achan to catch up, then set off in the direction of the stables. "Does he punish you often?"

Achan shrugged and fought the queasiness in his gut. "I don't know. Once, sometimes twice a week."

Sir Gavin halted. He went red again. Veins pulsed in his forehead and neck. He took a long breath through his nose and blew it out in a whistle. Without a word, he resumed walking toward the stables.

Achan scurried to keep up. The outer bailey was crowded after breakfast, but even more so with the coming-of-age celebration. Sir Gavin stopped behind a crowd.

"Make way!" someone yelled.

The people jerked back. Achan backpedaled to keep from falling down. The sharp movement roiled his still-queasy stomach. He should have insisted on grabbing mentha leaves before leaving the kitchens. He wheeled around and heaved his breakfast at the backside of the armory. The nearness of the chimney's bricks heated the right side of his face.

Sir Gavin's voice came from above. "Are you all right?"

Achan cleared his throat and spat. "I usually chew some mentha to settle my stomach. The tonic doesn't like to stay down."

"Then I'm sorry I kept you from it. But be glad the poison is out for the day. Your head will be clearer without it."

Achan wiped his mouth on his sleeve and stood. "You're certain the tonic is poison?"

"Aye. It won't harm you, but you shouldn't be taking it. I'll speak to Lord Nathak about it the first chance I get."

Achan nodded, though he wanted to know what the point of poison was if not to kill or make ill. Why poison a stray? Achan was nobody to anyone.

A chorus of gasps turned his head back to the crowd. Achan was tall for his age and could see easily from his position. A procession of black horses shrouded in green silk with silver trim passed by. The banners their riders held displayed a goat's head. Achan smiled, thinking of Dilly and Peg.

The men also wore green. Their skin was olive-toned, and they all had hair as black as their horses' coats. They steered their mounts into the inner bailey. A litter mounted onto four horses, two in front and two in back, jerked past. It was larger than the litter Prince Gidon rode around in, and just as ornate, though the wood was dark and polished rather than painted.

"Who are they?" Achan asked.

"Jaelport," Sir Gavin said.

A shiver ran up Achan's arms. Jaelport was a city in Darkness.

When the procession had passed and the crowd dispersed, Sir Gavin continued toward the stables.

They found Noam waiting with two saddled horses: a noble chestnut courser the color of Gren's hair and a grey and white speckled rouncy. The courser was lean and sleek. The rouncy was round and bulky, though smaller in stature.

Noam's small, brown eyes darted over Achan and Sir Gavin, and he smiled.

"Achan," Sir Gavin said, stroking the nose of the rouncy, "this is Etti. She's my pack horse but will be a good one for you to learn on. Take her reins and lead her into the field."

Achan swallowed hard, bubbling with excitement, and took the reins. Not only did he have the day off from his chores and all the preparations for the celebration, but he was going to learn to ride. He glanced at Noam and grinned before guiding Etti out of the stables.

Achan led Etti across the courtyard, feeling like a real squire. He jutted his chin at the guards on the wall and passed through the main gate, his new boots tapping on the drawbridge with Etti's hooves.

He stopped beside the moat and stared across the grassy field at the allown tree, feeling as though the tree were witnessing his life change. Etti began eating fresh spring grass at the side of the moat. Achan stroked her neck as she munched and waited while Sir Gavin led the chestnut courser over the drawbridge.

"This is Scippa," Sir Gavin said when he'd stopped his horse beside Achan. "He's the fastest horse I've ever seen, except the festriers in Xulon."

"He's beautiful," Achan said.

"That he is." Sir Gavin nodded to Noam, who stood watching from the drawbridge. "You ever see a festrier, Achan?"

"No, sir." Achan had heard of the horses that measured as high as twenty-four hands. He believed in them about as much as he believed in the giants who were said to ride them.

"Someday you will." Sir Gavin took Scippa's reins in his left hand and held them up. "When you ride, always mount on the left side." He reached up with his left hand still gripping the reins and fisted Scippa's mane. Then he put his left foot into the stirrup, his right hand on the top edge of the saddle, and jumped. He pulled himself up and swung his right leg over the horse's back.

It looked easy enough. Thankfully, Etti was small. Achan tried to imitate what Sir Gavin had done and just about fell into the moat. On the second try, Achan just barely managed to mount. He flushed to think how that must have looked to Noam. It was a good thing he hadn't been trying to mount a horse the size of Scippa.

"Nicely done, lad! Let's go to the field for a bit." Sir Gavin led Scippa toward the wheat field where Achan had spent so many hours with the waster.

Etti followed for a few steps then stopped, her head dipping back to the grass. Then she walked after Scippa again, only to stop a few paces later for more grass. Achan still gripped Etti's mane in his left hand, and he held tight. Her body rocked him from side to side when she moved. It was like being a giant, to sit atop a horse. He grinned, liking the height very much but wondering just how he was to control this animal.

He looked up to see Sir Gavin heading back to him. A cloud of dust rose to the north. Likely another procession headed to the prince's celebration.

Sir Gavin steered Scippa close. "Hold the reins loose but tight enough to pull if you need to. She's an easy one, so lifting the reins a bit to the right or left is all it takes to steer her. Turn your head the way you want to go as well. She can feel your body move and sense your intentions."

Achan tried a few turns on the road in front of the castle's entrance. Etti responded well to his guidance. It was an empowering feeling.

"That's right," Sir Gavin said. "Now, gently tap your heel into her side to make her walk."

Achan did, and Etti took a few steps forward. Then she stopped for more grass. He squeezed again, a bit harder, and this time she took off at a lazy amble.

"That's it! Always thank her for doing a good job and you'll win her over."

Achan patted her neck. "Thank you, Etti girl."

Etti snorted and followed Scippa out to the wheat field.

Achan steered Etti in circles around the field, practicing commands and reining until the sun burned high in the sky.

Two more entourages entered Sitna manor as they rode. Both groups carried banners of blue and black. Their passing filled the air with dust so thick it seemed like fog. One procession looked like tribal hunters draped in animal skins. The other group was neat and clean, like a bunch of scribes.

"Let's get away from all this dust, shall we?" Sir Gavin steered Scippa west, past the allown tree, and followed the road that ran alongside the gurgling Sideros River.

The horses' hooves clomped a steady rhythm in the dust. Achan swayed from side to side, starting to feel an ache in his lower back and thighs. Flies buzzed around Etti's mane, and she flicked at them with her ears. The wind was soft and warm today. Birds chirped from budding treetops.

Sir Gavin twisted to look back. "You see that ridge there?" He pointed to the western horizon where a bumpy darkness edged the skyline.

"Aye."

"Those are the Chowmah Mountains. We'll go as far as the Sideros Forest today."

Achan grinned. He'd never gone so far from home—or even seen a forest, for that matter. Their journey continued, always with grassy fields on his right and the smooth river on his left. Achan couldn't wait to see a change in the land.

Sir Gavin stopped under a small grove of poplar. They tied the horses to a tree and sat on the bank of the river for a lunch of apples, bread, and cheese. Sir Gavin removed a dagger from his right boot and gave a lesson in how to fight with it. Achan practiced some stabs on a sturdy tree, then they continued with their ride.

Achan could now make out the Sideros Forest. Hundreds of trees stretched from north to south as far as he could see. And the forest continued west, sloping up the side of the mountains until snow took over. Achan had seen snow a few times. It came down occasionally in Sitna but rarely stuck for more than a day.

Why would anyone want to live in endless fields when there was a beautiful place like this they could come to instead? The trees were taller than any he'd ever seen. If not for Gren, Achan might've wished that Sir Gavin would never take him back to the manor.

As they neared the thick forest, Achan noticed the fog that edged the skyline. A queer chill washed over him. He saw that halfway up the peaks, the snow transformed into a shifting grey cloud that seemed to stretch the length of Er'Rets.

The Evenwall.

Achan tried to look beyond it, but he saw only the mist. Yet he knew Darkness was there. The cursed land beyond the Evenwall hadn't seen the sun since King Axel and Queen Dara were murdered. The black shroud was said to be a result of the gods' anger. Punishment for the murder of their king. Achan had heard of the Evenwall but had never seen it himself. It looked like a fierce storm cloud approaching.

Sir Gavin stopped Scippa just outside the forest. "Eerie, isn't it?" He nodded toward the mountains.

"It's a nightmare," Achan whispered.

"Too true. Hear this, young Achan: never go into Darkness. Never even as far as the Evenwall mist. It calls to men. It lures them inside. A man can go crazy in the haze and never find his way out."

Achan had no intention of ever going into Darkness or the mist that was supposedly the doorway to the eerie place. "Do people actually live over there?"

"Aye, plenty. Therion used to be a land as fair as Nahar. But it's a different world since the death of the king. Thirteen years ago Darkness pushed all light from the western half of Er'Rets." Scippa shifted nervously beneath Sir Gavin, as if he didn't like the topic. "The lack of light is the lack of Arman," Sir Gavin said. "And the lack of Arman is Darkness indeed."

Achan considered this, not quite understanding what Sir Gavin meant. Arman was the father god. But Sir Gavin's story confused him. Couldn't a god go anywhere? How could darkness push a god away? Etti turned toward a tuft of grass, and Achan had to steer her back so he could see the forest.

"Some of the noble houses have endured despite the lack of light," Sir Gavin said, "although it is said that madness brews there aplenty."

Achan could only imagine what it would be like to never see the light of day, the sun, or even the moon and stars. How did people cope?

Sir Gavin turned Scippa in a half circle.

Achan twisted around. "Are we going back?"

"I am. You have a mission."

"I do?"

"Aye. Climb down."

Achan slid down Etti's side. Sir Gavin pulled the dagger from his boot and handed it down, hilt first. Achan took the weapon and looked up at Sir Gavin.

"It's tradition that every squire kill his first beast alone."

Achan's lips parted. He glanced into the forest, then up at the mountains, not wanting to go near the cursed mist.

"No need to go far. You'll find plenty of deer and fox in this forest here."

Deer and fox?

"That's right," Sir Gavin said, as if reading Achan's mind. "Don't come home without an animal. A bird doesn't count, and I don't recommend trying for a bear your first time out."

Achan stood gaping as Sir Gavin grabbed Etti's reins. Surely he couldn't be serious?

"I'm very serious, lad. To kill an animal takes wit, strength, and courage. I believe you have all of these traits in great measure, but to be publicly declared a squire, you must prove it to others. This is, and always has been, the way. Arman be with you, lad." At that, Sir Gavin yelled, "Hee-ya!" and Scippa and Etti took off at a gallop.

Achan stood watching the plume of dust that rose in their wake and stung his eyes. When the dust settled, Achan turned toward the trees.

"So much for my day off."

The trees stood before him, a legion of wood soldiers standing guard in both directions as far as he could see, separating the peaceful plains of northeast Er'Rets from the mountains leading to Darkness. He recognized allown, poplar, and pine trees, though they seemed bigger than those he was used to. He hoped the forest wouldn't mind sparing a small animal to help him on his way to freedom.

Yet as he faced the woods, a thrill coursed in his veins. Publicly declared a squire. Could it be true? Would a squire be worthy enough to speak with Gren's father? Achan winced, doubting that even a Kingsguard knight made as much income as a merchant. Likely Riga would inherit the business from his father.

He sighed. How exactly did one catch a fox? Certainly not by chasing it. Should he find a place to crouch and wait for one to wander by? And wouldn't a deer be able to smell him coming? Sir Gavin had never once spoken of hunting. Achan had no idea how to go about it. Why did Sir Gavin give him this task now? And why hadn't he left him Etti?

You must do this alone, Sir Gavin said.

Achan swung around, wondering why Sir Gavin had come back. But Sir Gavin had not returned. Where, then, had his voice come from? Had the Evenwall drifted further than Sir Gavin had thought? Was it already unraveling Achan's mind? The air appeared clear around him, the sky cloudless, the sun bright . . .

He shrugged. It was probably just that he knew Sir Gavin so well now he could guess the kind of thing he would've said. Achan swallowed, gripped the dagger in his left fist, and stepped into the forest.

The scent of pine filled his nostrils. It was dark and cool under the thick, green canopy of poplar, allown, and pine. Low bushes grew between the trees. The forest floor was dotted with dead pine needles, pine cones, and little white flowers.

Achan walked a few paces and stopped. If he went deep into the forest, how would he find his way out? He stepped to the nearest poplar and stripped a wedge of bark off with the dagger, exposing a swatch of moist, white wood. He did the same at another poplar ten paces in. He decided he'd mark only the poplars. For some reason, cutting an allown tree seemed sacrilegious. Not that Achan was a strictly religious or overly superstitious man.

He smiled to himself. He *was* a man now. His sixteenth year had come and gone with little fanfare. Thoughts of being a man reminded him of the gifts he'd received that day, which reminded him of Gren.

Thankfully, the wedding was not scheduled until Riga's father could build them a cottage. That gave Gren—and Achan—some time to get used to the sickening idea. Unfortunately, it didn't take long to build a cottage.

Normally a man had to build his own home. That very act proved him capable of providing for a wife and family. Riga was happy to cheat his way to manhood, letting his father pay a carpenter to build his home.

Poor Gren.

Something rustled to Achan's left. A jackrabbit bounded down a narrow trail between some waist-high rosehip bushes. Achan followed. If a rabbit went this way, perhaps something bigger had too. His tunic snagged on the thorny bushes.

Ripping it free made so much noise he decided to return to his original route.

Had Achan's father built a cottage to win his mother? Or had his birth been a mistake? Achan didn't know. Perhaps his father had been a soldier just passing though and never knew he had a son. But how, then, did Lord Nathak end up with Achan? He didn't want to follow that train of thought, for it led to frightful scenarios he refused to consider, even for a moment.

Most infuriating was that Achan had no memory of his mother—or his childhood at all, for that matter. His earliest recollection was of a young noble pushing him into the mud when he was seven. Gren had come along moments later and helped him up.

Most children had some recollections of what had happened to them before they were seven. What was wrong with him? Had the tonic somehow robbed him of his earliest memories? What did Lord Nathak gain by forcing it on him? Was his head truly clearer without it, as Sir Gavin had suggested?

Achan twisted around and found he could no longer see the prairie through the trees. Pressure built in his temples and his pulse raced. On some level of his mind, he sensed an emotion from outside himself. A sound too soft to be identified reached his ears, and he wheeled around, wondering if a person was nearby. He spotted a doe munching the buds of a poplar ten paces away.

Though such a thing was impossible, the emotion seemed to be coming from the deer. Curiosity, perhaps. Achan's eyes met the doe's, and their minds connected somehow. The pressure grew and Achan cringed. He could taste bitter leaves and branches. It disturbed him.

Come here, girl. He formulated the words in his mind, preparing to speak them aloud.

But before he could make a sound, the doe turned from the tree and, as if she'd heard his thought, trotted toward Achan.

Achan's lips parted in awe as the animal silently maneuvered over a fallen tree, around a briarberry bush, and came to stand in front of him. Achan held out his right hand, and the doe sniffed it, her nose cold and wet against his fingertips. Could she hear him?

Come closer.

The doe stepped nearer. Achan scratched her ear, gripped the dagger tightly in his shaking left hand, and gulped.

I sense you! a male voice hummed. *Tell me your name!*

Achan stopped and turned around in the tall grass of the prairie. He'd left the road for a bit, hoping to take a shortcut. The orange sun sat low and bright on the horizon, but he could see the grey plumes of smoke from the castle's chimneys in the distance, though the manor was still barely a speck on the horizon. He shielded his brow with his free hand but could see no one. The doe's warm body draped heavily around his neck. His head throbbed from the smell of its blood.

Hello, new one. Welcome to our ears. My, how strong your presence is. Who are you?

A woman's voice. Kind. Again Achan twisted around in the grass, nearly dropping the doe. "Who's there?"

Grass surged for miles around like a great green sea. He was alone. He swallowed, his heart pounding, and gripped the doe's legs tighter. Perhaps he'd been too close to the Evenwall after all. But wouldn't he know if he'd stepped into the mist?

He turned back toward Sitna Manor and waded through the grass. He wanted to reach the gate before they raised the drawbridge for the night.

Who are you, gifted one? a deep male voice asked.

What are you called? an old woman asked.

Please! the humming voice said. *What is your name?*

Achan cowered, wincing at the strain on his mind. Perhaps his headache was not from the stench of blood. "Stop it!" Achan yelled to the voices. "Don't speak to me!"

Do not be afraid, the kind woman said. *It is a gift.*

Achan screamed to block out the voices and staggered toward home.

Despite his efforts, it was after dark when Achan approached Sitna Manor.

The drawbridge was up. Arrow loops glowed brightly in the dark night. Yellow flames spaced around the parapet and listed to the east, flickering in the gentle breeze. Achan still held the slain doe around his neck, gripping two legs in each hand.

He stopped and yelled up to the guard. "Lower the drawbridge!"

Are you all right? the kind woman asked. *I sense blood.*

He cringed, by now hating the painful force the voices brought. Hating how they knew things. Hating how he couldn't silence them.

"State yer name and yer business," a voice yelled from the gatehouse above.

"'Tis Achan Cham. I've returned from an errand for Sir Gavin Lukos."

Cham? He's a stray!

Achan! Where are you, Achan? Is Sir Gavin with you? the deep-voiced man asked.

Achan stiffened. How did this strange voice know of Sir Gavin? He looked over his shoulder but already knew there was no one.

"Stay put," a guard yelled down.

Achan waited. His back and shoulders were numb from the deer's weight. The leaden stench of the doe's blood haunted him. Its stickiness drenched his left side. His fists trembled and his head ached from the voices calling out. He'd gone mad. It was a certainty he could no longer deny. The Evenwall must have drifted lower, or maybe killing the doe had somehow—

The familiar boom of the lock and the clinking chain snapped him out of his deranged fog. The drawbridge lowered slowly, revealing a lone man standing inside the outer bailey facing him.

Sir Gavin Lukos.

When the drawbridge hit the ground, Achan dragged himself across it. His new boots made dull, hollow clunks on the thick wood. He then clacked over the flagstones of the gateway and clomped onto soft dirt. The outer bailey was dark and nearly deserted. A few guards looked down on him from the sentry walk. The forge still burned in the armory.

"What yeh got there, boy?" a voice called down from above.

Achan flinched as the compression in his head grew and voices attacked at once.

What has *he got?* a man asked.

He's killed something, another said.

Killed? What have you killed, dear? the kind woman asked, a slight edge to her voice.

Achan stopped in front of Sir Gavin.

Are you well? Sir Gavin spoke inside Achan's head, just like the others.

Achan perked up, ignoring the pain, and stared at Sir Gavin. Then somehow, he sent a thought of his own. *How do you do that?*

Please tell me where you live, dear, the kind woman asked. *And if you are hurt.*

Where are you? the humming voice asked. *I must find you.*

Do not say, another man responded. *He'll only bring you trouble.*

But he must have training, the kind woman said.

If the gods will it, he will learn.

I can teach you much, droned the humming voice. *Tell me your location, and I'll send someone for you.*

Achan dropped to his knees and moaned. He clutched his temples, and the doe's body slid off his back and thumped onto the ground.

He's fainted. This voice was familiar. A guard. Achan looked up to the gatehouse.

Naw, he's hurt.

Think he stabbed himself? Dumb stray don't know which end of the knife is which.

You're a stray?

Speak to me for a moment, I beg you, the humming voice said. *Concentrate on my voice alone.*

Yep. That's the boy's blood, thought another guard. *He's keeling over. He's wounded for sure.*

You're a boy? How old? the humming voice asked.

Achan leaned forward and set his brow against the dusty ground. They could know not only his thoughts and words but the thoughts of others around him? How could this be? His head pounded as if it might burst. He rolled onto his side, clutched his hands over his ears, and squeezed his eyes shut. *Please stop!* "Stop!"

Sir Gavin knelt beside him and massaged the base of Achan's head, right where it hurt most. *You must shut the door, Achan. Focus on a quiet place. See yourself there. Focus on the silence.*

Sir Gavin's voice and tone seemed to cushion Achan's pain. The sensation was somehow familiar, like this had all happened before. But it hadn't. Achan tried to sit, but the pain surged.

Listen to the knight, Achan.

This was a new voice. Unlike the others, this one seemed to come from inside him, like a warm breeze confined to his body alone. Achan froze and blinked up at the night sky. What was that?

Focus, Achan. A quiet place. Sir Gavin's words flooded Achan's mind again, blowing away the warmth of the strange voice. *Only you can ease this pain.*

Listen to the knight. Focus. Achan thought of the allown tree by the river, in a summer sunset. A pleasant wind rustled the grass, and the flax fields bloomed with lavender blossoms.

The pain in his head diminished instantly.

"That's right. Concentrate." Sir Gavin stopped rubbing. He patted Achan's shoulder, then stood. "Now get up. Get your deer. Let's go."

Achan opened his eyes. The voices had gone, and the throbbing in his head remained manageable. He got to his feet and hoisted the deer over one shoulder.

"Let it be known," Sir Gavin called out, "that on this day, Achan Cham has killed his first animal and is worthy of the journey to knighthood."

Few people mingled in the outer bailey at this hour to witness his achievement. A handful of guards roamed the sentry walk. Harnu's father stared from the armory, most likely working late on armor and swords for the coming tournament.

Right now Achan didn't feel worthy to be a knight. He wanted to get the blood washed off him, crawl into his bed, hold a wet cloth to his temples, and sleep. He trudged across the outer bailey in a daze, following Sir Gavin past the stables and barn to the tanner's wagon, which smelled strongly of urine. A high trestle stretched along the side of the wagon. A cowhide hung on one end, the brown pelt glistening in the torchlight.

Sir Gavin helped Achan hang the deer from the trestle. "I'll see that someone takes care of this for you."

Achan nodded and stared at the deer's glassy eyes. "It had a fawn. I didn't see it at first."

"Most have fawns in spring."

"You don't understand." Achan's hands trembled. "The fawn is a stray now . . . like me . . . because of me."

"Aye." Sir Gavin stroked his beard. "And that's the reality of it, Achan. In war, people die. Every one of them is important to someone. A child, a husband, a father, a brother, a mother, a friend. War's ugly. And being a knight, you'll have to deal with that. You'll kill or be killed."

But the doe hadn't been at war, not with him.

Achan blinked. Being a knight was his chance at freedom, his only chance to win Gren. He wanted to learn to use a sword because it was exciting and made him feel strong and in control. But he'd never thought about actually killing anyone. His naïveté stung. Why else would he be learning to use the sword, axe, and dagger if not to kill?

Sir Gavin gripped Achan's shoulder and steered him around to the back of the kitchens. He stopped at the well and drew out a bucket of water.

"I cheated," Achan said. "I told the doe to come to me and she did. I'm no hunter. I'm a deceiver."

Sir Gavin's bushy eyebrows knit together. His one blue eye lay in shadow, making them both appear dark.

"Why could I talk to the deer? Why can you talk to my head? Why did I hear all those voices? One of them knew you were with me. How?"

Sir Gavin's eyes narrowed. "How many voices did you hear?"

Achan shook his head. "Dozens. The whole way back. I think the Evenwall somehow . . . " He looked at the knight. "Why didn't you leave me Etti?"

Sir Gavin's questioning expression faded. He slapped Achan's shoulder. "Stop whining. Go to bed. We'll talk about the voices in the morning."

Achan didn't complain. He used Sir Gavin's water to wash the blood from his body the best he could. Then he rinsed out his tunic. He didn't remember walking down the stairs to the cellar, but suddenly he found himself there. He hung his tunic on one of the ale spouts to dry then crawled onto his pallet under the casks.

Prince Gidon's coming-of-age celebration began tomorrow. Poril would be in a frenzy, and Achan wouldn't have a moment to spare. But Sir Gavin had declared him worthy of knighthood. Would Poril allow him to watch any of the tournaments?

The thought should've thrilled him. But at the moment, he didn't even care.

PART 2

VRELL

4

"Now pull the laces as tight as you can," Lady Coraline Orthrop said.

Vrell obeyed, then tied the silk strings in a tiny bow and tucked the ends into the scooped neckline. "It is more comfortable than the binding and all the tunics."

Lady Coraline stepped up to Vrell and ran her fingertips down the front laces. "And this will be easier than wearing so many layers. No one will suspect a thing."

Lady Coraline was a master with thread and needle. She had crafted Vrell's snug undergarment to be similar to a corset. This one had no uncomfortable whalebone at the waist, though. It was designed to give Vrell a small paunch of wool fleece rather than suck her stomach in. With Vrell's only confidante going to Carmine, she would not have help to bind her breast and dress each day. The new undergarment would enable her to do it alone.

Vrell gripped Lady Coraline's hands. "I wish I could go with you," she said. "Must you really leave?"

Lady Coraline's brown eyes met Vrell's. "My father is ill, and I am overdue for a visit. Plus I have not seen your mother in over eleven years. Do not fret. You will be safe here."

But Vrell wasn't sure. She had been safe only because of Lady Coraline's care. Lady Coraline had been like a mother to Vrell these past months, though she did not look like a mother of four, which she was.

She wore a maroon silk gown with green and gold embroidery. Every curl of her golden hair was pinned into place with a turquoise and silver circlet. At first sight, Vrell had thought Lady Coraline looked very out of place in this fishing town. A noblewoman from Zerah Rock, she was all elegance and decorum. She had married beneath her but did not care. In that, Vrell hoped to someday relate.

Lady Coraline walked back to her bed and began to pick up leftover scraps of fabric. The morning sun beamed though the closed shutters, painting stripes of light over the blue bedspread.

Lady Coraline's bedchamber was small compared to Vrell's chambers at home, and not more than a garderobe compared to Mother's room there. Still, there was something quaint and cozy about this manor. Walden's Watch was like a getaway cottage. This room consisted of a large oak bed and matching sideboard, a tall mirrorglass, and two chairs in front of a warm fireplace. An oval braided rug covered most the floor.

Vrell lifted the orange tunic from the sideboard and ran her thumb over the scratchy fabric. "I know I'll be safe, but I miss Mother so." *And Bran.* Her lips curved into a smile at the thought of Bran's sunburned face. It had been six months since

Vrell had gone into hiding here at Walden's Watch, the home of her mother's childhood friend.

Lady Coraline took Vrell's face in her hands and kissed her forehead. "Dearest, I cannot believe this will go on much longer. Your suitor will soon tire of searching and wed another."

Vrell hoped so. She had come to Walden's Watch last winter to hide from the horrible man. Mother had felt the need to conceal more than Vrell's location—thus the idea to take on a new identity and gender. Vrell's suitor might be scouring all Er'Rets in search of her, but he would not be looking for a fourteen-year-old stray boy.

"I hope you are right." Vrell pulled the orange tunic over her head and tied the brown rope belt. "Masquerading as a boy is fun, though. Trousers are so comfortable, but I wish I could have worn blue." She walked to the mirrorglass that stood in the far corner of the bedchamber.

At seventeen, Vrell was fully grown, but because of her small frame, Mother had suggested her boy persona be fourteen. Vrell examined her short black hair and fair skin in the mirrorglass. She wrinkled her nose and gave her round cheeks a pinch.

"Orange does nothing for my complexion, and strays are treated so horribly. When I return home, I vow to be kind to every stray I see."

Lady Coraline's rose leaf-toned face appeared in the mirror over Vrell's shoulder. "I am sorry you must take the part of a stray, my dear, but it is truly the safest hiding place. Few take notice of strays, and your sallow complexion better hides your beauty."

It certainly did. That and the fact that the padded garment made her torso chubby despite her skinny arms and legs. Her shaggy, chopped hair would not lie flat, and she could only describe the dingy, orange tunic as hideous. Would Bran still think her beautiful if he saw her now? Would he forgive her for running away?

Vrell pulled on worn leather boots and set her hands on her hips. "Well?"

Lady Coraline clapped. "Perfect! Now just you remember your words."

"I am trying!" She cleared her throat. "I mean, 'I be tryin' real hard, m'lady.'"

Lady Coraline giggled.

In Vrell's efforts at playing a stray boy around Walden's Watch, she most often forgot to speak like one. Thrice now she had ordered servants about in the manor before remembering her place. Lady Coraline had introduced Vrell to them as her husband's ward and had insisted *the boy* be treated as a guest and not a servant.

The servants did not like Vrell much.

For the first time in her life, she was thankful for her hoarse, gravelly voice. She had always hated sounding like she had a cold that would not go away. Finally it came in useful.

A pressure squeezed in on Vrell's mind. The thoughts of the little girl climbing the stairs at the end of the hall echoed through Vrell's inner ear. "Aljee is coming," she said to Lady Coraline. "She is hoping to wear your pearls and coral necklace."

Lady Coraline's face paled. "I wish you wouldn't do that."

"I cannot help it."

"You and your mother and your bloodvoices." Lady Coraline scowled. "Your mother played the most rotten tricks on me until she finally confessed her gift. I had feared she was a witch for the longest time."

Vrell laughed. "Yes, Mother told me." The gift had begun in Vrell a month before she had gone into hiding. Mother had explained that bloodvoicing was an endowment. It enabled Vrell to speak with her mother's mind when Mother reached out, but Vrell did not yet know how to reach for Mother. She found she could also hear the thoughts of anyone who was nearby. Some minds were easier to hear than others. Children were always susceptible.

Vrell had wanted to learn everything right away, but Mother said it would be safer to wait until this crisis passed so that she could be trained properly.

A knock sounded at the door.

Lady Coraline scowled.

"Sorry!" Vrell whispered.

"One moment, please," Lady Coraline called.

Vrell darted behind the mirrorglass. It would not do for even young Aljee to see a *boy* in her mother's bedchamber.

Lady Coraline's footsteps creaked across the wooden floor until the door grated open. "Hello, dearest."

Vrell peeked around the edge of the mirrorglass.

Nine-year-old Aljee, Lady Coraline's youngest daughter, stood in the doorway looking lovely in ruffles of blue silk. "Father is ready to see you off."

"Of course. Carry my purse?"

Aljee skipped to her mother's table, golden ringlets bouncing, and swung a red silk purse over her shoulder. "Can I play with your jewels while you're away?"

Lady Coraline sighed, and Vrell suppressed a giggle. "No, but you may use my purses and shawls."

"Hurray!"

Vrell smirked at the child who could not wait to be a young woman. It would happen all too soon, and once Aljee tried the corset and learned the politics of court life, she might wish to return to age nine. After Lady Coraline and Aljee left, Vrell sneaked from the room and went downstairs to bid her mother's dear friend farewell.

Less than an hour later, Vrell stood on the embankment with the four Orthrop children, just below the stone walls of Walden's Watch Manor.

Lord Orthrop had walked Lady Coraline and her serving woman onto the ship that would sail to Nesos. Vrell had heard Shoal, the Orthrops' eldest son, refer to the wooden boat as a cog. Vrell didn't think a cog looked at all safe. Lady Coraline and her serving woman would be riding with six men in a space no bigger than Lady Coraline's bedchamber. And the cog was stacked with cargo that caused it to sit low in the gentle waves. What if there were a storm? There had to be a better way to travel.

The unfamiliar warmth of the sea breeze tousled Vrell's short hair in and out of her eyes. Her skin felt damp with the abrasive smell of seaweed, fish guts, and paraffin oil from boat lamps. The smell stuck to her. With Lady Coraline gone, Vrell would not have a decent bath until her return.

The sea stretched out before her, calm and heavy. Gulls swarmed the rocky shore, nipping bites of whatever creature had died among the rocks. The beach rose sharply up the hill until sand gave way to green grass that ran all the way to the greystone manor walls.

Vrell always felt awkward at these family gatherings. Council law required strays to wear orange. But, as at Zerah

Rock and Carmine, Walden's Watch did not employ slaves or strays. That did not stop people from treating Vrell with contempt. The Orthrop children were kind to her, though. Eleven-year-old Gil more so than anyone.

Lord Orthrop walked up the dock and stood beside Shoal. At first glance, the two men looked like twins. Both had blond hair slicked back into a tail, brown eyes, tanned skin, and broad shoulders. But eighteen-year-old Shoal did not have the weathered face of his father.

A chorus of good-byes rang out from the children, and Vrell joined in, blinking away her tears. Aljee ran down the dock, tossing blossoms in the boat's wake and waving to her mother. Riif and Gil had already moved on. They were fighting with sticks on the grassy lawn behind the manor. Shoal and his father were discussing the tides.

Shoal was quite handsome. If he hadn't smelled like fish at all hours of the day, Vrell might've been tempted to get to know him better.

It was probably for the best. For one thing, Shoal believed in the Er'Retian gods, which Vrell held to be mythical. For another, Shoal was in love with Keili, a fisherman's daughter. It was a shame that Lord Orthrop would never approve the match. Such was life. But those two topics of conversation would certainly cause trouble. Vrell had a bad habit of setting people straight about *the gods* that usually ended in ridicule. Plus, her own thwarted love would prod her to romantic discussions no true boy would venture into willingly.

Best to steer clear.

Shoal, still engaged in conversation with his father, grinned at Vrell as she walked up the hill, practicing her springy boy walk. Unfortunately, after hearing his thoughts, she knew his smile was not for companionship, but at his memory of clobbering her with a sword. Her hand was still bruised. Vrell sighed and started for the apothecary, kicking pebbles on the dusty road as she went.

The village of Walden's Watch was crammed into a small flat space at the end of the Nahar Peninsula. Cliffs edged the ocean on both sides of the town. The houses were narrow, two-level stone dwellings packed close beside one another.

Vrell kept her head down as she walked, glancing up only to keep from running into anything. Strays were not to make eye contact with people above their station, and that took a lot of training on Vrell's part. A little boy chased a rolling leather ball into the road. She did not meet his eyes or try to hear his thoughts, but his sunburned face reminded her of Bran.

Seven months ago, Bran Rennan had asked for Vrell's hand. She longed to be his bride. He was her dearest friend and her only love. But Bran was only a lesser noble, and Vrell was heir to a duchy. She would be marrying beneath her, at least in terms of social station. To Vrell's delight, her mother had actually been considering the match when another suitor had come along.

The powerful and horrible Crown Prince of Er'Rets: Gidon Hadar.

Vrell had wanted nothing to do with him. Thankfully, Mother had agreed. But when the prince threatened to send guards to provoke a favorable answer, Mother sent Vrell into hiding.

The plan was simply to wait. As soon as Prince Gidon yielded and chose another woman to marry, Vrell would return home. At which point she would beg Mother to accept Bran's offer.

For now, Vrell was homesick but safe. It was winter's end, and if she were home she would still be wearing heavy woolen skirts and furs. Here she did not even need an overcoat. Walden's Watch was almost tropical, although it was more swamp than rainforest. According to Lord Orthrop, however, the gods always cursed the Nahar Peninsula in a winter drought.

She rolled her eyes at such foolish superstition.

The apothecary sat two streets from the manor house in a stone building with a large wooden shutter covering the window. When the shop opened, the shutter would serve as an awning to shade both customers and merchandise. Vrell approached the building and followed the path to the backyard.

The shop owner, Wayan Masen, served as the only apothecary for miles around. Lord Orthrop had arranged for Vrell to apprentice there. But Vrell found the work of Wayan's wife, Mitt Masen, much more interesting. Mitt was a healer and midwife. Vrell would have loved to see babies born, but under this disguise it was impossible. A boy apprenticed to a midwife was unheard of. And as far as the Masens were concerned, Vrell was a boy.

Thankfully, Wayan found Vrell a bother—an opinion somewhat helped along by Vrell—and was therefore quick to send her away to assist his wife. Though Vrell couldn't help her with the midwifery, she was learning a great deal about the healing arts. Mitt frequently spoke of her visits with patients, and Vrell soaked up all the information she could. Using plants to heal was fascinating.

She enjoyed the smells of herbs and blossoms, and learning the healing trade gave her a sense of home. She missed her private garden, her hybrid plant projects, and Mother's library. Lord Orthrop did not keep books or scrolls of knowledge—not that Vrell's boy persona would be able to read them even if he did.

Vrell entered the Masens' backyard, a small medicinal garden filled with all kinds of herbs and spices. Lines of twine zigzagged between the apothecary and the Masen's home next door.

Vrell found Mitt hanging sprigs of juniper and oregano on the lines. Mitt was short and round but very able. She always wore a charcoal grey dress with a white apron over it. Her face was as round as the rest of her, and her cheeks were always flushed.

"Morning, Vrell!"

"Good morning. May I help you with those?"

"You surely can." Mitt motioned to a basket of fresh blossoms. "Hang the lavender over by the wall, will you?"

Vrell took a bunch of lavender and a length of pre-cut twine and made her way to the wall. The lavender smelled heavenly, like Mother. Vrell's eyes watered as she thought of the wonderful visit her mother and Lady Coraline would be having soon. She blinked the jealous thoughts away, tied the sprig to the line, and went for another.

"Kehta Grett's twins come last night," Mitt said.

Vrell gasped. "How did it go?"

"Terrifying. For a time I wondered if I'd been wrong and there was only one. But when the girl come out weighing so little, I knew there was another. The boy was a jackal, though. Gave me a time of it. Come feet first with the cord around his wee neck. Survived in spite of it, and I praised the gods."

Vrell bristled at how everyone so freely gave credit to the gods. As if mythical beings could be capable of acts of healing and controlling the weather. She itched to correct Mitt, but that would only draw attention and questions. She forced her thoughts back to the twins. "How lovely for Kehta there was one of each."

"Yes. Though it's rare for a boy to notice such things." Mitt chuckled. "I suppose that's why we get along so well, you and me."

Vrell's cheeks flushed. Even when she purposely tried to avoid drawing attention, she managed to slip. It was just so hard not to be herself around Mitt.

"How is your salve coming along?" Mitt asked.

With Mitt's help, Vrell had been building her own healing kit. She had gathered quite the collection thus far. She was currently working on her first yarrow salve for cuts and bruises.

"It's nearly finished."

Mitt clipped a spring to the line and brushed her hands on her apron. She waved Vrell over to the garden. "Test time." Mitt pointed to a small daisy. "What's this?"

"Calendula? It's the main ingredient in my salve. Does wonders for bruising and inflammation. And . . . grows naturally in the Chowmah Mountains?"

Mitt nodded and pointed to a leafy tropical plant.

Vrell thought for a moment. "Kava kava? It's used to make a sedative."

"Yes, but how is it made?"

"You grind it and strain it to make a tea. And can you also chew it fresh?"

A strand of greying hair fell loose from Mitt's braid. "That's right. How about this one?" She pointed to a flat, petal-like, brown mushroom.

"That is reishi," Vrell answered right away. "It is good for a weak heart, dizziness, and high mountain travel."

Mitt led Vrell though the garden until she had questioned every plant. Then they went inside the shop, where Vrell helped make a large batch of clove oil for a customer with a toothache. Not long into the project, the spicy smell numbed her nostrils.

Vrell had just begun to grind willow bark for a tonic when young Gil raced into the shop, panting. At eleven, Gil was a weed. His body had reached that awkward stage where his head, arms, and feet seemed too big for the rest of him.

"Vrell! Father needs you at the manor straight away." Gil shook his shaggy blond hair out of his wild eyes. "Some men have come for you."

Vrell's heart took off at a gallop. Could she have been discovered? How? She reached out with her mind to seek Lord Orthrop's thoughts, but gleaned only his anxiety. "What kind of men?"

Gil's eyes bulged. "Kingsguard knights, and one's a giant!"

Mitt's chuckle rose over the scraping of her mortar and pestle.

"Do not be silly." Vrell tried to sound casual. She wiped her shaking hands on a towel and forced sensible words from her lips. "There are no giants around here."

Gil grinned, baring his new adult teeth that looked oversized on his childlike face. "Just you wait and see, Vrell. He had to duck to come through the door."

Vrell apologized to Mitt and walked back to the manor house with Gil, who prattled on endlessly about the Kingsguard knights. Vrell sought over and over but could not hear Lord Orthrop's thoughts or the strangers'. If only Mother had taught her more bloodvoicing skills before Vrell had left. What if Prince Gidon had somehow found her? Sweat beaded under her wool padding at what may lie ahead. She prayed Arman would protect her.

The manor house at Walden's Watch sat at the highest point on the cliffs. No wall or moat surrounded the sea stone dwelling. It was guarded by a single gatehouse entrance, which was the only way in or out. Vrell darted through the gate and pushed past the oversized oak door.

The manor was cool inside. She walked through the small foyer and down a narrow corridor. Her boots crunched over the dead rushes that were in need of replacement. Lord Orthrop's study sat directly across from the dining hall. Two bulky packs lay beside the closed door, one three times the size of the other. Vrell stood outside the room, seeking the thoughts inside. Finally, Lord Orthrop's amplified words rung in her head.

I'd like to travel again. It's been a while since I've gone anywhere but to sea for fish. Been waiting for Prince Gidon to take the throne. Wondered if he wouldn't make some changes to the appointed lordships.

Vrell groaned. If she had been discovered, they were no longer talking about it. But why else would she have been summoned? Lord Orthrop had always ignored her. Now that his wife had left, would he send her away? Sell her as a slave, despite Walden's Watch's laws? She did not know the man well enough to guess.

She raised her fist and knocked.

The valet opened the door, and Vrell stepped inside. Like the rest of the manor, the study was oak and sea stone. A large hearth lay cold behind Lord Orthrop's driftwood desk. Lord Orthrop stood in front of it, pointing up at a wooden carving of a swordfish that hung over the hearth. "This is a replica of one I caught two summers past. Took me an hour to pull him in."

Two knights stood before Lord Orthrop's desk looking up at the wooden fish. They wore black New Kingsguard capes embroidered with the golden justice scales of Mahanaim's crest. One man stood so tall Vrell understood why Gil had called him a giant. His head nearly brushed the timber ceiling. He was as wide as two men—but it was hard muscle, not flab. His legs were strapped in leather, sheathing daggers and axes. Most of his face was hidden behind a bushy black beard.

Vrell stepped up to Lord Orthrop's desk. The giant looked down at Vrell with brown eyes the size of goose eggs. A red scarf was tied over his hair like a nightcap, and a fat braid hung over one shoulder and down to his waist.

Vrell suddenly missed her long hair. She shook the thought away and sought the giant's mind.

She could not find it.

How strange. She could always read people this close, but when she tried for the giant, he was empty. The tops of her ears tickled suddenly, and she focused hard on drawing the curtains around her mind, as Mother had described the defensive action. One of these men must have the bloodvoices as well and was seeking her thoughts. Her ears always tickled the same way just before Mother communicated.

The idea brought a shiver of fear. If either of these men could bloodvoice, could they discover her true identity? Or did they know it already? Maybe this was about her being exposed, after all.

Vrell dragged her gaze to the other New Kingsguard knight. He was barely taller than she was. This scrawny man's greasy brown hair hung in his dark eyes. Scruffy cheeks, a wild mustache, and a long neck added to his weasely appearance. He wore a sword at his side almost as long as he was tall. It looked ridiculous on him, like he was just holding it for the giant.

Vrell did not risk opening her mind to try and hear his thoughts. She was pretty sure she didn't want to know what they were anyway.

Lord Orthrop turned to Vrell. "Ah. My good knights, this is the boy you've come for. Vrell Sparrow is what he's called. Don't know how you knew he was here. He's only been my ward these past six months."

Lord Orthrop walked from the hearth and sat at his desk. He motioned to the giant. "This is Jax mi Katt." Then to the short man. "And Khai Mageia. It's an incredible opportunity for you, boy. I don't understand it entirely, but apparently you have a gift."

Vrell's jaw fell open. How could anyone have known about her bloodvoicing ability?

Lord Orthrop's eyebrows rose. "You know of this?"

"I . . . " Vrell swallowed, hating to lie, but afraid to tell the truth. "N-None that I know of, my lord."

"Well, I suspect you'll find out soon enough. These men have come to take you to the great city of Mahanaim to apprentice for the Council of Seven."

Vrell could only gasp and sputter.

"You'll train under Master Macoun Hadar," Khai said in a nasally voice.

"Hadar is a royal name," Lord Orthrop said. "An amazing privilege for anyone—but of course even you must know this."

Indeed, Hadar was a royal name, but not one she trusted much. Besides, Vrell could not travel to Mahanaim with two men! She would not. She needed to stay here to hide until she could marry Bran. Plus, such a thing was unheard of. Noblewomen did not travel without a companion. It had taken her months just to get used to walking to the apothecary by herself. Of course, she couldn't say any of this without revealing her identity, or at least her gender.

Her heart rattled under her padded prison. "Forgive me, my lord, but Lady Coraline promised I could stay until my training with Master Masen was complete."

Lord Orthrop waved his hand around. "I've indulged my wife long enough in this matter. You must trust me, Vrell. A man knows what's best for a man. Serving a Hadar is a much loftier goal than apothecary in any city, especially Walden's Watch. We're at the edge of the world here, boy. No one much cares about this place."

"I do."

Lord Orthrop gave a small smile. "You're a stray. You could do no better if you worked hard your whole life."

All this would make perfect sense if Vrell were truly a boy and truly a stray. Lord Orthrop would never send a woman off with two men. Except he did not know she was a woman. He could not find out either—he might side against her. Vrell's heart was a lump in her throat, choking back her words, and thankfully, tears.

If only she knew how to bloodvoice Mother.

"We will leave the moment the boy is ready," the giant said in a booming voice.

Lord Orthrop's eyes met Vrell's. "Off you go then. Pack your things."

She bowed. "Yes, my lord."

After that, everything happened fast. Gil gave her a small leather satchel to stow her healing herbs and salves. She'd clipped a leather water skin to it. Vrell realized with a pang of loneliness that this was all she would leave here with. She had brought no personal belongings from home, so she had nothing more to pack.

When she came downstairs—with Gil sniffling at her side—Lord Orthrop, Aljee, and the knights were waiting in the foyer. Lord Orthrop handed her a small velvet bag of coins.

"My lord, I couldn't possibly—"

"You must, boy. And you'll take a horse too. I'll be in trouble enough when Coraline returns to find you gone. Accept this as a token of my apologies for rushing you off. You must understand: even if I wanted you to stay, the Council is law. I cannot speak against them. May the gods be with you."

Aljee rushed up and grabbed Vrell around the waist. "Oh, Vrell, I wish you didn't have to go. You've never teased me as much as my brothers."

"And you never beat me as much," Gil said, his posture slumped.

"It won't be much longer, son, before you'll be as skilled as your brothers," Lord Orthrop said.

"My lord?" Vrell asked. "Might I bid good-bye to Master Masen and Mitt?"

Lord Orthrop shook his head. "I'll send word. These knights have instructions to bring you back with haste. Isn't that right, Sir Jax?"

The giant nodded. "We must leave at once."

Vrell hugged Aljee one more time. She longed to hug them all and beg them to let her stay, but it was too risky. Arman would protect her, would he not?

"I'll tell Mitt for you, Vrell," Gil promised.

Tears blurred Vrell's vision. She followed the massive form blocking out the sun and his tiny partner to the stables. It would be a very long journey to Mahanaim—at least a fortnight.

What would happen if these Kingsguard knights discovered her secret?

Fear scuttled over her like a thousand beetles. She concentrated on closing her mind and putting one foot in front of the other.

5

Vrell's steps slowed at the sight of the giant's horse. It stood before the stables, saddled and ready to go with the other two horses, but its back was as high as the others' heads. Vrell had seen festriers at tournaments when she was younger, but none quite as large as this one.

Jax swung up onto the beast in a swift motion, his axes clanking against each other. The stirrup holding his massive boot dangled at the level of Vrell's chin. How thrilling it must feel to ride such a horse. She wondered how her horse back home, Kopay, would react to the sight of one.

Vrell mounted Nickel, the withered grey palfrey Lord Orthrop had given her, and followed the knights out of Walden's Watch.

The dirt road stretched out across the Nahar Peninsula with nothing but sagebrush, chaparral, cactus, and the occasional juniper tree for miles on either side. She wondered if the scenery would change on their way to Mahanaim. She had been to the stronghold several times but never by this route.

Jax stopped his horse and waited until Vrell came alongside. He looked down on her with his oversized eyes. "Have you ridden much?"

"Some, sir."

"What kind of horse?"

"Um . . . a . . . " Vrell faltered as she tried to decide how to answer. Kopay was a sleek courser. But a stray would have no business on such a fine animal. She feigned ignorance. "I don't know, sir."

Jax looked straight ahead. "It will be a hot afternoon. It's best we move mostly at night to avoid the sun. Have you traveled this road before?"

"No, sir."

"Where you from?"

Jax's deep, rumbling voice shook Vrell's already frazzled nerves. She would need to keep her answers short, as Lady Coraline had suggested. Since she had a tendency to forget her role and speak like a noblewoman, the less she said the better.

She decided to name the city her boy persona was supposedly from. "Zerah Rock."

Jax nodded. His red head scarf made his skin look darker. She knew from her lessons with Sangio, her tutor back home, that Jax was a yâtsaq giant. Since Darkness came, the giants had divided into two tribes: eben and yâtsaq. The ebens were said to be pale and fair-haired. Yâtsaq, the opposite. Jax's black braids were as thick as Vrell's wrists.

She hoped he would not try to make idle conversation the entire journey. She did not think she could handle the stress of coming up with the right answers. She allowed Nickel to slowly fall behind Jax's mount. Eventually, Jax spurred his festrier to Khai's side.

Vrell's every nerve was on edge. Her body ached more from tension than from the miles they had covered since leaving Walden's Watch that morning. She feared making a move that might give her secret away. Staying behind the two knights gave them less opportunity to wonder, but it doomed Vrell to witnessing hour upon endless hour of their crude behavior.

Khai craned his long neck around, his dark eyes plowing over Vrell as if to dig up her secret and anything else she held dear. He was probably only making sure she had not ridden off—as if there were any place to go. She focused hard on keeping her mind closed. Khai turned back and let out a loud, horse-like laugh.

Vrell cringed.

These knights were far from noble. They were soldiers who scratched and spat and smelled and swore—though Vrell doubted that even noble knights would behave chivalrously around a stray boy. Did Bran do such things when no ladies were present?

She should have told him the truth about the prince's proposal. By now, Mother would have done so. She hoped he did not do anything foolish when he heard.

Without any warning, Khai dismounted to relieve himself on the side of the road. Vrell gasped and spurred her horse to pass.

Men were revolting.

Vrell had to go herself, but she was not sure how to manage it. They were headed for the Nahar Forest, but it was three days away. She couldn't wait three days for the privacy of a tree, but how would she ever escape long enough to do her business?

The sun set quickly, casting a beautiful array of color over the flat horizon before vanishing. Jax lit a torch and held it high above his towering form to light their way on the dark, dirt road. It helped little. Natural darkness stretched around them on all sides. Within the beam of light, Vrell could make out only the silhouette of her horse.

She would rather wet herself than leave the small circle of light beaming from Jax's torch. The darkness had plunged the meadowlands into a black void. Behind her, a hollow squawk rang out and dwindled to a gurgling moan. Her horse jolted.

Vrell's breath caught and she patted his neck. "Do not fear, boy." She shuddered to think what kind of an animal made such a—

RAWHH!

Nickel reared up. Vrell gripped his mane, but the horse took off at a gallop.

"Vrell!" Jax called out as she passed.

The horse bolted out of the torch's beam and into a shroud of darkness.

Shadows loomed before her, making her afraid the roaring beast might attack at any moment. She gripped both reins and grabbed the roots of Nickel's mane with her fingers. She pulled back with her left hand, turning the horse's head toward her. Nickel slowed to a canter. Vrell pulled the left rein back to her hip and let the right slip through her fingers a bit, hoping to turn the horse's head more.

Nickel circled. The sensation was terrifying in the dark, but Vrell fought to maintain her calm since horses could sense their rider's fear.

When he stopped completely, Vrell patted his neck. "See?" she said in a soothing voice. "You are just fine. Yes, you are. You are a good boy, Nickel."

She stayed put, continuing to comfort the animal. She strained to hear any sound of the wild beast approaching again. Jax's torch bobbed in the distance, growing slightly with each passing second.

"Vrell?" Jax yelled from afar.

"Here!" Vrell called back, not too loudly.

Nickel stiffened beneath her palm, but did not bolt.

Slowly, the torch lit her surroundings. Jax and Khai trotted up and reined in their horses.

"You okay?" Jax asked.

"Yes. A wild animal scared my horse."

Khai snickered. "Jumpy little sprig is just like his rider."

Jax spun around, the torch's flame sputtering. "Enough of your gowzal calls, Khai. We don't have time for this foolishness."

Vrell gaped at the weasely knight. Had he purposely frightened her horse? She could have been killed.

Khai glanced away, still smirking.

Jax scratched underneath his beard and dismounted. The dead grass crunched under his footsteps and his axes jangled. "We'll stop here to get some food in our bellies. But only for a few hours. I want to travel as much as possible when it's cool."

"How will we get back to the road?" Vrell asked.

"It's just there." Jax pointed the direction they had come.

Khai wheezed a laugh. "Plus, the sun will come up soon enough, boy. This ain't Darkness, you know."

Vrell gritted her teeth and slid off the side of her horse. "I *meant to ask*, how can you be certain where the road is?

Everything looks the same here, even in daylight. We have been traveling all day, and I have not seen a single traveler. How do we know we are even on the right road? Have you a map?"

Khai mocked Vrell's raspy voice with a lofty tone. "Yes, Sir Jax. But how can you be *certain* where the road is? Everything looks the same and I'm tired and hungry and daft."

Vrell was thankful for the black void that hid her flushing cheeks. This was why it was best for her not to speak.

Jax rounded on Vrell and thrust the torch into her hands. "Hold this."

She pulled her neck back to keep her hair free of the flame and lifted the torch high away from her skittish horse.

Jax unfastened his pack from his horse and dropped it into the grass. He removed some rope from it and tossed it to Khai. "Tether and water the horses. Vrell, help him."

Khai gathered his and Jax's horses and stomped away, the parched grass swishing under their steps. The tip of his massive sword's scabbard dragged behind him.

Vrell stayed put, unsure of what to do with the torch. "Do you need the light, sir?"

Jax looked up and held out his large hand. Vrell passed him the heavy torch, and he drove it into the ground so it stood on its own. He got on his knees to go through his gear. In this position he was almost her height.

Vrell turned and blinked. The torch cast enough light that she could see where Khai had taken the horses. Bushes lit up like misty shadows. She led Nickel to the others. Khai had already stripped off their saddles and set out a bucket of water for each, including her own.

This surprised Vrell. "Thank you for pouring a bucket for my horse."

Khai grunted. “I didn’t do it for you. I did it to conserve water. If I see your skinny fingers on the water pack, I’ll break them. Understood?”

Vrell’s eyes widened, but she held her tongue. She turned away from Khai and tied Nickel to a chaparral bush. She took care of his gear, then returned to the torchlight. Khai and Jax busied themselves in their packs. If ever there was a time to steal a moment alone in the dark, this was it.

“I am going to . . . ” She pointed away into the darkness. “I need to . . . ”

“Fine.” Jax dug in his gear for something. “Don’t go far.”

Vrell inched away, looking over her shoulder with each step to verify both men remained at the camp and that she could still see the torch. She walked straight ahead, arms stretched out in front to feel for anything. She did not want to stumble into any cactus.

When the camp had shrunk to a small glow, and Vrell was confident she would not be seen, she crouched over the dead grass. For the first time in her life, she relieved herself outdoors. When she finished, she used water from her water skin to wash her face and hands. The road had been so dusty her nostrils were stiff and crusty. She did not have a handkerchief.

She did have a salve to protect her skin from sunburn, though. She had made it herself with chaparral from Mitt’s garden. How strange it had been to see so much of the desert bush in its natural state during her ride earlier. She rubbed the salve generously over her face. The cool mixture tingled the heat from her skin. She thought of Bran and smiled. He had such a fair complexion. She had often tried to convince him to use one of her salves, but he never had.

Vrell returned to the torch and found Jax and Khai eating. She settled down on the ground to Jax's left, putting the fire between her and Khai. Jax passed her a hard bread roll, some dried figs, and a chunk of dried meat.

"Thank you, sir."

Vrell bowed in silent thanks for the meal, then bit into the bread.

Khai was watching her, his brows heavy over dark eyes. "What'd you do? Bewitch it to taste like tarts?"

Vrell lowered her hands into her lap and swallowed the bite of bread before answering. "I always thank Arman for my food."

Khai bit into his roll. He tore off a chunk and spoke with a full mouth. "Arman? Why not Zitheos or Dendron? It's their provisions you eat."

Vrell huffed a sigh. "There is only one God: Arman the Father."

"Ohhh." Khai tipped his head back with a wide grin. "You're one of those crazy Waywarders."

"I am not crazy," Vrell pointed out coldly, "and it is called the Way."

"If your Way is true, why do so few follow it?"

"*Khai*," Jax's voice boomed. "Leave him be."

Vrell hid a smug smile. She ate her bread and meat first, saving the figs for last. The sweet taste reminded her of the plump raisins so plentiful back home.

The men ate in half the time Vrell did. She watched Jax while she nibbled her figs. The giant had removed his cloak and head scarf. He sat motionless, hands in his lap, head tilted up to the starry sky, glassy eyes staring at nothing.

His undershirt clung to his muscled torso. The iron cuffs gave the appearance of shackles on a convict bound for Ice

Island, although these were not the same kind. Guards often stopped in Vrell's hometown, transporting criminals to the icy prison. Those cuffs were always thin and chained to one another. Jax's covered both forearms and seemed to be painted or carved, but she could not tell in the low light of the torch.

A quick glance at Khai caught him leering again. Did he suspect she was a woman? Could he read her thoughts? She swallowed her fear and nodded to Jax. "What is he doing?"

Khai yawned, his tiny mouth stretching abnormally wide. "Reporting."

"To whom?"

"Your new master."

Vrell blinked. "You mean to say he is communicating with someone? Now?"

Khai leaned back on his elbows.

She stared at Jax's flickering eyes. "How?"

"Don't play the fool with me," Khai said. "You know how or you wouldn't be here."

Vrell pulled her knees up to her chest and took a bite of her last fig. Khai was implying that Jax was bloodvoicing someone. She realized she shouldn't be surprised. She had seen Mother do it before, but never with her eyes open.

Why had Mother not tried to bloodvoice her in so long? Was she in danger? Surely she hadn't forgotten her own daughter. Lady Coraline would not have arrived in Carmine yet. That journey would take at least a week. When she did arrive, Mother would certainly contact Vrell to let her know. Right?

Vrell sucked in a sharp breath. What if her avid focus to close her mind to the knights had blocked out Mother? That seemed a logical answer to Mother's lack of communication. There had to be a way to connect with one person and block out the rest, but Vrell had no idea how. Dare she risk asking Jax?

When they had finished eating, Jax ordered Vrell and Khai to ready the horses. Vrell obeyed, though she was so tired she was certain she would fall asleep in the saddle. Jax wanted to sleep during the day, though, so she obeyed without complaint.

They rode over the same barren desert plains until the sun brought sweat to her brow. Vrell was so tired she hardly remembered the day's journey. Jax stopped where a juniper tree and some chaparral bushes clustered together. Vrell tied up Nickel where Khai tethered the others. Jax took all three horses' blankets and draped them over the vegetation to make a shady place.

Jax unfastened his bedroll from his pack and tossed it in the shaded spot. He looked to Vrell. "You have no bedroll?"

Vrell paled. She had not considered sleeping arrangements. How foolish. Someone else always took care of such things when she traveled. "No, sir."

"Well," Jax said, "the grass is rough, but at least it's not rocky."

Sleep on the ground? Vrell looked at her horse, blinking away tears. Of course the men would not give up their beds for a stray. Maybe if she made her rank and gender known?

She pressed her lips together and found them dry. Her mind weighed the consequences of revealing her identity. If she did, Jax or Khai would likely offer her a bed. She could sleep soundly. The knights would behave in her presence and return her to Walden's Watch. She was not certain of Lord Orthrop's political views, but there was at least a chance he would not turn her in.

On the other side, if Prince Gidon had offered a bounty for whoever located his *intended*, the knights might know of it. In that case, one of them might give up his bed to see her comfortable tonight, but in the morning they would escort her to Mahanaim, where she would be forced to marry the pig.

Or they might attack her.

She would keep silent and be thankful to sleep on the ground. The grass would be heavenly compared to a lifetime of sleeping on a featherbed next to a cockatrice. She suddenly realized why she disliked Khai Mageia so—he reminded her of the prince.

Vrell found a flat patch of earth a few yards from Jax and stomped the dead grass stalks flat. She got down on her knees and brushed away the broken blades and bits of sagebrush until she had a clear place to sleep. When she was satisfied, she glanced at the men. Jax had lain down. Khai was digging in his pack, his longsword stretched out behind him like a third leg. She strode away from the camp. She found a place where some chaparral obscured her view enough that the men would not see her use her latest privy.

When she returned to the shelter, Khai's bedroll lay in the spot she had cleared to sleep in. She gasped. "What is the meaning—" She stopped herself before she spoke above her station.

One side of Khai's mouth curved into a grin. "I thank you for clearing a place for me, boy. Saved me some work. About time you made yourself useful."

Vrell seethed. Clearly that had not been a place for Khai. He had seen her clear it when Jax had told her the grass was softer than . . . Oh, why bother to think on it? The man had done it on purpose, and she would not let him see her anger.

She turned her nose in the air and started trampling a new spot on the other side of Jax.

Then she realized a boy—especially a stray boy—would probably not put his nose in the air, so she slouched down and stuffed her hands in her pockets. Yes. Much more like a sulking boy.

She lay down in her earthen bed and curled into a ball on her side. The bitter chaparral smell filled her nostrils. She watched Khai pour red powder into a small, wooden bowl. He added a drop of water from his water skin and stirred it with a stick. What was he doing?

A sharp kick in the side woke her. A dark form loomed above.

She cringed as Khai sneered, "Up, sloth!" Then he mumbled, "What Master Hadar sees in you is a mystery."

Vrell blinked wildly and scrambled back to avoid another kick. The sharp, dead grass scratched her palms. It was dark. Jax already sat atop his festrier and held the torch high. He held the reins to Vrell's horse in his other hand. Nickel was already saddled and ready to go. Vrell sat up. Her body ached from so much riding yesterday and from sleeping on the hard ground.

She yawned and mounted her horse. She took a drink from her water skin, only to find it nearly empty. It had probably been unwise to use it for washing. What would she do if she ran out of water? Khai's courser carried two jugs for the horses, but she had no desire to have her fingers broken.

Vrell's eyelids were heavy in the darkness. She was thankful she did not have to walk. Occasionally she remembered to worry about slouching in her saddle like a boy, but she was too tired to keep up the concern. They rode for hours with only the clomping of hooves and the crickets' song for company. Soon the darkness faded and the endless savanna lit up with the dull, grey dawn.

The air was cool, for now, and Vrell took a long cleansing breath. Her surroundings looked no better today than yesterday, however. Sagebrush and chaparral. A few juniper trees squatting here and there. But no streams, no ocean, no vibrant colors. With each step her horse took, the sun rose higher, the sky turned bluer, and Vrell grew more and more thirsty.

And now her water was gone.

Khai knew of Vrell's bloodvoicing gift. Jax probably did as well. Maybe there was no point in hiding it. She spotted Jax's red head scarf ahead. If she could get him aside, she could ask him how to bloodvoice someone directly. Then she could contact Mother. The instant Mother discovered Vrell's plight, she would surely send someone to her rescue.

But as much as Vrell wanted to be home again, she desired to wed that fool of a prince even less. He didn't love her. His attentions were strictly based on political gain. Carmine influenced much of northern Er'Rets. The prince likely figured that an alliance with Carmine would give him better control over the kingdom. But Prince Gidon's reputation already held doom for the future. His rule would not be a noble one.

For the sake of the kingdom and Vrell's future, she was safest hidden. If she could play her part, perhaps this apprenticeship in Mahanaim would be the perfect refuge.

Was she mad? The sun must be melting her good sense. She could not continue to travel with these Kingsguard ruffians. She should be seeking opportunities for escape. If she could get away and make it back to Walden's Watch, perhaps Mitt would take pity. But Wayan would never keep secrets from Lord Orthrop, and if Lord Orthrop discovered Vrell had fled the Kingsguards, the blow to his pride might make him cross enough to deliver Vrell to Mahanaim himself. If only Lady Coraline had not chosen this time to travel.

Khai's horse kicked up a plume of dust, and the wretched wind threw it back in her face. She coughed and spluttered and brushed the dirt off her tunic. As if her problems were not plentiful enough, where would she bathe?

Vrell's mouth and throat were parched, her lips were crusty, and swallowing had become difficult. They rode until Jax found another cluster of juniper to build a shelter in. As soon as they dismounted, Khai led the horses—and the extra water—away. Vrell halfheartedly stomped out a clear spot in the dead grass, then lay down and instantly fell asleep.

All too soon, Khai's kick jerked her awake. As they rode through the dark night, Jax demanded she pick up the pace, but she was so tired and thirsty. Her body would not stay focused enough to guide her horse. Every muscle throbbed and spasms of pain pulsed in her temples. Finally the sun rose, blurring the endless savanna like melted butter.

Jax reined in his horse beside hers. "You must move faster, Vrell. We can make the forest before dark."

Vrell blinked. Her horse had stopped completely. She looked at the giant, but his face went out of focus and she could not determine whether he was truly angry. Wasn't it time for bed? Her eyelids drooped, her head rolled back, and she slumped. Jax's ample hand gripped her arm, and she snapped to at his touch.

Her words came out in a whisper. "I shall try, sir." She blinked and wiggled her tongue, but her pasty mouth could gather no saliva to swallow.

Jax tugged the water skin off Vrell's satchel and shook it. "You have no water?"

Again her voice croaked, "I finished it yesterday."

Khai groaned to the sky.

Jax pushed Vrell's empty skin into her hands. She hugged it tight, cradling it like a broken child. The giant lifted a strap over his head and offered her his water jug. It was carved from some kind of gourd, the surface intricately burned with a picture of a tree. She clipped her empty water skin to her pouch and reached for Jax's jug.

The wet, cool liquid softened her shriveled tongue. She swallowed and swallowed and swallowed, until Jax pulled the sweet moisture away. Vrell whimpered and eyed the jug greedily as he hung the leather strap back over his head.

"You must take small drinks," Jax said. "Make your water last. How is it you live in Walden's Watch and don't know of the pre-spring drought?"

"Because he's a half-wit," Khai said. "Let him thirst. It will teach him to think next time."

Vrell scowled at Khai. She had not understood about the drought. Lord Orthrop had said it came from mythical gods, so she had dismissed it as mere legend. Besides, Lord Orthrop and Mitt had always had plenty of water to drink. She forced her befuddled mind to answer as the stray, Vrell Sparrow, would.

"Um . . . " Her pounding head made it difficult to remember. She was to give Lady Coraline's hometown as her own. That should suffice to explain to Khai why she knew little of Walden's Watch. "I . . . come from Zerah Rock."

Khai groaned again and looked away. "No wonder." He turned back and threw up his hands. "He's a sapient slave. Fancies himself worth more than he is."

Jax silenced Khai with a sharp look. "I will share my water, but we must keep moving if we are to reach the forest before dark. There are many streams in Nahar Forest to refill our jugs."

The drink revived Vrell enough that she could keep pace with the men's horses. She was further strengthened when Jax passed out another meal of bread, meat, and figs.

She didn't know why Jax treated her kindly, but she was glad. It had been fun, the first few days of playing a boy in Walden's Watch. But the first time she'd gone to apprentice at the apothecary, she had quickly learned what life was like for a stray. No one had made eye contact, no one had spoken to her, and when she had tried to ask directions, she had been shoved, cursed at, or ignored. They had treated her as Khai treated her. But Jax did not.

The journey continued. Vrell's eyes stung, begging to close. If Jax wasn't going to let them sleep, couldn't they stop to eat? Judging from the sun's place in the sky, it must be early afternoon. A strange shadow painted the horizon. Could the drought be coming to an end?

Vrell occupied herself with memories of Bran. She recalled his wide smile and brown eyes, the feel of her hand in his. How she missed his company. She prayed that he was not too cross with her having gone into hiding. She couldn't risk his knowing where she was. He sometimes did the silliest things for noble reasons.

An itch seized her left ear. A fly? She batted at the air, hoping to send the bug away, but the itch grew.

Vrell Sparrow.

Vrell halted her horse, clutching the reins until her knuckles whitened. Mother!

The call came again. *Vrell Sparrow.*

Jax glanced over his shoulder, then turned his horse around. "You all right, Vrell?"

Vrell Sparrow.

Did she dare answer Mother now?

The pressure increased. Vrell scratched at both ears, certain that Jax was now trying to pry into her mind as well. She concentrated on keeping her defense strong, fearful that she was about to be discovered.

Jax steered his horse back to her side. "Are you well?"

Vrell nodded. "Something bit me, I think."

Jax leaned close to examine her ear. He grabbed her chin and turned her head to look at the other. "Looks fine. We must ride."

Vrell nodded. As the party continued along the dusty road, a sorrow settled over her. What could her mother be thinking now that Vrell had not answered? Would she call out again? And how could Vrell know if it was safe to reply?

As the day wore on, the shadow grew until Vrell realized it was actually a forest stretching across the land. Her heart raced for the change in scenery. Shade would make such a difference in the temperature. To her distant right, water glittered in the sun. She thought back to her geography lessons and figured that it must be the Lebab Inlet. She longed to run and bathe, but it was miles away—and saltwater would not quench her thirst.

The road before them curved up a small hill and entered the woods. Yellowed grass gave way to green. New sounds of nature met her ears as her horse neared the trees. A rustling of branches, twittering birds, and . . .

A stream!

A bubbling brook curved out of the forest along the road then cut east through the dry earth to run toward the ocean. Vrell dismounted and ran into the shallow flow. She slurped with her hands until satisfied, washed her face, then pushed up her sleeves to clean her arms.

Khai squatted by the stream and submerged his leather water jug into the current. "Good thing you've not been recruited for the Kingsguard. You'd make a pathetic soldier."

Vrell ignored him and washed the dusty grime from her skin. She spotted leafy green sorrel growing along the bank. She dug in her satchel for her tiny knife and cut some. Mother's cook, Jespa, made a divine salad with sorrel, walnuts, and strawberries when they were in season. Vrell washed the leaves in the stream and ate some. It tasted fresh and juicy and welcome after days of dry food. Vrell cut more and wrapped them in the largest leaf for later. She also cut some white clover. If she could somehow dry it, it would make a hearty tea.

Jax knelt to fill his jug, He pulled off his head scarf and rinsed his face and hair. His gaze met Vrell's as he tied the red scarf back over his head. "I like your thinking, Vrell." He pulled a knife from his belt and cut strips of river cane as long as Vrell's arm. He tied them into torches with hemp twine and tucked them in his pack. "Ready to go?"

"Yes, sir." Vrell filled her jug and clipped it to her satchel.

They mounted and rode into the forest.

Never had Vrell seen such trees. Redpines and cedars stretched to the heavens, their trunks wider than four grown men. Branches intertwined overhead like a green, red, and brown canopy that let in shafts of light but blocked the merciless heat of the sun. Thick yellow moss carpeted the ground. Leathery orange ferns and tiny white flowers grew from it in a lush garden array. Even the dusty brown path they'd been riding on had now changed to red clay.

Such beauty distracted Vrell from her weariness, her plight, and her task of acting a boy. The next few hours passed pleasantly. She hummed softly with the rustling trees and chirping birds. Chunks of shell mushroom clung to the side of an oak tree. She reined Nickel and slid off his side.

Vrell stepped off the path, and her foot sank deep in the spongy moss. Maybe the worst of the journey was over. If they camped in the forest tonight, she wouldn't mind sleeping on such soft ground. She longed to snip some white flowers and thread them in her hair, but dared not pick one without an herbal excuse. She withdrew her knife and reached up to cut the mushroom.

"Boy!" Khai yelled. "We've no time for gardening."

Vrell wheeled around to see that Khai and Jax had turned their horses sideways on the road. "I only wish to cut some mushroom," she said. "It's quite good."

"Quickly, Vrell, then no more stops," Jax said.

She sliced off wedges of mushroom until her satchel bulged. A mentha plant waved in the breeze only two paces away. She glanced at the men. They were engaged in conversation with each other. She crouched to cut as much mentha as she could.

Khai suddenly cried out.

Vrell looked up to see him scrambling into her side of the forest on foot, his horse galloping away. Jax dismounted, slapped his horse's rear, and crouched in the middle of the road. His horse ran on ahead. Jax yanked two axes from his leg sheaths, one in each hand. Vrell's eyes widened.

A song-like cry warbled in the distance. It sent a tremor to her heart. Something whooshed past her arm and thunked into a nearby redpine trunk. She stepped toward it to get a closer look. It was an arrow with a crude, black, obsidian head and—

"Vrell!" Jax yelled. "Look out!"

Vrell darted behind the redpine just as another arrow pierced the trunk.

"Wee ahlawa men teeah!"

Vrell peeked around the tree to see a man as tall as Jax but pale as a lily. His long blond hair hung around his face like a curtain. Animal skins were draped over one shoulder, across his white chest, and down around his hips like a skirt. He clutched a spear in one hand and a curved axe in the other. Both weapons were chiseled out of obsidian and lashed to wooden handles with leather.

He stood on the road facing Jax.

Jax bowed to the giant. "We seek passage through Nahar Forest."

The giant pointed down the road, back toward Walden's Watch. "Wee ahlawa men teeah!"

Jax shook his head. "We will not go back. We must take this road to Xulon."

The pale giant tipped his head back and bellowed a trilling cry into the treetops.

A chorus of voices returned the cry from all sides. Vrell's horse turned and trotted back toward the peninsula. Vrell scowled and whipped around, her back pressed against the redpine trunk.

Two more pale giants approached where Khai stood in the forest. Another three walked up the road and stood behind the leader. Jax stood motionless before the four giants, clutching his axes, waiting.

Scraping metal on wood turned Vrell's gaze back to Khai. The knight had drawn his monstrously long sword. He held it at the two giants who faced him, waving it back and forth to keep them at bay.

Vrell bounded over the soft ground to an oak tree with low branches and scurried up. Climbing trees had always been something she enjoyed, as much as it vexed her mother. She had barely settled on a thick branch halfway up when the clash of weapons sent her spinning around.

The two giants had attacked Khai. One swung an ax and another stabbed with a long spear. Khai chopped the tip off the spear, parried the axe, sliced its wielder's leg, and spun back to lop off the hand of the giant holding the remainder of the spear.

Vrell gasped. The little weasel could actually use that weapon. She tore her gaze away to look at Jax.

The four pale ones rained blows upon him with club and spear. His red scarf shone bright against their bleached skin and hair. She had never seen men fight with anything but swords. Jax swung his axes in a blur and blocked his opponents' attacks with the iron cuffs on his forearms. So that was what they were for.

Khai vaulted over the mossy ground and onto the road, barging into Jax's fight. Vrell climbed to a higher branch to get a better view. She glanced back to where Khai had first fought and found his first two attackers slain. Their pallid bodies lay on the yellow moss as if they were asleep.

A heavy tear fell down her cheek. She squeezed her eyes shut and fought the bile rising in her throat. She must not panic or weep like a girl. These giants had attacked without cause. Jax and Khai had killed in self-defense. Had they not, the pale giants would have killed them.

She choked back her tears. A sudden silence caused her to look back to the road. The battle was over. Khai had left two dead in the forest. And now four more ashy giants lay dead on the road. Blood oozed from their skin and seeped into the red clay road like red rivers converging. Khai and Jax appeared unharmed. Khai crouched and wiped his blade on the moss.

Jax peered through the trees then spun around. "Vrell?"

She croaked, "I am here."

Jax's long legs carried him to the oak in four long strides. He lifted a blood-spattered hand to her. She hesitated, then gripped it and jumped down into the spongy moss.

"Who were they?" she asked, wiping her hand off on her tunic.

"Ebens."

Vrell nodded and followed Jax to the road.

Jax squatted and cleaned his axes on clumps of moss before pushing them back into their sheaths. "Khai, we must retrieve the horses and keep moving."

"Aye." Khai jogged down the road, farther into Nahar Forest.

"Why did you dismount?" Vrell asked.

"They might have slain the horses otherwise." Jax stepped past her and strode back toward the peninsula, studying the ground as he went. "There will be more, Vrell. We must find your horse quickly."

More ebens? Vrell's toes curled in her boots as she fought to conceal her fear. Jax didn't stop, so she hurried after him. "Why did they attack?"

Jax veered off the road and around a thick oak. "When ebens come out of Darkness, it is for mercenary work. These ebens were well paid."

Vrell traipsed over the soft moss and spotted Nickel ambling under the low branches of an oak tree. She swallowed. "You mean they were here to kill us?"

"No, boy, they were hired to kill giants. Although they would kill anyone who tried to pass through Nahar Forest right now."

"But they *are* giants."

Jax took Nickel's reins and handed them to her, his face hardened. "They *were* giants, Vrell. Darkness changed them." He cast his eyes to the sun, as if judging the time. "Now, no more questions. Their battle cries will have alerted their comrades. We must move quickly and quietly. Can you do that?"

"Yes, sir." Vrell led Nickel back to the road and mounted. Khai was waiting with the other two horses. Vrell urged Nickel slowly up the road as she waited for Jax and Khai to mount. She passed the dead giants on the road and gazed down at one of the massive pale men. His glassy blue eyes stared into the canopy of branches above.

They rode for hours without encountering any more ebens. Vrell hadn't slept in way too long, but Jax wanted to press on until he felt it was safe to stop.

When they finally did stop, Khai went off hunting on his own.

Jax sat against a tree and removed his black cape. The left arm of his white shirt was matted with blood just above the elbow.

Vrell gasped. "Jax, you are hurt." She hurried to his side and saw a broken stick protruding from his arm.

"One of their arrows struck me. It's not bad."

Vrell lifted the strap of her satchel over her head. "I have been learning the healing trade. May I help?"

Jax smiled. "You may assist. I've likely mended more battle wounds than you."

Vrell knelt beside him and nearly fell over in the deep moss. She settled herself and met Jax's huge, brown eyes.

His grin warmed her cheeks. "The first thing you must know in treating an arrow wound is what kind of arrow you are dealing with. Best way is to find one and look at it." Jax shrugged. "I know ebens well. Their arrowheads are barbed obsidian."

"Yes. I saw one," Vrell said.

"Barbed arrowheads are harder to remove. It's best to use something to pry them out with. But mine is not deep. What do you have in your pack?"

Vrell laid out her assortments of herbs and jars. "I have a yarrow salve I made myself."

Jax beckoned for the jar. She pried off the lid and handed it to him. He took a long sniff and raised his brows. "That will do fine."

Jax removed the arrowhead easily. Vrell helped him clean the wound and added her salve. He bandaged it with strips from his spare shirt. She listened avidly to his battle tales of how healers worked on wounded soldiers. She found Jax a fountain of wisdom and questioned him on herbs and healing, until Khai wandered up with a dead rabbit.

They made a wonderful meal of the rabbit and Vrell's mushrooms. Vrell also shared some of her sorrel lettuce with Jax. Khai refused any.

When it was time for sleep, Vrell snuggled into the deep softness of the moss. It was indeed as comfortable as she had imagined. She let her mind wander to the last time she and Bran had been together.

She had met up him at the southwestern vineyard and led him to her special corner, where she had been experimenting with cuttings of a thunbergii mountain vine, hoping to blend it with the local vinifera. Not much had grown yet, but Bran had sat beside her, listening avidly as she'd explained her hopes for the test. She had wanted to—

Vrell Sparrow.

It was her mother, calling out to her again. Vrell was still too afraid to answer. Jax and Khai were awake, murmuring to themselves a few feet away. Had they heard Mother's call? She pushed the fears from her mind and fell asleep thinking of Bran.

The next morning, Jax shook her awake. She much preferred his gentle hand to Khai's kick. She rose quickly, and they set off on the road, heading south.

"When we come to the King's Road, we'll head north," Jax said.

Vrell pictured the map of Er'Rets in her mind. The King's Road stretched the length of the kingdom, from Tsaftown in the far north all the way down to Er'Rets Point in the far south. They still had a very long way to travel. If ebens were being paid to keep people from entering Xulon Forest, all roads would be guarded. This would only lengthen the time she would have to spend with the knights and increase her chances of being discovered. Vrell did not want to be a stray boy anymore.

She wanted to go home.

6

Vrell cowered under the canopy of a leathery fern. Rainwater poured over the edges, but the plant's vastness offered a semi-dry sanctuary. It also provided camouflage, its orange and red surface blending with Vrell's tunic. She had been covering her head with her arms for so long they had grown stiff. The patter of rain, screams, grunts, and clanking metal rang out from all sides. She dared not move.

Jax had shoved her under the ferns before lunch, when another group of ebens had attacked. The fighting had only gone on a few moments before some different giants had joined in to help the knights. Yâtsaq giants like Jax, not the pale-skinned ebens. Vrell found the battle sounds petrifying, although they had faded some. The sun sat low on the horizon, squeezing rays of orange light between the thick tree trunks. Had the fighting ended? Now that Jax and Khai had help, would it be over for good?

Something poked her in the back. Vrell jumped inside her skin, then berated herself. She should have played dead.

"Oi! I found one hidin' in the ferns, Po!" The voice was young and girlish.

Swishing pant legs grew close, and a young boy's voice said, "Think it's alive?"

Something poked harder and Vrell twitched.

"You see that?" the girl said.

"Poke it again!"

If her two Kingsguard escorts could fight mercenary giants for weeks on end, Vrell could best a couple of children. She sat up and snatched the stick. "Do you mind?"

Two children stared at her with huge brown eyes and dirty faces to match. At least, they looked like children. Their heads were bigger than normal. The boy matched Vrell in height, the girl nearly so, but their faces were childlike. Both had long hair that hung in braids. The girl had two braids. The boy had three. They both wore leather clothing.

"How old are you?" Vrell asked the boy.

"Eight. Name's Po. This here is Nina. She's six."

Six! They must be giants' children. Yâtsaq giants, perhaps, since they had black hair and tan skin like Jax.

The girl flashed an insincere smile. "Our pop pop is going to kill your pop pop."

The statement shocked Vrell, and she looked out from under her fern to see where the knights were. She spotted Jax's red scarf through the red and brown trees. He was very much alive, swinging two axes and growling.

"He is not my pop pop," Vrell said. "They are taking me to Mahanaim."

"Our pop pop lets no one go to Mahanaim without a fight." Po folded his arms as if he were one of his father's soldiers. "Most travelers work for the Council, and the Council's evil."

"Why do you think the Council is evil?"

"'Cause they tell lies," Nina said, her large, brown eyes fixated on the stick Vrell had taken from her.

"And they make secret votes, and they work with ebens," Po said. "Pop Pop says Prince Oren should be king, not the puppet prince."

Puppet Prince? Vrell straightened. "You mean Prince Gidon?"

Nina's dark eyebrows sank. "He don't deserve to be king, our pop pop says. He's a puppet, which is like a doll. I've a doll at home. Do you?"

"Don't be thick, Nina. Boys don't play with dolls." Po pushed Nina's arm and scowled. "Pop Pop says if the puppet prince is king, it'll be the end."

"The end of what?"

Po shrugged. "Enough talking. You're our prisoner, eben-lover."

"That's right, human." Nina picked up another stick and jabbed at Vrell. "We're taking you to our nest where you can't help the puppet prince."

"But I do not want to help the puppet prince."

Po's nose wrinkled. "You don't?"

"No. I have met him on several occasions. He is an absolute snake."

Nina giggled. "He's slimy?"

"Very," Vrell said, enjoying herself despite the violence that might still be taking place around her fern haven. "He snorts a lot, and he chews with his mouth open."

"Po does that."

"Do not!"

"Do too. Mama always says to shut your yap."

"Does not!"

A deep and rumbling voice called, "Po! Nina!"

Nina's eyes went wide again. "That's Pop Pop. We've got to go. You stay here, and if you see the puppet prince . . . skin him alive!"

Vrell cringed at the cruelty of little Nina's words.

"I skinned a reekat once," Po said. "Then Mama made me these boots." He held up one foot clad in thin brown fur.

Vrell had never heard of a reekat.

"Nina! Po!"

"Bye!" Nina dropped her stick and scurried off through the leathery ferns.

Po smiled and saluted. "Skin him alive!"

Vrell stayed under her fern, watching Po's reekat boots squish over the wet moss. Her mind repeated their conversation. The idea that some felt that Prince Oren should be king was new to her. Vrell had met Oren—Prince Gidon's uncle—at court many times over the years. He never seemed a bit interested in ruling.

Months ago, Bran had mentioned that Sir Rigil, the knight he served, was loyal to Prince Oren Hadar. She had not thought anything strange about that comment at the time. Who would not loyally serve Prince Oren? He was a wonderful man. But could Bran have been hinting at treason? Was he loyal to Oren but not Gidon? She knew how much he admired Sir Rigil. Did Sir Rigil and Po and Nina's father serve the same cause? Could Prince Oren Hadar be looking to take the throne from his nephew? She did not believe it.

Vrell listened to the gentle patter of rain. She wondered how her new master, Macoun Hadar, fit into the royal family. He had obviously been passed over.

Soggy footsteps caused her to cower back out of sight, but Jax's familiar voice came like a gift from Arman.

"Come on out, Vrell. It's all over."

Stepping out, she disturbed a pool of water that had settled on top of the fern. It spilled down the back of her tunic, and she gasped at the coldness. Jax looked down and smiled. His handkerchief sat crooked on his head, and his black hair frizzed out at odd angles. Other than that, he appeared to be in one piece.

Did she dare hope? "Is Khai all right?"

"He's with Lord Dromos. Come, we are invited to dine and rest."

Dine? Vrell bounded over the springy moss after Jax, which was the only way to keep up. She was so hungry. Because of the battle, Vrell had not been able to eat lunch. And now it must be nearly dinnertime. She wondered who Lord Dromos was. She did not recognize his name from court. They walked a long while, weaving around immense tree trunks and brushing past wet ferns. By the time they ventured onto a red clay road, Vrell's tunic was soaked.

They followed the road south and met up with an amazing sight. Khai stood with all three horses beside a giant, who sat on his own giant horse.

"I see you survived the attack," Khai said to Vrell. "How ever did you manage?"

Vrell did not acknowledge Khai. The giant man and festrier captivated her.

The man seemed taller than Jax, but maybe only because he sat on his horse. The huge beast was at least a head taller than Jax's horse. It was silky brown and wore checkered banners of grass green and emerald. Like Jax, the giant man had black hair. Three thick plaits hung over one shoulder to his waist. A jumping brown stag was embroidered on the front of his beige tunic.

"Lord Dromos," Jax said, "this is Vrell, our charge to deliver to Mahanaim."

Vrell nodded. "It is an honor, my lord."

Lord Dromos nodded in return and spurred his horse onward.

Vrell, Jax, and Khai mounted their horses and followed Lord Dromos down the road. The rain had stopped, but the forest continued to drip. Before long, Lord Dromos ventured west into the forest over no discernable trail. He stopped suddenly. His demeanor was that of a man arriving at the front door of his home, but though Vrell turned full circle, she could see no manor. Not even a cottage.

"Pethach!" Lord Dromos called out.

Vrell jumped at the sound of a clicking of chain against metal. A section of the forest slid away not fifteen feet from her horse. The moss-covered door had blended in so well with the surroundings, Vrell had not noticed it.

Lord Dromos led them into an oversized fairytale village. Hulking stone cottages, overgrown with yellow moss, sat beside one another. The air was sweet inside the gate. Honeysuckle and bluebells edged the wide dirt road beneath her feet. The road curved around tree and bush, as if it would've been a sin to cut down any living plant to make room for the path.

Large faces glared out windows and cracked-open doors as they passed. Did the giants dislike visitors? Certainly they could not dislike her. She had never met them.

Then she saw the giant girl, Nina, clutching the leg of the biggest giant yet.

She reached out for the girl's thoughts and heard, *Skin him alive!*

Vrell smiled. Nina's father was a watchtower, and Vrell craned her neck to get a good look as she passed. All these giants were black-haired with dark eyes. This man was no different. His long hair gathered in a single braid, and his short, bushy beard clung to his chin like moss.

Lord Dromos led his horse down the winding dirt road and across a stone bridge that arched over a sparkling stream. As Vrell's horse crossed, her gaze followed the stream to where it disappeared into an opening in another wall of leaves. Lord Dromos led his horse around a curve in the road and up to the wall. Sure enough, before Lord Dromos reached the wall, metal clinked and the gate slid to the right. Vrell spurred her horse to catch up.

Beyond the gate, the sun lit a vast, grassy field. The color was so vibrant Vrell gasped. She turned to find where the crystal stream came in and traced its flow along the edge of the curtain wall. It turned in front of an immense greystone manor house and plunged off a mossy-green rock into a bubbling pool. The manor was built into a steep hill. On the far end, the walls rose five levels high, but on the end where the stream plummeted into the pool, only the top two levels emerged. An arched stone bridge crossed over the bubbling pool and met a set of carved stone doors twice Jax's height.

The whole place reminded her of the quaint rock garden and fountain in the courtyard back home. Only ten times larger.

Lord Dromos dismounted the festrier in front of the waterfall. A young giant boy, just taller than Khai, led the animal away. Vrell dismounted as well and handed her horse off to another giant boy. She met his eyes, awed at his height and youth.

A tinkling bell caused her to turn away from the boy just in time to see a gargantuan dog bounding toward her. He was tan with black jowls, nose, and tips of his long ears. He came straight for her face, his curling pink tongue—with a long stream of drool—swinging under his chin. She cried out and tucked her face into the crook of her elbow, but the beast was not dissuaded. His wet jowls flopped on the top of her head and his sniffing nose tickled.

Laughter rang out all around. Vrell's pounding heart slowed, and when she no longer felt the slobbering mouth on her hair, she peeked out. The dog had found its master and was jumping up against Lord Dromos's legs.

Lord Dromos gave a hearty chuckle. "Missed me did you, Cheyva?"

Vrell loved animals, but this one was no pet. If saddled, it could be ridden by a grown man. A man who didn't mind drool. She caught Khai's smirking stare. "What?"

"Scared you, did he? He's just a little doggie."

"*Little?*"

The giant lord walked across the stone bridge and entered the manor. Vrell paused on the bridge and stared into the water, where thousands of smooth pebbles sparkled in the sun.

She caught her disheveled reflection in the glassy surface and cringed. How horrible she looked! If Mother could see her now, she would faint from shock. It had not helped that the beast-dog had drooled all over her head. His stench added to her own, and she longed to be clean. But she doubted a stray would be offered the hospitality of a bath.

"Boy!" Khai snapped.

She stepped though the massive doors and the temperature dropped. She followed Khai through a spacious greystone foyer and stopped at a half wall that wrapped around the perimeter of a vast atrium. The sun lit up a colorful courtyard below. From Vrell's viewpoint, she could see all five levels of the manor and each staircase that connected them. She stood three levels up from the garden, but the levels were much taller than those from any manor house Vrell had seen. Lord Dromos, Jax, and Khai had already descended to the second floor. Vrell ran to catch up.

Lord Dromos led them down a cool stone hallway and turned into a warm sitting room. A fireplace crackled on the outer wall. A kinsman woman and two girls sat on a stone bench by an arched window. The human females looked terribly small in Vrell's eyes. She had heard that giants did not keep slaves. Perhaps they were servants.

"Papa!" A girl, smaller than Vrell, with black ringlet curls, jumped up from the bench and ran toward Lord Dromos. He scooped her into his arms, twirled her once, and kissed her cheek. "Are you staying for dinner?" the girl asked.

"Yes. And I've brought guests. Xylene, this is Jax mi Katt and Khai Mageia of the New Kingsguard, escorting young Vrell to Mahaniam to apprentice."

Xylene beamed, her sweet round face filled with joy. "Welcome, welcome to you all!"

The woman and an older girl made their way across the room. The girl's thick brows furrowed at Vrell, whose cheeks burned knowing how wretched she looked, even for a boy.

Yet the girl thought, *He's filthy, but it's cute how he blushes.*

Vrell fought back a smile.

The woman, big boned and tall for a human, looked down on Vrell. "Oh, you poor thing! Did Cheyva get you? If you see him coming again, say *atsar*."

"Atsar?"

"He'll stop, won't he?" The woman looked to Lord Dromos.

Lord Dromos nodded. "Yes, of course. This is Lady Kiska, my wife. And my daughters, Zoea and Xylene."

Vrell studied the women again. It had never occurred to her that kinsmen could marry giants. Lady Kiska was tall and big boned. She had light brown hair that hung in four long braids to her thighs. She wore a gown of green wool embroidered with leaves.

Her girls wore their dark hair in the same manner, but neither seemed to have inherited their mother's height. Both were shorter than Vrell. Little Xylene had rosy round cheeks and a dimpled smile. Zoea was as slender as a blade of grass and could not yet fill out the womanly gown she was wearing. It was way too long for her. It crumpled around her feet as if it belonged to her mother and she were playing dress-up.

"I'm sure you would all like to wash before dinner," Lady Kiska said. "Ez will take you to the steams, won't you, Ez?"

A wispy poplar of a man appeared from the shadowed corner of the room. "This way."

Vrell followed the Kingsguard knights, who followed Ez. She had never heard of steams. Most gatehouses had a bathhouse for the guards. Were steams like a bathhouse? Either way, she could not risk being ushered in with the men. Not knowing what to do or say, Vrell followed the men to the lowest underground level. Ez drifted down another cool stone hallway until he came to a thick green tapestry hanging across an entrance. He held it aside, and a cloud of steam puffed out.

"I thank you," Jax said, ducking to go inside. Khai entered without a word.

Vrell stopped and asked, "Might you have a privy?"

Ez nodded and trailed further down the hall. He held aside another green tapestry. "In the far corner."

"Thank you." Vrell slipped under the stiff curtain and tied it closed. She stood in a small, stone antechamber. A deep wash basin sat empty on one wall. Pegs protruded from the opposite wall in a straight line. Another green curtain separated the privy from the antechamber. She slipped inside, blinking at the extra large privy hole, and surveyed her only option—a small basin of water meant to rinse one's hands after using the privy. It would have to do.

Ez led the knights and Vrell to the great hall for dinner. The ceiling was at least four kinsmen levels high. Fat candles burned in brass fixtures that hung from the ceiling, casting shadowed light over the room. Wall sconces held more thick candles. A long stone table stretched across the far end of the room. Lord Dromos and Lady Kiska sat at the center of it. Three tables lined each of the side walls, but they were mostly empty. A few giants sat at the lowest tables, those farthest from the high table.

Ez seated Jax and Khai to Lord Dromos's right. He seated Vrell to Lady Kiska's left—a shocking, and completely unheard of, honor for a stray. Zoea sat on the other side of Vrell, batting her eyes. Xylene sat next to Zoea.

Zoea had changed into a dress that fit her slim body. Maybe she truly had been playing dress-up earlier. She touched Vrell's shoulder and gazed into her eyes. "In what will you apprentice at Mahanaim?"

Vrell knew she at least looked clean now, but the idea of looking handsome to this kinsman-giant girl turned her stomach. Plus she had a headache. She worded her answer carefully. "I do not know the specifics yet."

A line of serving giant girls entered the room carrying various things. One set a stone platter before Lord Dromos. Another servant set one before Zoea. It was covered in a pile of dark meat that smelled like venison. Another tray was heaped with steamed vegetables. Zoea waited for a servant to set down a stack of flat stone disks. She lifted one and began to pile food on it as if it were a trencher.

A stone trencher. How interesting.

Vrell filled a round trencher with food and thanked Arman for her meal. She took a bite of the venison, which was salty and very rich. Zoea watched her every move. Vrell had learned from Ez that Zoea was thirteen and Xylene, seven. That fact brought little comfort when Zoea scooted down the stone bench, inch by inch, until her arm brushed against Vrell's. Vrell did not even want to try and read the girl's thoughts.

Lady Kiska turned to Vrell. "Yulessa, my eldest, is married now. She just birthed darling twins, she did. They weren't too big, so they're likely not true giants. One of each, named Dunfast and Paisley. Aren't those nice names? Yulessa's husband is human. Royalty, he is. Not in line for the throne, but kingly blood is in his veins as much as Prince Gidon himself."

"What is his name?" Vrell asked.

"Donediff Hadar. He's Prince Oren's son."

Vrell nodded. No wonder the giants—the non-eben ones—supported Prince Oren for king.

Lady Kiska went on. "Donediff has been given the assignment of warden at Er'Rets Point. That's a lordship, that is. Makes our Yulessa a lady all over again."

Seeing Lady Kiska's pride brought a smile to Vrell's face. "How lovely."

She winced inside. Again she had used the word *lovely.* Well, it was not exactly easy to carve certain words from her vocabulary. At least she had not yet used it on a man. Besides, she had met Donediff Hadar at court on several occasions. He *was* a lovely young man. Handsome. Kind. A little boring, perhaps, but Yulessa was lucky indeed. Many noblewomen found far less favorable matches in marriage.

Which brought her mind back to why she was here pretending to be a boy. But Vrell did not want to think about that right now. Her head was throbbing as it was.

She did wonder how tall Yulessa was, having had a tall mother and a giant for a father. Last she had seen him, Donediff was at least six feet tall. All the Hadars were tall men. And even though Lady Kiska was the tallest human woman Vrell had ever seen, her children were much shorter than giant children. She could not imagine Donediff with a woman taller than him.

Vrell scooped up another bite of venison and tuned her ear to Lord Dromos.

"I do try to stay neutral," he said. "The Mârad oppose the ebens' mercenary work."

"Then they oppose the Council," Khai said.

"They operate outside my authority," Lord Dromos said, reaching for his goblet, "but we bring many wounded into Xulon."

"Wounded ebens?" Jax's tone implied the mere mention was scandalous.

"Never. Only yâtsaq giants are brought into Xulon."

"How can you tell which ebens are mercenaries and which are only passing through?" Vrell asked.

The room silenced, and Vrell flushed at having spoken out of turn. At home she was able to speak whenever she pleased, even given the floor. But here in Xulon, under the guise of a stray boy, speaking to the lord of the manor without having been spoken to was far too bold.

Lord Dromos seemed of good cheer, however, and answered without scolding. "Ebens live on the Dark side of the Cela Mountains. They never leave for innocent reasons. If they do enter Light, it is because they have been hired. The Council of Seven has chosen to employ them, so I do my best to support that, though I cannot understand why Kingsguard knights cannot do the work. Er'Retians would trust them more."

Zoea leaned close. "Because of ebens, it's disgraceful to be born blond. Though sometimes when you marry a human, your children are born blond. That's why very few yâtsaq marry out of our race. Yulessa was an exception. And Mother. But they married Kinsman men. Still, *I* won't marry a human."

Vrell turned away, annoyed at the young girl's prejudice. The kinsman people were those descended from Echâd Hadar, the first king of Er'Rets. They had dark hair, brown skin, and blue eyes. Vrell's hair was dark, but her skin was pale and her eyes were green. Was little miss Zoea suggesting Vrell would not make a good match for her?

It was true, but terribly rude to speak of such things. Strays were not permitted to marry in most parts of Er'Rets. Vrell knew little of Nahar Duchy, but few nobles got away with marrying that far beneath their stations. Still, Zoea's pointing it out was in poor taste.

Vrell wondered where Lady Kiska hailed from to have taught her daughter so little decorum. How she managed to marry her eldest to a prince's son, Vrell could not fathom.

That night, Vrell snuck down to the bathhouse. The scrubbing she had given herself in the privy had made her temporarily presentable, but it had been weeks since she had had a proper bath. Grime coated her from head to toe. Only hot water, like the steam she had seen when Ez opened that green curtain, would pierce her greasy shell. It might also clear her head. The headache had grown stronger, almost bringing tears to her eyes. If only she had lavender or chamomile tea.

Her heart throbbed as she walked along the stone corridor leading to the steamy chamber. Giving in to this small temptation could ruin everything. She peeked around the heavy green tapestry.

Steam clouded everything, and, for a moment, Vrell could not see. She slipped inside and crouched down where the air was cooler. Water rushed somewhere nearby. The smell of minerals was strong. Hazy light flickered above her and appeared to come from two torches on the walls. She saw no one.

Like all the others, this room was grey stone, but the floor ended two yards out from the entranceway, like a pier. Beyond it, a steamy underground river lazed by just below floor level. She walked in a crouch to the edge and peered down a black tunnel on either side but could see nothing but a fine net draped across the openings. She shuddered, wondering what it was meant to keep out.

She turned back to the emerald tapestry and could hardly see it. She sighed. There was no tiny corner to bathe in here. If anyone entered, she would be discovered in all her feminine splendor. But at least the steam provided some protection. If she heard someone enter, she could likely get dressed in time.

The steam had already loosened her pores, and so, with a quick prayer that Arman would keep her safe, Vrell gave in to the watery temptation. She stripped off her clothing. Her chest heaved when she removed the undergarment that had not been taken off since Lady Coraline had helped her tie it almost a week ago. She lowered herself into the hot spring and gasped at the water's scalding temperature. She would be pink from head to toe when she got out.

She kept to the front of the stone ledge against the net. Kicking out her foot, she found that the net continued under the surface. What strange creatures might lurk in an underground hot spring that only a simple net could keep out?

Vrell washed quickly and thoroughly, scrubbing the layer of grime from her body with heavenly honeysuckle soap. Then she scrubbed her clothes. When she finished, she reluctantly returned to her padded prison and stray's tunic, both sopping wet, and snuck back up to her bed for the night.

Vrell entered the large room, realizing it was likely considered small by giants' standards. A plain fireplace filled the wall opposite the door. Two long beds occupied the side walls. A small straw mattress had been placed beside the door for Vrell to use. Jax and Khai sat near the fireplace whispering. Vrell settled onto the firm mattress with a smile on her face and stared at the stone beam of the high ceiling above. Wet or not, she was clean. Joy filled every tingling pore. She laid her head on the pillow and shut her eyes.

A thick pressure flooded her mind. On top of her already aching head, the tension brought a tear down her cheek. Had the hot water aggravated her headache? Or maybe the venison had worsened it. It had been very rich.

I sense you! an elderly man's monotone voice droned in her mind. *Tell me your name!*

Vrell stiffened and yanked the covers up to her chin. She fortified the walls around her thoughts, but the pressure grew. She sensed confusion. A bright orange light. Heat and . . . iron? Wetness? No, that was her clothes.

Hello, new one. Welcome to our ears. My, how strong your presence is. Who are you?

Mother? Vrell sat up in bed and twisted around. Khai and Jax had stopped whispering. Both sat very still. Vrell's heart pounded in her chest. Was her mother nearby?

A man yelled, *Who's there?*

Blood! Blood was on her arm! Vrell swiped her shoulder, but the wetness would not dissipate. Something had died. Tears streamed down Vrell's cheeks. So sad. The baby. An orphan. All alone. She shook her head, confused, and pulled her blankets up to her chin. Something tickled her legs and she twitched. She threw down the blankets and swatted at her legs. A spider?

Who are you, gifted one? a deep male voice asked.

What are you called? an old woman asked.

Please! the elderly man said. *What is your name?*

Vrell cowered, wincing at the force in her mind. Perhaps her headache was not from the hours on the road, the hot water, or the venison. These were bloodvoices she was hearing. She turned back to the knights. Were they hearing it too? And why was she unable to block them out?

Stop it! the man yelled. *Don't speak to me!*

Vrell clutched her ears. So loud, this voice. So heavy the weight it brought to her mind.

Do not be afraid, Vrell's mother said. *It is a gift.*

Vrell waited to hear more, curious what else her mother would say, but the sensation faded. Jax and Khai whispered to each other again, nothing she could overhear. She sank into her mattress and pulled the covers over her head.

She thought over the bloodvoicing conversation. Apparently a man had discovered his gift, but he was confused, alone, and possibly bleeding. Something had happened to his legs or his shoulder. Why had his thoughts brought such tremendous strain to Vrell? When she had discovered her gift, she had accidentally spoken to her mother's mind. That was all. Mother had heard it and started to teach Vrell. But this . . . this was . . . frightening.

Vrell's ears had not even tickled first, so this person had not been intentionally seeking her mind. But she had not been able to block him either. Without trying, his thoughts had bled over into dozens of minds. What could someone so strong do with his gift? Was that why the people had called out to him? Why Mother had called out?

And why hadn't Mother tried to call her again? Vrell would have answered when she was in the steams. Why couldn't Arman work the timing out so that Vrell and her mother could speak?

Vrell dwelled on the voices until she drifted to sleep. She dreamed of Mother comforting the frightened man. Mother wanted to know if he was okay and where he lived. Vrell wanted to know too so she could help him. There were so many voices, and he did not know how to block them. Vrell could teach him.

In her dream, the man dropped to his knees and moaned. He was in pain. There was still blood.

Your home, dear, Mother said. *Where is it?*

The man yelled, *Please stop! Stop!*

And then all was silent.

Part 3

Unwelcome Changes

7

A rap on the skull woke Achan.

Groggy, he rose onto one elbow to find a dozen serving women fussing about the cellar, throwing potatoes, turnips, and onions into wicker baskets. Why were they in the cellar at this hour? He blinked his sleepy eyes, trying to remember the occasion, thankful he had slept in his trousers.

Poril scurried by the ale casks and reached down to knock Achan on the head with sharp knuckles again. "Up! There's much to do, and Poril needs yeh up and able."

Ah, yes. Prince Gidon's coming-of-age celebration began today. And Achan hadn't even milked the goats. He reached up, wincing at his sore shoulder muscles, and grabbed his tunic, which had dried in a stiff, triangular shape over the spout of the ale cask. He pulled it over his head and struggled to straighten it while lying down. He tied the rope belt and crawled out.

Achan's head pounded, so he took the narrow stone steps slowly.

The kitchens bustled with activity, warmth, and a mixture of scents: robust spices, fresh herbs, burnt toast, steamy soups, fish, and bloody meat. The meat smell turned Achan's stomach, bringing the doe to mind. And that reminded him of the voices—the culprits behind his throbbing skull.

Poril had apparently recruited every serving woman in Sitna Manor to help prepare the dinner feast, and they were deep into gossip as usual.

"What you s'pose his skin looks like under that mask?" one of them asked, chopping a carrot into slices.

"I've heard it's dark, like dried venison."

"Well, if I's the Duchess, I'd not marry him neither, him bein' half a man."

Achan dodged between elbows, reaching arms, and twirling brown skirts, navigating toward the exit. He grabbed the milk pail from the shelf above the door and went outside heading for the stables.

The outer bailey had never been so crowded before dawn. Throngs of foreign servants darted around on various errands. Pages led horses—some already wearing their jousting armor and banners—to and from the stables. A dozen slaves dragged long slabs of wood toward the drawbridge. The butcher—apron soaked in blood—had wheeled his cart close to the kitchens. His apprentice fought to hold down the wings of a flapping goose. Achan passed by just before the chop of the axe severed the bird's neck.

In the barn, Achan milked the goats quickly despite his exhaustion. When he set the milk on the table in the kitchens, Poril shoved a mug of tonic into his chest. "Drink."

The bitter smell jogged Achan's memory. Yesterday, Sir Gavin had suggested the tonic was poison—not able to kill, but bad in some way. Certainly not healthy.

A sharp throb bit through his skull.

Tell me where you live.

Are you there? Speak to me!

Achan's heart rate increased at the voices in his head. He closed his eyes and focused on the allown tree, the sunset, the wind.

Something hard cracked on his head. "Ow!"

Poril stood before him, his knuckles raised to strike again. "Poril has no time for games today, boy. Drink now. And let Poril see yeh do it."

Pig snout. Achan would get the truth from Sir Gavin today about this tonic.

He guzzled the bitter goo and stumbled to the mentha basket. He chewed a few leaves and began to feel better.

The serving women continued their gossip about Lord Nathak and the Duchess of Carm. One of them heaved a plucked goose from one table to another and began to stuff it with spices. "Does he really think cuttin' off her supplies is gallant?"

"He's got no sense," said another, waving a wooden spoon. "Just look how Prince Gidon treats his women. 'Twas Lord Nathak who raised him, that's clear enough."

Achan went for firewood. The morning dawn had cast its pale light over the manor. The sky was clear. It would be a warm day. He found the outer bailey even more crowded now and was thankful the firewood was near the kitchens and he did not have to carry it far. By the time he returned, his head and stomach felt fine.

As he stepped into the sweltering kitchens he spotted Sir Gavin. The old knight had cornered Poril near the ovens. Achan dropped the wood beside the largest hearth and added a few pieces to the fire. He watched Sir Gavin and Poril between the bustling skirts and strained to hear their conversation.

At length, Poril shouted, "Boy!" and the women cleared a path.

Achan hurried over, hoping to be sent with Sir Gavin again, but the knight had left.

"Yeh'll go with the good knight, yeh will. Soon as yer done, get back, yeh hear?"

Achan swallowed his smile. "Yes, Master Poril." He scurried out of the kitchens, running to catch up with Sir Gavin, whom he spotted striding toward the inner bailey.

The knight glanced over his shoulder. "We've little time to dress you for tournament."

Achan stopped. Tournament? "You can't think I'm ready to *compete*?" He made himself run to catch up again. "I've never even touched a sharp blade."

"Whether you're ready or not, you'll do your best. A squire must see his blood flow and feel his teeth crack under an adversary's strike. Just standing in the ring is an act of courage, and you need to work on yours."

Achan didn't like the sound of fighting squires who were much more advanced, but he wasn't about to let Sir Gavin call him a coward. "I'm brave."

"In some things, aye, in others . . . "

Achan frowned and followed Sir Gavin through the gate that led to the inner bailey.

To their left, the keep stretched six levels into the pale blue sky. A grassy courtyard spread out between it and the hedged walls of Cetheria's temple gardens. The temple itself lay at the far right of the inner bailey. Achan rarely came this far into the fortress, unless he had direct orders to. Doing so without permission was a good way to earn an extra beating. Still, he occasionally snuck as close to the temple garden walls as possible to leave an offering. He wasn't allowed inside the temple itself.

The fortress was crowded. Servants, stewards, valets, and maids from all over Er'Rets dashed about on errands for their masters. As Achan climbed the narrow steps that led to the upper levels of the keep, he paused to peek from an arrow loop. Outside the manor, dozens of tents and pavilions had popped up like tarts in the northern field, each waving colorful banners and crests. Most the guests had arrived yesterday while Achan was hunting. Skilled knights and squires from distant cities had come to—what was it Sir Gavin had said?—spill their blood and crack their teeth?

The jousting field sat farthest away. A long white tent with a red and white striped awning covered the grandstands beside it. Achan could see a horse and rider dart down the field in a practice run. Closer to the manor, square pens were set up to host a variety of events: hand-to-hand combat, the axe, the sword. Achan would've liked to spend the day out there, watching, learning, and, maybe someday, competing.

He followed Sir Gavin to the fourth floor and down a dark hallway to the knight's bedchamber. It was a nice room with a bed, a sideboard, a fireplace, and a chair by a window that overlooked the tournament field.

A boy Achan's age stood near the fireplace, two stools beside him—one empty, the other holding a basin of water.

"Off with your clothes and sit," Sir Gavin said. "Wils will get you clean."

Achan eyed Wils warily. "I washed last night at the well."

Sir Gavin raised a bushy white eyebrow, his moustache arcing in a frown. "You're the most obstinate squire I've ever heard of. Will you simply obey without question, for once?"

Achan's cheeks burned. He stripped down to his linen undershorts. "I can wash myself."

"Sit in silence, Achan, please!" Sir Gavin walked behind Achan. "If you are to be a squire—" He gasped. "Eben's breath, lad. What have they done to your back?"

Achan shifted and folded his arms. So he had a lot of scars on his back. What stray didn't?

Sir Gavin's calloused finger tapped Achan's left shoulder. "You have a birthmark."

Achan twisted his neck. He could never see the brand clearly. "It's the mark of the stray, sir. Don't you have such a mark?"

"No, I do not, but that is not what I refer to. The skin is red *under* your brand. A simple brand doesn't do that."

Achan looked again, pawing at his shoulder to see, but it was physically impossible to get a look. "I don't know. Maybe I do have a birthmark."

Sir Gavin walked to the window. He fell into a chair and sighed. "I was unable to speak with Lord Nathak yesterday. He was 'not to be disturbed.'"

The serving boy, Wils, rubbed a small brush over a brick of soap and attacked Achan's back, dipping the brush into the water basin and applying more soap after every few scrubs.

Achan scowled, feeling awkward and exposed. "Is that bad?" He was too distracted by Wils's brush to remember why Sir Gavin had wanted to speak with Lord Nathak.

"Not necessarily. I wanted to make it official with him before entering you in the tournament . . . out of courtesy." Sir

Gavin stood. "I'll try once more. Wait for me here. We'll go to the field together."

They'd better. Achan certainly wasn't going out by himself. He wanted to say something to Sir Gavin about the tonic, but he didn't want Wils to hear. So he sat still and allowed the valet to scrub him until his skin turned pink.

Never in all his life had Achan been so . . . fragrant. On the top half anyway. He wouldn't let Wils near the rest of him. The valet had washed Achan's hair with rosewater and braided it. Achan fingered the plait. A tail tied with a leather thong was all the patience he'd ever had for such things.

Wils held up a mirrorglass. Achan stared at it, glanced at Wils, then leaned forward. He'd never seen a mirrorglass. He'd never seen his face at all, except in the river or the moat or the dishwater. He studied his reflection, pleased he didn't find himself ugly. His skin was tan like the shell of a walnut. Black hair was pulled back into the braided tail, straight and smooth. Did that make his heritage kinsman?

He had a good face, he thought. A bit square, but not long and oval like Noam's or fat and round like Riga's. Wils had even shaved him, something Achan had never done despite the few wisps of hair on his chin. His cheeks and neck still tingled from the razor's edge.

Achan leaned closer to the mirrorglass. His eyes were blue. He hadn't known that about himself. Blue eyes were also a kinsman trait. He leaned back and nodded to Wils, who set the mirrorglass on a shelf over the fire. Achan smiled. He was kinsman.

Wils helped him dress. First a thin white linen tunic and scratchy black wool leggings, then a padded, long-waisted wool tunic with long sleeves. After that, Wils had Achan sit on the bed so he could lower a thick coat of steel chain over his head. It draped heavily on his shoulders.

"How am I supposed to swing a sword with this extra bulk and weight?"

Wils shrugged and pulled another tunic—this one of fine yellow linen—over the chain. Fancy ties hung from the neck. Achan tried to lace them.

Wils swatted his hands away. "I'll do it." He ignored the ties and, with a small smile, presented a black leather jerkin. "Last one."

Achan held out his arms so that Wils could slip the vest-like garment onto him. The leather was soft and a bit worn, but of high quality. Gren would approve.

Achan never realized how much clothing noblemen wore. He hoped Master Fenny might see him dressed in such finery. Maybe he might change his mind and give Gren to him after all. Not even Riga had a coat of chain.

Riga. Achan suddenly wasn't sure he wanted anyone to see him. What if Achan were humiliated? What if he were killed?

One of the loops on the chain coat irritated his neck, and he scratched at it while Wils laced up the tunic and jerkin. It would take Achan an hour to get everything off.

"Ready for your belt and sword, Master Cham?"

Wils had been doing that, calling him Master Cham, like he was someone special. Achan had burst into laughter the first three times, but this time his mouth hung open. He was to have a belt and sword? A real steel sword? "Where?"

Wils went to the window and returned with a brown leather belt studded with steel and pale blue stones. A carved wooden scabbard hung from the belt, holding a sword that had an ivory grip. Achan could only gape as Wils fastened the belt around his waist. His life was worth far less than one jewel on this belt.

When Wils backed away, Achan drew the sword. The sound of metal scraping against wood sent a tingle up his arms. He studied the carved ivory grip wrapped in worn leather, the long steel blade with one raised rib along the flat and a rounded tip—no good for thrusting—and the engraved copper and steel crossguard with some sort of ivory fish set into the center. He could almost imagine himself a Kingsguard knight.

The door burst open, and Sir Gavin spoke, out of breath. "Pompous man. Can't be bothered, not even for a—" He stopped and looked Achan up and down, jaw hanging open as if he had remembered something important. He shook it off. "Good, you're ready. I've entered you in the first round lists. If we don't hurry, you'll miss your chance."

Achan held up the sword, eyes wide. "This belongs to you?"

Sir Gavin thumped Achan on the back. "Belongs to you now."

"But sir! I can't possibly accept something so fine. I'll be killed for it in my sleep."

Sir Gavin's eyes twinkled. "Then sleep lightly, Achan. This belonged to a dear friend. Take good care of it."

"What's it worth?"

Sir Gavin blew out a long breath. "Oh, I don't know. Decent blade like this, minus the hilt, would go for at least thirty pieces of silver, maybe as much as two golds depending on the smith. Add ten to twenty golds for the stones, ivory, and workmanship. Then there's the value to the family, which . . . Well, as far as you're concerned, it's priceless."

The blood drained from Achan's face. The most a paid laborer could hope to earn in a year was about two pieces of gold. He forced himself to ignore the value, though he knew that just wearing it in public would make him a target for every thief in Sitna.

"D-Does it have a n-name?" Achan had to stop thinking about it. No one would steal a sword on the prince's coming-of-age day. Right?

"Well, of course it has a name, lad. All fine swords do."

Achan waited, and when Sir Gavin remained silent, he asked, "What is it then?"

"What is it?" Sir Gavin frowned and stroked his beard-braid. "Eagan . . . Elk."

"Eagan Elk?" What kind of a sword name was that?

"*Eagan's* Elk." Sir Gavin nodded and grinned, as if pleased with himself. He looked Achan up and down again, a far-off look in his eyes. "It suits you."

Achan felt ridiculous. Who was he trying to fool dressed in finery and carrying a priceless sword? He raised the blade to middle guard. "Is this a longsword or a short sword?" The grip felt shorter than the blunt he'd been using, but the blade looked longer.

"Kind of somewhere in the middle."

"But I should use it like a longsword, right?"

"Longsword is tomorrow. Today, I've entered you in the short sword and shield lists."

Achan sucked in a sharp breath. "But I've never practiced with a shield!"

"Which means you'll need this." Sir Gavin fetched a round, badly beaten, wooden shield, edged in peeling brown leather, from the corner of the room. The same spiky fish was painted dead center, but much of the paint had faded and chipped away.

Well, Achan thought, *I'll likely die today anyhow. A shield will make little difference.* "Sir Gavin, I don't know how to use this."

The knight sniffed long and slid the shield straps onto Achan's forearm. "Aye. Probably should have gone over it. Probably should have started with the short sword and shield and saved the longsword for later. Probably should have called for Sir Caleb or done a thousand things differently."

He waved the thought away. "Well, I did what I thought best. Just . . . hold the shield between you and your enemy. Keep your blade in middle guard, tucked behind the shield, see." He moved Achan's arms into position. "Make your cuts and thrusts around the shield. The shield is a weapon. Parry with it. Thrust it against your opponent's sword or body. Watch your head and legs. They'll be primary targets."

It all sounded good in theory, but without practice Achan may as well try the joust. "How many squires have you trained, sir?"

"You're my first."

"What?"

Sir Gavin shrugged and held out a plain steel helmet. "I was busy. Now, off we go. Thank you, Wils."

Wils bowed and departed. Achan struggled to sheath Eagan's Elk one-handed. He failed and had to use his shield arm to hold the scabbard still. Once the sword was sheathed, he took the helmet and followed Sir Gavin to the stairs in a daze. The scabbard's end clunked on the stairs behind him, and he pushed the pommel down to keep that from happening. Enamored with the jewels, he stumbled and decided now was not the time to be staring at anything but the ground in front of his feet.

They marched from the manor. Achan's clothing weighed him down. He'd been watching squires practice as long as he could remember. They always fought terribly when they first wore armor. They could hardly walk, let alone wield their weapons. Achan gulped.

At the gate to the outer bailey, a knight passed wearing full plate armor and a helmet. Achan staggered about as he shoved his own helmet on his head. The inside was padded with stiff, worn wool. Sir Gavin had dressed him in antiques. The helmet had no visor, just a long slit for the eyes that hindered Achan's peripheral vision. How was he supposed to fight with his vision impaired?

They walked over the drawbridge. The footsteps and the surrounding voices of the guests and guards sounded oddly muffled inside the helmet.

"I've negotiated a cow for you."

Achan turned his whole head to find a limited view of Sir Gavin's face.

"She's sick, likely to die any day. When she goes, they'll take her coat for leather. But instead of burning the carcass, they'll give her to us."

"What do we want with a diseased carcass?" Achan's voice sounded hollow beneath the steel.

"You have to learn what it feels like to cut a man. You need flesh to practice on, to gauge the power needed to strike someone down in battle. A cow will be perfect."

Achan was suddenly glad he hadn't eaten breakfast.

They reached the eastern field where the tents began. Sitna manor was not big enough to house all the tournament guests. Only the highest nobles were staying in the keep. Everyone else had brought along their own tents. Achan would have preferred to stay in a tent to keep him close to the festivities.

Sir Gavin led him to a square pen with long wooden benches along each side, crowded with peasants, slaves, and strays. Nobility preferred the shaded grandstands on the other side of the grounds, where they could sit on pillows and have servants bring them trays of tea and tarts.

A herald paced along one end of the pen watching two squires circle each other, each armed with a short sword and shield. The smaller squire, dressed in black and white, wore no armor. He had grey skin and a puff of bushy black hair. He was quick and darted around the pen like a firefly. His opponent, stronger and slower, wore shabby gold and maroon over chain armor. His shield donned a familiar image of red grapes. Carmine. Achan had seen the neighboring city's flags before.

The Carmine squire swung his sword hard. Too hard. It thwacked into his opponent's shield again and again, more like swinging an axe than swordplay. Achan grew tired just watching. The grey squire circled carefully, letting his opponent tire. Carmine stumbled. In a blink, the grey squire rained two crippling blows, knocking the Carmine squire to the ground, and poised his blade above his opponent's chest.

The herald called the match in Barth's favor. Achan frowned and studied the grey squire closer. Barth was a city in Darkness.

The Carmine squire pulled off his helmet to reveal a shock of short brown hair, frizzing in all directions. His face appeared flushed with anger, then Achan realized he was only badly sunburned. He lumbered to his feet and climbed out of the pen as Sir Gavin approached it.

Achan's heart pounded under all five layers of dress as Sir Gavin conversed with the herald. The sun beat down on his helmet, drawing sweat from his brow before he even lifted his sword. Would they let him compete? Would his animal surname cause a scene?

Sir Gavin stepped back, and the herald said, "Master Silvo Hamartano of Jaelport against Master Achan Cham of Sitna."

A murmur rose in the crowd. Achan stiffened as heads turned toward him. His cheeks flushed under his helmet and he was thankful for the mask. He stepped over the wooden rail of the pen and waited, scanning the crowd for his opponent from the city in Darkness.

An olive-skinned squire wearing green and grey moved through the crowd with the grace of a dancer. He was about Achan's size. He laid a hand on the rail and vaulted the fence with his legs to one side as simply as if he were yawning. He and Achan were now alone in the pen. The squire wore a hooded coat of chain under his green jerkin and stood with regal posture, his brown lips twisted up to one side. He looked to the herald. "Seriously? I'm to fight a stray?"

Achan stepped back to one side, drew his sword, and held his shield like the squire from Barth had. Were there rules to follow? What if Silvo struck him? Would the herald stop the match? Why hadn't Sir Gavin explained—

"Begin!" The herald scurried out of the way.

Silvo charged, sword above his head, shield lax in his other hand, apparently believing a stray equaled zero skill.

Achan took the staggering blow to his shield, thankful the old wood didn't crumble under the force. Achan couldn't believe his good fortune. The overbearing move had left Silvo wide open for all kinds of trouble. Sir Gavin's blunt had bruised Achan again and again for doing the same thing.

Achan stepped back and swung Eagan's Elk around the shield. The blade grated against the arm of Silvo's chain coat.

Silvo stumbled from the impact. Achan stepped around him and kicked him in the rear. Silvo crashed face first into the dusty red clay.

Laughter rumbled through the crowd. Achan leaped forward and pressed Eagan's Elk against the back of Silvo's neck. The crowd laughed harder, some applauded.

Achan fought the smile that wanted to claim his face. Silly, since no one could see under his helmet. He'd only won because of Silvo's arrogance. The herald declared Achan the winner. Silvo jumped to his feet and fled as gracefully as he'd arrived.

Achan joined Sir Gavin outside the pen. The old knight smiled and winked his brown eye. Achan couldn't believe it. He'd won a match! He'd had visions of humiliating defeat, not of actually wining. He stood tall beside Sir Gavin, feeling like it might actually be possible to carve a niche for himself in this place.

"What next?" Achan asked.

"We wait until you're called again. Each event is single elimination. You lose, you're done." Sir Gavin patted Achan on the back. "We'll stay here until you lose."

They watched a few more matches, and Achan studied how the squires used their shields.

Then the herald's voice called again. "Master Achan Cham of Sitna against Master Shung Noatak of Berland."

Achan had to look up at his next opponent. Shung, a beast of a squire at six-foot-plus, was the hairiest man Achan had ever seen. Huge tendrils of black, frizzy braids hung long and loose around his head. Wide curly sideburns traced his jaw to a beardless chin. Even his shield was hairy—covered in coarse, black fur. It was a much smaller, handheld shield called a buckler.

Shung grinned down on Achan, baring his yellow teeth. "You ready for Shung?"

Achan's eyes stung, and he realized he was staring at the circle of carved bone that looped through Shung's ear. "Aye."

The herald's voice started the match, but Achan and Shung remained still, each waiting for the other to make the first move.

"How old are you anyway?" Achan asked.

"Two and twenty."

That explained it. "Shouldn't you be a knight by now?"

Shung sidestepped. "In Berland, peasants can't rise above rank of squire."

Yet another city in Darkness. Achan stepped back and right. "What's Darkness like?"

Shung cracked his neck. "Dark." His long legs brought him within striking distance, and he swung his sword with immense power, screaming as he did.

Achan tensed, pushed his shield into the blow, and the force rattled his chain coat. He swung for Shung's arm as he had with Silvo, but his opponent blocked the strike with the edge of his shield then cut for Achan's legs with another piecing cry.

Forgetting his shield, Achan barely managed to parry with his sword, but Shung's force drove his guard back and the blade nicked Achan's shin.

He danced out of reach and tried to look as if he wasn't hurt. The cut sent throbs of pain up his leg. Achan grew instantly frustrated. He didn't know how to use a shield as well as Shung, let alone a sword. What was Sir Gavin thinking?

Shung crept nearer, and Achan put all his force behind his shield and rammed into his opponent. Wood, leather, and fur scraped against each other. Achan swung for Shung's legs and met plate armor under his trousers.

Oh, well, that was fair. Where was Achan's leg armor?

Shung's sword came over the top of Achan's shield and struck his helmet. Achan ducked back and swung Eagan's Elk out blindly. It clattered uselessly against Shung's shield.

Achan circled. "So, is Berland dark like twilight or dark like a moonless night?"

Shung came back with a downward cut from high guard, growling as he did. Achan parried with his shield, and Shung's blade cleaved into the wood, stuck.

Achan spun to the side, hoping to rip the sword from Shung's grip, but the sound of splintering wood sent him running as he realized he'd left his back unguarded. In the corner, he turned back to see Shung advancing.

"Dark like black," Shung said.

For a long while, nothing but the muted crack of swords on shields, and Shung's yelling, rang in Achan's ears. He focused, his heart stampeding, his body sweating—partly from fear—but he breathed, he followed through, he moved his feet, and he made a point of glancing into Shung's beetle-black eyes as much as possible.

And for some reason, he kept up the conversation. "So was that concerning? When Darkness came? Do you remember?"

Achan's head suddenly filled with pressure, and he gleaned Shung's desire to strike at his legs. The thought confused his actions, sending his feet hopping about awkwardly.

Shung easily drove him back against the fence. Their shields clunked together again. On a whim, Achan thought of the allown tree. The pressure, and Shung's strategies, faded from his mind.

Interesting.

When they broke apart and circled again, Shung said, "Therion forest always dark. Briaroaks and snarespruce grow thick." He adjusted his grip on his furry shield.

"Sounds painful." Achan lunged forward and struck Shung's wrist hard and fast.

Shung wore chain mittens, but the force of the blow caused him to drop his buckler. He backpedaled, using his sword two-handed to deflect Achan's offense. "Only if you forget your handaxes."

Achan didn't know what handaxes were, so he focused on where Eagan's Elk would strike next. Shung's jerkin roused Achan's interest. Black suede, fur, and dozens of dangling brown tails. "How many animals did you kill for that vest?"

Shung grunted and stabbed under Achan's shield, into his hip. "Seven and thirty."

Achan jumped back, stunned and furious that Shung did as well without his buckler. Achan needed much more practice with this ridiculous shield. He reminded himself that most squires had practiced daily for the past five or six years. Shung, closer to ten. Achan should be thankful to still have all four limbs.

He lowered the shield a bit, emulating the grey squire from Barth, then rained his favorite combination of strikes on Shung. The moves felt strange and awkward one-handed.

Shung darted forward with a cry and gave Achan's forearm a bruising blow, splitting the strap on Achan's shield. It clattered to the ground, and Achan stumbled over it. He gripped Eagan's Elk in two hands and they fought on.

Achan felt better this way. This was familiar, what he'd been practicing day after day. Still, his side pinched from fatigue, and his hip, shin, and forearm throbbed from Shung's strikes. "I'm tired."

Shung laughed, a deep throaty sound akin to gargling. Maybe he was tired too.

Achan felt pressure under his boot. His ankle twisted, and he stumbled back, catching his balance too late. Shung struck, and Eagan's Elk betrayed him by zinging from his hand and clattering to the ground. Achan dodged a thrust by falling onto his stomach and found himself lying on his shield, the cursed object he'd tripped over. He picked it up and cowered behind it.

Shung barred his yellow teeth in a wide grin. "Maybe you should give up now."

"Likely." Squatting, Achan twisted on his toes as Shung circled. "But I'm stubborn."

Shung swung again, silent this time.

Achan heard Sir Gavin's voice. "Yield, Achan."

Yield? He wasn't about to yield. Eagan's Elk was only a few paces away. If only—

Shung came at him again, silently. Achan, still crouched on the ground, parried a staggering wallop with the shield. The force knocked him to his rear. He planned to inch his way around the pen toward Eagan's Elk, but Shung stepped on the shield.

For a lighter man, this would have been a mistake. Achan could have pushed up or twisted the shield to the side and caused his opponent to fall. Shung, however, pressed Achan into the dirt like butter between two cuts of bread.

The herald proclaimed Shung the winner—although technically, Shung hadn't pinned him with the blade. Perhaps the herald was as tired of this match as Achan was. The sparse crowd clapped as if they'd rather be somewhere else. Apparently a squire from Berland and a stray brought little excitement.

Shung offered his hand. Achan gripped it, and Shung yanked him to his feet. "You well to talk to, Achan Cham. If ever you venture to Berland, we will hunt the beast of your name."

8

The next morning, Vrell stood in a steamy chamber similar to the bathhouse but three times as long. Torches flickered in rings on the walls. Mosquitoes swarmed. Instead of a stone floor that dropped off at the underground river, here a dirt floor sloped like a beachfront into the same vaporous tide. The river looked to be twice as wide as Jax was tall.

Lord Dromos and Ez stood in the chamber with Vrell and the knights. Six animal-skin boats were anchored to the shore by ropes looped around stone spikes, their wide ends bobbing in the rippling current. Ez, the wispy manservant, lowered two burlap sacks into the boat on the far left and strode to the chamber's wall. Khai darted forward and dropped his pack in the boat. Ez returned carrying a long staff with a glowing lantern on the end. He lowered it into a slot in the bow.

The slimy, brown tunnel wall gleamed in the lamplight. The walls were not clean here as they were in the bathhouse upriver. Over time, moisture and minerals had created gnarly textures along the walls like the roots of a tree.

Khai walked past Vrell for another pack.

"What about the horses?" Vrell asked him.

"They'll stay here. We can always get more horses. But gods forbid we lose your precious face to an eben spear. Master would rage. Therefore we go under the ebens, by boat. It's safer for everyone."

Lord Dromos stood with Jax, both giants ankle-deep in the hot springs. The giant lord pointed down the dark tunnel. "It's a two-day journey to the Lebab Inlet. You'll have to take shifts piloting the boat as there is nowhere to stop for the night."

Jax swatted a mosquito away from his face. "We appreciate your hospitality, my lord."

Lord Dromos walked backward and raised one hand. "Gods be with you all."

Jax, Khai, and Vrell climbed inside the boat. Ez untied it and pushed off. The humid air rushed past Vrell's face as the current sucked the boat into the dark tunnel. Jax had placed her in the bow, but moving at such speed into unknown blackness sent a tremor through her limbs. She turned her back and burrowed down into the boat's narrow front.

The current was so swift here that rowing wasn't necessary. Jax and Khai did not speak. Both held oars out to the side, stoic faces focused ahead. Every so often the boat jolted when one of them pressed an oar against the tunnel wall to steer the boat back to the center of the river.

Vrell did not like how the men's dark faces seemed to be looking at her. She twiddled her fingers, scratched a fresh mosquito bite on her wrist, then traced the tight stitches in the seam of the boat with her right forefinger.

She looked up. Craggy dripstones of various girths—some long and smooth, some tiny and jagged—covered the tunnel ceiling. A drop of water landed on her cheek, then her nose, then her forehead. With the intense humidity, she had not noticed the gentle shower.

A thick pressure filled Vrell's ears. It was the man newly gifted in bloodvoices. He was thinking of poison.

The low-voiced old man begged, *Tell me where you live.*

Another man said, *Are you there? Speak to me!*

Then the connection vanished.

Vrell's eyes flicked to Jax's. The giant's gaze was focused straight ahead. She glanced to Khai and met his black-eyed stare. She looked away, wondering if they had heard the voices as well. How could this man make everyone hear him? At least he appeared to have learned to close his mind. Perhaps he was someone's apprentice, as she would soon be.

Khai's oily voice echoed off the rock walls. "Clearly you know you have the gift or you wouldn't be so skilled at blocking others."

Vrell stiffened. "What gift?"

Khai cackled. "I'm no fool, boy. We were sent to bring you to Master Hadar. He wouldn't send Kingsguardsmen on a mission for nobody."

Vrell looked back to Khai. "But I am no one of consequence."

"Not now." Khai's eyes darted away as his oar clunked against the tunnel wall. "It's a long journey ahead. We could practice bloodvoicing, communicate with that new boy, help him."

Boy? His voice had not sounded like a boy's to Vrell.

"*Khai!*" Jax's booming voice made Vrell twitch.

"Well, why not?" Khai slapped a mosquito on his cheek. "We could ready this boy for his apprenticeship and find out about the other one for Master."

"What Vrell hides is his own business. We were sent to fetch him, not to poke around in his head."

"His secret could be valuable to someone. Perhaps we could both profit from it." Khai looked from Jax to Vrell. "There are ways to force it from him."

"I won't sink to witchcraft, nor will you in my presence," Jax said. "We'll deliver Vrell unharmed, nothing more."

Khai mumbled to himself.

Vrell's heart quaked beneath her layers of padding. Both of these warriors obviously knew she was hiding something, and at least one of them wanted to sell it to the highest bidder.

She did not know how or why her defense against their ability was so strong, but thank Arman it was. Should Khai discover her secret, his reward would be great and Vrell's life would be over. She could not allow the weasel to intimidate her into letting her guard down. Jax was a good man. If she stayed close to him, she knew he would protect her from Khai's greed.

But that alone was not a good enough plan. Vrell needed to learn to protect herself, and she needed a weapon. Her persona's age was fourteen—almost a man. She could not rely on others to save her for long. It would brand her a coward. She wanted to grow a fine reputation as a young man. Who knew how long she would have to live as Vrell Sparrow.

Hopefully not long enough to rouse suspicion about her lack of height—or whiskers.

Thankfully, Khai did not speak to her again until he passed on figs and bread for lunch. Vrell thanked Arman for her meal and munched on the bread slowly, glad to have something to pass the time.

Mid-bite, a great force thumped under the boat, knocking it against the tunnel wall. The frame scraped along the rock face. Vrell dropped her lunch and pressed her hands against the sides of the bow. Had they hit the roots of a tree?

Jax was crouched on his feet, axes drawn, when another impact struck the hull, lifting the boat off the water for a brief moment. Jax fell and the boat slapped back to the surface.

The combination sent a wave of hot water splashing up over the bow, soaking Vrell. She gasped and held back a scream as the boat spun around to the side. "What is happening?"

Jax's face tensed. He sheathed his axes, grabbed the oar, and paddled fiercely to straighten the craft. Khai's right hand clutched one side of the boat, his oar nowhere to be seen.

A third strike lifted the boat again, bringing another wave of hot water over Vrell when it splashed back into the current. The boat spun out of control, Jax's paddling useless to right it.

Vrell peered over the boat's edge. She could not be certain, but she thought she saw a large, dark body vanish into the waves like a giant fish.

She rolled back and sunk into the bow in time to see Jax duck. Vrell cringed, wondering what could possibly cause a giant to cower. Seconds later, the staff holding the lantern struck a low, fat stalactite. Glass shattered overhead and everything went black.

Vrell plastered herself against the side of the boat, choking in gasps of steamy air.

A piercing howl echoed in the darkness, the volume so terribly extreme it seemed to come from the walls themselves.

Vrell froze. "Wh-What was that?"

Jax's voice was soft in comparison. "A reekat."

Vrell thought back to Po's fur boots. "What is a reekat?"

"A problem," Khai said as if this were a routine chore he would rather assign to someone else.

Something rustled near Vrell's feet, then grazed her foot. She screamed and scrambled up into a squatting position, pressing back into the bow as far possible.

"Keep it down, you coward!" Khai hissed. "I'm only looking for my pack."

The reekat bumped the boat again. Then the ear-splitting howl came, beside her head this time, vibrating her cheek against the thick sheet of animal skin that formed the hull of the boat. Vrell held her breath, trembling in perilous silence. Were the Kingsguards going to do anything? Both had weapons, but could they use them in the dark?

Her dizzy head confirmed the boat was still spinning. It had been several seconds since the reekat's last scream. "Wh-What are you going to do?"

"Shhh!" Khai hissed. "Jax is seeking its mind."

Vrell frowned. What did that mean? Could Jax hear the thoughts of the creature? Could bloodvoicing be used on animals? Even if it could, what good would it do?

"There are two," Jax said.

Vrell prayed Arman would protect them and keep them safe. If she could live, she would be more obliging to her mother when she returned home—less stubborn, even giving up Bran if her mother wished it. She could learn to love another, could she not? She vowed to try if Arman would only deliver her from this ordeal. She breathed the words under her breath. "If it is your will, Arman, I give him up." Tears ran down her face at the sacrifice she had made.

Or maybe that was only the dripstones.

Two wailing howls shattered the silence, a lower-pitched one starting first, followed by a higher one, like a song sung in a round. Jax's words haunted her to the point of nausea.

There are two.

A force knocked the bow, slapping the boat against the stone wall with a loud crack. Vrell's head smacked the bone frame, shooting pain through her ear. Another force hit the stern, lifting the boat from the water. Before it could reconnect to the surface, something butted the hull, tipping the boat onto its side. Vrell tumbled into the steaming hot springs.

She gasped, hands gripping at the slimy textured wall, but found no hold. The current pulled her along, banging her body against the wall again and again. She was going to die!

Her life would end here, alone in pitch-blackness, drowned or perhaps eaten by a reekat, whatever that was. She would never see her mother or her sisters or her home again. Never grow her hair back out long enough to braid, ride Kopay, or snuggle with her cats. Never marry Bran or anyone at all. Her body would likely float out to sea and be netted by fishermen or drift into the canals of Mahanaim and be picked at by fish and birds.

The beasts' screeches came from behind, followed by the clash of steel on rock, a series of grunts from Jax, and a horrific ripping.

Vrell focused on her own situation and struggled to stay near the wall, but it suddenly vanished from beneath her fingertips. She surged forward and groped for the deformed stone, wanting to call out to Jax, afraid the reekat had eaten him and would eat her if she made a sound. There was only water where she felt the wall should have been.

Had she turned a sharp corner? Perhaps the tunnel had only grown wider? Her body whipped around in a small whirlpool. As she spun, she thought she saw light. Her stomach roiled from the tiny circles, and in a huge burst of effort, she swam free.

She bobbed in place, no longer caught in the current. She blinked as the darkness around her slowly took shape. She had drifted into some pond-like appendage of the underground river. A golden light glowed in the distance. She swam toward it as silently as possible, not wanting to alert any water beasts.

As she drew closer, the cavern around her came into focus. Stalactites covered the ceiling and dripped over the water's surface in a tribal rhythm. The dull, yellow glow illuminated the entrance to a cave, the opening as wide as two doors from Walden's Watch. On the bank, in front of the cave's entrance, several large stalactites had twisted together until they reached the ground, forming a tree of sorts. A massive cluster of thin, craggy dripstones on the ceiling above looked like icicle leaves.

As Vrell swam near the "tree," the cave behind it glowed fiery orange. Her feet found loose soil. She stood on shaky legs, waded toward the riverbank, and stepped onto a sandy shore.

A swarm of mosquitoes attacked, and she swung her arms around to ward them off. The steam carried a putrid stench that choked her. As she neared the cave's entrance, the light grew enough to see the ground. It wasn't sand she walked on, but some sort of pellet-like excrement . . . and a few shiny black beetles. She shuddered, quickened her pace, and stepped through the doorway into a long narrow cavern.

The light turned out to be from a flickering torch stuck in a crevice in the wall on one end. The space was no bigger than two servant's quarters end to end. Too small for a giant. And a reekat, whatever that was, could not light a torch. There had to be a human around somewhere.

"Hello?" she called.

A well-walked trail through the droppings stretched to the opposite end of the cavern, away from the torch. Vrell crept along it with soggy steps, dodging beetles. She found a gaping hole in the wall, waist high. It led to a narrow tunnel that burrowed up through the rock.

She stood staring into the shaft, unsure what to do. The tunnel could lead to a human who could help her . . . or hurt her. It could also be a cave for the water beast.

Perhaps it would be best to stay with the torch. She walked back toward the light, but the sound of splashing and grunting stopped her feet. Something was out there. Vrell darted out of the cave and behind the dripstone tree. She peeked through a gap where two stalactites narrowed.

It was Khai, staggering to the shore.

A shudder shook her limbs. Where was Jax? If something had happened to the giant . . .

Khai trudged up to the light, just as Vrell had. She stepped carefully around the dripstone tree to avoid being seen. She watched Khai lift the torch from the crack in the wall, examine it, and return it to its place. Then he looked down.

Vrell cringed. Her wet footprints would give her away.

Sure enough, Khai followed them to the other end of the cavern where the tunnel was. He lingered out of sight, but Vrell knew he would follow her footsteps back to the dripstone tree. She froze. Could he sense her presence? Vrell concentrated to close her mind, to be invisible, having no idea if it would work. Her ears suddenly tickled.

"Boy?"

Her breath caught in her throat. He could sense her. Could he sense her fear? Her location?

She could no longer see him from her position on the riverbank. She watched the edge of the dripstone tree trunk, listening for his footsteps over the patter of raining stalactites. His shadow loomed on the cavern wall, placing him near the cave's entrance, coming closer. She stepped back carefully over the gnarly base of the dripstone tree.

"I won't let the reekat get you, boy." Khai's voice was smooth and low and very close. He meant her harm. She could sense it. He wanted her secret. He could force it from her.

His shadowed face poked around the side of the tree. Vrell darted backward and leaned against a tall, thin stalagmite. The formation snapped against her weight. She crashed onto the hard ground, turned to her hands and knees, and scurried over the droppings in a crawl to her feet.

Khai jumped out in front of her, having gone the other way instead of following her over the craggy stalagmites. He grabbed her shoulder and lifted a dagger to her throat.

Vrell cringed. She had never in her life been treated so, not even as a stray. Her body quivered, her knees buckled, and although Khai tried to hold her up, his grip was not firm enough. She dropped to her knees.

He crouched beside her and gripped her shoulder tighter.

She scrunched her eyes shut. "Wh-What do you wa-wa-want?"

He reapplied his blade to her neck. "Your secret."

A shiver gripped every pore. She was cold despite the steamy heat. Vrell kept her voice low, doing all she could to keep him from guessing her gender. "I c-cannot tell you. I would d-die." In a sense that was true. Her spirit would die if she was forced to marry such an arrogant buffoon.

Khai pushed the blade against her skin. It pinched, but she did not think it had cut her. He released her shoulder and fumbled with a pouch on his belt. He drew out a small vial. "I made this over the past few days in hopes I'd get a chance to use it."

Vrell's eyes widened as Khai took the cork stopper in his teeth and worked it free. He spat it to the ground. The moist air tingled her eyes, and she blinked.

"Don't look at me like that, boy. It's not the witchcraft Jax spoke of. I haven't the time or materials for such ceremony. This"—he tapped the mouth of the vial to the tip of Vrell's nose—"is simple nature. A special blend to weaken that fortress around your mind." He straightened and kicked Vrell's arm. "Get up!"

Vrell slowly rose to her feet.

"Back," Khai said. "Into the spikes!"

Vrell obeyed, unsure what else to do. She backed up until she was wedged against the trunk of the dripstone tree and the slimy formations were rubbing against her wrists.

Khai pressed the blade to her throat and held the vial to her lips. "Drink."

Vrell shook her head, lips pursed. Without knowing the ingredients of this tonic, she would not ingest it. Master Masen and Mitt had both told horror tales of those who swallowed something wicked and suffered until death.

Khai pressed the dagger firmly against her throat. "Drink, I say!"

Something fluttered overhead. A bat! There were bats on the ceiling!

Vrell hated this place. She hated Khai. She hated having to play Vrell Sparrow to avoid a horrible marriage. Her arms and legs were free. She could fight, but she was uncertain about the blade. Dull as it may be, she did not doubt it would do damage with a powerful thrust. Khai might not be able to maintain control if he lost his temper.

He lowered the blade to where Vrell's neck met the top of her shoulder and drew the steel along the side of her throat.

At first she thought he had done nothing. Then a terrible sting throbbed where the knife had passed.

Khai leaned in, baring every flaw of his porous, sweaty skin. He remained there, pressing in on her mind, breathing his hot, stale breath in her face. He wiped the flat of the blade over her wound and leaned back, holding the weapon where she could see the dark blood smeared across the flat.

Tears welled in her eyes. Where was Jax? Had the reekat—

"That, boy, is your blood," Khai said. "I'm quite prepared to spill more of it, next time where it counts." He shoved the vial to her mouth. "Drink!"

She opened her lips and drank. It was gooey like honey but horribly bitter. Her stomach heaved as she held the repugnant liquid in her mouth, determined not to swallow. Khai's eyes glittered as the vial drained, and the pressure of his dagger's point lessened on her skin.

Vrell kneed Khai in the place that hurt a man most. He groaned and doubled over enough for her to slide between the dripstones, away from his weapon. She ran to the river, stumbled over the broken chunk of stalagmite, and spat the mixture from her mouth. She slurped a handful of hot, putrid water and gargled the bitterness away.

Khai grabbed her hair and pulled, lifting her out of the water. She took hold of the broken stalagmite and turned and bashed it against Khai's head. The stalagmite crumbled into smaller chunks. Khai's eyes bulged and he collapsed at her feet.

Served him right.

Vrell removed her soggy satchel and dug out her small knife. She cut two long strips off the hem of Khai's cloak. She propped him against a fat stalagmite and tied his wrists behind it. She also bound his feet, just to be sure.

Then she walked into the cave and kicked away the droppings and beetles to form a clear spot under the torch. She sank against the stone cavern wall and wrapped her arms around her knees, as sobs gently rocked her.

9

Achan clambered over the rail of the short sword pen and stumbled through a group of peasants, who laughed at him. He pawed at his helmet, but it seemed welded to his skull. Sir Gavin tugged it off. The cool air tingled Achan's sweaty face.

"Are you all right?" Sir Gavin asked.

Achan took a deep breath. His arms trembled from the fight with Shung. His hip and leg still throbbed, but the adrenaline coursing through him dulled the pain. "Aye."

"You should have yielded when you lost your sword. You risk getting killed dodging around like that. If he had hit you with his full power . . . "

Achan turned to see Shung stalking away through the crowd. "You think he went easy on me?"

"No. He fought hard until you lost your sword. Once you weren't a threat, he eased up. There are few who would kill another in tournament."

"But you said never underestimate an opponent. I could have gotten my sword back—"

"Don't be naive. In a real battle he'd have killed you the instant you dropped it. The only point of wielding a sword is to kill. Never forget that. Are you certain you're well? Your leg?"

Achan swallowed further debate and looked down at the dark wetness plastering his leggings to his shin. "It will be fine. A bruise or two will rise to the surface by tomorrow. But aren't you pleased? At least I wasn't humiliated."

"If I thought you'd be humiliated, I'd not have entered you."

Sir Gavin's backward way of teaching irked Achan. "I *should* have been humiliated with all the training I've had with a shield." Achan cast his eyes to the ground, shamed at his own attitude. This knight had no reason in all Er'Rets to train a stray. Achan needed to remember that.

But Sir Gavin only sniffed and bobbed his head. He tied the shield's strap in a knot and helped Achan loop it over his head and one shoulder so it hung off his back.

"It was hard," Achan said, trying to soften his complaint with discussion. "I couldn't guess when he was feinting or striking."

"Aye. That takes practice. You've had little."

The herald called out two new names and Sir Gavin led Achan away from the short sword and shield pen.

Achan stumbled alongside Sir Gavin. Only two fights and already his body craved his bed. Yet his mind couldn't sleep. All his life he'd watched tournaments from afar. Now he was a participant. The fact put a bounce in his weary steps. "Why did Shung scream so?"

"Gives him more power and unnerves his opponents."

"And he stopped screaming toward the end." So Shung *had* gone easy. Achan scowled. "Why didn't you tell me about the screaming?"

Sir Gavin shrugged. "I've never been the best teacher."

Achan inhaled to argue, but he could think of nothing to say that would make any difference. "What next?"

Sir Gavin stopped. "Why don't you wander a bit? There's someone I must speak with. I'll meet you back here shortly and introduce you." With that, he turned and strode into the crowd.

Achan looked around himself. He stood near the hand-to-hand combat pen, where two squires were rolling in the dirt. Peasants were chanting, "Ne-sos, Ne-sos." Two large red tents obscured his view of the longsword and axe pens.

In the distance, a cloud of dust rose before the red and white striped awning of the grandstands overlooking the jousting field. Achan drifted that direction, hoping he could see at least one match. But before he'd gone very far, his stinging hip reminded him of his wounds, so he stepped between two tents to inspect them.

He lifted his layers of shirts and drew the waistband of his leggings away with his thumb. The tip of Shung's sword had pierced the chain and grazed off his hipbone, a gash as wide as two fingers. The bone itself was tender, but the cut didn't look too bad. He checked his leg wound and found a shallow scrape. He'd cut himself worse peeling potatoes.

Squeals of laughter rose from nearby. Achan wove between the colorful tents in search of the source. He emerged in a clearing shaded by several poplar trees about twenty feet from the open tent where squires were helping their masters dress in armor for the joust.

A group of squires and maidens about his age ran about laughing and shrieking, playing hoodman's blind.

Achan shouldn't linger. Despite his armor and jerkin, he was a stray, and he doubted very much—judging by the lavish attire—that these people were. But their game migrated closer, and soon Achan stood in the midst of it. He quickly spotted the hoodman: a maiden with long curls so golden they were almost white, and tiny braids in a crown around her head. She wore a blue embroidered dress with layers of skirt. A grey blindfold covered her eyes.

The sunburned squire from Carmine who'd been defeated in the short sword pen bumped into Achan and laughed. The maiden came closer, the hem of her dress swishing in the grass, her arms outstretched, feeling the air. An olive-skinned maiden with dozens of oily black braids tipped with wooden beads, snuck up, whispered in the hoodman's ear, then darted behind a poplar.

The hoodman spoke, her voice filled with spunk. "I'll get you, Jaira, you wicked!"

The hoodman backed against Achan's chest. Her wild curls smelled like jasmine. Before he could remember the rules of the game, she whirled around and grabbed him in a hug.

"Got you!"

Achan jerked back in surprise and pulled free, causing the maiden to trip on her skirt. She screamed, and he reached out and caught her under the arms.

She giggled madly, gripped his forearms until she was steady, and tore off the blindfold. "What hero saved me from that fall?"

Achan blinked. The maiden was Cetheria in human form. The goddess protector, beautiful and golden. Her eyes were blue crystals that sparkled as she studied him. He stepped back, her scrutiny bringing a wave of uncomfortable heat. A crowd clustered around, waiting to see who the next hoodman would be.

"Well, who are you, hero?" the maiden asked.

"Achan."

"Just Achan?" Her lips parted in a teasing smile. "What knight do you serve?"

"Sir Gavin Lukos."

"The Great Whitewolf?" the Carmine squire asked.

Jaira, the maiden with the oily black braids, stepped out from behind the poplar and said, "He's ancient!"

The Carmine squire folded his arms. His sunburned nose was peeling. "He's not jousting, is he?"

"I doubt he could hold the lance," a scrawny, brown-haired boy said. "He's so old."

"Isn't he a stray?" Jaira asked.

Achan shrugged, hoping to appear like he belonged. "Lots of Kingsguard knights are strays."

"A handful. Of *Old* Kingsguards." The scrawny boy plopped down under a poplar and leaned back against the trunk. "The Council doesn't trust strays anymore. And with good reason. My father will never budge on *that* law."

Some grunted in agreement. Achan swallowed his unease and sought a polite way to exit.

Jaira pulled her black braids to one side of her neck and ran her fingers though them. "It's frightful that strays still have any authority in Er'Rets."

The blonde who had been the hoodman addressed Achan. "You have competed, I see. Did you win?"

His chest swelled. "Won one, lost one."

She smiled, but Achan wasn't sure if she was impressed, indifferent, or sympathetic. "Are you from Tsaftown?" she asked. "You wear our crest on your shield and our colors."

Achan blinked and looked down at his black vest. Tsaftown's crest and colors? "I'm, uh, from Sitna."

"What's your surname?" the Carmine squire asked. "I'd like to tell Sir Rigil who the Great Whitewolf has convinced to squire. He's never had a squire that I've heard of."

Why hadn't he? Sir Gavin appeared strong and bright. Doubt crept over Achan. Maybe Sir Gavin had gone mad in his old age to take Achan for a squire.

The group had gone silent waiting for Achan's reply. The Carmine squire must have left the short sword pen before Achan's lack of surname was announced. Achan could guess how this group would react once they heard it. He glanced at the pretty blonde with the sparkling eyes, the cause of his knotted tongue. He didn't want to see her fair face scowl and be the cause of it.

But now, with Eagan's Elk at his side and a legitimate victory under his belt, he didn't care what they said. "I'm Achan Cham."

Jaira gasped. "You're the stray who beat Silvo! He said you cheated."

"I did not!" Achan straightened to his full height. "His arrogance cost him the match."

The Carmine squire grinned. "Silvo *is* arrogant."

Jaira shoved the Carmine squire's chest. "Shut up, Bran!"

Bran barely swayed from her assault. "You'd know best, Jaira. He's your brother."

"*Lady* Jaira," she snapped. "And Silvo is better with a sword than you."

"Aye," Bran said. "I didn't say he wasn't good with a sword. I said he was arrogant."

Jaira's sculpted eyebrows sank over her narrow eyes. She turned her scowl to Achan. "Why are you here, anyway? Who let you compete?" She whipped around to face the scrawny boy under the tree, the beads in her braids clacking. "Reggio? Would your father approve?"

Reggio glared at Achan. "Most certainly not."

Jaira turned her pointed nose to Achan, lips pursed in victory. "Then why don't you scurry off to the stables or barns or wherever it is you strays live."

"Leave him be," the blonde said. "There is nothing wrong with being a stray."

Achan raised his brows. Nothing wrong with being a stray? He'd never heard anyone say such a thing.

"I beg to differ, Tara." Jaira wrinkled her nose. "They stink."

Reggio, the scrawny runt, burst into laughter.

Achan didn't care. He had just learned the blond girl's name. Tara. And Tara felt there was nothing wrong with being a stray.

Their mockery entered again into his awareness. Achan raised one eyebrow at Jaira, who was beaming at the attention. "Because we sleep with the animals in the barn, is that right, *my lady*?"

Jaira's gaze snapped back to his and she frowned. "Well, don't you?"

The canvas tents flapped in the wind. Everyone stared. Achan searched his memory for Sir Gavin's lessons on Jaelport, Jaira's city. He recalled their almost exaltation of women, which explained Jaira's countenance. They employed slaves and more eunuchs than the rest of Er'Rets combined. They worshipped Zitheos, god of animals.

Achan smiled wide. "Can you fault me, my lady? You prefer the company of animals yourself, do you not? Tell me, does not your god, Zitheos, have the head of the goat? Having met you and your brother, the rumors are confirmed. Those from Jaelport do take after their god."

Some of the boys laughed, but Jaira's chest swelled with a long intake of air. She looked Achan up and down with flashing dark eyes. "How dare you!"

Achan shrugged then bowed his head slightly. "You asked, *my lady*."

"Come, let us play." Tara forced a smile, wide peacemaking eyes darting between Achan and Jaira. She held the blindfold out to Achan. "I tagged you, so it is your turn."

Achan studied the faces around him. All but Jaira and Reggio looked content. It appeared as though they would let him play. He took the blindfold from Tara, and the touch of her hand sent tingles up his arm. She blushed and looked at the ground. The moment he pulled the blindfold up to his eyes he heard a dreadful nasal voice.

"Stop, Achan, this instant!"

Achan froze. He knew that voice. He took one last beholding gaze at Lady Tara, whose sapphire eyes had doubled in size, then reluctantly turned to his lord and master.

Sir Luas Nathak, Lord of Sitna Manor, strode toward them from the jousting field. His emerald cape billowed in his wake. A black leather mask completely covered the right side of his face. Dark, shriveled skin peeked out from the edges. His beard forked in two, half black, half white. His hair split also—the white half partly covered by the mask, the black half oiled back in a swell over his head. He wore a black leather glove on his right hand to hide the ruined flesh.

Gossip varied regarding Lord Nathak's condition. Some whispered of a rare skin disease. Others claimed a fire had burned him horribly. No one knew for certain.

The squires and maidens shrank back a few steps, leaving Achan to face Lord Nathak alone. Achan squared his shoulders. He knew better than to speak first. He bowed his head and prayed Cetheria would have mercy.

Pressure built at the base of his skull as a great fear washed into his mind. At first he assumed it was from someone in the group, but when he looked up and met Lord Nathak's eye, the feeling vanished. An icy tremor ran through Achan as if from an invisible breeze. He glanced at the budding branches on a nearby poplar and found them still as a statue. No wind had given him that chill.

How odd.

"Explain your presence here." Lord Nathak spat out his words like they tasted sour.

"I'm entered in the tournament, my lord . . . " Achan swallowed . . . "as a squire."

"On whose authority?"

Achan glanced up and found Lord Nathak's one eye horribly intimidating. "Sir Gavin Lukos, my lord."

Understanding tightened the visible half of Lord Nathak's face. "*You* are his new squire?"

"Yes, my lord."

"I heard he was training someone," Lord Nathak mumbled and tugged on the chin strap of his mask. "Then you have no time for games, do you? You should find him right away and see he has help dressing for his events. Is that not what squires do? Master Rennan?"

The Carmine squire, Bran, jumped, his sunburned face pinker than ever. "Yes. Yes, it is, my lord."

"Get to it, then. All of you!" Lord Nathak stormed past, bumping hard against Achan's shoulder. The other squires scrambled off.

Jaira gripped Tara's arm. "Come! Let us find seats for the joust. I'll introduce you to Sir Nongo. He's desperately handsome."

"It was nice to meet you, Master Cham." Tara rested a hand on his shoulder, bobbed up on her toes, and kissed his cheek. "Thank you for catching me."

Jaira rolled her eyes in a huff and pulled Tara away, but Tara looked back over her shoulder at Achan twice before disappearing around the corner of a blue and white striped tent.

Achan stood staring at the place where he last saw her, the scent of her jasmine hair lingering in his nostrils.

Achan left the shady clearing and made his way back to the hand-to-hand pen, where two different squires were fighting. Sir Gavin was nowhere to be found.

Achan watched the match while he waited. One squire wore blue and white. He had a full, black beard, grey skin, and was two heads taller than his scrawny, bleeding opponent. The freckled redhead, who couldn't be more than thirteen, seemed to favor the run-and-cower strategy. His purple, red, and silver striped tunic draped over his small frame like a shroud. Neither wore armor.

The big squire punched with such force that the boy made a dent in the dirt. Achan winced and ran his tongue over his teeth. For some fool reason, the boy scrambled to his feet and jogged around the perimeter of the pen. Begging for more pain, Achan guessed. Soon enough, the boy's wish was granted. The big squire cornered him and rained blows like Poril kneading bread dough. Why didn't the herald put a stop to this?

Thankfully, the boy finally stayed down. The herald called the match in favor of the squire from Hamonah. Achan couldn't recall from his lessons with Sir Gavin where that was.

Sir Gavin had still not returned, so Achan approached the herald. "Excuse me, sir. Have you seen Sir Gavin Lukos?"

"Not since this morning."

Achan surveyed the crowd one last time, searching every bit of red, hoping to spot the Old Kingsguard cape. He turned back to the herald. "Sir Gavin wanted me to compete here. Must I wait for him to enter?"

"What's your name?"

Achan took a deep breath. "Achan Cham."

The herald looked Achan over, clearly confused about Achan's rank. "Lord Nathak says you're to report to the kitchens . . . sir."

Achan nodded. He stepped back from the pen, then spun around and stormed toward the manor, loosening his jerkin as he went. The kitchens? By Lord Nathak's direct order? Why couldn't he allow him to serve Sir Gavin at least for one day? Lord Nathak had plenty of servants. Poril had plenty of help.

Achan stalked to the keep and up to Sir Gavin's bedchamber. The room was empty. Wils was probably off dressing some other poor sap. Achan jerked the shield over his head and let it clatter to the floor. He fought with his clothes until he got them all off, pulling out a tuft of hair along with the chain shirt. After folding them as neatly as his temper would allow, he left them, the shield, and Eagan's Elk lying atop Sir Gavin's bed.

He stared at the beautiful sword and scabbard. For a morning he'd been a real squire. He sighed. No reason to keep the blade now, though. It looked like Lord Nathak was denying him his knightly apprenticeship. Besides, the sword was much too good for cutting vegetables.

He washed his wounds and dug around until he found some strips of cloth to bind them. At least he would not die from infection. He fought two matches today, met a group of nobles who could have had him arrested, and came face-to-face with Lord Nathak. He should be thankful to be alive.

Achan spent the rest of the day in the kitchens running errands for the frantic Poril. As if the gods didn't feel this day was humiliating enough, Poril told Achan he was to serve at the feast. Poril made Achan wear a fancy green servant's uniform. It made him look like a jester.

Any other day Achan would have been thrilled for such an opportunity. But he'd been an equal with squires today, even insulted a noblewoman. To serve them now . . . well . . . he'd rather not.

Poril gave him instructions in the kitchen. "Yer not teh speak unless yer spoken to. Pages and squires will serve food to their lords, so yeh'll not be causing any trouble there. Once the squires sit, yeh'll serve them."

Fabulous! Perhaps Achan could offer up some ale or choice wine to Reggio or Bran or Shung or Silvo. He scowled at the floor.

Achan took his place in the serving room off the entrance to the great hall. Dozens of identically dressed servants crowded the tables and filled platters with food. No one had recognized Achan yet. He did see Reggio arguing with Poril about the best cut of lamb for Sir Jabari. Thankfully Poril dealt with the pompous runt himself. Maybe all would be well. Maybe no one would recognize him at all.

He waited for his turn to serve by peering through the doorway into the great hall. He had never seen the room during mealtime, and nothing could prepare him for the clamor of two hundred voices, ripping meat, chewing, and slurping. Brightly colored gowns and embroidered doublets complemented the polished poplar beams holding up the high ceiling.

As if circumstances didn't cause him enough sweat, the dozens of torches on the walls and so many bodies crowded together raised the temperature to such a degree, Achan was tempted to go dive into the moat.

A table draped in white linen stretched along a platform at the end of the hall. Prince Gidon Hadar sat in the center on a throne-like chair with a high, carved back. He was tall and strong. A jagged crown of gold sat over his oily black hair. A short, black beard shaded his chin. He looked ridiculous in his gold silk doublet with the red, ruffled sleeves of his shirt flouncing down to his bejeweled fingers. Gren had likely spent hours dyeing the fabric to achieve such a rich shade.

Lord Nathak and his wife sat to the prince's right. Sir Kenton Garesh, Prince Gidon's personal protector, also called the *shield,* sat at Gidon's left. Everything about Sir Kenton was thick but his black hair, which hung like a curtain about his pale face.

Two dozen others sat around them, dining and laughing above those unworthy to sit at the high table. Two more tables extended the length of the great hall, one along each wall, each seating eighty. All seemed to savor Poril's feast.

When the high table was served, Achan and nine others dressed like him carried tray upon tray of food to the lower tables in the great hall. Achan quickly spotted Lady Tara and her friends on the left wall facing the high table. He made a point of serving the far end of their table, where he would be neither seen nor summoned. When every trencher was full, the servants took their places along the walls. Five on each side stood in a line against the wall three paces back from those seated at the long tables.

Achan stood last in his line, nearest the door, and on the same side as Lady Tara. He watched the back of her head for a while then glanced over the shoulder of a fat man in front of him, who had already emptied his trencher twice. The man looked around greedily. Achan wondered if he might eat the trencher itself. Achan and the servants waited silently against the wall, moving only when summoned.

Someone to Achan's left snapped his fingers. "Servant. Some wine."

Achan retrieved a jug from the serving room and filled the man's goblet. He turned to go back to his place, but a woman dressed in turquoise held up her glass in silent request. Achan barely managed to fill it around her billowing sleeve. More glasses went up. Achan made his way down the table as guest after guest seized the opportunity for a refill. They raised their goblets and continued their conversation, as if the wine magically poured itself.

He spotted Jaira, the catty, braid-wearing, stray-hating noblewoman from Jaelport he had insulted earlier. She was sitting beside Lady Tara. A chill washed over Achan when Jaira lifted her goblet in the air, her olive-skinned fingers clad in copper and silver rings.

The way she held it, high up under his nose while she chattered to Silvo, made it difficult to pour. It would help to get a better angle. The last thing he needed was to spill on this infernal woman. So he plucked the goblet from her hand.

She gasped. "How dare you touch me!"

Conversation around Jaira dwindled and onlookers stared. Achan ignored them, filled Jaira's goblet, and set it in front of her plate. Out of nowhere a tiny, hairless dog leaped out of Jaira's lap. It dunked its head inside the goblet and started drinking.

Achan slid back against the wall and bumped into an overweight servant standing there. He flattened himself beside the pot-bellied man. Though he averted his gaze, he felt the burn of many sets of eyes, including Jaira's. A sinister pressure built in his mind. Trouble.

"Silvo." Jaira's chair scraped on the hardwood floor. "Look at this!"

A request for wine at the end of the table sent Achan scurrying in that direction, but someone caught him by the arm and squeezed.

"Pretty strong arm for a servant," Silvo said.

Achan jerked free and walked toward the passage leading to the kitchens, praying he'd get outside without a scene. A trencher flew over his shoulder. Something whacked the back of his head. He didn't stop.

"Hey! I'm talking to you, stray!"

Achan paused, breathed deeply, then turned and growled through clenched teeth. "*Sir?*"

Silvo stood, hands on hips, a single dark eyebrow cocked. His narrow eyes glittered. "Get us some wine down here."

The entire row of guests seated on the left wall seemed to be staring at Achan. Behind Silvo, he could see the blur that was Lady Tara's golden head turn his way.

"My jug is empty, *sir*," Achan said. "I need to refill it."

Something cool nudged his shoulder. Another servant traded a full jug of wine for Achan's empty one. Achan glared at the servant. Perhaps he could meet this boneheaded slave in the hand-to-hand pen immediately following this humiliation. Where was Sir Gavin anyway?

Achan strode back to Silvo, Jaira, and the rat-dog. He filled Silvo's goblet. Then Jaira's. The drunken mutt lay curled by his lady's trencher, sleeping. Silvo had drained his goblet by the time Achan filled Jaira's, and the impudent squire clunked it repeatedly against Achan's jug. Achan filled it again, all the while warmly aware that Lady Tara was watching the scene.

"Tell me, *stray*." Silvo took another sip. "How does this squire-servant thing work?"

"It doesn't really," Achan murmured.

"I would think not." Silvo snorted, then snarled, "I demand a rematch, *stray*. You embarrassed me in front of a lot of people today and—"

"You embarrassed yourself, Master Hamartano," Lady Tara said.

Silvo's eyes widened. His olive cheeks flushed maroon.

Lady Tara cocked an eyebrow and held up her goblet. "May I have some wine, please?"

"Of course, my lady." Achan took his time filling Lady Tara's goblet, his own cheeks burning from the effect of her stare.

"I think a man of many talents is quite the man indeed," she said. "Tell me, Master Hamartano, can you serve wine with one arm? Most servants I've seen use two to hold the jug. It must be very heavy." She looked at Achan. "Pass the jug to Master Hamartano, good sir. I fear Sir Nongo is parched at the high table. We cannot have Master Cham serving *your* knight, can we, Master Hamartano?"

The boiling rage in Silvo's eyes brought a grin to Achan's lips. The squire snatched the jug from Achan and glided on agile feet to the high table.

"I see we are even, Master Cham," Lady Tara said with a coy smile. "Now *I* have rescued *you*."

Achan smiled down on her. "That you have, my lady."

"Could you not tell me how you went from squire to servant in half a day?" She sipped her wine, her eyes never leaving his.

His stomach danced a jig. As much as he wanted to talk with her, he remembered his place, and bowed. "Is there anything else you need, my lady?"

"Only your company. Could you not pull up a chair?"

"I could not, my lady. Forgive me." Achan bowed again, feeling the fool, but enjoying himself nonetheless.

Lady Jaira clucked her tongue. "Really, Tara. You degrade yourself. I don't understand why you must—"

"Achan!"

It was Sir Gavin's voice. Achan spotted the knight sitting at the end of the high table itself. The knight was waving him over, his eyebrows trying to send a message Achan couldn't translate.

Could it have something to do with a servant holding conversation with a noblewoman in the great hall? Although he didn't sense anger from the knight, Achan blew out a deep breath, turned to Lady Tara, and bowed once more. "Excuse me, my lady."

He turned to walk the long way around the room to Sir Gavin—in order not to have to pass Silvo at the high table—and met Poril at the entrance. A sense of foreboding closed in on his mind, and, judging from the cook's bloodshot eyes and clenched teeth, Achan figured he'd also seen Achan's exchange with Lady Tara. Well, why not add a beating to this momentous day?

Knowing Poril would rather die than make a scene in the great hall in the middle of the prince's coming-of-age celebration, Achan passed him right by and went around to Sir Gavin. He squatted beside the knight's chair.

"For Lightness's sake, lad, stand up," Sir Gavin hissed.

Confused, Achan stood. He preferred the cover of squatting behind the table. He was tired of being stared at and longed to leave the great hall.

"Achan, I want you to meet a friend of mine. This is Prince Oren Hadar."

Prince? Achan knew of no claimant to the throne beside Prince Gidon. Achan averted his gaze for a moment, then curiosity won out. He looked up at the man seated beside Sir Gavin. Prince Oren Hadar had black hair, blue eyes, and a long, narrow nose. He wore a thin crown of gold on his head. It was so thin, in fact, that Achan might not have seen it if the torches on the wall hadn't reflected off the shiny metal. The prince studied Achan with narrowed eyes, as if searching his memory for something.

Achan's thrilling moment with Lady Tara had left his brain on the other side of the room. He put it to work at once. Was this man in some way related to Prince Gidon? Achan glanced to the center of the table where the prince sat presiding over his coming-of-age celebration.

"Prince Oren is King Axel's baby brother," Sir Gavin said. "Second in line for the throne, behind only Gidon."

Achan went straight to his knees.

Prince Oren chuckled. "None of that for me, lad. And I'm no baby, 'baby brother' though I be." He winked at Achan. "I think my nephew, Gidon, gets his handsome face from his mother."

"Bah!" Sir Gavin waved his hand. "Dara was beautiful. That—" he nodded to the prince—"is far from beautiful."

Achan failed to bite back a laugh. Sir Gavin had better watch himself or he'd be hanged for insulting the prince. People had been hanged for less around here.

The thought of unnecessary cruelty brought Lord Nathak to mind. "Sir Gavin, I need to tell you about what happened today—"

"How did you do?" Prince Oren asked. "Gavin tells me you clobbered Silvo Hamartano."

"Only because he was overconfident, Your Highness."

Prince Oren raised an eyebrow. "Modest."

"No, really," Achan said. "He assumed because I'm a stray I'd be weak. He led with a move easily deflected by any beginner, leaving him wide open and off balance."

Again Prince Oren laughed. "I hear Sir Gavin's logic in your words, my boy."

"Achan." It was Poril's thin voice.

Pig snout! Would no one let him be for five minutes? Achan turned.

Poril walked toward him as if each step brought the old man closer to death. Approaching the high table without food, wine, or invitation was a good way to meet a noose. Poril's gaze flickered between Lord Nathak and Prince Oren as if he were unsure who might banish him first.

Achan sighed and looked back to Sir Gavin. "I waited for you at the hand-to-hand pen, but you didn't return, and Lord Nathak told them I couldn't compete. Now if you'll excuse me, I'm about to be beaten for my dual roles at Sitna Manor today." He glanced across the hall and caught Lady Tara watching him. He grinned. "It was worth it, though."

Poril whispered, "Achan!" The cook now stood three yards from the high table. He beckoned Achan toward him with the jerk of his head.

Achan had never seen him act so strange. "Farewell." Achan bowed his head to Prince Oren. "It was an honor, Your Highness."

Sir Gavin grabbed his elbow. "See here, you'll not be whipped because of me."

Achan waved him off. "Oh, it's not really your fault, sir, and a very long story."

Sir Gavin chuckled. "See what I mean? He has that way about him, does he not?"

Prince Oren flashed Achan a curious smile. The stares of both men brought a flush to Achan's cheeks for no reason he could explain. He sensed a secret in them, something clandestine that somehow involved himself. He swallowed, bowed again to Prince Oren, and started toward Poril, who turned and made a beeline for the kitchens.

Achan was surprised to find Sir Gavin at his heels.

"Sir Gavin!" Lord Nathak's nasal voice amplified over the chatter, sending an icy chill up Achan's arms. "A word?"

"I'll be right back, Achan. Don't go anywhere."

But Achan desperately wanted to exit the great hall. He watched Poril's back, wondering what his reaction would be when he found Achan not following. He sighed. He'd almost take a beating just to feel some cool air on his face.

He stood where Sir Gavin had left him, torn between whom to obey. Then he saw Silvo's dark eyes spot him. The thin squire stood and started his way, no good on his mind. Achan wasn't willing to take *that* kind of beating. That settled it. He made a quick exit from the great hall.

He found Poril waiting outside. The cook gripped Achan's arm as if squeezing juice from a lemon. "Yer through serving, yeh are. Talking with noble folk like yer one of 'em? Never has Poril been in such a place to be forced to interrupt a prince. Gods have mercy on poor, miserable Poril. Lord Nathak said to keep yeh away from the knight, but yeh went right to 'im. What's Poril to do, I ask yeh? Into the kitchens until Poril can get his belt teh yer hide. That's what."

Lord Nathak would never allow Achan to train as a knight, and this proved it. Achan stalked out of the inner bailey. The sun beat down on him as if to laugh at his feeble attempt at a new life. He passed through the outer bailey and stepped into the kitchens.

He stood in the doorway and watched the women bustle about preparing desserts. He had never been filled with more rebelliousness in his life. The gods had given him a taste of noble life today and, with the exception of his bath, he didn't want to lose it. He stepped into the kitchens, lifted a briarberry pie from the table, and slipped away.

Normally he would've sought out Gren, and they could've shared the pie together in secret. But she was engaged now. And besides, he had only bad news to share. Lord Nathak's discovery of his training would likely mean the end of Achan's dreams of knighthood, which crushed his hopes of rescuing

Gren from a life with Riga. So instead of heading to her home or even the Corner, Achan carried his pie over the drawbridge and toward the river.

The sun shone high in the sky as Achan sank against the allown tree. He shoved a bite of pie into his mouth. The sweetness brought comfort, but it changed nothing. It was foolish to hope. No stray could serve in the Kingsguard. Achan knew the law. Why had Sir Gavin insisted on breaking it?

Achan sat under the allown tree until the sun sank behind Sitna Manor, watching the rushing river and picking at the pie until it was gone. He should return and take his beating like a good stray. Instead, he lay down and dreamed of Lady Tara's kiss.

10

"What's this?"

Vrell could see Khai's boots through the cave entrance from her position under the torch. He was still unconscious. It was not his voice that spoke. Nor was it Jax's.

"Somebody done a number on him," the voice said. "That's quite a wallop."

Vrell leaned to the right until she saw the speaker. A hunched man stood at Khai's side, wearing only blackened undershorts. He had a narrow, skeletal build, but his sinewy arms and legs burst with muscles. A few wisps of black hair lay matted to his bald head. It looked like he'd tried to shave his head but had missed a few spots.

Jax stepped into Vrell's line of sight. Her heart leapt to see him alive and well. He crouched behind the stalagmite where Khai's wrists were bound.

"No!" Vrell scrambled to her feet and ran to the men, who turned to her in surprise. "Leave him!"

"Vrell!" Jax stood, his wide smile baring two rotten bottom teeth. "I thought the reekat ate you for sure." He motioned back toward the river. In the dim light, she saw a wet form at the craggy base of the dripstone tree. A swollen brown beast lay where the water met the shore. In the shadow of the dripstone tree it was difficult to make out anything specific.

"Is it . . . "

"Dead," the near-naked man said. His skin was winkled all over as if he had been in water his whole life.

Jax pointed down at Khai. "Did you do this?"

She looked at Khai's face. A small turnip had swelled from his temple, shiny and purple. "He attacked me." She pointed to the sticky cut on her neck. She had forgotten to clean it, not that it would matter in such a filthy place.

Jax's bushy black eyebrows sank into a scowl. "Why would Khai attack you?"

Vrell looked at her feet. "He said he wanted my secret. He forced me to drink something bitter, but I spit it out."

Jax sighed. "I'm sorry, Vrell. I meant to keep an eye on that." Jax rubbed his face, fingers lingering on his right eyelid. "But I can't leave him like this. Khai's greedy, but he's my partner. I need to untie him, make him comfortable. You understand?"

Vrell swallowed but nodded.

The giant pulled a dagger from his boot and cut Khai free. He lifted the unconscious Kingsguard over his shoulder and carried him into the cave.

Vrell glanced back at the wrinkled man. He was watching her with raised eyebrows. Feeling self-conscious, Vrell walked into the cave. She cleared a spot in the droppings across from the dark tunnel that led up into the cave wall and sat. She watched Jax out of the corner of her eye, but he spent only a moment settling Khai under the torch before joining the wrinkled man by the dripstone tree.

The two men dragged the reekat into the cave. Under the torchlight, the beast came into full view. It was a slug-like creature covered in short brown fur. It had the whiskers and scrunched face of a bobcat, a short tail, and webbed feet with thick claws on each toe.

Jax glanced over his shoulder to Vrell before giving the front left limb of the reekat a final tug. "Peripaso here saved me."

"Ah, you'd of done all right." The man—Peripaso, apparently—stood and stretched his arms overhead until his bones cracked. "We'll just leave her for now. I'll skin her tonight."

"It is huge," Vrell said.

"Aye. She's a big one," Peripaso said.

"But how? What do they eat that makes them so big?"

"Oh, they got themselves a filter in their mouths like a whale to swallow tiny fish from the springs. Garra, dace, suckers, and chubs."

"Then why do they attack?"

"They're real territorial. They got at least one nest up river. Likely have a young one. It's the right time of year."

Vrell kicked a beetle away from her foot. "What are we going to do now?"

"Peripaso has invited us to dine with him," Jax said.

The wrinkled man burst into laughter. Jax joined in, the sound so jolly Vrell smirked.

A groan from Khai silenced them all.

Jax squatted beside his companion. "All right, Khai?"

The knight rolled to his side and up onto his knees. "What happened?"

"Met some help upriver," Jax said. "Peripaso here killed the reekat."

"Jax nicked the first one," Peripaso said.

"Scared it away."

"Well, that's a big one," Khai said, staring at the beast. He turned to Peripaso. "You live down here?"

"Up in a cave. Reekats don't leave the water much, and when they do, they're too fat to get in my tunnel."

Khai fingered the lump on his head and rose to his feet, glaring at Vrell. "Was the boat destroyed?"

"Only torn," Jax said. "Peripaso says he can mend it, but we'll have to fetch it first. It anchored when it tipped. It's upstream a ways." Jax tugged the handkerchief from his hair, wrung it out, then retied it. "Vrell, if you don't mind helping Peripaso bring down supplies from his place, Khai and I will fetch the boat."

Vrell's eyes bulged. "Me? Go up there?" She stared up the dark tunnel.

Jax nodded. "Once we've eaten and the boat's mended, we can head out again."

"But how will you swim upstream?" Vrell asked. "The current is too strong."

"I'm tall enough to walk it. I'll carry Khai on my back."

"Just leave me," Khai said. "Thanks to the boy, I feel ill. I'll only be a burden."

"I'd let you rest if I could," Jax said. "But I'll need help should another reekat come along."

Peripaso turned to Vrell. "What you say, laddy?"

Vrell stood. If it got them out of the underground river faster, she would do her part. "What must I do?"

"You jest follow me. Tunnels are a maze and blacker than tar. Stay close now."

As Peripaso turned and hoisted himself into the tunnel, Vrell caught a glimpse of the brand on his back. A curly *S* the size of her fist popped out on his right shoulder in raised, white flesh. The mark of a stray. Vrell shivered. If anyone ever looked, they would find no such burn upon her skin. She was glad for that, of course, but it would instantly destroy her disguise.

With one last glance to Jax and Khai, Vrell heaved herself up. The tunnel was tall enough that she could walk in a squat. Humid, stale air closed in as she inched up the steep tunnel grasping onto slick, craggy rocks for leverage. Vrell's nerves tingled with each step up and away from the light. She turned to see the entrance, a beige circle below. She did not like the idea of going into a tunnel that was *blacker than tar*. "Could we bring a torch along?"

"Nah. Air's not so good. Snuffs 'em out. Long as we keep movin', we'll be fine."

Vrell twisted back to the dark path and scooted after Peripaso's fading silhouette. "How far is it?"

Despite her attempts to keep up, the old man's form vanished. His voice drifted back from the blackness.

"We're 'bout a quarter of the way. Tunnels wind all over Nahar and Arman. If you know the way, you can go almost anywhere. I've traveled 'em all. Took one all the way to Darkness. Scare me half to death when I come out to find ebens havin' some sort of tribal ceremony. Bonfires everywhere. Watched long as I dared, then turned and come home. Caved that tunnel in right after. Didn't like the idea of them sneakin' up on me, like I did them."

The tunnel leveled out. Vrell bumped into Peripaso, who had stopped. She jumped and fought back a scream.

"Feel." His wrinkled hand patted Vrell's shoulder, down her arm, and stopped at her wrist. He drew her hand against the stone of the passageway. It slid along, and then fell away. A side tunnel. "This one run down to the Lebab Inlet. Take almost a week to crawl through here. You could always go this way. Though it makes better sense to fix your boat and take the river. Besides, your giant friend won't fit up here."

All the way to the Lebab Inlet? Vrell's mind ticked off possibilities. If she could take the tunnels, she could escape from the knights, Khai, especially. She could stay hidden from the prince and the ebens. She could talk to Mother. "Can you go to Walden's Watch through there?" If she could get back there, she would ask Mitt to hide her until Lady Coraline's return.

"Sure. Can even climb your way as far as Arok Lake."

Vrell's heart raced. Maybe she could sneak away. If Peripaso would show her the right tunnel . . .

Something grabbed Vrell's hand and she gasped and swatted at it.

"Is jest me now." Peripaso pulled her hand along the rock to the right until she could feel a small opening. "Passed by this one hundred times 'fore I found it. Takes me right to Xulon's dungeons." He released Vrell's hand.

"Who built all these tunnels?"

"They say King Granton I had the heart of his granddaddy, King Trevyn the Explorer. But ol' King Trevyn discovered pretty much all there is in Er'Rets, so King Granton found new places to explore. He liked the idea of being able to sneak his men up to jest 'bout anywhere too."

She heard his steps scratching away and stayed close behind, occasionally smacking her hands or head on the invisible rock. Not being able to see him brought stabs of fear. She sought out his mind.

Seven . . . eight . . . nine . . . ten . . . left. Six more paces to the fork.

Peripaso hobbled forward a bit more and stopped. "This fork will get you to the sea that lies south of Nahar Peninsula."

Vrell reached out with her hands, feeling for the hole. She would never venture into one of these tunnels alone, unless . . . "Could you tell me how? I am hoping to travel to Walden's Watch."

"You jest come from there, boy. Goin' to Mahanaim, aren't you?" There was a moment of silence in the dark, then, "You a prisoner?"

If you only knew. "Not exactly. I am being taken there for an apprenticeship."

"Well, that's promisin', then. Few strays get such opportunity."

But she was not a stray! Vrell groaned inside. She heard Peripaso shuffling onward and hurried along. "Why do you live down here . . . up here . . . wherever this is?"

Peripaso chuckled. "I'm also a stray, laddy."

"But it is so dark down here. Life as a stray is not so awful."

"Oh, I don't mind dark." He chuckled. "You know the story of King Axel's death?"

"Of course."

Vrell's knees were sore from crawling on the rock. She raised herself onto her toes, but her back struck the ceiling. The most comfortable position was back on her hands and knees.

At least the humidity had died down some, which also made the rocks less slippery.

"Lived in Armonguard at the time." Peripaso's voice faded some as he continued on.

Vrell leaned her shoulder against the tunnel wall and crawled after his voice.

"Met the king twice, I did. Worked in the falconry, mostly cleaning cages. My master was kind. Let me feed and hold the birds. King Axel had a gyrfalcon, finest I ever seen. Spent hours visitin' that bird, takin' it huntin'. Both times we met, he's kind to me. Didn't mind strays. Queen Dara, now she's another matter. Look. We's almost there."

Something silvery glowed in the distance.

"Do you have a torch lit?" Vrell asked.

"Candle."

"It glows brightly for a candle."

"You'll see."

Peripaso's crouched form took shape as it silhouetted against the silver light. He swung out of sight into the silver opening. Vrell's heart pounded. She hurried forward and looked out. What she saw ripped the breath from her lungs.

A cavern with a vaulted ceiling, twice the size of the one by the dripstone tree, shimmered before her eyes. The walls rippled like the tunnel of the underground river, but instead of roots, this looked like ice. Yet the room was hot and muggy and smelled of smoke.

She could see the makings of a home below. A bedroll, a collection of cooking utensils, a fire pit, stacks of fabric, and tools. Vrell crouched in the opening. A smooth stone ledge tapered down to the floor below. A rope ladder also hung from the ledge as a way to climb back up.

"Slide down." Peripaso scuttled below on the clean stone floor gathering things from around the cavern.

Vrell sat on her rear and pushed off. Her hair blew back from her face as she flew down the stone slide. She smiled when she reached the bottom. That was fun. She got to her feet and walked to the wall.

She ran her fingers over the shiny ripples on the wall. "Are they crystals?"

"Silver. Cave's full of silver. Hot springs cause dripstones to form from the minerals in the soil. Nice, ain't it?"

"It is wonderful."

"Maybe you'd better not mention it to that little man."

Vrell sniffed a laugh. "You are right. Khai would surely mine the silver from your home."

"It ain't much silver." Peripaso twisted twine into a large ball. "Someone greedy enough could destroy the cave and not end up with enough for one goat."

Vrell nodded. "I will tell no one about your home."

"Much appreciated. Don't usually talk to strangers passing through."

"Well, Jax is kind."

Peripaso shoved the twine into a burlap sack and grunted. "For a giant. I ain't the most fond of 'em. Know they ain't all bad. But I can't help but think of ebens when I sees one."

"Why did you help Jax, then?"

Peripaso shrugged. "Right place at the right time. Was hunting me a reekat."

"Are they terribly vicious?"

"They can be."

Vrell strolled around the cavern and surveyed Peripaso's belongings. A brown fur bedroll on a raised ledge of rock appeared to be made from reekat fur. Bits of hay and dried-out rushes of sweet flag grass lay strewn over the floor. There were no pellet-like droppings to be seen here, but Vrell did spy a few black beetles creeping about under the rushes. Water trickled down a crevice in the opposite wall, where Peripaso had organized a kitchen of sorts. A small hearth blackened the stone around it and the ceiling above.

Peripaso came to her side. “Can’t let a fire go long. Smokes me out.” He picked up a wooden mug and held it under the stream in the crevice. “Like a drink? Water’s cool.”

“Thank you.” Vrell took the mug and drank. The lukewarm liquid tasted thick with minerals. It was not until she finished that she realized how dry her throat was. She thrust the mug back under the flow for a refill as Peripaso went about his business. When Vrell finished drinking, she said, “You never finished your story about how you came to live here.”

“Well, the king and queen got killed by a stray up north, and Armonguard Castle went into a fit. Kingsguard knights arrested every stray they could find. Tossed ’em in the dungeons. Friend of mine worked as a guard. Told me of a tunnel that went out from there. He wasn’t certain, but rumor said it went all the way to Tsaftown. For me, it was tunnel or prison. So I packed up and went for it. And no. They don’t go to Tsaftown. Tunnels only go as far north as Arok Lake.”

Vrell smiled at the image of a man crawling the entire length of Er’Rets. “You have truly lived in this cave for thirteen years?”

“This cave? Only nine. Took a few years to learn the tunnels. Go as far as I could, start to run out of food, and have to go back. When I found this place,” he said, gesturing around the glittering cavern, with its safe location and running water, “I knew I’d found home.”

"It is very unique."

Peripaso held up a burlap sack with a long strap. "Mind carrying this? I'll take the others."

Vrell draped the sack over her shoulder.

"Best be heading back. Like another drink first?"

Vrell helped herself to one more mug of water before following Peripaso up the rope ladder and back into the tunnel. As with most journeys, the trip back went much faster.

Jax and Khai were waiting with the torn boat when Peripaso and Vrell arrived back in the sweltering cavern. Vrell watched as Peripaso and Jax mended the boat with a sheet of reekat skin, twine, and some very smelly, clear gel.

"What is that?" Vrell asked.

"Reekat fat," Peripaso said. "Seals up the seams. Waterproofs it." He turned to Jax. "You should sleep here and wait for it to dry. Moist as this cave is, though, won't ever dry completely. Should be strong enough in a few hours to get you to Mahanaim. Jest don't run into no more reekats."

Vrell was sick of reekats. When Peripaso passed around dried reekat meat for dinner, she wanted to throw it in the river. What she really wanted was a large bowl of grenache grapes and a wedge of goat cheese. Instead she bit off a chunk of the greasy meat and chewed it into leathery mush.

As they sat around waiting for the fat to dry, Peripaso told more stories of his exploits in the Nahar underground rivers and tunnels. Vrell loved his twangy voice. If she hadn't been so ill from the smells, the mosquito bites, and the reekat meat, she would have liked a long visit with him. When he announced their boat would be fine to set off, Vrell sighed with relief.

She hugged the wrinkled man, which hopefully was not too strange for a boy, and climbed into the bow of the boat.

The lantern had been destroyed, but Peripaso gave them a small torch and two spares. He said they would stay lit as long as they were kept low, out of the wind. Peripaso pushed the boat off, and Vrell waved good-bye to her strange, half-naked friend.

She settled down in the bow to sleep, annoyed to find the stench of reekat fat by her head.

PART 4

NEW MASTERS

11

Achan awoke under the allown tree.

It was past dawn. His hair and clothing were damp with dew. His legs itched under the wool stockings.

He jumped up and wandered back to the kitchens to change, dreading the inevitable confrontation with Poril. He'd talked with nobles, snuck off with a pie, slept outside, and had yet to milk the goats. He could already feel Poril's belt on his back.

Would Sir Gavin be upset as well? The knight had told him to stay put, and he hadn't.

The tournament was still in full swing. Nobles, servants, and peasants crowded the manor inside and out. It was another clear day and already much later than Achan first thought. He walked quicker. Dilly and Peg would be about to burst.

Achan entered the kitchens. The old cook glared from the fireplace, then pointed to the mug on the table. The tonic.

Achan slunk toward it and chugged it down. Back to life as usual.

"Yer teh see Lord Nathak."

Achan cringed. That was worse than a beating. Poril must have been plenty angry to report his behavior. Perhaps he shouldn't have returned at all. He could have hiked up the Sideros River and—

"Get goin'!"

"What about the goats?"

"Mox has seen to it."

Mox? Achan grabbed a few mentha leaves and trudged across the inner bailey toward the keep. Truly, he should flee and take his chances in the Sideros Forest. It would be a lonely life. Maybe he could talk Gren into coming along. He stopped and considered it. Would she go with him?

Go to the keep, Achan. I shall direct your path.

Achan glanced around. This voice was so odd, so different from the way Sir Gavin and the others had spoken to his mind the night he'd killed the doe. This voice brought intense warmth to his veins. It did not press as if invading. His eyes locked on the roof of Cetheria's temple poking out of the lush gardens. Could the goddess protector be speaking to him?

Achan swallowed and hastened to the keep, now afraid not to—Cetheria might strike him down if he disobeyed her. He climbed the narrow stairs to the sixth floor and entered a drafty corridor. Achan wasn't positive where he was going. He only knew Lord Nathak's chambers were on the sixth floor. Chora, Prince Gidon's valet, stood at a carved door. His long brown robes blended in with the wood so well that Achan almost didn't see him.

Achan was about to inquire where he might find Lord Nathak, but Chora opened the door, blinked over his bulbous nose, and in a disdainful voice announced to those inside, "The stray, Lord Nathak."

"Send him in."

Achan entered a sweltering solar that was partitioned off by vibrant tapestries that told the story of how Lord Nathak found the infant prince wandering in the fields. The room was likely much larger, but Achan knew that the tapestries were used to keep the heat in. At night they would be moved around the bed.

Hay and rushes crunched under Achan's boots. He stopped on the center of a garish red and gold rug edged in black fringe. This was a corner room. Two large windows took up half of the outer walls.

Lord Nathak sat at a window in a high-back wooden chair, overlooking the delta where the Sideros River poured into the sea, his back to Achan. The ties of his black leather mask were cinched over his two-tone hair. Achan inched closer, hoping to see something more of Lord Nathak's disfigurement. Maybe he could gather some feeling from the man that could—

A slurping sound turned Achan's head.

Prince Gidon slouched on a chaise lounge eating grapes from a tray held by a servant boy. Though the prince was fit and almost exactly Achan's age, he was propped up like an invalid by tufted velvet cushions in shades of emerald and red. He wore a maroon velvet robe embroidered with gold ribbons. A delicate crown, studded with rubies and garnets, squished his oiled, black hair against his forehead. A short, black beard shaded his chin.

Seeing the heir to Er'Rets so close, Achan's heart went wild, as if trying to break free of his body and flee. Unfortunately, his feet didn't obey this instinct. Despite his fear, he focused, seeking the pressure in his head, searching for any clue his intuition could discover. Nothing came. Both Lord Nathak and the prince were empty as far as he could tell. Achan frowned. How could that be? He'd never sensed emptiness in anyone.

A chill caused Achan to shiver, and he wondered how the temperature had changed so quickly. He waited as Lord Nathak gazed out the window and the prince munched grapes with the manners of a hound. The longer the men ignored him, the more the horror of being in their presence faded. He grew bored and looked around the chamber.

Achan had never seen so much finery. The red and gold rug covered most the floor, edged with rushes of sweet flag and chamomile that made the room smell fresh. Elaborate brocades upholstered the polished furniture. A silver tray heaped with fruit, two ornate goblets, and some of Poril's fancy cakes sat on a table behind the prince's chair. The cream filling from a half-eaten tart dripped from the center and pooled on the silver tray. Achan puzzled over how he could be shaking with cold while it was hot enough to melt Poril's cream filling.

"Sir Gavin has left us," Lord Nathak said finally, still facing away. "He will not return."

Dizziness swept over Achan. Left? Without saying farewell? Was it because Achan had placed so poorly in the tournament? That wasn't all his fault. He might've held his own in other matches had Lord Nathak not banished him to the kitchens. Besides, Sir Gavin hadn't seemed upset at the feast.

A sudden thought gripped his heart. Would Achan be punished for training as a squire? He'd broken Council law and trained behind his owner's back. Would he be executed? Achan wanted to run. He remained frozen, though, almost captivated by the rhythmic slurping of grapes.

"Sir Gavin claimed you are a squire." Lord Nathak continued to gaze out the window.

Achan glanced at the prince then back to Lord Nathak. An eagle soared outside the window. Achan could almost see the corner of the grandstands at the jousting field.

"It is my purpose in life to protect the Crown Prince at all costs." Lord Nathak turned to Achan, his one eye staring as if awaiting an answer.

The sight of that one dark eye sent a molten shiver through Achan that he feared would melt him into a puddle on the fine rug.

Achan didn't know where to look. Lord Nathak's leather mask clung to the right side of his face as if held there by something sticky. Achan's eyes darted from the mask to the shriveled skin he could see near Lord Nathak's nose, to his two-tone hair, to his forked beard, to his visible eye.

Achan cleared his throat and said in a small voice, "A noble purpose, my lord."

"Indeed," Lord Nathak said. "And one you will help me with."

Achan gulped. "My lord?"

"Since you think yourself worthy of squiredom, I shall grant your wish."

Achan froze. "My lord?"

"You shall serve the Crown Prince as squire. He has several, of course, but you shall clean his chambers, ready his horse, and fetch anything—"

"No." Prince Gidon sat up. His tone was defiant. "This one will serve as my sparring partner."

Lord Nathak bolted to his feet. "I cannot allow that, my prince."

"And since I cannot compete in my own tournament," Gidon said, "I will fight the stray in front of an audience. That will teach him to insult my guests."

Achan's jaw sagged. He could only mean the venomous Lady Jaira. How thoughtful that she'd further torment him by tattling to the prince. Achan's mind whirred to find an excuse, but his overly quick tongue now left him speechless.

"It would be too dangerous," Lord Nathak said.

An abnormally wide smile stretched across Prince Gidon's face. "It was *your* idea to invite my guests to watch me practice. Now they may witness my skills firsthand."

So Achan would be the lucky recipient of the prince's skills. The man had been trained by the best weapons masters since birth. Was this a trap to frame Achan or put him in harm's way? Perhaps a fancy execution?

Lord Nathak looked slightly green. Certainly he wasn't afraid Achan could best the prince?

Prince Gidon reached for a bunch of grapes. "Report to the practice field after lunch, stray—and don't wear those serving clothes. Chora will provide proper attire. Dismissed."

Lord Nathak stared at Achan, his visible eye wide and fearful.

Achan turned on his heel and exited the solar, the air in the hallway hitting him as if he'd stepped into the kitchens when all the pots were boiling. As Chora led him down to the fourth level, Achan's mind replayed what had just happened.

He was a squire to the prince now? Was that on top of working in the kitchens, or was he now permanently free from Poril? He'd been through so many reversals in the last few days he didn't know what to believe. And what had Lord Nathak been afraid of? His concern for the prince's safety with Achan as a sparring partner was laughable. It was Achan he should worry about, not that he ever would.

Chora knocked once on a narrow door and pushed it open. This appeared to be a sewing room. It was long and narrow with a single arrow loop window at one end. Bolts of linen and silk in a rainbow of colors lined one wall. Along the other wall, two women sat sewing, a third worked a loom, and a fourth cut red velvet on a table in the corner.

A short, pudgy woman with straight pins tucked into the cuffs of her sleeves turned from a bin of shirts and perched her fists on her wide hips. "What's this?"

"Lord Nathak wants this one dressed as a soldier. He's to squire for the prince."

"Is he now?" The woman waddled to Achan and looked him over. Several moles dotted her flabby face. A large one hovered over her left eye. She was so short that her scowling face barely reached Achan's chest. "He's as tall as the prince. His Majesty don't like having his squires so tall."

"Just dress him, Shelga." Chora opened the door to leave, then said to Achan, "Once she's through, come to the armory for a sword."

Achan nodded, and Chora swept from the room.

Shelga motioned to the arrow loop window. "Get yourself into the light where's I can look at you."

Achan stepped into the stripe of brightness stretching across the thread-strewn floor.

Shelga snapped her fingers. "That's far enough." She drew a cord from around her neck and set about measuring him. "How'd you come by this assignment?"

"Luck, I guess."

Shelga snorted. "'Tis not luck. The gods have cursed you. Haven't you seen the prince's squires limping about? Most are only able to tie nettle-hemp into fishing nets when he's through with 'em. Unless he injures their hands."

"What do you mean?" Achan had heard rumors of Prince Gidon's temper with women, but nothing about his squires.

"You'll find out. Least you're his size. Maybe you'll fare better than the runts he usually takes on. Off with your clothes."

Achan stood still as she waddled to a row of baskets along the interior wall and pulled an item from each. She waddled back holding a stack of clothing. "Off with 'em! I haven't got all day to waste on the likes of you."

Achan groaned inwardly and soon found himself in his undershorts in front of an audience for the second time in as many days. At least he was free of the itchy leggings.

Shelga set the bundle of clothes on a stool and twisted her pudgy lips together. "Well? Think I'm going to dress you?"

Achan snagged the white shirt off the top of the pile, pulled it on, then reached for the trousers. Shelga slapped his hand.

"Take it off. 'Tis too tight. If you can manage to swing at all, you'll tear it, and I've no time for extra mending with the prince's new wardrobe due."

Achan stifled a retort. He pulled off the shirt and found Shelga rummaging through a basket across the room. Several of the women had stopped working and were watching him. Achan quickly traded the shirt for the trousers and pulled them on. The shirt slid off the stool onto the floor behind him. He tied the trousers before turning to reach for it.

Shelga gasped.

Achan jumped to his feet and spun around. The woman's face had turned white, her eyes bulged, and her bottom lip quivered.

"Are you well?" he asked.

She shook out of her trance. "Do they know what you are?"

He blinked at her. "Ma'am?"

"Think with a serving uniform and that handsome face you'll fool everyone, do you? Well, I'll not be party to your treason. Kiera! Fetch me Chora straight away."

"Yes'm." A portly woman with thick brown braids lumbered for the door. Her face had gone white as well.

Achan couldn't guess what Shelga was on about. Again he crouched to retrieve the shirt.

Shelga snapped her fingers wildly. "Just you keep your front to me. That clear? I'll not be looking on that cursed mark again."

Oh. The mark of the stray. Achan reached across his chest and over his shoulder to finger the brand on the back. "Lord Nathak knows what I am, ma'am. I'm sorry it . . . surprised you." But he wasn't sorry. People had ignored him and bullied him all his life, but never recoiled in horror as if he carried some disease.

Kiera returned. "Chora says he knows, ma'am. He says it's all right." She bowed her head to Shelga and scurried back to the loom.

Shelga shot Achan a piercing glare, then thrust another shirt at him and waddled away. "Can't believe I'm wasting my time dressing a stray. What madness is Lord Nathak up to now?"

Achan shrugged and dressed quickly. This second shirt fit to Shelga's satisfaction. He pulled a plain black cloak over his head. It didn't bear the embroidered crest of Mahanaim like Prince Gidon's personal guards. It was just the uniform of a low-ranking soldier. Still, Achan left the sewing room a little taller. No stray he'd ever heard of had such a position. So far, his punishment felt like a reward.

He doubted the feeling would last.

Achan went straight to the kitchens to explain to Poril, but the cook had left to take lunch to the keep. Achan pulled off the thick, black gloves Shelga had given him and grabbed a chunk of bread. He went downstairs to stow the serving uniform under the ale casks, dreading his upcoming match with Prince Gidon. Achan guessed the prince wanted to humiliate him, perhaps cripple him—hopefully not kill him. But Achan had no intention of going down easily. In fact . . .

Eagan's Elk lay tucked under his blanket, the pommel sticking out of one end. Achan dropped to his knees at the ale casks, a soggy clump of bread in his mouth. He threw back the covers and pulled the sword onto his lap.

A sheet of parchment fluttered behind him, and he turned to pick it up. Achan stared at the smudged ink and swallowed the lump of bread. *Tonic* was the only word he recognized. He studied the letters, compared them to what he knew from reading Poril's lists, and managed to decode most of the short note.

> Don't drink the tonic. I'll be in touch.
> Sir Gavin

He didn't know what t-o-u-c-h spelled and couldn't manage to sound it out to any clarity. Could it be a town Sir Gavin had gone to? The scratchy writing looked as if it had been written in a hurry.

Achan stood and buckled Eagan's Elk around his waist. He took the cellar steps two at a time. He tossed the note into one of the blazing fireplaces before starting off to the stables, pulling on the gloves as he went. Since he no longer needed a sword from the armory, he had enough time to see Noam before he was expected on the practice field.

Achan stepped into the outer bailey and saw a group of nobles leaving for a hunt. Over two dozen fine horses trotted single file toward the gatehouse, their riders carrying birds or bows. Hounds scampered ahead, excited about the coming chase. A crown of platinum braids caught Achan's eye. Tara rode full saddle on a chestnut mare, a brown and white merlin perched on one hand. She smiled at Achan.

He had never seen a woman ride like a man. Her blue skirts draped over the animal like a tent. Jaira rode beside her on a black courser, sidesaddle, holding a violet and black speckled bird. Achan bowed to the ladies, returned Tara's smile, and entered the stables.

The scent of hay and manure filled his nostrils. The building was set up similar to the barn, with timber walls and a high, thatched gable roof.

Achan found his friend in a stall grooming a white destrier. He crossed his arms atop the fence-like gate. "They're keeping you busy, I see."

Noam whistled. "Where'd you get that uniform? Is that a sword?"

Achan fought back a smile. "First tell me this: did you happen to meet Tara?"

"Tara who?"

Achan shrugged. "I don't know. I saw her on a chestnut mare just now with the hunting party. She rides like a man."

"A young blonde wearing blue?"

"Aye," Achan sighed the word.

Noam chuckled. "Yep. I met her. Lady Tara Livna of Tsaftown. She's very kind."

"She kissed me—my cheek. Yesterday."

Noam's lips parted until his mouth hung wide. "How in all Er'Rets?"

Achan told Noam his tale of the previous day, the fine clothing, Eagan's Elk, Silvo, Shung, Jaira, and Tara, how he served at the banquet, and meeting Prince Oren.

Noam tugged his comb through the destrier's tail. "You do get all the excitement."

"Well, you must have met a lot of the nobles."

"I met their horses," Noam said. "Or their servants. Only three nobles spoke to me, one of which was your Lady Tara."

Achan shut his eyes. "Say that again."

"What?"

"'My Lady Tara.'"

Noam whacked him with the comb. "Get over it, halfwit. Now, what's this you're wearing today? This is a Kingsguard cloak, not a leather jerkin."

Achan stepped back and slid down the post across the aisle from the stable Noam was in. He sat on the hay-strewn dirt floor and watched through the gate as Noam braided the horse's tail. "I'm to serve the prince as squire."

"What!"

Achan recapped his morning visit to the keep.

"Achan," Noam's frown elongated his narrow face, "this is what comes from trying to be something you're not. This can't be a promotion."

Achan lifted a strand of hay in his fingers and twirled it. "What can I do?"

Noam sighed. "Fight as well as you can, keep your eyes open, watch your back, and pray to Cetheria. That's all you *can* do. You could ask Gren to make an offering for you."

Achan considered this. All his offerings of late hadn't changed Gren's betrothal to Riga. He had nothing of true value to offer Cetheria, except his sword, but he couldn't give that up in the face of Prince Gidon's skill. Still, if the goddess was speaking to him now, he should do what he could to stay in her favor. He almost told Noam about the voices, but the mere thought of confessing such a thing out loud was inconceivable.

He changed the topic. "Did you see Sir Gavin leave this morning?

Noam pulled a leather thong from his pocket and wrapped it around the end of the braid. "Aye. Lord Nathak came himself with the instructions to ready Sir Gavin's horses."

"I'd hoped he'd take me with him."

Noam pulled an apple from his pocket and fed it to the destrier. "That would've been something."

Achan's thoughts drifted to Gren. "Did Gren tell you about Riga?"

"Aye. Poor lass," Noam said. "I'd poison myself before committing to a life with a Hoff—especially Riga. I see you've forsaken her already for *your Lady Tara*."

Achan's chest swelled with rage, but he let it out in a groan. He hadn't thought of Gren since yesterday. How quickly he had allowed life to distract him from her bad fortune.

He silently compared the two women. Both were beautiful. He'd known Gren all his life and would marry her in a breath if he could. He scratched the dirt floor with his gloved finger and cursed his overactive imagination. Lady Tara was of noble birth. If he wasn't allowed to marry Gren, a peasant, then Noam spoke true. He really was a halfwit to even waste thoughts on Tara. He sighed.

"Why do you think Sir Gavin bothered with me? A stray is not to be trained for the Kingsguard—that's Council law. Yet now Prince Gidon disregards the law as well. Why?"

"It wasn't always so," Noam said with a sad smile. "Strays have only been singled out since one killed the king and queen. And they only knew that because a Kingsguard bloodvoiced it."

"But there's no such thing as bloodvoicers," Achan said. "People who talk through their minds? It's myth." But his laugh quickly faded and he blinked. No. Bloodvoices couldn't be what he experienced the night he killed the doe. He'd been delirious, that was all.

Noam raised an eyebrow. "Myth or not, you and I are marked for life as a result of that story. Myth doesn't make laws, Achan. Reality does."

Achan shoved thoughts of bloodvoices to the back of his mind as he wandered from the stables.

The noon sun shone brightly as he entered the inner bailey. He drew near the grassy courtyard that sat between the keep and the temple gardens. Grandstands had been built for Prince Gidon's practice bouts. They sat so that they formed three sides of a square, boxing the area against the brownstone wall of the keep.

Chora paced along the wall, cloak billowing. He looked up and huffed. "Where have you been? You didn't report to the armory."

"I have the sword Sir Gavin gave me. Will it do?"

Chora shrugged. "A sword is a sword as far as I'm concerned."

"What about a shield or armor?"

Chora shook his head. "His Majesty doesn't spar with shields or armor."

"What?" Was the prince a fool?

Chora stepped close to Achan. "Our king is brave. Besides, he never chooses an opponent he cannot beat. Not that there are many who could best our king. Now wait here and *hold your tongue*!"

Achan stared at Chora for a moment, uncertain why the valet referred to the prince as king, when he had not yet been crowned. He leaned against the wall of the keep, resting the sole of one boot against the stone behind him.

The sun had warmed the wall, and he basked in the comfort while he could. From his position, he faced the grandstands. For now, they were empty. Beyond, the stone colonnades from Cetheria's temple peeked over the green hedges that separated the gardens from the rest of the inner bailey.

He thought over Chora's statement. The prince never chose an opponent he couldn't beat? How terribly brave. Achan shouldn't be surprised. His presence on this field was likely an execution anyway.

Nobles drifted toward the makeshift arena in packs. Apparently Achan's execution was going to have an audience. The small crowd consisted mostly of elderly lords and ladies, with a few young maidens. Achan was thankful Lady Tara and her friends had gone hunting. A piper stepped into the center of the field and began to play a festive tune. Achan wanted to break the instrument over his knee.

A murmur rose from the grandstands. Achan followed the turn of heads to see eight Kingsguards approaching in diamond formation. The group was led by Sir Kenton, Prince Gidon's Shield. A tall, grey-skinned man lumbered in back. All eight wore black capes with the high-ranking gold crest of Mahanaim sparkling in the sun. Achan spotted specks of crimson flashing between the black uniforms. Prince Gidon Hadar walked in the center.

The Kingsguards poured into one corner of the field at a spot where two of the grandstands met, then peeled away. Prince Gidon waved at the crowd without so much as a smile. The audience applauded their future king.

Achan studied him. His hair was slicked back with oils and tied into a tail. His coloring was the same as Achan's: dark hair, brown skin, blue eyes. It almost made Achan wish he hadn't recently discovered that he was kinsman. He didn't like having things in common with this man.

The prince moved with more grace and confidence even than Silvo. A fine, red linen shirt, tucked into black trousers, billowed in the wind, outlining a strong upper body. Oddly enough, Gidon wore no jerkin or doublet. Polished black leather boots rose to his knees. He wore a plain, leather sheath at his side that held a plain practice sword.

Seven of the Kingsguards sat on the lowest level of the center stands. Sir Kenton stood with Chora in the gap where the entourage had entered. Prince Gidon strode to the center of the field, spat on the ground, and drew his sword.

Achan licked his lips and swallowed. It was a good thing that intimidation was part of his everyday life. He stepped away from the wall and drew Eagan's Elk—

Barely in time to stifle a cut from the prince's blade. That was a dirty trick. Achan's estimation of the prince dropped even lower, if that were possible. He pushed off and jumped back to get a better position.

The prince huffed and threw up one hand. "Stop!"

Achan lowered his sword.

The prince thrust his blade into the grass and turned to Chora. "What is he fighting with?"

Chora scurried over, his bold demeanor gone in the prince's presence. "What are you fighting with, stray?"

"A sword."

Chora turned back to the prince. "He fights with a . . . a sword, Your Majesty."

The prince propped a hand on one hip. "I know it's a sword, you ale-soused buffoon! Where did he *get* it?"

Chora, pink-faced, turned back to Achan. "His Royal Highness would like to know where you got your sword."

"I told you, it was a gift from Sir Gavin."

"He cannot wield a finer weapon than me," Prince Gidon whispered. "Weren't you supposed to dress him, Chora? Didn't you provide a sword?"

Chora's voice croaked, "He never came for one, Your Majesty."

Achan held up Eagan's Elk for Prince Gidon to see. "Because I already had one."

Sir Kenton stepped between Achan and the prince. His curtain of black hair swung about his face like a chain hood. "We practice with plain swords here, stray. And watch your tone."

Achan looked from the prince to the Shield to Chora. He had no desire to make trouble. Perhaps holding his tongue would be his best plan.

Prince Gidon turned to Sir Kenton and continued in a hushed voice. "His job is to make me look like the best swordsman in all Er'Rets. He's failed already."

Achan scowled. That was his job, was it? Well, he wasn't about to go down easily. Achan would give him everything he had.

"Where is Polk?" Prince Gidon asked.

"Lord Nathak dismissed Polk," Sir Kenton rumbled.

"Then fetch him back."

"He sent Polk with the emissary to the Duchess of Carm," Chora mumbled.

"*My* squire?" Prince Gidon's posture swelled. "Who is king? Lord Nathak or me?"

Achan raised his eyebrows. So Prince Gidon had already proclaimed himself king.

Chora's spine drooped.

"Well? Am I king?"

"Not yet," Achan murmured.

Prince Gidon whipped around to face the grandstands. "Who said that?" His eyes scanned the crowd until his dark gaze fell to Achan. He stepped forward. "Was it you?"

Achan's cheeks burned, but he maintained eye contact and shrugged one shoulder. Disrespecting the prince in public. Clever. What happened to holding his tongue?

The corner of the prince's mouth twitched. "Chora, fetch me Ôwr."

A murmur rose from the stands behind Achan. He shivered. What was Ôwr?

"But . . . f-forgive me, Your Majesty, they will not . . . release it to me."

The prince waved his hand toward the keep. "Take Sir Kenton along."

The Shield strode away, hair swaying, Chora scurrying alongside.

Achan stood staring at the prince in the sweltering sun. Prince Gidon snapped his fingers and two attendants ran out from behind the stands. One set a crimson pillow on the end of the center bench in the shade. The prince sat. The other attendant waved a large, wicker fan at his face. Achan raised his eyebrows and retreated to lean against the warm brownstone wall.

After a long wait, the valet and Shield returned carrying an ornate jeweled scabbard. Prince Gidon stood and Chora buckled a silver, jeweled belt around the prince's waist. When it was secure, the prince strode back to the center of the field and drew a blade that sang as it scraped against its scabbard and gleamed in the sunlight like a white star.

"The Kingsword!" someone shouted.

The crowd murmured.

Achan turned his head in blinded surprise. "What sort of metal is that?"

"White steel." Prince Gidon's blue eyes glared. "A gift to King Willham from Câan, the son-god warrior, after his rebirth. No other weapon is made from this metal. It cannot be broken."

The tale of Ôwr was another thing Achan had thought to be myth. Câan had used a special blade, named Ôwr, in a battle to free the kinsman people. But he'd died, having been captured by kinsman traitors and tortured. A few days later, the legend went, Arman had breathed life back into his son.

An impressive story, but few temples were built in Câan's honor. Most minstrels sang no songs of Câan, or if they did, they were comedies. The god killed by men was considered weak.

The weapon itself held great mystery. It was slightly longer than Eagan's Elk. A narrow fuller ran down the center, catching the sun on its ridges. The tip was sharp and narrow, unlike Eagan's Elk's rounded point. Achan made note that, with this blade, Prince Gidon could cut *and* thrust.

Achan stepped away from the wall and breathed deeply. A sword was a sword. Myth didn't make one better than the other. He drew Eagan's Elk, which now looked very dull and grey in comparison, and waited for the prince to make the first move.

The sun blazed down. A hush fell over the crowd. Prince Gidon attacked. He swung Ôwr with amazing power for his lean frame. Achan parried, staggering back a step from the impact.

He focused on the prince's every move, memorizing his cuts and thrusts. He circled just out of reach, but the prince came after him like a mosquito, annoyingly persistent. Achan dodged, deflected, and stifled, spending every bit of energy on defense. It was smarter this way. Achan knew precious few offensive moves. Until he got a feel for Prince Gidon as a swordsman, or until Achan could learn more attacks, it was better just to let him tire himself out.

The match went on to the cheers of the crowd, until Achan's knees wobbled, his arms tingled, and his lungs were void of air.

Prince Gidon changed strategies. Instead of trying to attack him with elaborate moves, now he was simply herding him. He worked Achan back toward the wall of the keep. Every time Achan tried to step around, the prince cut him off, his footwork excellent. Achan drew back to parry, and his elbow struck the stone wall so hard he dropped his sword. He cringed, both in pain and at the realization that Prince Gidon had boxed him in. The crowd cheered. Achan froze as the prince pushed Ôwr's sharp tip against his left shoulder.

"Do you yield?" Prince Gidon's oily voice oozed amusement. He didn't even sound out of breath.

Achan nodded, panting. "Aye."

Lips pressed into a thin line, Prince Gidon jabbed the tip into Achan's flesh. "Do you yield?"

Achan sucked in a sharp breath. "Yes! I said yes."

The prince pushed a bit further until he drew a ragged gasp from Achan. "Do. You. Yield?"

What did he want to hear?

A familiar green shifted in the distance. Achan glanced over Prince Gidon's shoulder to the captivated audience and caught sight of Gren standing between two grandstands, a pile of green fabric in her arms that was nearly the same color as her dress. She stared at him with wide eyes and mouth. He would not allow himself to be killed in front of her.

He clenched his teeth to work up the courage. Like lightning, he gripped the end of Ôwr's blade with both gloved palms, kicked Prince Gidon's stomach enough to startle him, pushed the blade back, and dodged free.

The prince staggered back and regarded Achan with narrowed eyes. He pursed his lips and stepped forward. Then, just as quickly as Achan had broken free, Prince Gidon bashed Ôwr's pommel against Achan's temple.

As he fell, Achan heard Gren's scream and a mixed reaction of cheers and gasps from the crowd. He hit the ground on his hands and knees. His head throbbed. The blades of grass blurred before his eyes.

Prince Gidon's disdainful voice floated down from above. "Tomorrow. Same time. And for future reference, stray, it's, 'I yield, *Your Majesty.*'"

Achan sat back on his haunches in time to see the prince hold Ôwr out to the side as if to dispose of it. Chora scurried forward to claim the weapon.

"Make my new squire clean the blade," Prince Gidon said. "It is *his* job."

With that, the prince strode away, crimson shirt fluttering in the wind. The Kingsguard hurried to form their protective cordon around him. The crowd began to disperse.

"Never you mind about Ôwr," Chora said. "I'll see it cleaned. No stray should touch the Kingsword." The valet scurried after the prince, cradling the blade like a child.

Achan trembled. His shoulder stung, as did his fingers and head. He lifted his hands to see blood seeping through gashes in the black leather gloves. The crowd drifted away in the prince's wake, and when all were gone, Achan slouched back against the brownstone wall.

Gren approached and crouched beside him. "Oh, Achan. Noam told me about your new position. I came straight away. Are you all right?"

He looked up into her worried face. "He stabbed me."

"I saw."

"Why?"

She shrugged. "He stabs all his squires . . . or cuts them or . . . knocks them about with the pommel." She tugged at Achan's cloak, and he leaned forward so she could pull it over his head. "I've never heard of him using the Kingsword before. Not ever. It's said to be kept under lock and key until his coronation."

"Well, I humiliated him by owning a sword. Apparently he's the only one allowed—" Achan gasped as Gren pressed her apron on his shoulder. "Will I die?"

Gren giggled and the sweet sound lessened his pain. "Of course not."

Achan regarded Gren's tanned, freckled face and dark hair. How different she and Lady Tara were. One golden, one bronze. Achan decided at that moment that he preferred Gren's coloring. Tara's resemblance to Cetheria almost made her intimidating. Gren was familiar and warm and sweet.

Gren looked at him sympathetically. "You're a mess, Achan. Your hair . . . " She fingered his frizzy braid. "Did you braid this?"

"My valet," Achan said, thinking of Wils.

Gren giggled again. "Your valet. You're one for surprises, Achan Cham." She took his hand and brought it up to his shoulder. "Press down."

Achan did, a bit softer than Gren had. She moved to her knees and patted the grass in front of her. "Sit here."

He scooted into place, his back to her, and she combed out his hair with her fingers. Achan closed his eyes. The sensation distracted him from his stinging wounds.

"I skinned your deer," she said.

Achan opened his eyes. "You did? I thought the butcher had claimed it."

"He took the meat. I didn't think you'd mind."

"How'd you even know about it?"

"Father left the keep late that night. He'd been working all day on a brocade for the prince's coming-of-age ensemble. He saw the whole thing."

So Gren's father knew of Achan's . . . position? Did Achan even have a position now? Squire to the prince sounded good in theory, but like Shelga had said, most ended up tying nettle-hemp. Gren would say something if there was anything worth saying.

But she didn't. She rebraided his hair and came to kneel before him. She tugged off the glove on his free hand. "I'm tanning the deer's hide to make you a jerkin. Shelga has taken me as an apprentice. It will keep me busy when I'm . . . married." She didn't meet his eyes.

Achan winced, but not from the pain of Gren scraping at his fingers with her handkerchief. "Gren, if I could do anything, I—"

She pressed a finger to his lips. "I don't like you serving Prince Gidon. He's cruel. You know what they say here about a maid with a bruised face?"

"What?"

"That she must have displeased her prince. Yet you purposely provoked him today. That's unwise, Achan. When I finish your jerkin, you should leave. Run away north to Carmine or Zerah Rock or Tsaftown. The people up north are kinder, so I've heard. They don't keep slaves in those cities. And when I'm done with you, you won't look a stray, plus carrying a sword like that . . . "

Run away. Without Gren.

Achan knew he should be concentrating on Gren's words, but the idea of leaving Sitna without her brought his thoughts back to Lady Tara. Lady Tara of Tsaftown.

Thinking of one pretty girl while in the presence of another was probably something that would get him in trouble. Not that he had any experience with such things. Why did he feel compelled to follow a woman? Why not go alone? Yet his mind did wander north. Tsaftown was the northernmost city in all Er'Rets. Perhaps Lord Livna could use another guard for his watch.

"Would I freeze in Tsaftown?"

Gren twisted her lips in a frown. "You prefer Tsaftown?"

He shrugged and looked at a tuft of grass beside his leg.

"If you make it there before summer's end," she said, "you could hunt on your way and trade the furs to a seamstress who could sew you something warm."

Achan let his imagination drift to a snowy city he'd never seen. A sharp pain in his finger jerked him back to reality. "Ow!"

"Hold still," Gren said. "You've got a sliver of leather wedged into the cut. Why would you grab his sword?"

"I've seen knights do it."

"With mail mittens!" Gren rolled her eyes and stood. "Let's go for my needle."

Achan rose. He paused for his head to clear, then picked up his sword and sheathed it, grabbed his cape, and followed Gren out of the inner bailey toward her family's cottage. "I can't believe he stabbed me!"

"It's his way." Gren weaved behind the armory to a narrow corridor between cottages.

Achan stepped to the side to allow two boys to run past. "I looked a fool. I wanted to win, but I don't know him well enough to even try."

Gren stopped beside him. "Win? Achan Cham, do you know how it would look if the prince's squire beat him in a practice match? A match performed before the nobles to make *His Highness* look good?"

Achan grinned.

Gren swatted his stomach with the back of her hand. "Don't be foolish! You've already pushed your luck. He'll worse than prick you next time."

Inside Gren's family's cottage, Achan sat at the oak table and waited for her to find a needle. She returned to the table, lit a candle, and held the needle in the flame. "Give me your hand."

Achan obeyed. Gren dug into his finger with the hot point. It tickled, and her expression as she bit her bottom lip amused him greatly. His laughter shook his hand and the needle poked. "Ow!"

She glared at him, then went back to her task. "You're much handsomer than the prince, you know."

He huffed a laugh. "Of course I am."

She slapped his leg. "Modesty, dear stray."

Achan sighed. "But what matter my very good looks if I'm dead?"

"I think the maids—and even some of the noblewomen—were hoping you'd live."

He fought another chuckle that trembled his hand.

She looked up, her face serious. "You fought well, Achan. Sir Gavin would be proud. You did so much better than the day you bested the tree."

12

A cool breeze woke Vrell. She felt a gentle rocking. She opened her eyes to a sky so bright she had to immediately shut her eyes again.

The boat was in the ocean. They'd left the tunnels. Praise Arman!

She sat up and turned to see Jax paddling, alternating his oar from side to side. Khai slouched against the side of the boat, asleep, his neck tipped over the edge at an awkward angle. Apparently it was his turn to rest.

Slate grey waves surrounded every side but the left. A rocky coastline topped with a thick forest stretched in both directions as far as she could see. The sun shone down from a cloudless, pale blue sky.

"Good morning," Jax said.

"How much farther?" Vrell asked.

"We should reach the first gate before lunch. Then it's another hour to the city."

Gate? She focused for a moment to remember where they were going. Right. Mahanaim could be reached by water from the south through the Reshon Gates.

The dream she had been having came back to her mind full force. The man with the bloodvoices had been hurt. "Jax?" She glanced at Khai, heard his low snore, and continued. "What happened that night in Xulon? When the voices called out?"

Jax nodded. "Someone discovered his bloodvoice."

Vrell had guessed that much. "But why did people call to him? And how is it we heard the exchange?"

"His gift is greater than any I've sensed in a long while. It does not happen that way for many."

"Who is he?"

Jax propped the oar on the side of the boat and water poured off the blade and into the ocean. "That's what we all would like to know. It's why so many called out—to ask him."

Vrell twisted her lips and looked out over the peaking waves. "You have sensed others who are great?"

"I've never sensed such strength in someone's discovery. The greatest power I have felt has come from old men. Macoun Hadar, your new master, for one. King Axel was another."

"You sensed the king?"

Jax dipped the oar back into the water and stroked. "Aye. When I first joined the Kingsguard as a young soldier. King Axel led us in battle against Cherem."

"That must have been exciting."

Jax nodded. "Bloodvoicing is a great power when used for good." He paddled two great strokes and his bushy, black eyebrows furrowed. "Be wary of your new master. He was once a very powerful bloodvoicer, but his stamina has decreased over time. Now he's simply conniving. He uses his apprentices for strength, teaching them only enough to manipulate them into tools for his own agenda."

He glanced at Khai, then back at Vrell. "Thank Arman for your unique gift, Vrell. You may not be as strong as the newly gifted one, or many bloodvoicers before you, but your ability to block is unprecedented. Continue to guard yourself at all times. Remember, no one can own a man. Stay true to yourself, no matter what your master commands you to do. Someday we all will have to answer to Arman for our actions."

Vrell swallowed this information, thankful that Jax had confided it to her, but terrified of what lay ahead. She wanted to ask if he believed in Arman as the only true God, as she did, for she had never heard him mention His name in such a way, but before she could form the question, he spoke again.

"I sense Macoun Hadar hides much from the Kingsguard and the Council of Seven. Arman does not like when His gifts are misused. Hadar knows this, but I think he grows overconfident in his old age, despite his weakness. Or desperate. Another reason to keep your wits about you."

Vrell looked over the side into the water. She could see nothing beneath the dark waves. She glanced up at the forest and saw that it would soon end in a jagged cape. "I have never heard of Macoun Hadar. Is he related to the prince? Why does he live in Mahanaim?"

Jax nodded. "He is very old. He was related to King Johan, Axel's grandfather. He has lived in Mahanaim since Lord Levy's grandfather ruled the stronghold. Which is probably why Lord Levy has let him stay."

Vrell wished for more of Peripaso's cave water to soothe her parched throat. She had not considered what she would be doing when they actually got to Mahanaim. Jax's warning sent a shiver along her bones. Hiding out in Mahanaim until Prince Gidon married another did not seem as appealing as it had under the blistering sun on the Nahar Peninsula. Nothing about the place she was headed felt safe.

"The drink he gave you," Jax said, jutting his chin at Khai, "was it red?"

Vrell looked down to a stain of the gooey mixture on the hem of her tunic. "Yes."

He nodded. "The âleh plant stifles bloodvoices and opens your mind to be read. If you are ever forced to take some, eat karpos fruit. It counteracts the âleh."

Vrell filed this knowledge away. "Jax, could you teach me to fight? I would like to have a trick up my sleeve should anyone decide to force such a drink on me again."

The boat rocked with Jax's booming laugh. "I don't know, Vrell. You might be small, but you did manage to knock out a fully trained Kingsguard knight and tie him to a stalagmite. Not bad, if you ask me."

Vrell's cheeks burned and she glanced at Khai. "Still, there may not always be dripstones to aid me. I used to practice with Lord Orthrop's younger sons. They taught me the basics. But Shoal always bested me in a heartbeat."

Jax chuckled again. "There is little I could teach you in one day, Vrell, but you are right. You cannot hide under a fern your whole life. Still, in a fight, there are advantages to being short."

Vrell swelled with excitement. "That is what I must learn."

She listened as Jax shared stories of crippling blows humans had used on him over the years. She would hide and duck if need be, but she wanted to learn to defend herself at her full height, short as it might be. The next time Khai or someone like him tried to attack, she would be . . .

The boat slowly rounded the rocky cape, and the land ahead came into view. Vrell gasped. The rocky coast on her left came to a point where it nearly met the flat, grassy land that curved down from the right. Two colossal pillars—clearly man-made—rose from the land on either side, each one wider than three redpines. An iron portcullis stretched across the sea between the pillars, its black bars woven in a tight, intricate pattern.

Beyond and slightly to the right, she could see the second set of the Reshon Gates standing sentry, looking much smaller from her position. Further right, in the distance, the stone city of Mahanaim sat like stacked yellow, brown, grey, and orange blocks against the velvety backdrop of Darkness.

Vrell shivered at the sight of the Evenwall. She had been to Mahanaim several times but had never gotten used to seeing the cloudy mist fogging half the city like a rainless thunderstorm. She had never set foot on the side of Mahanaim that was in Darkness.

Jax rowed the boat toward a small dock jutting out from the gatehouse at the foot of the northern pillar. A guard wearing a black Kingsguard cloak with no embroidery walked toward the boat, his footsteps hollow on the wooden dock.

"Sir Jax. We worried you had fallen off the edge of Er'Rets. I see Khai is making himself useful as always."

Jax chuckled. "The Mârad has been making trouble to the south. We had quite a battle before Sir Dromos took us in."

Vrell wondered why Jax didn't mention the ebens, who seemed more to blame for the trouble than the Mârad rebels.

"I hope to get the full story of it tonight in the barracks." The guard glanced at Vrell. "Well, I'll get the gate so you can be on your way."

He walked back to the shore and around the pillar to the edge of the gate. He gripped a black handle and turned a crank. A small gate within the large one clinked as it rose into the air. Khai stirred but did not wake. When the clinking stopped, Jax paddled the boat toward the opening and under the first Reshon Gate.

"Will we go under both gates?" Vrell asked.

"No. Our boat's small enough to take the Arob Canal straight into the city."

Vrell had only ever come to Mahanaim on horseback. She had seen the slimy canals from the safety of the keep but had never traveled one. They were not considered safe for a lady, so Lady Fallina Levy had said. As Jax rowed nearer to the city, Khai slept and Vrell worried.

The hour passed quickly. The temperature rose and the air became moist and muggy. Soon Jax steered the boat into a bog-like canal walled in stone. It was early afternoon, but the nearness of the Evenwall made it seem as if the sun had passed behind a thick cloud. Vrell could not see her reflection in the murky water. Lime foam clustered around weeds that climbed the stone wall as if hoping to escape their swampy home.

A sandstone curtain wall loomed ahead, stretching across their path in both directions. Jax slowed the boat alongside a large stone ledge that shot out from a gatehouse on the right. An iron portcullis gate blocked their path into the city.

"We're back." Khai's nose twitched and he opened his eyes. "I could smell it."

Jax took a deep breath and bellowed, "Lo! Jax mi Katt wishes to enter."

A voice floated down from the gatehouse. "Jax is back!"

Vrell could not see any men, but the portcullis started to rise. Jax paddled under it and into the city of Mahanaim.

Buildings made from all colors of stone loomed above like hundreds of fortress keeps side by side. Swampy canals separated them from each other like miniature moats. The thick mist of the nearby Evenwall moistened Vrell's face. Every so often their boat passed long canals that stretched west and gave Vrell a glimpse of Darkness. Vrell couldn't imagine why people lived on the dark side of the city.

Jax guided the boat through the maze of canals without hesitation, though Vrell couldn't tell one canal from the next. She would be lost here on her own. Grungy men shot dark looks down on them from the buildings above, as if casing their boat. Jax's size repelled their gazes as quickly as they came. Vrell drew her arms around herself.

Lord Levy's manor seemed to hover before them like a mountain cliff. It stood at least ten levels tall. Only the curtain wall separated them from being inside the fortress now. Three towers divided the southern wall, each twice the width of a redpine and built from a different color: yellow, grey, and brown. The jagged orange parapet that edged the curtain wall was slightly familiar, though Vrell had never entered Mahanaim by this route. A few boats were out, but none were headed into the manor itself.

"What day is it?" Khai asked with a yawn.

"I don't know," Jax said. "It's taken us much longer than expected. They may be gone."

"Who?" Vrell asked.

"Lord Levy and his family," Jax said. "Prince Gidon's coming-of-age celebration was due around this time. I'm not certain of today's date, but it could be that Lord Levy is still in Sitna for the event."

Vrell considered what this meant for her. She had visited this fortress many times. The Council of Seven meetings were held here, and her mother was on the Council, so Vrell had often accompanied her. Even so, she had never been formally introduced to Lord Levy, the master of this stronghold and chairman of the Council. She had played with his spoiled daughters years ago but doubted they would recognize her now.

Jax stopped the boat before another portcullis gate and the guards cheerfully let them enter. It seemed that Jax was well liked wherever he went. Vrell wasn't surprised that no one spoke to Khai. Jax paddled the boat a bit farther and coasted to a stop beside a stone pathway. Khai hopped out and looped a rope around a peg on the path. Vrell looked up to the jagged orange parapet of Lord Levy's manor. They had arrived.

They exited the boat. Jax led her to a narrow stone stairway that climbed three flights along the curtain wall before exiting at the back of the gatehouse, just inside the Mahanaim stronghold. Jax and Khai went inside to speak with one of the guards. Vrell waited outside in the humid air and looked across the fortress.

Voices, squawking fowl, and the sounds of animals met her ears. The smell of the canals was not as strong up here—or else it was overpowered by the scents of animals, roasting meat, and incense.

This fortress was unlike most castles. Here, the inner bailey and keep were contained all under one roof. The outer bailey consisted of a cobblestone courtyard that stretched out from the gatehouse to the castle on all four sides. Vendors and traders sold their wares from tents or wagons during the day. Vrell remembered shopping here with her mother.

In the center of the courtyard, a grand fountain circled a bronze statue of the Mahanaim justice scales. The scales were the symbol of the Council of Seven, which had been started to rule Er'Rets until Prince Gidon came of age and took the throne.

A little girl with a filthy face and bare feet approached carrying a basket of orchids. "A flower for your love?" she said, holding out a purple bloom.

Vrell smiled and took the flower. "Thank you." She reached for the velveteen bag of coins Lord Orthrop had given her, but it was not on her belt. Her heart thumped in a panic. She had had the bag when she had left Peripaso. Perhaps she had dropped it in the boat.

She handed the flower back to the girl. "I'm sorry, beautiful one. It seems as though I have lost my coin purse."

The child took the blossom back and threaded it under the handle of her basket. She batted her eyes at Vrell and padded away.

Vrell's heart raced. There was a great deal of money in that pouch, and she wanted it. She inched toward the gatehouse, hoping to catch Jax's eye without interrupting. She stopped under his elbow.

"Hello, Vrell. Sorry we've kept you waiting. I'm sure you're anxious to get settled."

"It seems I have lost my coin purse. I wanted to run down and see if I left it in the boat."

Jax frowned then turned to Khai. Had he taken it? Since he had not been able to sell her secret, would he steal her money?

Jax seemed to think so. He pulled Khai away from his conversation by the shoulder.

"What?" Khai asked, struggling to free himself.

"Give up Vrell's coin purse. Now."

Khai snorted. "I don't have his coin purse. Why ever would you think such a thing?"

Jax gripped Khai by the hair and lifted.

Khai squealed. "Okay! Okay. I'll give it back. Let go."

Jax put Khai down and the scrawny Kingsguard jerked back and smoothed his oily hair flat again. He reached into his shirt, pulled Vrell's velveteen pouch out, and tossed it to her feet.

"I was only testing him to see how bright he was. Took him long enough to find it missing." Khai scurried back into the gatehouse.

Vrell picked up her coin purse and tied it to her belt.

"He's not a thief," Jax said. "Or at least not primarily a thief." He bent closer to her ear. "It's easier to reach into someone's mind if you have a personal belonging."

"You think because he had my coin purse he could have succeeded?"

"Probably not, but Khai isn't one to give up easily." Jax settled one beefy hand onto Vrell's shoulder. She stiffened under the weight. "Let's get you inside before he can do you any more harm."

Vrell smiled and followed the giant across the courtyard. Anxiety fought with her excitement. Mahanaim was a wonderful place to visit, but she did not look forward to meeting Macoun Hadar, especially after Jax's warnings. They passed a vendor selling golden cups, which caused Vrell to look over her shoulder to where she remembered the temple was.

A circular colonnade filled the northeastern corner of the courtyard. Black and white banners draped around the roof. Mahanaim worshipped Dâthos, the god of justice. Vrell recalled how suspicious the people of Mahanaim could be, attributing good fortune to the amount of good deeds done and decreeing that those who suffered bad times had brought them upon themselves by doing too many bad deeds.

Vrell turned back and followed Jax around a fur trader's wagon. On the other side, she had a clear view of the entrance to Lord Levy's manor. Two doors as tall as those in Xulon marked the entrance to the grand building. They were propped open and guarded by two New Kingsguard soldiers. Jax nodded at them and passed through without stopping.

They walked into a vast foyer. Decorative limestone columns painted bright yellow held up the high ceiling every ten feet. The floor was covered in a mosaic of multicolored bits of stone. At the far end, a grand staircase spilled out into the foyer. Around the back of the staircase, the steps continued down.

Halfway across the foyer, along the right wall, they passed the golden doors that led to the Council of Seven's meeting chambers, where Lord Levy presided as chairman. Vrell remembered that the room was round and filled with grandstands that sat five hundred spectators. Her favorite part of going inside had always been the hallway that led up to the auditorium. It was decorated with displays and statuary commemorating the great warriors and leaders in Er'Retian history.

A red-haired servant girl met them at the foot of the staircase. "Ah, yes," she said after Jax introduced them. The girl's name was Mags. "Master Hadar's been s'pecting you," Mags said. "I'll fetch him."

Vrell and Jax waited in the vacant foyer. Several minutes passed before another servant came down the stairway and continued down to the lower levels. Perhaps Lord Levy and his family *were* still at Sitna. It did not seem that Mahanaim was very busy at the moment.

A long wait later, the serving girl walked down the steps beside an old man wearing a grey satin tunic and black leggings. The man reminded Vrell of a white jackrabbit. He had lots of thick, white hair tied in a low ponytail, large ears, and small brown eyes. Vrell reached out and sensed his excitement. His thoughts came easily.

He doesn't look like much. At least he's alive. The master will be very pleased.

This was not Master Hadar? Vrell looked to Jax, her brows furrowed.

"That's Master Hadar's man, Carlani."

Carlani inched along as if his legs had been injured in some way. Clearly he did not move like a jackrabbit. Perhaps it was only his age. His tunic looked draped over bones.

"Welcome, young man," Carlani said in a rasping voice. "The master has been eagerly expecting you."

Vrell forced a smile and bowed. "It has been a long journey."

Again Jax's heavy hand settled on her shoulder. "Good luck to you, Vrell."

"Thank you, Jax." How she longed to throw her arms around him and kiss his big, hairy cheek. Instead, she reached out her hand. He took it gently in his huge hand, and they shook.

"I'll show you to your chamber," Carlani said. "Mags. Run ahead and prepare the boy's room."

Mags, the red-headed servant girl, nodded and scurried up the stairs. Vrell followed Carlani, wiggling her fingers at his infuriatingly slow pace. Carlani hobbled up the first flight of stairs.

"I'm sure you're tired from your journey," Carlani rasped, "but the master is anxious to meet you. He greatly opposes the uniform of a stray, so you must change first. I've set out your new clothing in your chamber."

When they reached the third floor, Carlani moved down a long corridor. They passed Mags on the way.

"The room's ready," she said.

Thankfully, Vrell's status as a stray and apprentice would keep her closer to the ground floor. The last time she had stayed at Mahanaim, her chambers had been on the seventh floor. It would have taken Carlani another hour to get there.

Carlani stopped at a room at the very end of the corridor and pushed the door open. "Change as quickly as you can and meet me on the eighth floor. I'll be waiting for you there."

As slow as he moved, he would need to start now. Vrell stepped into the dark chamber and closed the door. A single candle flickered on a waist-high sideboard. Once Vrell's eyes adjusted to the dark, she took in her new home. The room was tiny and narrow, only as wide as the straw mattress at the end. A set of clothes lay folded on the stiff mattress. A basin of water—warm, she hoped—sat on the narrow sideboard.

She knelt on the bed to look out the small arrow loop window. At first she thought the window was false because she could see nothing but blackness. Then a few vague yellow glows came into focus and she shuddered.

Her window overlooked Darkness.

It was the only logical explanation. It had still been light when she and Jax had entered the castle not long ago, so it couldn't be nighttime already. She turned and sank against the wall, the reality of her location continuing to make her tremble. She had never wanted to set foot in Darkness, ever. Now, without knowing it, she had wandered right into it. May Arman keep her safe.

She sighed deeply and carried the change of clothes to the doorway. Standing with one foot keeping the door shut, she changed into a pale satin tunic and black leggings, thankful to be rid of the hideous orange tunic. Probably no one would enter without knocking, but she would not take that chance. Her padded undergarment was still damp from her swim in the hot springs. She hoped it would not mold in the Mahanaim humidity.

Once she was dressed, she caught up to Carlani on the stairs just past level seven. He smiled, panting, and lifted his foot to tackle another step. At the top of the stairs, he led to the right and knocked twice at the third door.

A muted "Enter" drifted through the thick cypress door.

Carlani pushed it open and inched inside a small, stone antechamber. The room was like standing in an oven: dark and very hot. It was empty but for a blazing fireplace straight ahead and a bald man sitting before it in a wicker chair. Two doors led off the room on each side wall.

The bald man rose from the chair. He was draped in a thick, charcoal cloak. His skin was milky and semitransparent, revealing blue veins and liver spots. He had sunken grey eyes in hollow sockets and no eyebrows. It was as if they had been burned off. He rose to his feet and took two steps forward, the hem of his cloak falling around bare ankles. He wore black satin thong slippers revealing long yellowed toenails.

Vrell averted her gaze to the fire and fought back her revulsion. She fortified the walls around her thoughts, just in case.

"Carlani," the man said.

The valet hobbled forward. Vrell watched in frustration at the feeble man's slowness. Carlani picked up his master's chair and turned it.

The bald man settled back down. "You're the one from Walden's Watch?" he asked, his voice a monotone hum.

"I am, sir."

"Very good. You are how old?"

"Fourteen, sir."

"You will call me *Master* or *Master Hadar*. Are you tired?"

"Yes, Master."

"Then we shall let you rest, after a small test." Master Hadar glanced at Carlani. "Tell me what Carlani is thinking."

Vrell's stomach churned. That was not a very kind thing to do with poor Carlani right here, but the valet did not appear to be paying attention. He was picking hairs and fuzz from his master's cloak. She sought Carlani's mind again.

. . . should have a cloak of silk or satin. Wool does tend to pick up every little thing in this drafty castle. But the wool keeps Master warm. Maybe I should suggest a bonnet. It would keep the heat in . . .

Vrell pulled back and cocked an eyebrow. "He is concerned with your cloak, Master. Every little thing clings to it. He knows the wool keeps you warm, but he thinks a bonnet might do the trick and maybe a cloak of silk or satin."

Master Hadar's sunken eyes bulged. "Good! Very good!" He purred and rubbed his gnarled hands together. "Carlani's mind is like a child the way it's so easy to read. Still, you're more advanced than I expected. Excellent. One more test."

Master Hadar stared at Vrell, his eyes as grey as his cloak. Her ears itched, so she swallowed and focused on closing her mind. He raised a hand and waved her closer. She took one step forward, but he continued to wave. She walked until her knees touched his. He reached up, pressed his wrinkled thumb in the softness under her chin, and his fingers against her temple, cupping her face. His intimate touch startled her, and she glanced into the orange flames to remain calm and focused. Her face burned from her nearness to the crackling fire.

A tiny pinch started in the base of the back of her skull. The sensation grew slowly until it felt like a fist had reached inside and squeezed her brain. She let out a ragged breath and swallowed again. A tear trickled down her cheek, into the place where his thumb touched her chin. Her limbs trembled. She fought to steady them. Her arm twitched involuntarily and slapped his. He did not flinch. He did not release her.

Vrell uttered a small cry, sucked in another breath, and steeled herself against the ferocious pain. Her forehead grew damp with sweat. She glanced down to her master's storming, enlarged pupils, and her knees buckled. She pulled back to catch her balance and severed his grip.

Master Hadar hummed. "Excellent! Your tolerance is incredible. Had you not met my eyes you'd have lasted longer. I could get nothing from you. Nothing at all."

Vrell couldn't stop shivering. She did not want to last longer. She never wanted him to touch her in such a way again. What horrible magic did this man wield?

"What are you called?" Master Hadar asked.

"Ffff . . . " Vrell paused and sucked in a deep breath. "Vrell Sparrow," she whispered.

"You may go, Vrell. Join me here for breakfast tomorrow morning."

"Ye-y-yes, Master."

Vrell turned and strode as fast as she could without looking like she was in a hurry. Once the door clicked shut behind her, she fled down the stairs and back to her chamber. She pulled back the covers of her bed, climbed underneath, and sobbed.

13

Over the next few days, Achan woke to his usual chores and tonic with Poril, then sparred daily against Prince Gidon in the inner bailey courtyard, under the captive eyes of the noble tournament guests. He fought hard, despite his tender shoulder wound.

Although the prince never left him unscathed, Achan didn't receive another cut as deep as he had the first day. He was quick to remember His Majesty's title when he yielded, and the prince was slightly more forgiving with his final blows. Still, the multiple cuts and bruises on Achan's body made him feel like a patchwork quilt. He would have much rather fought other squires out in the tournament pens. He wondered how far Shung had made it.

Each day the crowd grew, though Gren had not been able to come and watch again due to the amount of work she had.

But on the final day of the tournament week, Lady Tara came to watch with Silvo, Jaira, and Bran.

Achan couldn't resist the spunk that rose inside him in the presence of Lady Tara. He kept her light blue gown in his side vision without actually staring at her. Maybe he could manage to speak with her after today's match. One thing was certain: he wasn't about to lose today if he could help it, although he'd never beaten Prince Gidon and his body ached for a month of rest.

Again Achan took the field with Prince Gidon. Chora stood beside Sir Kenton at the edge of the field. The other seven Kingsguards sat in their usual spot along the bench. Gidon wore a quilted, red jerkin over a white shirt. The question was, would the prince manage to keep it clean today?

Their swords clashed. Achan's and the prince's feet trampled the grass. The crowd gasped or cheered on every cut. Achan remembered Sir Gavin's counsel. He was never to think about his opponent's station or skill. He was never to fear what might happen. He was to be confident in his own ability, remember his training, and do his best to win.

Achan had another advantage over his opponent. Since that first day, the prince had grown predictable in his movements. His lone strategy was to push Achan back into the wall or the stands, then strike. As long as Achan kept circling to the side, the match would drag on and on.

Achan also knew that Prince Gidon favored strikes from the right. Perhaps if Achan switched to a left-handed grip for the briefest moment, it would throw the prince off enough so Achan could strike. He'd have to be careful. Because the prince wore no armor, any hit could kill. And killing the Crown Prince would surely be a death sentence.

Achan had heard the whispers: the people were saying that these demonstrations were rehearsed. Prince Gidon either didn't think so or didn't care. Achan did. He wasn't about to let Lady Tara or Silvo think him an actor.

Achan worked up to his attack, waiting for the perfect moment. He sidestepped Prince Gidon's lunge, tossed Eagan's Elk into a left-handed hold, and cut low and left.

His blade struck true.

Prince Gidon yelped and Ôwr thumped into the grass.

The crowd gasped. Achan thought he heard Tara's voice above the rest. What had she said? He turned to where she sat, but Sir Kenton's angry face blocked his view.

"Hold!" The Shield sprinted onto the field.

Prince Gidon clasped a hand over his left thigh and snapped his other fingers. "Chora!"

Chora scurried forward, but Sir Kenton arrived first. He examined the prince's wound, then turned and smashed his fist into Achan's mouth.

Achan crumpled to the ground and rolled to his side, tasting blood.

Well, at least Sir Gavin would be proud.

Chora's blubbering voice met Achan's ears. "Yes, Your Majesty? Are you all right, Your Majesty?"

Still clutching his leg, Prince Gidon glared down at Achan.

Sir Kenton kicked Achan in the stomach, rolling him onto his back. The Shield gripped the neck of Achan's cape and yanked him to his feet. Achan staggered, his palm clamped over his bloodied mouth. Sir Kenton clutched his throat in one beefy hand and thrust him against the wall of the keep. Achan's head clunked off the stone, dazing him.

Sir Kenton lifted Achan off the ground like he weighed nothing. "Do that again, and I'll kill you."

Achan licked his swelling bottom lip and grunted in agreement. Sir Kenton dropped him.

"Take the stray to Myet," the prince told Chora, "then have him report to my chambers in twenty minutes. Be quick about it." He limped away with Sir Kenton, to the soft applause of his shocked subjects.

Achan's body throbbed. He clambered to his feet and located Eagan's Elk in the grass. He wiped the bloodied blade off on his trousers and sheathed it, then glanced to where Tara sat. Judging by her tense expression and Jaira's pink cheeks and waving hands, they seemed to be engrossed in argument. He didn't know who or what Myet was, but it probably wasn't something he was going to like. He sighed. At least he'd made a good showing for Tara.

Chora signaled to two guards. "You heard the king. Be quick about it."

The men each seized Achan by an arm and dragged him away.

Myet, it turned out, was a man. A very cruel man who operated out of a dark room in the dungeons. The guards delivered Achan to Myet for twenty-three lashes. Then they dragged his sagging form up to the sixth floor.

With each step all Achan could think was, *Where is Cetheria's voice now?* So much for her protection. From now on, Achan would eat his offerings. He distracted his anger and frustration with sarcasm. *Why twenty-three lashes? Why not twenty or twenty-five? Could Myet not count?*

The guards left him at the door to Prince Gidon's solar. Achan pushed it open and stepped inside.

At first the room appeared empty. The tapestries were arranged differently than the last time Achan had been in the room. The eastern windows were blocked off today, revealing the prince's bed and the open doorway that led to the balcony. Lord Nathak's voice drifted in from outside.

"Give up this ridiculous obsession and let me send him back to the kitchens where he will be forgotten."

"I have no desire to forget him until he is dead," Gidon said. "He is a nuisance in every way."

"My prince, I beg you to heed my warning. We must not harm the stray. Let him rot in obscurity. Find someone new to amuse yourself with. But leave him unharmed."

Achan froze at the foot of Gidon's massive bed. Lord Nathak didn't want him hurt?

"Why do you protect him?" the prince asked. "His attitude and behavior toward me is scandalous. He should hang. If I allow him to treat me this way with no consequence, word of it shall spread to every rebel in Er'Rets. I must crush him in public where the people will see and take heed. I want my people to fear me, Lord Nathak. To know *I* am in control and my power cannot be taken from me."

Achan inched closer to the doorway.

"I have always advised you well," Lord Nathak said. "Do not forget you have not yet been voted in as king. That can still change. Focus on choosing a bride, I urge you. And forget the stray. I leave it to you to end this."

Footsteps clunked across the floor, and Achan darted back outside the chamber. The door opened and Lord Nathak stepped out. He jumped when he saw Achan and clasped a hand over his chest. He took a long breath and stalked away.

A chill danced over Achan as he watched the man go. Why would Lord Nathak urge the prince not to harm him?

Achan took a deep breath and reentered the room, this time walking all the way inside. Chora spotted him and led him to the balcony overlooking the inner bailey courtyard and tournament field. Prince Gidon lay on a wooden chaise lounge wearing a red silk robe. He didn't look injured. Achan hadn't swung very hard anyway.

Achan's own shirt stuck to his throbbing back. He didn't want to know how bad it looked after Myet's handiwork. He shifted his weight and tugged at the back hem of his shirt to loosen it. His wounds tingled at the rush of cool air.

Prince Gidon raised one hand and snapped at a servant who stood in the corner of the balcony. The servant stepped around Achan and held the fruit tray in front of the prince.

"Well, stray," Prince Gidon said, "in order to take the throne, Lord Nathak insists I choose a bride. This very night."

Achan wrinkled his nose and glanced at the servant, who kept his eyes down. Achan could care less about Prince Gidon's marital options. Did the prince expect him to respond? "He . . . wants you married? Tonight?"

The prince took a handful of grapes and shooed the servant away with a snort. "No, fool. I must choose who I want tonight. The marriage will happen later. If I don't choose, Lord Nathak will choose for me."

Achan didn't know why he was here. Why would Prince Gidon want him around if he wanted him dead? Clueless to the rules of this game, he could only play along. "Is that bad, Your Highness?"

"Possibly." The prince sucked a grape into his mouth. "Have you seen Lady Gali? That beast is among my prospects."

Achan failed to stifle a snicker, which hurt his back. At twenty-two, Lady Gali of Berland stood over six feet and was as broad-shouldered as Sir Kenton. Besides her height, she wore bone bangles around her neck and arms, "jewelry" that looked more like shackles. What an intimidating couple she and the prince would make.

"Then you see what I'm up against." Prince Gidon popped another grape into his mouth. "The pickings are slim indeed. Who would you choose if you had to?"

Lady Tara's golden hair filled his thoughts. "I wouldn't know, Your Highness."

Prince Gidon stood and grabbed Achan's chin in a vice-like grip. He steered Achan toward the edge of the balcony. "I wish your opinion, stray. Who? The fairest? The wittiest? The curviest? I wouldn't expect you to understand the politics of houses, so we'll keep things simple. Who do you favor?"

Achan stepped to the ledge in an act of obedience, but he merely wanted free of Prince Gidon's touch.

Below them, the inner bailey moved at a slower pace than what Achan was used to in the outer bailey. Pairs of young ladies strolled arm in arm near the temple gardens, picking flowers and feeding the ducks. Achan recognized a few faces from the hoodman's blind game but knew none of them by name. He looked from lady to lady in the courtyard below, seeking the most vile.

A familiar giggle rose from the side yard where a peasant boy was making a dog do tricks. Lady Tara clapped her hands, her lustrous hair shining brighter than Ôwr. Her blue gown was the color of the sky. He'd never recommend Lady Tara. Prince Gidon would ruin her.

"You choose Tara." The prince's blue eyes flashed to Achan's, then back to Lady Tara below.

"No." Achan said quickly. "She's kind, that's all."

"Kindness." Prince Gidon grimaced. "A weakness in a queen."

"Why?"

"Because she would pity the people. Every beggar in Er'Rets would make the trek to Armonguard just to spin their tale of woe for her sympathy. And she would give it. She'd bankrupt the treasury in a season."

Lady Tara was no fool. She'd be kind to those who needed it. But Achan was relieved the prince did not desire her for a bride.

"She *is* beautiful." Prince Gidon paused to pour a fistful of grapes into his mouth. "Perhaps I will take her as a mistress."

Achan gripped the railing until his knuckles turned white.

"But"—the prince smacked his lips—"nobles don't make good mistresses. Too demanding. Plus it upsets their fathers, and there you edge into the politics that would melt your dim-witted mind. Who is that pretty brown maid who speaks to you so often?"

"Gren?" Achan answered before thinking. How did the prince know who Achan talked to?

"She is a peasant?"

Achan could only stare.

"Now she would make me an excellent mistress. I shall inquire about taking her with me to Mahanaim."

Achan sputtered. "I . . . uh . . . she's betrothed . . . to Riga Hoff."

"Hoff, you say?" The prince snorted. "Then I would be doing her a favor." He popped another grape into his already full mouth.

Achan trembled. "If you say this is to punish me, Your Majesty, I beg you to choose another method. I'll gladly face Myet again."

"Punish you?"

"Gren is a quiet girl who dreams of raising children and chickens. She loves her family and would die without them. There are many others you could take on your journey."

The prince shrugged and looked down on the noblewomen. "But who will I marry, stray? Lady Halona is but a child. Lady Jacqueline would give the Council too much control of me. My cousin, Lady Glassea, would give the rebels too much control of me. Lady Mandzee is the best political match, but her sister, Jaira, is far prettier, though she'd rob me blind." He pounded the tray and sent grapes flying. "There is no one worthy!"

Achan thought back to Sir Gavin's lectures of the nobles in Er'Rets. "Does not Lord Sigul have a daughter? Lady Tova or something?"

The prince scoffed. "I would rather wed a peasant."

"Could you?" Perhaps if Prince Gidon were to actually marry Gren it wouldn't be so—

For the briefest moment, the prince looked ghostly white. Then a wide smile spread over his face and he laughed. "Never. With a noble bride comes a dowry and land and an army and power . . . for me. And since there is nothing more important than my throne, I shall have to settle. Gods know who I want, but Lord Nathak has failed me there."

"Who do you want?"

Prince Gidon fell back on the chaise lounge and propped both red satin slippers up on the back, crossing his ankles. "You need a shave, stray. I'll not have a squire who looks older than me."

Achan ran his fingers over his scratchy, swollen jaw. His whiskers had grown fast since Wils's shave. "I *am* older than you," he paused, then quickly added, "Your Majesty."

"Ridiculous. Tomorrow be cleanshaven or you can fight me without your weapon."

Achan opened his mouth to protest, but when he took in Prince Gidon from head to toe, he saw the prince was right. It was ridiculous to think Achan was older than this man. He looked well over sixteen years of age. Maybe it was from eating so heartily his whole life.

"You will accompany me on my journey to Mahanaim, of course," Prince Gidon said. "Lord Nathak has dispatched my other squires on various errands, so you will have to do everything yourself. We leave in two days. You're dismissed."

Achan's jaw dropped. "Yes, Your Majesty."

Achan begged Noam's help to put salve on his back. Then he washed out his shirt and put on his stray's tunic. He took a knife from the kitchens and went to the river to shave.

He knelt on the bank and leaned over to see his reflection. The sky was cloudy, so all he could see was a dark blob. Still, he scraped the blade over his cheeks again and again, trying to cut the hairs. He'd never seen a man shave and had no idea how to go about it. He jerked each time the blade nicked him, and cut himself more than his stubble. In the end his cheeks not only still felt prickly, but he'd drawn blood in several places. He tried again. Eventually he gave up and stalked to Gren's cottage.

She opened the door and gasped. "What's he done to you now?"

"No." Achan held up the knife. "I did it to myself . . . trying to shave." He forced his voice to imitate Prince Gidon's lofty tone. "My prince demands it."

Gren rolled her eyes. "You silly boy." She took Achan's hand and led him to a chair by the table, then went to the fireplace. She rose on her tiptoes and reached onto the mantle searching for something. Her brown skirt swung like a bell above her bare ankles. "But your lip, Achan, how did you do that?"

The Fenny cottage was like most in Sitna: a small main room with a fireplace and a table, then two more rooms in back.

Achan sighed. "Ah. Well, Sir Kenton punched me."

"No!" She carried a roll of leather to the table, lips parted. "What happened?"

"I struck Gidon."

Gren's gasped. "You what?"

Achan told Gren about his day as she filled a basin with cold water and set it on the table. Then she lifted the kettle from the hearth and added hot water, testing it with her fingers.

She clicked her tongue, her eyes darting about his face. "What a mess, Achan. We can't have you looking half dead if you're to go to Mahanaim with the prince. You might even stand before the Council."

"No one will pay any attention to me. I'm sure Gidon will have a hundred errands to keep me occupied, like fluffing pillows and feeding him grapes."

She swabbed a wet rag over his face, then lathered soap over his cheeks. She unrolled the leather and held up a knife-like razor. "The right tool helps." She sharpened the blade on a leather strop, set it at the top of his left cheek, and slowly drew it down.

As Gren scraped the hairs from his face, Achan studied her brown eyes, her dark eyelashes, and each freckle on her nose and cheeks. She wiped the razor on a rag and a wispy chestnut curl fell over one eye. She raised the razor to his face again and blew the tendril aside.

"Thank you, Gren. You're a true friend."

She beamed.

"Where did you learn to do this?"

"Father. He's been making me practice on him for . . . when I'm married."

Achan looked to his lap. He didn't want to speak of this again. There was nothing to be done.

Gren's voice came soft. "I'd much rather marry you, you know."

He flushed, feeling awkward in the silence that followed. When he looked back to Gren, she was busy on his right cheek. He changed the subject. "Gidon asked about you. About taking you with him . . . as his . . . uh . . . mistress."

Gren's eyebrows sank. "Why would he want me?"

"Who wouldn't want you?"

She smirked and worked the razor over the strop again. "That's sweet, Achan, but Prince Gidon can have anyone. He was probably only trying to upset you."

Achan hoped that was all. "Would you . . . want that, though?"

She scowled and softly slapped his cheek. "Achan Cham, what a thing to ask a girl! Of course I wouldn't want that. No amount of wealth could make that a desirable life. Not that I'd have a choice in the matter if it were so."

Achan went red again, but relief melted his anger some, knowing he was right about Gren, that neither wealth nor title would sway her heart.

She darted behind him, pressed one hand to his forehead and the razor to his throat, and hissed in his ear, "But if it were so, he wouldn't take me without a fight."

Achan laughed at her caviler attitude, but he had a feeling it was the fight Prince Gidon enjoyed most. He kept that thought to himself.

When Gren finished with his face, she held a finger against his chest. "Wait right there." She scurried down the hall and returned with a vest. She held it up. "It's finished."

His eyes bulged. This was more of a doublet than a jerkin or vest. It was sleeveless except for little caps shooting off the tops of the shoulders. A v-neck yoke cut across the chest, and below, tailored seams encased the waist before flaring out in a short peplum. It was tan, doeskin suede. And altogether beautiful. "My doe?"

She nodded, eyes sparkling. "Try it on."

She helped him pull off his cape, then put on the jerkin. He held his breath to stifle his reaction to the pain when he reached back for the second sleeve. He didn't want Gren to know about Myet's workmanship. She fastened the silk ties into bows down the front. His chest swelled. She was so thoughtful to make this from his deer.

"It will look even better with the brown shirt." Gren swiped her hands over his dingy white Kingsguard sleeve. She ran her hands down either side of the laces, as if inspecting her own handiwork, then looked up, smiled, and took his face in her hands, one on each stinging cheek. "You're destined for more than the life of a stray, Achan Cham. That I know." She rose onto her tiptoes and kissed him on the lips.

Heat flashed over him as if he'd stepped out of the shade into the sun. Gren had kissed his cheek lots of times but never—

The door swung open. Gren's mother stood in the sunlit opening, one hand on her hip, the other holding a bundle of fabric against her chest. She shut the door quickly. "You both are too old for these types of visits. This is vastly inappropriate, more so than ever with Grendolyn's betrothal."

Achan looked to the floor, seized by a different kind of heat. He shuffled his feet and desperately wished he could vanish.

Gren stepped away and set about clearing the shaving materials off the table, her voice shaky as she defended herself. "Achan needed help shaving because the prince—"

"Achan will have to take care of himself from now on." Her mother set the fabric on the table and sighed. "I know you're friends, but this must stop. Forever. Now, say your farewells. Your father is not far behind." She walked past the table and into the back room.

Gren rolled the razor and strop inside the swatch of leather and did not look up when she whispered, "Farewell, Achan."

A horrible ache welled in his throat. He glanced at Gren, who returned the leather roll to the mantle and stood poised like a statue.

In a hoarse whisper Achan said, "Gren, I . . . "

She looked up and shook her tear-streaked face. "Don't."

He walked to the entrance, dragging his feet. His boots scraping over the dirt floor sounded extra loud in the silence. He turned back and met her forlorn gaze. She glanced away.

He stood at the door. "Thank you, Gren. For everything."

14

As much as Vrell did not want to see Macoun Hadar again, she guessed she had better report to breakfast. The sooner she learned how to contact Mother, the better.

She took the time to pray, then wandered up the staircase uncertain of what she would do when she arrived. If only she could find Carlani first. He did not threaten her, and she thought of him as an ally. They both served the same master, anyway.

A chambermaid carried a basket of clothing down the stairs.

"Excuse me," Vrell said. "Where could I find Carlani's room?"

"He sleeps on a pallet in his master's chamber," the girl said. "Master Hadar is very demanding."

"Thank you." Vrell continued to the eighth floor. She should have guessed. Servants often bunked in their master's room in case they were needed at any hour. Someone as old and odd as Macoun Hadar would not want to be kept waiting. Strange that he relied on such a snail of a servant.

Vrell knocked on the antechamber door. When no one answered, she crept inside. The antechamber had cooled since her visit the previous evening. A few glowing embers smoldered in the fireplace. The other two doors were identical to the first: cedar panels held together by a diagonal plank and rounded at the top. She knocked at the one on the left first. When no answer came, she pushed it open and saw that it led to another dark antechamber. This room had no other doors, no windows, and no fireplace—just a completely empty stone room, like some sort of dungeon cell.

Vrell closed the door, noting that it locked from the inside only. For some reason this brought relief. She could not be locked in. She walked to the other door and knocked.

Master Hadar's muffled voice said, "Enter."

Vrell took a deep breath and pushed open the door. She entered a bright, sweltering room. This appeared to be Master Hadar's bedchamber. It sat on the east side of the stronghold. The morning sun shone through three large windows on the east wall, spilling long beams of sunlight across the wooden floor. Despite the natural heat, a fire blazed in a hearth twice the size of the one in the antechamber.

Master Hadar sat on the end of a canopied bed like a mini king, his feet resting on a small stone slab, ugly toes poking out the ends of his satin slippers. Thick, grey, wool tapestries hung around his bed. He did not seem fond of color.

Master Hadar's sunken eyes watched her, but he said nothing, compelling Vrell to speak.

"Good morning, Master. Am I late?"

"No. Carlani has not yet returned with breakfast."

Vrell wondered how long ago Carlani had left and if he would return before lunch.

Master Hadar pointed a gnarled finger at a small table sitting under the center window. "Bring that here."

Vrell blinked, then walked across the room. She stole a glance out the window. The entrance to the stronghold stretched out below, the shining sun casting a golden glow onto the stone buildings. In the distance, beyond the parapet wall enclosing the city, the Lebab Inlet edged the skyline like a shimmering, silver blanket.

Lovely.

The table was tall and awkward but not heavy. Vrell lugged it toward the bed.

"Here." Master Hadar pointed to his feet. "Then we can eat."

Vrell positioned the table over the stone slab. Master Hadar pointed to a stool in the corner. Vrell fetched that as well, which he had her set opposite him.

Then he pointed to the mantle above the hearth. "There's an old bronze ring. Fetch it."

The mantle sat a foot higher than Vrell's eyes. She reached up to the dusty surface and felt along the top. Carlani was not much of a housekeeper.

"No, no. The other end."

Vrell moved to the opposite end and found the ring. She held it up.

Master Hadar nodded. "That's right. Bring it here."

Vrell carried the ring to her master and set it in front of him on the table.

He did not pick it up but looked at her with his sunken grey eyes. "Sit."

Vrell sat on the stool.

"Find Carlani."

Vrell blinked. "Master? You want me to find him?" Perhaps Master Hadar was as hungry as she was. Waiting for Carlani on a regular basis must get frustrating.

"That's right. Close your eyes and concentrate."

Of course. Time to learn. She hoped he would not touch her again. Jax's warning came to mind. She would be wary of becoming this man's pawn. Vrell closed her eyes and focused. A massive coldness loomed before her and she shivered. She assumed that was Master Hadar closing off his mind. Strange that she could sense his closed mind but had not sensed anything from Jax or Khai. Did that make the knights stronger or weaker?

She pictured the old servant in her head. She thought about Carlani's wrinkled face, his hunched posture, his white ponytail, and his tiny brown bird eyes. She furrowed her brow but could not sense him. That either meant he was too far away or he was blocking her. She opened her eyes.

Master Hadar was staring, the wrinkled skin hanging from his cheeks as if it might slide off. Crescents of pink flesh peeked out from under his sunken eye sockets. How was it a man could have no eyebrows? He reached his twisted fingers above the ring and slid it toward her with one finger, the bronze scraping across the polished wooden surface. "Try again, holding this." He lifted his finger off the ring.

Goosebumps broke out over Vrell's arms at the curious humming tone of his voice. He expected a different outcome with this ring. Was it magic? Vrell did not want to play with mage magic. Arman would not approve.

She gulped and picked up the ring. She gripped it in her fist and closed her eyes again. Before she could even try to picture the white-haired valet, she found him in a kitchen.

". . . doesn't like it. But add a bit of bacon for the boy and some milk. Skin and bones, he is," Carlani said.

"Would you like if I carried it up for yeh?" a girl's voice asked.

"Oh, that would be nice, Mags. It's such a long walk, and I could use the company."

Mags sighed. *"No. I meant I'd deliver . . . oh, never you mind."* She picked up a tray, and the aroma of bacon, tea, and toast filled Vrell's nostrils. She inhaled a deep breath.

A throaty chuckle popped Vrell's eyelids open. Master Hadar's thin lips twisted in a smile, revealing brown teeth. "Found him, did you?"

Vrell nodded. "I smelled the bacon."

Master Hadar wrinkled his nose. "I don't eat meat."

Vrell set the ring back on the table. "Is it a magic ring?"

"Magic? No. It belongs to Carlani. I use it to find him quicker. The older I get, the harder it is for me. I have to resort to the tricks of my youth."

"Tricks?"

"The ring." Master Hadar reached out a crooked finger and pulled the ring toward him. "What do you know of bloodvoicing?"

"Very little."

"Well, bloodvoicing is the ability to hear the thoughts and share the experiences of others. You can learn to use it on any living thing. However, those who have the gift can learn to block others out. That you already know how to do."

Vrell nodded.

"If you tried to seek out a friend, someone you know very well, you should be able to find them without help. But if you haven't seen them in a while or don't know them, are out of practice or weak from illness or age, it helps to have something of theirs. Personal belongings increase connection."

Which was why Khai had stolen her coin purse.

"You've a question?" Master Hadar asked.

"No." Vrell shifted on her stool, not liking that this man could tell when she was thinking, if not what. "Yes, actually. Why me? Why did I get this gift?"

"It travels through blood, hence its name. It's an ability that was bestowed upon King Echâd, the first king of Er'Rets, when the father god, Arman, gave him rule of this land. To be able to hear and influence the thoughts of others is a gift only the gods have. But King Echâd was given that ability to aid in his rule. The gift passed through his bloodline the same as any human trait: brown hair, blue eyes, crooked teeth . . . "

Master Hadar coughed. "Not all his descendants were born with the ability. Of those who were, each had a variation of the gift. No one has ever had the full power that King Echâd originally had."

"So I am a descendant of King Echâd?" Vrell knew this already, but she wanted to confirm she understood the gift properly.

"You must be."

"How was it you sensed me in Walden's Watch?"

"I've been around long enough, boy. I know everyone who has the bloodvoices and where they live. No one in Walden's Watch had it. But recently, I sensed the gift there. So I sent the Kingsguards to fetch you."

Vrell took a risk and asked, "How did you know where to find me and that I was a boy?"

"I didn't . . . at first. But there are always clues. I sent Jax and Khai to Walden's Watch. As they neared, I could sense you through them even though they couldn't sense you. This is called jumping. Jax is stronger than Khai. Upon entering the manor house, Jax sensed a bloodvoice presence, but he couldn't discern who or how old or the level of ability. You walk about with your shields up, which is wise. Through Jax, I could sense you were someone young and someone who didn't belong."

Heat flushed over Vrell. How close he had come to knowing the whole truth.

"Once Jax spoke with Lord Orthrop and discovered he had a new ward, I figured that was who had the gift. When Jax saw you, I sensed your power."

"But you could not hear me?"

"No. You block too well. I sensed you were there, heard your conversations with Jax and Khai through their thoughts, but I could not hear your thoughts directly."

Vrell thought about the newly gifted man. "There is one voice, a new one whom Jax, Khai, and I heard on our journey here. His thoughts blast into my mind, even though my guard is up."

"Yes." Master Hadar's eyes sparkled. "The boy. Achan. I've been seeking him."

Achan. He hadn't sounded like a mere boy to Vrell. "Why do you seek him?"

"His strength would be of great use."

Vrell tilted her head. "Why do you think him a boy?"

"Clues. You heard all the voices?"

"Yes."

"Good. But I listen to what they said. Some referred to him as a boy. These were likely the thoughts of regular men who were near him at the time. He was transferring their thoughts for all bloodvoicers to hear without realizing it. It's like the reverse of jumping. Very hard to do."

Vrell glanced at the ring. How strange that thoughts could be sent so easily, yet she could not contact Mother. Had she been away from Mother too long to reach her? She had none of her mother's belongings in her possession. Would that help if she did? Would a possession keep others from listening in? "How could I call out to you, Master, without Jax or Khai or someone else hearing me—sensing me?"

"That's called messaging. I'll teach it to you soon enough. It will be important for you to be my eyes in places an old man is not able to go."

Vrell wondered what sorts of places Master Hadar had in mind. Did he intend to make her into a spy?

Someone tapped on the door.

Master Hadar called out, "Enter."

Carlani inched his way inside. Mags, the thin, red-haired servant girl, walked with him, her steps fidgety, her expression tense. Vrell jumped up and took the tray from her hands. She must have had a very long and frustrating walk beside Carlani. Mags's eyes fluttered over Vrell. She smiled, then left the room. Vrell set the tray on the table before Master Hadar. Carlani hobbled to a sideboard in the far corner that held a water pitcher and mugs.

Vrell turned to Master Hadar. "How can I speak to Carlani? To send him a message?"

Master Hadar dug into his bowl of gruel, sloppily putting some to his lips. "You can't. Carlani does not have the gift. But you can influence him."

Vrell narrowed her eyes.

Master Hadar's thin mouth twisted into a sinister smile, globs of gruel showing between his lips. He slurped. "These are things I'll teach you over time. Things some consider . . . immoral."

Vrell shivered in the hot room, not liking the sound of that.

15

Lord Nathak canceled the prince's sparring practice due to his *injury.* Even though it was not for his benefit, Achan was grateful. He wore his Kingsguard uniform anyway and carried Eagan's Elk at his side. He didn't want to be caught off-guard and without a weapon, nor could he simply leave a priceless sword lying around.

He spent the morning peeling potatoes under Poril's mournful eye and planning his escape to Tsaftown. Deserting the prince was punishable by death, but death was just what Gidon had in mind for him, so he may as well get away while he was still whole.

Chora had informed Poril that Achan would be traveling to Mahanaim. Poril moped around the kitchens, suddenly unable to do anything without Achan's assistance. The old man still stood sentry until Achan drank his tonic. Achan wanted to heed Sir Gavin's warning not to drink it, but he didn't want to start a war with Poril on their last day together.

Achan was melancholy but couldn't fathom where the feeling came from. He shook off thoughts of Poril and focused on the potatoes. His dreams of leaving were going to come true at last, but not how he'd hoped. Tonight he'd flee Sitna a fugitive rather than a free man. And Gren would not be coming along.

Gren.

She refused to run away. Achan wasn't surprised. She loved her family and home. Still, he felt like she had chosen Riga over him. Could Achan simply leave her here? Maybe he could come back to make sure that Riga was treating her well. The thought of Riga quickened his knife, and soon all the potatoes were peeled and chopped.

A page raced into the kitchen. "Master Poril, sir." The boy paused to catch his breath. "Prince Gidon requires the stray's presence immediately."

The stray's presence.

Achan slid off his stool and stormed outside. He would face this tyrant for the last time. Prince Gidon was nothing but a glorified Riga or Harnu. Achan's back still smarted as he bounded up to the sixth floor, boots stomping all the way.

Chora hushed him at the door, then let him through. "Master Cham, Your Highness."

Achan strode into Prince Gidon's solar. The prince stood on the balcony, arms propped on the railing, hip jutting out to the left. He wore a deep maroon doublet and brown leather trousers bound below the knees with gold garters. Achan started toward him, but someone cleared his throat. Achan turned to see Lord Nathak at a desk in the corner of the room reading a scroll.

Lord Nathak tossed the scroll aside and looked at Achan. The ties of his mask had come undone under his chin, letting the mask gape slightly. Achan caught a glimpse of the ruined flesh. "You are ready to leave in the morning?"

Achan stiffened. He'd be leaving before then, but he couldn't reveal that here. "Yes, my lord."

"I will not be coming with you. I will follow behind with the nobility."

Achan knew all this already. Prince Gidon's procession would ride out first, accompanied by the knights and squires. Lord Nathak would follow at a slower pace with the lords and ladies and their children who were going south. Some of those would attend the Council vote in Mahanaim, but many—including Lady Tara, Achan had discovered—were going home until the actual coronation that would commence in the fall.

"I'm counting on you to serve his every need, as his attendants are not used to travel."

Achan fought to keep his face passive. He'd never spent time as a personal servant and had no intention of starting now. Come morning, he would be deep in the Sideros Forest on his way to Mitspah.

Lord Nathak went on. "Chora will be with him, as will Sir Kenton, but should anything happen, are you prepared for battle?"

Battle? Achan blinked. "Yes, my lord." But he wasn't. Not really. Who would be insane enough to attack a procession of Kingsguard knights? Achan searched his memory. Had Sir Gavin ever mentioned anyone who might want to kill the prince? Hundreds of people, probably, but Achan couldn't remember anyone specific.

"Try not to make him angry and you should live until I get to Mahanaim."

Why was Lord Nathak telling him this? Achan sought the man's feelings but found only a chill in the air, as if Lord Nathak himself were the source of the cold. How did he do that?

"Well? Your prince is waiting."

Achan walked out to the balcony, and the heat of the late morning warmed him. What a magnificent view the prince had. To his right, Achan could see where the Sitna River met the ocean. Straight ahead the multicolored tents on the tournament field were being dismantled. To the west, he could just barely see the dark ridge that was the Chowmah Mountain Range. "You wanted to see me, Your Highness?"

The prince stared at the river. "You will do something for me, stray. Your friend, Wren."

Achan furrowed his brow. "Gren?"

"I want her to come along. I'm not returning to Sitna. The Council will undoubtedly vote in my favor, then I will continue on to Armonguard as king. She should say her farewells to whomever."

"But . . . I told you. Gren is betrothed to Riga Hoff."

Prince Gidon straightened and gripped the railing. "I do not care about Riga Hoff. Bring her with you in the morning."

"You can't just—"

Prince Gidon turned. "Am I king?"

A rush of heat seared through Achan and he snapped, "Not yet, Your Highness."

The prince stiffened then smiled, blue eyes flashing. "You are dismissed."

The blood boiled in Achan's veins. He turned to go.

"Do not do anything foolish, stray," the prince said to his back. "Should you and the young lady go missing, I shall kill her parents first, then hunt you both down."

Achan stormed from the room, down the stairs, and into the inner bailey. He paced toward the gate to the outer bailey, then turned back. As if Gren's betrothal to Riga hadn't been bad enough. At least with Riga she'd be near her family, her home—she'd have some . . . stability. Prince Gidon was about to be married to some random noblewoman! Gren would be nothing to him. How could he be so . . .

Why would Cetheria let this happen? And after she had told him to go to the keep that day. Achan could have left long ago. He could have been gone, and Gren safe. Achan stormed to the temple.

A guard stopped him at the colonnade. "Only nobility can enter."

Achan drew Eagan's Elk. "I am here on a very specific errand involving Prince Gidon."

The guard stepped back, eyes wide. The man had his own sword, but Achan doubted anyone had ever threatened violence simply to enter the temple.

Achan strode forward and climbed the steps two at a time. He slowed on the porch and crossed the threshold with wide eyes. Inside the cella, marble pillars rose three stories high long the side walls. Incense filled his nostrils. The statue of Cetheria stood at the end of the room, her head nearly reaching the roof.

He froze when he saw her, his anger dwarfed by her size and splendor. Her skin was ivory, her gown sheets of gold leaf. She clutched a golden spear in one hand, a shield in the other. Her eyes, some sort of blue gemstone, stared forward, sparkling from the hundreds of candles burning at her feet. Treasure was piled there: gold cups, jewels, coins, toys. Perhaps the guards were posted outside mainly to keep people from stealing the offerings.

Achan approached the altar slowly, staring up at the jeweled eyes. "You're not so beautiful. Not like Tara." He winced, waiting to be struck down, hoping, almost, to be put out of his misery. Nothing happened.

"Why do you speak to me? I have little in this world, goddess. Why toy with a stray? Is this fun for you?" He scowled and threw Eagan's Elk on the pile of offerings. "You want that? Is that what you want? It's all I have. Take it. Take everything, but—" He fell to his knees, clutching his hands into fists. "Please leave Gren be."

Heat swept around him like a summer wind, seeping through his skin and into his veins. He gasped.

Watch yourself carefully, Achan, so that you do not corrupt yourself with an idol of any shape, whether formed like man, woman, beast, or nature.

Take your sword and go. You know what you must do.

Achan cowered to the floor, trembling. The burning heat brought sweat to his brow. "Is it not Cetheria who speaks to me?"

But the voice did not answer. Achan gulped and rose to his knees, his gaze flitting back to Cetheria's jeweled eyes. Was she really only an idol?

Achan jumped up and fetched his blade from the hoard. He sheathed it and fled. The guard stopped to search him at the gate, but let him go without further questions.

Achan set off at a jog for Gren's cottage. The voice had said he knew what to do. All he really knew was that he could not allow this. Future king or not, Prince Gidon had no right to take Gren. Achan might not be able to flee, but that didn't mean there was nothing he could do.

He pounded on the door of Gren's cottage. "Master Fenny!"

The door opened a crack, and Gren peered out. "Achan. What is it?"

"I must speak with your father. Is he home?"

Her eyes went wide. "Yes. What are you going to do?"

That she thought he might be speaking to her father against Riga flooded him with guilt. He pushed the thoughts aside. "Please, Gren. Now."

She rolled her eyes and shut the door. A breeze gushed through the corridor between the cottages but did not quell the heat in Achan's chest. The burn of that voice lingered.

Master Fenny opened the door. "What is it, boy?"

"Forgive me, but I must speak with you. It's partly the business of Prince Gidon."

"Oh. Do come in."

"If you please, sir, this involves Master Hoff as well. Could we go to his home?"

Master Fenny was tall, but his shoulders were hunched from years over the loom. He ducked out the door with ease and closed it behind him. The sun glared off his balding head. "Lead the way."

Achan walked across the outer bailey, trembling with every step. His actions were openly treasonous, but he didn't care. Let Gidon hang him.

Riga's mother led them inside the cottage, which was bigger than the Fenny home but not as clean. Father and son were eating lunch at a long table, a sight almost as disgusting as Prince Gidon eating grapes. Gren's future prospects truly disappointed Achan.

Master Hoff stood, pea soup dripping down his fat chin. "What's this?"

"The boy is on a task from the prince himself," Master Fenny said.

Riga shot Achan a glare with his beady eyes and crunched down on bread roll. His round, pink cheeks bulged more with food in his mouth.

"Well, out with it, boy. We're busy men here," Master Hoff said.

"The prince leaves tomorrow for Mahanaim to appear before the Council," Achan said. "Then he'll go on to Armonguard, where he—"

Riga huffed a loud, groaning sigh. "Everyone knows this."

"He wants to take Gren with—" Achan coughed, his throat too dry to force out the vile words.

"Take her where?" Master Fenny asked. "He shouldn't need a seamstress on the journey. I'm certain there are seamstresses in Armonguard."

Achan studied the floor, and the truth came out in a whisper. "Take her . . . as his mistress."

Master Fenny paled. "What?"

Riga jumped to his feet. "But Gren is betrothed to me."

"I told him that," Achan said. "His answer was, 'I don't care about Riga Hoff.'"

Riga's pudgy face turned pink.

Master Fenny slouched into an empty chair at the table. "This cannot be. Not my little girl."

"She could run away, until he's left," Master Hoff suggested.

"No," Achan said. "He said if she ran, he'd kill her parents first, then hunt her down."

"What madness is this?" Master Fenny said. "He's never once shown interest in Grendolyn."

"If I may," Achan croaked. All three looked to him. "I'm to fetch Gren tomorrow morning for the prince. If I were to find she'd already been—" he closed his eyes—"married, I could tell the prince I was mistaken that she was only betrothed."

Master Hoff's eyes bulged. "Married today?"

"He knows Gren and you are friends?" Master Fenny asked.

"Aye."

"Then he won't believe you didn't know."

"He might not." Achan glanced at Riga. "But after all, I'm just a stray. Why would anyone share such *intimacies* with me?"

"That's true," Master Hoff said.

Riga's coloring returned to normal. His everyday glare had vanished. His face softened, and Achan could see his pale blue eyes.

"There's no time!" Master Fenny said. "We need three days for a wedding."

"We could say the ceremony had already begun," Master Hoff said.

Gren's father shook his head. "Still, Gren needs to make temple offerings of her childhood clothing and toys. With a priest present."

"Go and do that now." Master Hoff pushed his chair in and wiped his face with a napkin. "Riga and I will tend to the feast. We'll need guests to stand up as witnesses."

"The women can see to that. Perhaps she could wear her mother's veil."

Master Hoff paused. "Such deceitfulness could anger the gods."

"Better a cursed marriage than have my daughter made a concubine!"

"Well, I don't desire a cursed marriage for my son! He's my only heir, as Gren is yours. If the gods are angered, they could curse her womb. Where would that leave us both?"

"Do I have a say?" Riga looked to Gren's father. "The dowry has already been agreed upon. I've made dozens of sacrifices for this union. The gods won't curse us. It's my dedication to the gods that brings this warning to us. It is their gift to us in our time of need."

Achan bit back a sarcastic remark. If the voice was right, and all the gods were idols, what did any of this superstitious talk matter?

Master Fenny sighed. "It shall be done then, if you agree, Vaasa."

Master Hoff scratched his chin. "The cottage isn't finished, but it's livable. I'll go to the priest this moment and ask him to perform the ceremony tonight. Word should spread fast."

Achan slipped to the door and let himself out, unable to bear any more. He stopped to suck in a long, fresh breath. He could see the barn from here and the plumes of smoke from the kitchen chimneys. The door opened behind him. He turned to see Riga pulling it closed.

"You think she'll be happier with me than the future king?"

Achan grimaced. "I do."

"Why?"

"Because Gren loves Sitna, and you're in Sitna. Be kind to her. Be kind to her family. If I ever hear you weren't . . . " Achan set his hand on the hilt of his sword. Riga's squinted eyes flew wide. Achan turned and stalked away.

That night he lay under the ale casks, mourning the death of the girl he loved. Come morning, she'd be a married woman.

He had once watched a wedding from a distance. In the final act of the ceremony, the unveiling of the bride, the father had announced to the groom, "In front of these witnesses, I give this girl to you."

Tonight, Gren's father would say that to Riga, and she'd be his.

Achan would not torture himself by watching the ceremony, even from afar.

His stomach churned. Now his own plans had been foiled as well. He couldn't flee for fear of Prince Gidon's wrath against Gren and her parents. Tomorrow they would both start a new life. Gren as Riga's wife and Achan as the prince's personal slave.

The next morning Achan lay staring at the casks overhead. He hadn't slept well. Memories of Gren haunted his every thought.

He tugged his blanket over his head and noticed a jagged tear in the top corner. Someone had cut a square from the thick wool. Trivial as it might be on any other day, this morning Achan seethed. Could he have nothing that wasn't rags? He'd just been given a new Kingsguard uniform, which Prince Gidon had shredded little by little each day. At least his sword was still intact.

He pondered his coming adventure as he dressed, then rolled the brown shirt and the doeskin doublet inside his blanket. Gren would make clothes for Riga now, but these might yet come in useful. He tied his blanket with his old belt and carried the bundle upstairs.

Poril stood at the bread table. He sprinkled flour on the surface and dumped out a lump of bubbly dough. Achan's tonic sat on the table, but Poril made no mention of it.

"I'm leaving for Mahanaim."

"That yeh are." Poril sprinkled more flour over the dough, then kneaded his hands into it.

"I don't know when . . . " Achan shifted his weight from one leg to the other.

"Yeh'll be fine, yeh will. And if yeh never see Poril again . . . Poril wishes yeh well."

A tight ache welled in Achan's throat. Would he actually miss this old goat? "Well, I . . . thank you." Achan stood in the entrance to the kitchens, watching Poril go about making bread. He wanted to leave, but his feet wouldn't move. His eyes misted and he clenched his jaw. "Farewell, then." Achan turned and fled.

He was five steps from the entrance when Poril yelled, "Achan!"

Achan turned, expecting to see the cook holding up the mug of tonic.

Instead, Poril hobbled up and handed Achan a bulky sack. "'Tis a long journey ahead. Maybe yeh'll be hungry. Guards can't cook worth much."

Achan dropped the bag and hugged the old man. "Thank you, Master Poril."

Poril wiggled away, rubbing his eye. "No trouble, boy. No trouble at all."

Achan sniffed and shoved his blanket into Poril's bag. Did the old man regret naming him Achan—"trouble"? Was he trying to say he was sorry? It was a nice thought, and he tried to keep it in the center of his mind as he hurried to the Fenny's cottage, anxious to get this over with and be gone from Sitna. He'd had his fill of emotions.

He knocked on the door and stepped back, secretly hoping Gren would open the door like always. Instead, her mother did.

The woman squealed and pulled Achan into a hug. He stood stiffly as her body trembled with sobs. He patted her back.

Thankfully Master Fenny came to the door. "Ah, Achan. What can we do for you this fine morning?"

His words came out monotone. "I . . . I've come for Gren. Prince Gidon requests her company on his journey."

Gren's mother reeled into a new chain of sobs and squeezed Achan so tight, he feared she might sever his body at the waist.

"I'm sorry," Master Fenny said. "You'll have to check with her husband. She's a married woman now."

Achan couldn't help but smile at his performance. "Oh, that is new information. I'll relay that to His Highness." Achan peeled away from Gren's mother. He wanted to see Gren, but that would be hugely inappropriate. "I cannot write . . . so I couldn't say farewell . . . could you tell Gren I—"

Gren's mother burst into tears again. Master Fenny clapped him on the back. "She already knows, Achan, but I'll tell her."

"Thank you, sir."

Achan left Gren's cottage behind and ran over the drawbridge. There, the caravan of horses and wagons was lined up along the river. He stood with Noam as his friend harnessed a horse to a wagon, neither saying a word.

Finally Noam spoke. "Chora says you aren't allowed a horse."

Achan closed his eyes and smirked. "That sounds about right."

"You won't miss this place, Achan," Noam said. "You won't even think of us when you're living in the palace at Armonguard."

"I might never live in the palace. I might be back in a fortnight. I might be dead."

"Nah. You're too lucky to be killed. Cetheria has always watched over you, even though you think she hasn't. I'm almost certain you'll stand in the Armonguard palace someday. Maybe I'll come and visit."

"I thought you didn't like adventures."

"Don't." Noam pulled a scrap of parchment from his pocket. "Gren brought this by yesterday."

Achan's brow furrowed as he stared at the curled parchment in Noam's hand.

A red and gold litter approached, carried by four men. Achan had seen the litter travel in and out of the Sitna Manor before, but never had he loathed it so. It was a floating bedchamber painted red with golden trim and carved scrolling. Thick gold fringe and tassels outlined the roof. Birds were carved at each corner. The heavy, red wool curtains were drawn closed.

The men stopped and lowered the litter near the front of the procession. Prince Gidon exited, dressed in a red embroidered silk doublet over a white shirt with flowing sleeves and golden leather trousers cinched below the knees with scarlet garters. A thin gold crown studded with rubies and diamonds held his slicked-back hair in place. He stood with his hands on his hips as a large wagon, stacked high with ornate trunks, came to a halt behind the litter. The prince's luggage perhaps?

Prince Gidon's gaze met Achan's. "Stray!" He snapped his fingers in the air.

Achan sucked in a deep breath and snatched Gren's letter from Noam's hand. He crammed it into the bag Poril had given him, and strode toward the prince. "You snapped, Your Highness?"

"Where is Wren?"

"I don't know any Wren, Your Highness."

Prince Gidon pursed his lips. "You know who I mean. Where is the girl?"

"She's not here, Your Highness."

"And why not?"

"It seems I was wrong about her betrothal, Your Highness. I was happy to find her already married. Apparently I was not invited to the ceremony, nor did she share the date and time with me. I am, after all, only a stray."

The prince's eyes narrowed. "Married?"

"You didn't want me to take her from her husband, did you?"

"Of course not." Prince Gidon folded his arms and looked back to the manor. "This is most disappointing. In fact . . . " He strode toward the manor. "Come."

Achan glanced back to Noam, then jogged after the prince.

Chora scurried up to them from the back of the procession. "Your Majesty, where are you going?"

"The stray and I have an errand."

"But we are ready to leave. We've already lost an hour—"

Prince Gidon stopped and grabbed the valet's shoulder. "Am I king, Chora?"

Chora nodded and circled back.

Achan and the prince walked in silence until they reached the drawbridge. A trader's wagon blocked the way as the guards checked the cargo.

Prince Gidon stopped behind it and paced, arms crossed. He turned to Achan. "The thing is, stray, it's all a little too convenient, don't you think?"

"What is, Your Highness?"

"The whole—"

"It's His Royal Highness!" a guard yelled from the sentry walk.

"On foot?"

As the wagon rolled forward, Achan feigned interest in a fresh patch of mason work on the brownstone walls.

The prince cleared his throat and held a hand out in front. "Lead the way, stray."

"Where, Your Highness?"

"To the married woman's new home. I'd like to see where *Riga Hoff* lives."

"I don't know where they live."

Prince Gidon's eyes went wild. "Then let's find out. Lead the way to her old cottage, and we shall ask her father."

Achan blew out a deep breath and trudged to the Fenny home. It was very early and the outer bailey wasn't crowded, but whenever someone recognized the prince, they fell to their knees, head bowed. Achan reached the Fenny's cottage. He knocked on the door and stepped back.

The door opened a crack. "Achan! Is something wrong?" Gren's mother pulled the door in, but before she could step out, the prince pushed past her into the house. She squeaked and knelt in the doorway. "Your Highness! To what do I own such an honor?"

"You have a daughter, woman?" Prince Gidon's voice came from the back bedroom. He moved from one room to the next, searching. "Who sleeps in these rooms?"

Still on her knees, Gren's mother said, "I . . . my husband . . . He's gone to fetch water for the wash. I'd do it, but I sprained my wrist."

Achan took her elbow and helped her to her feet. "It'll be all right. Tell him."

She gulped and said, "M-My husband and I are on the left, and the other room belonged to my daughter, G-Grendolyn."

"Where is this Grendolyn?"

"She lives with her husband now."

"Show me."

"Certainly, Your Majesty." Gren's mother bowed and scurried from the house.

Achan waited for Prince Gidon to pass before closing the door behind him. Gren's mother led them though the maze of tiny thatched cottages to a fresh one crammed against the northern parapet wall. Sawdust peppered the dirt around the entrance. Instead of the wooden shutters that covered most cottage windows, sheets of undyed wool were nailed over the openings. The sound of maidens singing rose softly from inside.

Achan's stomach muscles tightened. He didn't want to go in and witness the celebration that was not yet over.

Gren's mother pushed the door in softly.

The prince grabbed Achan by the back of the neck and shoved him inside. The singing stopped. Candles flickered along the walls and floor, incense burned, and the pale faces of Gren's four maiden friends stared in shock from where they sat at the table.

"It's him," one of the girls said.

"What's he going to do?" said another.

This cottage looked just like all the others. It had a table and fireplace in the front room and a hallway leading to the bedrooms. The only difference was that it encompassed everything Achan could never have. He did not want to be here. He did not want this thrown in his face.

A third maiden squeaked. "It's the prince!"

The girls jumped from their chairs and knelt on the floor. Prince Gidon ignored them and scanned the room.

Harnu stood in the hallway before a closed door to one of the bedrooms. According to wedding night ritual, the best man must guard the happy couple from intruders. Harnu's face paled so quickly it almost made Achan laugh. Which would he honor: his duty to the groom or his duty to the prince?

The prince pushed him aside. He found the door locked and pounded on it. "Open up for Prince Gidon."

Achan wondered how often the prince had to announce himself.

Riga opened the door in his nightshirt. He flushed like a maid and awkwardly lowered his bulky form to his knees in the bedchamber doorway. The sight of Riga, the louse who stole Gren from him, shot fire through Achan's veins.

The prince stepped over Riga. He caught his jewel-encrusted boot on Riga's sleeve and tripped. Achan smirked—until he heard Gren's small scream.

Riga clambered to his feet just as Achan reached the door. The two crashed into each other. Achan clenched his fists and let Riga go first.

He followed him inside and found Gren on her knees in a long white nightgown. Prince Gidon towered above, one hand clutching her hair in his fist, the other hand perched on his hip. Riga paced at the foot of the bed like a scared bulldog, until the prince dropped Gren and rounded on him. Riga cowered.

"This cottage is unfinished," Prince Gidon said.

Gren's mother, gods bless her, was in rare form. She moved toward the prince. "They were so in love, Your Highness, that they couldn't wait for the house to be finished."

The prince forced a smile. "When was the happy day?"

No one spoke or met Prince Gidon's eyes. It was obvious the wedding guests were still here. Achan looked from Gren to Riga to Gren's mother.

Riga finally said, "Yesterday, Your Majesty."

Prince Gidon turned to Achan and raised a dark eyebrow. "I see." The prince looked down his nose at Gren and strode from the room, banging the front door closed behind him.

Achan shuddered and stepped toward the entrance.

"Achan, wait!" Gren hopped to her feet and gripped him in a hug, reminiscent of her mother's from that morning. Her hair smelled like orange blossoms, but her eyes were bloodshot. He gritted his teeth, not wanting to do or say anything that might get Gren in trouble. He wanted to carry her away from here. He wanted to kill Riga and take his place. He didn't like the way he felt like he was losing control.

"Thank you, Achan," Gren said.

He could only nod.

Gren released him. Her mother kissed both his cheeks. Then Riga opened the door and gave him to Harnu, who towed him out the front door and slammed it in his face.

Some gratitude.

Wanting to get as far away as possible, Achan ran through the maze of cottages, out the drawbridge, and toward the procession. He caught sight of the prince a few yards ahead and hung back.

But Prince Gidon rounded on him. "You think me a fool, stray? I know you did this. Stay close to me on this journey. If I even think you've deserted me, that 'happy couple' will be dead before you can bother to explain."

The prince stomped to his litter, which was now harnessed to two horses, one in front and one in back. He climbed inside and whipped the curtains closed. His jerky movements upset the animals, and Noam and two guards did their best to calm them.

Achan stood simmering in the morning sun. It was simple then. As long as he endured Gidon's wrath, Gren would be safe. So be it. He'd never have been free anyway. He might be leaving Sitna, but his life really wasn't changing. He was still a stray—only now his master would be a king instead of a cook. He didn't imagine things could get much worse. He looped the drawstring of Poril's bag of food over one shoulder and waited.

A cloud of dust billowed into the air at the front of the line. The caravan was moving. It took over ten minutes before the litter was able to move. Achan gave Noam one last wave and trudged along beside it. He didn't look back again.

16

Vrell reported to her master's chamber, only to find the dull, grey room empty. The only color in the room came from the sun shining though the windows on the eastern wall across from the chamber's entrance. Master Hadar's bed sat against the northern wall. The southern wall held a huge fireplace near the entrance, and a sideboard and shelves near the window wall. An alcove jutted out in the center of the southern wall, where an oak desk sat cluttered with scrolls.

She helped herself to a mug of water from the sideboard in the corner, then inched toward the fireplace, sipping her drink and taking everything in as she went. Halfway to the fireplace, she paused at her master's oak desk. A small stack of scrolls lay piled on one side. A bottle of ink with a quill poking out sat beside a sheet of parchment in the center of the desk. The letter had likely been left out to dry. The quill was plain. A gull's feather, perhaps. Mother always used a lovely peacock quill when she corresponded with—

The name on the top of the letter caught her eye: *Sir Luas Nathak, Lord of Sitna*. A chill raked her body. Lord Nathak? That man had pined for her mother's hand for years following Father's death. Vrell hated men who sought a wife when they already had one. It was the deepest form of cruelty and selfishness. Worse was the fact that Lord Nathak only wanted control of Carm. Apparently, he had advised his ward, Prince Gidon, to accomplish what he could not.

Lord Nathak's eerie mask and disfigurement did not help his reputation. Nor did his behavior since her mother's refusal. He had used threats to try to get his way. He had even resorted to force once, but Mother's guards had been quick and thorough.

In Vrell's mind, the man was pure evil. And his ward was worse. She walked around to the other side of the desk to read the letter.

> My Good Sir Luas,
>
> Thank you for accepting my invitation to meet. I look forward to your coming visit.
>
> Macoun Hadar

Vrell frowned and glanced at the stack of scrolls. Why did her master want to meet with Lord Nathak? She closed her eyes but sensed no sign of Master Hadar's cold-walled mind. So she set down her cup and reached for the scroll on the top of the stack. She unrolled it and read.

> Master Hadar,
>
> I will be travelling in the second party, sending our king ahead with his attendants and knights. Watch over him as he prepares to meet with the Council. All is going according to plan.
>
> Luas

Plan? What could these two men be plotting with Prince Gidon? Vrell shivered. The prince was coming to Mahanaim? Did that mean his coming-of-age celebration was at an end? Had he chosen a bride?

She lifted another scroll, but a coldness pressed in on her mind. Master Hadar was near. She quickly returned everything to its original position and hurried to the center window. The warmth of the sun and the drink now back in her hand calmed her thumping heart as the door squeaked open. She turned to see Carlani scooting inside.

"The master requires your presence."

Vrell set her mug on the sideboard and joined Carlani at the door. "Where is he?"

Carlani nodded across the antechamber to the second door, the one that led to the empty stone chamber. Vrell's lips parted. What would her master be doing in such a cold and empty room? He'd been so near while she'd read his letters?

Carlani inched his way across the antechamber, knocked twice on the door, and pushed it open. He raised his hand, urging Vrell to enter first. As she swept past, he whispered, "I'm not allowed to enter this room."

Carlani closed the door behind her, and Vrell fought the chill that tickled her spine. She turned to see Master Hadar sitting on a small stool, eyes closed. The room was empty, like a dungeon cell, but cleaner and without a cot or privy bucket.

A second stool sat empty beside Master Hadar. A lantern on the floor by his feet splashed golden flecks of light over his dark robes. She watched, fidgeting with the hem of her satin tunic. With the exception of his steadily rising and falling chest, and the occasional flicker of his eyelids, he remained motionless.

Vrell swallowed and began the mundane task of counting the bricks along the outer wall. She counted to sixty-three before her master spoke.

"This is my quiet room." He motioned to the stool beside him. "Bloodvoicing is best done in a room like this. No distractions."

Vrell sat on the squat stool, its lowness and her short height put her shoulder at Master Hadar's elbow. Something red glistened between his gnarled fingers: a ruby cabochon belt buckle. A jewel that exorbitant could only belong to royalty. She pointed at it. "Whose is that?"

Macoun opened his palm, displaying the cabochon under Vrell's nose. "This belongs to Prince Gidon Hadar."

Vrell shuddered. "Surely His Royal Highness would miss such a jewel?"

"On the contrary, boy. Prince Gidon has more jewels than he can keep track of, especially red ones. Besides, Lord Nathak of Sitna sent this to me. He's the young prince's caretaker. Do you know the story of how this came to be?"

"Aye." Vrell couldn't imagine a soul in Er'Rets who did not. Though she despised Prince Gidon, she wouldn't wish that kind of sorrow on anyone. Vrell herself had lost one parent, but to lose both at such a young age, without having known either . . . so sad.

Even more so to be raised by such a horrible man. It explained a great deal about Prince Gidon's callous reputation. Having those two in charge did not bode well for the future of Er'Rets.

"Lord Nathak depends upon my gift to look over the prince," Master Hadar said. "It helps to have another set of eyes when rumors of assassination blow like the wind."

If the prince wanted fewer enemies, he should try being more kind. Once he took the throne, the attempts on his life would no doubt increase. With a scepter in his hand, Prince Gidon would dole out one horrifying order after another. Vrell hoped to be safe at home by then.

Master Hadar nudged her shoulder and held out the cabochon. "Take it."

Vrell opened her hand, and her master dropped the heavy, smooth stone. She fingered it. It was lovely. An oval ruby set in engraved gold. So much artistry and money to hold up the prince's trousers. What a waste.

"Seek him."

Vrell's jaw dropped. She looked up at her master with wide eyes. "Seek the prince's mind? Surely that cannot be acceptable?"

"For a prince to be truly protected, much privacy is sacrificed. Trust me, this man cares not what anyone thinks of his actions. He won't feel violated. He won't even know. Besides, you might fail. This is a difficult task, seeking one you've never met. Concentrate."

Vrell swallowed the truth, hoping it did not show on her face. She *had* met the prince before, more times than she liked. She sucked in a deep breath and closed her eyes.

She sought his narrow face, his dark hair . . . and something rattled. A heaviness closed in on her mind. Grass, horses, and the faint smell of lavender gripped her senses. A purring rose around her, spasmodic—snoring. A light breeze rippled red curtains around the sleeping prince. Muted voices . . . laughter . . . the clomping of hooves along dirt.

Like a feather caught in a gust of wind, Vrell whipped out of the curtains and floated into a soldier's mind. Everyone around this young man rode a horse, yet he trudged along on foot in a cloud of dust, caked from head to toe. His cape was tossed up over his shoulders, covering his nose and mouth to keep from breathing the filthy air. His cheap boots hurt his feet. His heart overflowed with grief. He did not want to be here. He hated Prince Gidon.

What is your name? Vrell asked him.

The soldier tensed and drew up his walls, spitting Vrell out.

She flew into the air and into a black cloud. Her head nodded forward with a jerk, and she opened her eyes. She gasped, shocked at the fatigue gripping her bones. She looked up to find Master Hadar looking down on her hungrily.

"Well?"

"He travels, asleep in his litter." She held the stone out to her master, anxious to be rid of this draining connection with Prince Gidon and his soldier.

Master Hadar's jowls gathered into a devious smile as he accepted the stone. "Excellent! How quickly you succeeded. Delightful, the vigor of youth." He reached under his stool and pulled out a straw basket filled with small items. He tossed the cabochon in as if it were a mere pebble. "You'll practice with these. Try another. Tell me what you see. Take your time. We have all day."

Wary of taxing herself further, Vrell accepted the basket and studied the objects inside, careful not to touch any. There were dozens of swatches of cloth, a few ribbons, a turquoise bracelet, several brooches. Had these things all been pilfered from their owners? Would she have to resort to thievery to become proficient in bloodvoicing? And what about her energy? How would she last all day if one look at Prince Gidon drained her so? Or had it been his soldier who had drained her?

A lock of auburn hair in the basket caught her eye. She dug it out from under a swatch of leather, consumed by the color and curl. She lifted it to her nose, but it only smelled of the straw and metal surrounding it.

"A romantic, are you?" Master Hadar raised the skin above his eye where an eyebrow should be. "Go on then."

Vrell closed her eyes, gripped the silky hair, and thought of its russet color.

A familiar laugh grew in her mind. The subtle scent of grape blossoms brought a gasp to her lips. It was Mother!

A warm breeze flittered across her mother's face, blowing her auburn hair about. Honeybees buzzed around her. Someone held her arm. A friend.

It's been a warm spring, Mother said. *We've had an incredible crop. Lost nothing so far. But once the grapes set, we'll have to put out bird nets.*

Lady Coraline's voice came loud, as though spoken in Vrell's ear. *Bird nets?*

To keep them from eating the grapes, Mother said. *Orioles and cardinals are the worst. I cannot blame them—the grapes are very sweet. Everything will have to be netted.*

Is that difficult?

Yes. It takes the workers several weeks to cover all the crops.

The smell is enchanting. All these years, and I still haven't gotten used to the fishy smell of—

The sun blazed overhead. Vrell was not with her mother anymore. She was back with Prince Gidon's caravan. And the young soldier. He tossed his cape up over his shoulders again to let his skin breathe. He wore far too many layers for such a journey on foot. His linen shirt clung to his chest with sweat.

Why had he pulled her away from Mother? *What do you want?* she asked him.

The soldier tensed, but this time he spoke back. *What do I want? It's you who are in my head. I didn't invite you.*

Yes, you did. Stop pulling me here.

Vrell tried to leave, to focus again on Mother and Lady Coraline, but she hit something hard. Her eyes flashed open and she wheezed.

She found herself lying on her back on the cold floor of the chamber. She tried to lift her head but couldn't. She opened her hand, and the lock of hair fell to the floor. Good. She still had some control of her limbs.

Master Hadar peered down from his stool, the golden glow of the lantern casting black fissures over his lumpy skin. "What did you see?"

Vrell closed her eyes and tried not to show her alarm. Why did Master Hadar have a lock of her mother's hair? Was he spying on her? And why hadn't she tried to communicate to Mother when she'd had the chance? She breathed deeply until the pressure faded from her mind. When she opened her eyes again, she met her master's hollowed eye sockets. They were wide, watching.

"I couldn't see . . . " She took a deep breath, half exhausted, half exaggerating her state. "Why does this weaken me so?"

"Perhaps you've not practiced enough. There are ways to get stronger. I'll teach you everything in good time. Let us stop for breakfast. Food gives strength as well, and you've not eaten, have you?"

Vrell shook her head.

Master Hadar rose and swept to the door. "Breakfast then." He left her lying on the floor.

She stared at the timber ceiling and shivered.

How dangerous this bloodvoicing business was. Not only did it weaken her, but also she had almost given away her identity. Master Hadar could not sense her thoughts, but she supposed he might be able to jump through her to Mother. Maybe it was best that she hadn't had time to try to send her a message.

And what of that soldier? Who was he? How could he pull her mind into his without meaning to? Clearly he knew nothing of his own power. Could he be the one called *Achan,* whom Master Hadar thought was a boy? Surely one so powerful wouldn't be relegated to walking in the dust while so many horses and wagons were available with the prince's entourage.

It was nice to know the crop at home was good. Carmine would eat well for the next year unless a storm came, which was doubtful now that they were well into spring.

Vrell's energy returned quickly, and she joined Master Hadar and Carlani for breakfast. The master had business afterward and sent her away. With relief, she went outside the keep.

The courtyard was bustling with activity. Vrell wove between people, horses, and wagons, looking at the things for sale. She was thankful she had the bag of coins from Lord Orthrop. She purchased small linen cloth and a sage tooth scrub so that she could clean her teeth. She also bought a small antler bone comb. She could hardly wait for the cleansing she would give herself that night.

She came to Dâthos's temple. The round structure, surrounded in regal pillars, was beautiful, but it gave Vrell a chill. Vendors had set up booths on all sides selling gold, silver, and bronze cups in all shapes and sizes. People plunked down a lot of coins to give temple offerings to gods who were false. Guards stood at the entrance, keeping the peasants, slaves, and strays from entering. Such lowly worshippers left offerings around the outside of the temple instead.

Vrell walked on. She enjoyed the feel of the breeze, but it was not the same as the haunting smells from home. Mahanaim was a port city, and as such it smelled of fish and the rancid saltwater that filled the canals. Vrell bided her time, browsing the carts of merchants selling furs, fabrics, wooden bowls and cups, tools, and weapons.

She paused at the local smith's workshop and watched from a distance as he pounded red-hot iron into a long shape. She stepped closer, enthralled by the flying sparks.

The smith's apprentice was a short, husky boy in his early teens. The youth filed another blade. He glanced up through sweaty dark blond hair, meeting Vrell's gaze with a bored expression before turning back to his work.

Vrell stepped closer. "Do you sell any swords, sir?"

The smith looked up. His dark skin was caked in sweat, black smudges, and pockmarks from sparks that had scarred his skin. "You're in the market?"

"Aye. My master wants I should buy one."

The boy glanced at Vrell again, this time with curious eyes. "Who's your master?"

"Jax mi Katt," Vrell said.

The boy's mouth lifted in a one-sided grin.

The master smith turned to her, his face wrinkling with amusement. "*You're* training in the Kingsguard?" He looked at her disdainfully.

"Aye," Vrell said, straightening her posture.

"Why come to me? Kingsguard knights get their weapons from Kingsguard smiths."

Oh. Well, if Vrell had known that, she would not have weaved such a tale. She furrowed her brow. "I am not training to be a knight. Still, my master says I should buy one. He is going to show me a thing or two once I get myself a sword."

"Is he now? And just how much money do you have, boy?"

Vrell was no fool. "First tell me the cost."

The smith laughed. "And if I said a sword costs a hundred silvers?"

Vrell smirked and glanced at the apprentice, who had stopped filing to watch this exchange. "Then I would have to keep looking, for that price is thievery. Surely you are not the only one selling weapons this fine morning. Maybe I would do better to purchase a bow or axe."

At this, the young apprentice burst into laughter. "You'd be struck down thrice over before managing to swing a battle axe. Even a bow requires more muscle than you have. I suggest a set of handaxes or a dagger. Perhaps you could use them while your enemy sleeps?"

Vrell huffed and said to the smith, "Thank you, sir, for your time." She turned away, scanning the carts for a peddler with premade weapons.

"Come now," the smith called after her. "Don't mind the boy. If you've got ten silvers, we can make you a fine short sword. Nothing fancy, but it would hold its own for you to learn on."

Vrell turned back to the smith and beamed. "When can I have it?"

The smith took the blade he was working on and thrust it into a drum of water, sending a cloud of hissing steam around his face. "Pay half up front, and you'll get it in a week."

"Agreed." Vrell pulled out her coin purse and counted out five silvers.

"I'm going to teach you two new things today," Master Hadar said.

It was after breakfast. They were sitting in the empty cell across from Master Hadar's chambers. The room was cold and dark, but for the lantern.

"These are very important to the work you'll be doing for me. First, you must learn to recognize a *knock*. This is when someone is trying to message you while your mind is closed. And you must also learn to *message,* to speak to one person without anyone picking up on your conversation. First we will practice messaging."

Vrell fought to keep herself from beaming. She was going to learn to contact Mother! She waited patiently for Master Hadar to explain.

"Speaking to one person at a time is all about concentration and control. You must allow one person inside, blocking off an area for them in your mind, careful to hide everything else from them. The stronger your mind, the easier this is to do. You will exercise by jumping from one individual conversation to another, trying to keep them each private as you go. You'll practice today with Sir Jax, Khai, and myself. Once you understand the concept, we will practice knocking."

Master Hadar brought out his basket of trinkets and dug through it. He selected a little stone horse and a charm made from feathers and beads and set them on the table. "The horse belongs to Jax. The charm is Khai's. Reaching me shouldn't be difficult since I'm right here. Begin."

Vrell practiced. With bloodvoicing, that seemed the only way to learn.

She gripped the little stone horse and focused on Jax's face. *Jax mi Katt*, she called to the picture she visualized in her mind. *Jax mi Katt.*

Hello, Vrell. Jax's voice boomed in her head. It startled her so much she dropped the horse and lost the connection.

"Well?" Master Hadar said.

"It worked!" Vrell said. "But I lost him." She picked up the stone horse. "Are you certain he cannot know all my thoughts when he speaks to me?"

"Not if you are guarding them."

Vrell tried again and had a successful conversation with Jax. Master Hadar made her practice that for a while, then he moved on to conversations with multiple people at once. She spoke to Jax and Master Hadar at the same time.

Khai made things difficult, always barging in uninvited. Vrell solved this problem by setting up a cottage in her mind and organizing her thoughts into rooms. A *knock*, as Master Hadar called it, felt like a heavy itch to her ears or a quick stab to her temple, depending on whether it came from Jax or Khai. It was followed by the voice of the person trying to reach her saying her name. This was what Mother had been doing to reach Vrell, but Vrell hadn't known how to answer at the time.

Khai knocked over and over, bringing a dull headache to Vrell within minutes. To combat him, she added a foyer to her cottage. The next time Khai knocked, she invited him inside there to wait his turn. Soon she had Khai and Master Hadar waiting in the foyer while Vrell and Jax had a private discussion about skinning reekats.

Master Hadar was thrilled with Vrell's progress. Although she got better and better at the process, her energy continued to drain just as fast. Master Hadar could find no reason for this.

It had been a blessing, finally learning to bloodvoice someone securely. Vrell made good use of her new skill that very night.

Alone in her chamber, she fortified her mind. When she was certain no one could overhear, she focused on the memory of her mother's face and called out to her.

Within seconds she got an answer.

Vrell? Is that you, dearest?

Mother! Vrell laughed though her tears. *Mother, forgive me. I have been so frightened. I wanted to answer you, but . . . Oh, Mother. I am in Mahanaim. I have been taken as a bloodvoice apprentice to Macoun Hadar. Do you know of him? I had wanted to confess to Lord Orthrop when the Kingsguards came to fetch me, but I was afraid. You had said to trust Coraline, but I did not know how Lord Orthrop would respond.*

You are still disguised as a boy?

Yes. I am almost certain that none suspect. Master Hadar is training me. I learned just today how to message.

My dear child, tell me everything.

Vrell started at the beginning and told her mother all she had gone through from Walden's Watch to her new training with Master Hadar.

I know of no man named Macoun Hadar, Mother said. *You say he is old?*

He must be in his eighties.

I will write my brother and ask if Father ever spoke of such a man. I am not sure where else to inquire. You say the giant cautioned you against him?

Yes. Jax said that Macoun Hadar was not to be trusted.

I do not like this, my love. I want you home.

What shall I do?

Prince Oren will be in Mahanaim soon for the Council meeting. You should be able to find him without much difficulty. I will tell him to be looking out for you. Sir Rigil will be there as well. He may be more easily approached by a stray than the prince. Find him or Prince Oren, and either will see you safely from Mahanaim.

But you will be coming as well, will you not? Mother held a seat on the Council of Seven. If they were meeting, she would be there.

Only if I can be assured that my land will be safe in my absence. Lord Nathak is up to no good. Though I know he will be at the Council meeting, I do not trust him. His men have been spotted on our land. They claim to be hunting. If I think there is any danger of trouble, I will not leave. I will send my proxy with Anillo.

Anillo was Mother's trusted advisor, a man Vrell had recently discovered had the ability to bloodvoice. He was a logical choice to send in Mother's place as he would be able to instantly relay to her all that was taking place.

Vrell did not like to hear of trouble at home. Regardless, after that talk with her mother, she slept soundly for the first time in months. Her days as a boy were numbered now. Soon she would be going home.

17

Achan traipsed alongside the prince's litter, dust from the horses clouding him in a fog. He threw his cloak up over his nose to try and filter the air, but the dust stung his eyes as well. He considered walking a few yards out, but he didn't want Gidon to think he was running away.

He tried not to focus on anything, but his mind kept flitting back to Gren. He didn't want to dwell on her, that he'd never see her again, that she was Riga's wife. He gritted his teeth and counted to twenty, hoping to distract himself. He wanted to leave. He hated Prince Gidon.

A scratchy voice said, *What's your name?*

Achan froze at the voice in his mind and thought of the allown tree.

"Hey! Keep moving!"

Achan turned to see a mule in his face. The beast was pulling a cart. The man steering held up both hands. "Is there a problem?"

"No. Sorry." Achan scurried after the litter and resumed his pace beside it, tensing against the flood of voices that were sure to fill his mind. Were they going to come back? What had kept them gone for so long?

A charcoal palfrey trotted off to the side of the procession, traveling in the opposite direction. Achan recognized the squire from Carmine, Bran Rennan. He steered the strong horse toward Achan. Bran looked bigger than he truly was on such an animal, though no squire could hope to look fierce with a peeling, sunburned nose like Bran had. He turned the animal to walk alongside Achan. "You were given no horse?"

Achan looked up. "You're observant."

Bran frowned. "Sir Rigil suspected as much. He sent me to check on you. Have you got water?"

"No." Achan hadn't thought to ask Poril for a water jug.

Bran lifted a strap from over his neck and lowered a water skin down to Achan. "You're welcome to it. We always carry plenty anyway, and this is a short trip, so running out isn't a concern."

Achan draped the strap over his head and worked the cork free. "Thanks."

"I'll see you at camp."

Achan nodded. Bran's horse cantered away. Achan hadn't expected to befriend anyone. The idea lightened his mood somewhat. He guzzled half the water and replaced the cork in time to dodge a trail of horse dung. The sun blazed above. He tossed his cape back up over his shoulders and reveled in the cool air on his arms. His linen shirt clung to his chest, drenched in sweat.

What do you want? the scratchy voice demanded.

Achan tensed, but this time he left the connection open. *What do* I *want? It's you who are in my head. I didn't invite you.*

Yes, you did. Stop pulling me here.

Achan waited for the voice to speak again, but it didn't. He constructed a theory. Somehow, the tonic quieted the voices. Since he hadn't consumed it this morning, the voices were coming back. But why Lord Nathak insisted he take the tonic, and why Sir Gavin insisted he didn't, baffled him. He considered Noam's mention of bloodvoices, but the idea seemed too far-fetched. This was life, not a bedtime story. There were no such things as bloodvoices.

Or strange voices who rejected other gods.

In the early afternoon, the procession paused at the foot of the Chowmah Mountains to water the horses at a rocky stream. Achan was drawn to the forest. It was thick with allown trees. He wished he could someday live in such a place.

Achan came back from filling his new water skin to find a chamber pot sitting outside Prince Gidon's litter. He thought nothing of it until Chora came by and said, "What are you standing around for? Do you think this empties and cleans itself?"

Mortified, Achan carried the stinking bronze pot toward the river. He dumped it in the bushes and sloshed it about downriver. When he returned, a young lord and lady stood talking to the prince. Chora had drawn back the curtains on the litter to each side, and the prince sat on the floor of the litter like it was a throne.

Thin and tall with shocking orange hair, the young lord pleaded his case. "It's just that the heat is so much stronger than we expected. Kati nearly fainted twice from heat stroke, and this the first day of the journey. I fear she may fall from her horse."

Achan wondered why the fool had insisted on bringing along his wife—dressed in twenty-five pounds of embroidered wool—when all the other women had waited to travel in the slower moving party.

"I would love to have company." Prince Gidon offered his hand to the pretty, plump, grey-skinned lady. "I am bored to weeping in here all alone. Gods know my squire is as dull as the dust coating his hair."

Lady Kati burst into a screeching giggle and spoke with a strange accent. "Oh, Your Highness. You are being so funny."

Achan groaned inwardly. His only hope was that with the lady present, Prince Gidon would make less use of his chamber pot.

Soon it was time to move on again. The prince drew the curtains shut as he and his guest conversed. As the day wore on, Achan grew ill of the lady's laugh and more so at the idea of what the prince could possibly say or do to illicit such reactions.

They made camp early at a clearing on the edge of the Sideros Forest. The mountains rose up to the north. The sun had already begun to sink behind them. A grassy prairie stretched out to the south as far as Achan could see. It was filled with the sweet-smelling white blooms of daisies, asters, and yarrow.

Some of the knights went hunting for dinner. Night fell quickly. Achan wasn't sure what to do with himself. A group of soldiers erected a massive red tent for Prince Gidon, but the prince yelled at Achan when he tried to help. So he lay down in the grass between the litter and the tent and stared at the stars. Lady Kati and Prince Gidon's voices murmured inside the new tent, interrupted by the lady's occasional high-pitched giggle.

Achan's stomach growled. He sat up and drew Poril's bag of food close. He looked at all the tents in the clearing. There were several striped tents, some of the same ones that had been set up on the tournament field. There were also many smaller, white, soldiers' tents. The soldiers had also driven poles into the ground that held single torches at the top. These lit up the camp. Achan pulled out a meat pie from his bag and bit into it. The gravy had jelled, but the flavor was decent. He was considering reading Gren's letter, when Bran came over and sat beside him.

Bran held out an apple. "Want it?"

"Thanks." Achan took the fruit and held it in his lap.

"If you don't mind my asking, what happened to Sir Gavin?"

Achan looked at the squire's peeling nose and shrugged. "I don't know. Lord Nathak said he left and wouldn't return."

"I heard Lord Nathak sent him away."

"Really?" That made much more sense. "He left me a note saying . . ." Achan paused, not wanting to admit he could hardly read. "Well, it wasn't clear where he went or why."

Bran propped his elbows on his knees. "Sir Gavin can bloodvoice. Do you know anyone else who can? Maybe he'd try to contact you through them."

A cold tingle seized Achan. "I thought . . . Aren't bloodvoices a myth?"

"Of course not. Haven't you heard of the Council's bloodvoice mediators?"

"No."

"They use bloodvoicing to tell if someone is lying. Very useful. I take it you don't know anyone who could bloodvoice, then."

Achan was beginning to suspect that he could himself, although the idea still seemed outrageous. He met Bran's questioning brown eyes. "I-I'm not sure. Maybe."

Bran nudged Achan's leg. "So have him contact Sir Gavin for you. Then you wouldn't have to wonder."

Contact Sir Gavin? How?

Bran made small talk about the journey and Mahanaim. Achan was fascinated with his description of a city built in water, half of which was in Darkness. Sir Rigil called Bran for an errand, and Achan went back to his cold dinner. He tried to talk to Sir Gavin with his mind, but succeeded only in feeling foolish.

Apparently he dozed off, because the shout of "Stray!" shocked him out of a slumber. He sat up straight and looked about. Prince Gidon stood outside his tent, holding a decorative jug. "Fetch some water."

There was no river near camp. "From where?"

"Am I king? Use your head, dimwit."

Achan got to his feet and snatched the jug. He wove between tents until he found a large bonfire where the Kingsguards' cook had prepared dinner. A meaty gravy smell hung in the air. A crowd of knights, squires, and Kingsguard soldiers congregated around the bonfire, laughing and eating and drinking. A soldier-turned-minstrel thumbed a lute and sang:

The heir to Shamayim fallen and slain,
Failure and tragedy meld with his name.

Achan approached the cook. "Pardon me, sir. Could you spare a jug of water for Prince Gidon?"

"Help yourself," the cook said without looking up from turning the spit.

Achan filled the jug from a cask and started back to Prince Gidon's tent. A sinister pressure built in his head as he walked. Someone meant him harm. He slipped between two tents, hoping to avoid trouble.

A beefy, olive-skinned knight with long, dark hair slicked back over his head stepped out from behind a green tent, arms folded. Achan turned to weave the other way, but the young squire from Barth, who'd defeated Bran in the sword fighting pen, stood in that path, his black hair puffed out like a seeding dandelion.

Looming behind that squire like a shadow stood a towering full-grown knight version. An older brother, Achan assumed. The torchlight flickered off his black armor. He wore no helmet. Could a helmet even fit over such hair? Achan should have taken the time at the tournament to match faces with the names Sir Gavin had spoken of. He turned again, head pounding, only to narrowly miss crashing into Silvo Hamartano, who must have slithered up behind.

"Servant or squire?" Silvo asked in his silky voice. "Which is it, stray? One minute you're in a tournament for nobles, then you're serving wine. Now you cart around a priceless sword and a jug of water. Why?"

"The prince is thirsty, I suppose, or wants to wash."

"And always so witty."

Achan sighed. "I'm the gods' plaything, meant only to amuse."

All four men closed in. Someone pulled Achan's hair tail from behind, jerking his head back. Silvo snatched the water jug away before Achan could use it as a weapon and passed it to the squire from Barth. The older brother backhanded Achan with his black iron gauntlet.

The force blasted Achan's jaw, which was still sore from when Sir Kenton had struck him. He crashed back into the green tent and slid down the coarse fabric.

Despite the throbbing, he rolled into a crawl and darted between legs, hoping to escape. Someone grabbed the waist of his trousers. A boot met his temple, another his ribs.

He gritted his teeth through the blows and grabbed the closest pair of ankles. He ducked his head between the low boots, protecting his skull for the moment. He wanted to draw Eagan's Elk, but it was too long to wield from his position. Instead he bit down on one of the legs beside his head. Unfortunately, this not only lost him his shield, but he took a boot to the ear.

He spotted a good-sized rock, grabbed it, and pitched it up over his head. Someone grunted and the rock clumped into the dirt to Achan's left. He reached for it again, but a black boot crushed his hand. He sucked back a cry, gripped the ankle with his other hand, and pulled, managing to scrape his hand free. A strike to his lower back knocked the breath from his lungs.

The zing of a sword leaving its scabbard paralyzed him.

"Can we play too?"

Achan didn't recognize the voice, but the assault stopped long enough for him to pull to his knees. The movement burned his pummeled torso. Two more weapons sang from their scabbards.

"This is not your concern, Sir Rigil," an oily voice said. "Take your sunburned squire elsewhere, lest you lose him. I hear he's slower with a sword than this stray."

Steel clashed against steel. Achan took advantage of the swordplay to crawl free and rise to his rubbery legs. He licked his bleeding lip and looked into the brawl.

Bran and Silvo squared off against one another, as did the olive-skinned knight with Bran's companion, whom Achan guessed was Sir Rigil. All four tangled in a fierce dance. Bran was faring far better tonight than he had in the tournament. Maybe he didn't like being compared to a stray.

Sir Rigil, who looked to be in his early thirties, had a wild air about him. A thin, reddish beard shaded his jaw, but his hair was short and blond. He wore midnight blue trimmed in black. Golden lightning bolts studded his black leather belt.

The black-armored knight turned from watching the scuffle and locked eyes with Achan. He drew a black sword.

Limbs shaking, Achan tugged Eagan's Elk from his sheath and scrambled back. "Have we met?" Achan asked.

"No." The knight grunted the word.

"Then why—"

The knight lashed out, his sleek blade whipping through the air, the tip slicing into the green tent. Achan parried and ducked. The swords clanged, and Eagan's Elk vibrated in Achan's sore hands. He gripped it tighter and blocked another series of strikes. He had no desire to attack, only to evade and deflect. His opponent's blade clipped his chin.

Achan growled. He was still misjudging his parries. The closeness of the tents offered little room for anything but a massacre. Achan needed to get away, but the black-armored knight had blocked him in. Why were these men trying to kill him?

Clashing swords rang out all around, but Achan couldn't be bothered by any battle but his own. Sweat or blood, or a combination, dripped off his chin. The knight attacked fiercely. The blades blurred in between them, and Achan's burning arms could barely hold off the knight's relentless rhythm.

Again and again his parry fell back under the force of his opponent's strikes, and the black blade nicked him in small, teasing cuts. His forehead, his knee, his shin, his forearm. Achan ground his teeth. Why couldn't he get it right? After a rapid combination of attacks and parries, Achan's grip slipped. The knight lunged past Achan's guard and sliced his bicep.

Achan yelped, more in shock than pain, and reeled back. He tripped over a tent peg and crashed to the ground. The knight leaped forward. He pressed his blade against Achan's throat and stepped on his wounded arm.

Achan choked back a scream. Swords clashed behind the black-armored knight, but Achan couldn't see their wielders. He stretched for Eagan's Elk, but his blade was out of reach.

He looked into the knight's grey eyes. He saw no hatred. Only an expression of superiority. Maybe he wouldn't kill him. Maybe he was only toying with him.

Achan panted out, "Looks like you win this time."

The knight only stared. Apparently, conversation was not on his list of skills.

"What's this?" Prince Gidon's regal voice pierced the mêlée, and the swordfight ceased. The prince stepped around the black-armored knight and peered down at Achan, his crown and jeweled belt glittering in the torchlight. He raised one dark eyebrow. "Well, Sir Nongo, I see you've bested my squire. What has he done now? Made fun of your hair?"

Sir Nongo, the black-armored knight, turned to the prince. "My hair, Your Highness?"

"Forgive me, Your Majesty." Silvo stepped forward and bowed. "Your *squire* insulted me and my sister, Jaira."

The prince's brows shot up to his greasy hairline. "Lady Jaira is here?"

"No, Your Highness. This was days ago."

"Yet you waited for Sir Nongo to do your dirty work?" The prince gave Silvo a bored stare. "I'm sure your claim is valid, Silvo. My squire does have a hinged tongue and a tendency for insubordination. Regardless, he's all I have. Lord Nathak sent no one but Chora and this stray to serve me. So unless any of you wish to take my squire's place, I suggest you let him live. I could care less who serves me. Any of you will do, and this stray does vex me greatly." The prince looked from face to face. "No volunteers?" He sighed. "I suspected as much. Let him up, then."

Sir Nongo stepped back, and Achan staggered to his feet. He retrieved Eagan's Elk and sheathed it with shaky arms. The cut on his arm stung terribly. Blood soaked his sleeve to the elbow. The knights and squires dispersed, leaving Achan alone with Prince Gidon. Achan was glad to see that none of those who had come to his aid appeared to be wounded.

The prince sighed and strode off in the direction of his tent. "Don't forget my water, stray."

Achan found the water jug, still full, and lugged it after the prince using his good arm. His torso ached with every step. He spat blood out on the ground.

Those who crossed their path fell to their knees before the prince.

He turned to Achan and pointed. "See how my people revere me, stray?" He cocked his head to the side. "Why is it that you do not do the same?"

Achan shrugged, though the gesture stung his arm. He did his best to be obedient. If the prince wasn't such a beast, he might try harder.

Prince Gidon persisted. "You have never once kneeled in my presence. Why?"

Achan didn't answer as they approached the litter. It was true. He'd never kneeled before Prince Gidon, yet when Sir Gavin had introduced Prince Oren, Achan had fallen straight to his knees. Strange. "I dunno, Yer Highest." He spat out another mouthful of blood. It hurt to talk.

The prince threw up his hands. "You don't know. Well, I demand you start!"

Achan set the jug on the ground and lowered his bruised body to his knees, one at a time.

The prince looked down his pointed nose at Achan and sighed. "Oh, get up!"

"As yoo yish, Yer Highest."

"And shut up!"

Achan was more than happy to, but raised one eyebrow just for fun.

That night the voices came in his mind, louder and more persistent than ever before. Achan remained open and silent, trying to listen for Sir Gavin, but the knight didn't speak.

The person with the scratchy voice did. *You have learned to close your mind, have you?* Scratch said.

Aye. Achan was finding it easier to send thoughts back. *I was just listening for someone.*

Who?

I'd rather not say.

A woman's voice spoke, *Who are you?*

What's your name? a man asked.

You're very talented. I should like to know you.

Can you all just be quiet? Achan said. *I'd like to talk to Scratch.*

Who is Scratch?

Block us out then. Have you no one to teach you?

Oh, never mind. Achan reached out for the allown tree.

The next morning, Chora and the Shield found Achan as the caravan readied to leave.

Chora held up a flask. "You are to drink this." Chora twisted off the cap and offered it.

The Shield stepped toward Achan. "Now."

Achan snatched the vial and smelled it. The tonic. If he took it, he wouldn't be able to hear if Sir Gavin called to him. But his body had already been pounded like clay. He didn't need to give Sir Kenton another reason to strike. He swallowed the bitter goop and handed the vial back. Chora nodded to Sir Kenton and they both walked away. No mentha. Clearly these fellows didn't have all the facts.

He considered digging out a bread roll, but without any mentha leaves, the tonic would likely come up soon. Why waste breakfast?

Sure enough, a few minutes later, Achan retched into the bushes.

The morning was cool and cloudy. The procession was all lined up and ready to go. Achan hoped he could manage to keep up. His body ached terribly.

Bran approached. "Are you all right? Did they hit your head last night?"

Achan spat the nastiness from his mouth. "No. Ate something sour. Thanks for last night, by the way. I'd likely be dead if you and Sir Rigil hadn't stepped in."

Bran nodded, then said in a low voice, "Do you enjoy serving your prince?"

Achan furrowed his brow. "Aye. So much as I enjoy the tip of a sword against my throat."

Bran smirked and scratched the back of his head. He glanced around and stepped closer. "Sir Rigil says, should you seek a different master, he'd welcome you."

"Leave Prince Gidon to serve Sir Rigil?"

"Not exactly. We're joining with the Old Kingsguard. Sir Gavin's Kingsguard. They serve Prince Oren."

Prince Oren? Second in line to the throne behind only Gidon. Achan's mind raced. Could this be a conspiracy rising up against Prince Gidon? How he'd love to be a part of that. But for Gren. "I . . . can't. Prince Gidon, he . . . threatened my friend back in Sitna if I should try to . . . leave his service."

"Who?"

"Gren Fen—Hoff. The Fenny and the Hoff family."

Bran nodded, his brow pinched. "Prince Gidon's good at scaring people. He learned from the best." Bran looked away and sighed. "With your permission, I'll convey this information to Sir Rigil. There may be something he could do to help."

"I don't know what anyone could do, but you have my permission."

A cloud of dust in the distance signaled that the caravan had pulled out. Bran glanced at Achan one last time. "Sir Rigil says the Great Whitewolf was the greatest Kingsguard commander ever. You're fortunate to have learned from him, even for a short time."

Achan nodded and watched Bran jog to his horse. If he could contact Sir Gavin, he might know what to do with himself. Join the Old Kingsguard? Had that been Sir Gavin's plan all along?

The procession marched on. Achan emptied the prince's chamber pot, fetched water, and delivered message scrolls to Lady Kati, passing her husband's angry remarks back to an amused Prince Gidon. The voices seemed to be coming to him again. At least he'd still be able to listen for Sir Gavin and talk to Scratch.

Achan's left bicep looked wretched. Sir Nongo's black blade had sliced a deep gash three fingers wide. Achan had cleaned it as best he could, but the pink skin around the incision boasted his failure. Most of the smaller cuts had healed. His torso was badly bruised and sore, but the bones seemed to be in place—not that he knew what broken bones felt like. His face and jaw ached. Thankfully, mirrorglass was scarce on the road. Achan didn't want to know how his face looked.

He tried to speak to Scratch. They managed a few words here and there, but someone in the caravan always interrupted. So far Scratch had told him nothing useful. Achan wasn't enjoying bloodvoices much. Perhaps he was too practical to invite dozens of people into his head. He had so little control and privacy in his life. His mind was the one thing people couldn't beat, manipulate, or force to obey. He didn't want people trampling his last sanctuary.

He hadn't heard from that other warm and powerful voice since Cetheria's temple. Was Cetheria really an idol? That would certainly explain a few things. He shrugged and walked on, choking on the dust of the road.

As they neared Allowntown, the Evenwall loomed to their right. The Evenwall, as Achan understood it, was a gateway to Darkness and all that hid within it. The air grew thick and misty. Achan didn't like the feel of the moisture on his face. He remembered Sir Gavin's warning never to set foot in the mist.

In the wide prairie to their left, women worked the potato fields, their skirts hiked up above their knees. Several soldiers hooted and called out to them. Pretty as some of them were, they only reminded Achan of how fetching Gren had looked as she stood in a tub of wool. He was thankful when the sun set on the day and the memories.

They stopped in Allowntown for the night. The procession filed through a narrow gate and into an old motte and bailey-style manor. Guards began to pitch tents within the wooden curtain wall. Prince Gidon dismissed Achan and went inside the manor to sleep. Achan wandered around, looking for Bran.

A distant allown tree caught his eye between two tents. He stepped back and stared at it from afar. It was the famous tree, the one from all the stories of King Axel's murder, the day Darkness came. Achan walked to the tree and stood before it, mesmerized.

Warmth surged inside him and the majestic voice coursed through his veins.

Before I formed you in the womb I knew you, Achan Cham. Before you were born I set you apart.

Achan sucked in a sharp breath and glanced around. No one was paying him any mind. The heat inside him was already fading. Was that all the voice had to say? Set apart? Like this tree, set off from all the other trees? He looked up at it.

Half of the tree was dead. Half was alive. This was surely the tree from the legends. The living half, so like the allown tree back on the Sideros River, calmed him. But the other half . . .

Gnarled, black branches twisted in the air like monstrous claws, the mist so thick around them, they blurred into the black sky. A heavy wind rustled the leaves on the living side, but the barren branches on the dead side cracked and swayed like they were reaching, hoping to squeeze the life out of Achan.

He shivered, torn. It was as if the tree was his heart. He'd always felt a kinship with allown trees, as ridiculous as that sounded. This one, more so. But it repelled him at the same time. It was a most awkward emotion.

Despite the dead side of the tree, Achan lay down on the soft grass under the rustling leaves, feeling like he'd finally come home, and fell asleep.

Yet into his peace came horrifying dreams.

The voices called out. He tried to concentrate on the allown tree in Sitna to silence them, but an image of this eerie tree filled his mind instead. They knew he was here. Under the allown tree, where life meets death.

A woman screamed. A baby cried. A horrific sound split the night like one massive roar of thunder.

Warriors would go through the mist and bring back food. The women and children would have to wait until their return. The pale ones were hungry.

They were coming.

Part 5

The Gifted One

18

Vrell moaned and rolled all night, so vivid were the voices, the fear, the hunger in her mind. Something terrible was about to befall the young soldier. A sharp prick to her temples woke her.

Macoun Hadar.

Master Hadar was knocking. She let him inside the foyer of her mind.

Boy! he bloodvoiced. *Did you hear him? The gifted one?*

He must mean the soldier. *Yes, Master.*

Come to my chambers at once.

Vrell dressed and hurried to the eighth floor. She had not told Master Hadar about her conversations with the soldier, but she was almost certain he was the one her master sought.

She found Master Hadar sitting on the end of his bed, grotesque feet propped on the stone slab. A lantern hung on a stand beside his bed. His eyes were wide and glassy in the dim light. Out the windows, the sky was charcoal grey. Dawn had not yet broken.

"Vrell," Master Hadar said, "you'll go north with Jax mi Katt and find this gifted boy. He's in danger, and we must locate him quickly."

"You know his whereabouts?"

"He slept in Allowntown last night, under the Memorial Tree. Prince Gidon's party camped there. If he's with them, they'll be headed here, so finding them should be no problem. Go and bring him to me."

"How will I know who he is?"

"Don't be a fool. With your mind, boy, how else?"

"Yes, Master." Vrell bowed out of the chamber.

She went to her room and fetched her pouch of healing herbs and ointments. If there had been a battle, she might be able to help the wounded. She filled her water skin in the courtyard fountain. She wished her sword was finished. Going into a battle without a weapon, or with a weapon but without the training to use it, seemed terribly foolish. She found Jax at the stables and was shocked to see a squadron of Kingsguard knights ready to depart.

"Vrell!" Jax greeted her with a smile. "We journey again."

The familiar, little, white courser Jax presented thrilled Vrell's heart. He reminded her of Kopay, her horse back home. Jax sat atop a massive, black festrier. Vrell felt like she was riding a colt in comparison.

The strain the young soldier brought to her mind pressed against her all morning, but she could not see him clearly. His power was close, though, and she sensed great fear. Judging from the concern on Jax's face, he could too. He did not try to pace the horses but galloped north at top speed.

After an hour of hard riding, Jax pulled up at the top of a hill overlooking a vast green valley. Vrell stopped beside him.

Darkness rose like a wall to the west, stretching for miles in each direction, separated from the green prairie and forest by the vaporous Evenwall. There was no sign of Prince Gidon's procession. A great foreboding hung over the squadron like a cloud. Vrell opened her mind slightly to those who were gifted. All sensed the same thing from their fellow Kingsguards who escorted Prince Gidon: fear.

"What is it?" Vrell asked Jax.

"Poroo."

Vrell's heart quaked. The poroo had once been a peaceful race of men, but Darkness had driven them mad. It was rumored they ate anything they could catch, humans included. "But they live in Darkness."

"Aye. That they do. They must be very hungry to cross into Light."

"Do you sense the soldier?" Vrell asked.

"Barely. He fights. They all do. The poroo attacked from the Evenwall at first light." Jax wheeled his massive horse around and addressed the soldiers. "Our prince is in trouble! We must aid our Kingsguard brothers to see him brought safely to Mahanaim. The poroo attacked from the trees with spears and rocks. Go carefully." Jax yanked an axe from the sheath on his left thigh and raised it high above his head. "For our prince!"

The other soldiers and knights each waved their weapons high and echoed, "Our prince!"

Jax turned to Vrell. "Wait here for our return. If we should fail, report to Mahanaim."

With that, Jax kicked his horse in the side. It galloped down the hill, raising a cloud of red dust behind. The squadron followed.

Vrell sat atop her horse, staring after them, lips parted. Her orders from Master Hadar were to find the gifted one and stay with him. How could she do that from more than a mile away? And did she really want to?

Vrell carefully closed her mind and concentrated, sending a knock to her mother.

Vrell? What is it, dear?

Remember the soldier I told you about? There's been a battle. Master Hadar sent me to bring the soldier back. I hesitate to deliver him to Master Hadar, but I also do not want to leave him with no training.

When the fighting is over, take the boy to Master Hadar, Mother said. *But warn him to be wary. When Sir Rigil arrives, make sure he knows who the boy is. He may be able to help.*

Vrell closed the connection to her mother and sought out the soldier. She could barely sense him. His distracted state acted as a closed door against her search.

Below, Jax's squadron had reached the valley and was galloping toward a tree line at the far end. Vrell watched them move across the plain, the poroo battle nowhere in sight. Surely she could get a little closer than this. She steered her horse back onto the road and cantered down the hill.

Scattered trees on her right grew thicker, and soon Vrell found herself in a kind of corridor. Dense, green forest on her right. Grey, misted Evenwall on her left. It was cooler here than Mahanaim's humidity. A breeze blew the stale, Evenwall mist over her, dampening her skin. An army of poroo could be standing just inside the cloud, watching, and she would never know until it was too late.

At the clash of metal, Vrell halted her horse. The sound had come from the forest on her right, but she sensed that the soldier was not there. She turned her head to the left, zeroing in on the mist, and a shiver raked her soul.

The soldier was in the Evenwall.

Vrell stared into the churning vapor, her shaking hands clutching the reins. She thought she heard a whisper somewhere close. "Hello?" Her eyes darted around the mist but detected no living thing.

Perhaps it had been only the wind. She nudged her horse forward, toward the Evenwall, but the beast was smarter than that. She nudged harder, and the horse jerked forward. The air cooled instantly. Dampness clung like dew.

Contrary to what she had expected, the Evenwall was not pitch black. It was like standing in a forest on a rainy day. Everything ashen, somber, and chilled. Like twilight.

Vrell steered her horse slowly, able to see only a few yards in any direction. She wove around drooping willows and redpines. Under their leafy canopy, the shadows deepened, limiting her visibility.

She sensed a presence, a foreboding that someone was watching. A hiss to her left stiffened her posture. But she saw no one, only mist wavering around tree branches. She pressed on in the direction of the soldier. She sensed his fatigue. He needed rest.

Muted sounds of blades clashing, men grunting and screaming, and frightened horses grew as Vrell forged through broken branches and over trampled ground. She had gone too far. She had only meant to get a little closer, but now Jax would be cross. So would Mother. She did not even have a weapon.

At least she was in the wake of the battle and not in front of it.

A body came into view, lying on the turf to her right. She approached slowly and saw that it was only an arm, severed just above the elbow. Vrell looked away, horrified.

A few more paces revealed the body the arm had come from. Mud had been painted on his milky white skin like war paint. His glassy eyes stared into the sky. He wore a knotted combination of animal pelts and fabric.

A poroo, she supposed.

A crude spear lay beside him, its head a chiseled, leaf-shaped stone. Vrell dismounted, careful to hold the reins in case her horse decided to abandon her, and stepped over the pine needles to retrieve the weapon. The forest seemed to whisper indiscernible words. Or maybe it was the mist itself. She did not look at the dead man until she was safely back on her horse. Feeling better with a weapon, she urged her mount toward the sounds of the distant action.

She could not see anyone through the thick, green forest, but she did hear far-off sounds of men yelling and steel clashing. It reminded her of a dreadful haunted swamp, without the watery ground.

Vrell should have stayed on the hill.

She saw movement and stopped. The pearly skin of poroo soldiers popped in the distant, shadowed wood. It was harder to see their Kingsguard opponents. Vrell's white horse would be a beacon to her presence. The thought sent a tremble up her spine. She dismounted and tied the courser to the nearest tree. Vrell would blend in better without it.

She crouched low and darted from tree to tree, clutching her spear. The cries of dying men tugged at her heart strings. She had brought her satchel. Perhaps she could help some of them.

But she pressed on, ignoring the wounded and the whispering forest—to find the gifted one.

She waded across a shallow stream. Several dead bodies lay on the forest floor. Vrell identified two Kingsguards and a half dozen poroo without having to look too closely. A steep hill rose up before her. She climbed it, heading in the direction she sensed the soldier. She wove around briarberry bushes and grappled for tufts of grass to pull herself up the incline, but the mist had dampened her hands and she slid backward every few steps.

Pain shot through her skull. She cowered in a briarberry bush, clutching her temples. The soldier was close, debilitating her with the pressure of his untamed bloodvoice.

She concentrated on closing her mind, something she had never needed to do simply to keep from experiencing pain. The pressure eased some, and she crawled to the top of the ridge and peeked over.

Shrouded in fog, a Kingsguard soldier fought two poroo in a small clearing, his movements quick but careful.

Vrell darted behind an oak tree to get a clearer view and clutched the scratchy bark. She had been right. The gifted one was a soldier. Younger than she had expected, but no mere boy. He was tall, strong, and wounded. Plum bruises covered his handsome face. His dark, wet hair and soggy Kingsguard cape whipped about as he swung his sword. Studded jewels on the ivory crossguard caught Vrell's eye. He must be a noble to wield such a weapon, yet she had never seen him at court. And he'd been walking instead of riding.

Movement to the far left turned her head. Prince Gidon! The heir to the throne of Er'Rets leaned against an allown tree, watching the soldier fight. A hedge of briarberry bushes concealed him somewhat. She and the prince stood on the same ridge that sloped down the hill to the stream. He was simply further down. Vrell crouched lower, heart thudding.

Where were his distinguished guards? The mighty Shield? And why was His Highness just standing there? He was quite gifted with the sword, or so his reputation said. He could be helping the soldier fight off the poroo.

Vrell snorted. Our new and noble, lazy king.

A third poroo charged up behind the soldier.

Look out! Vrell yelled to his mind.

Scratch? The soldier spun around just in time to parry the jab of a spear. He scurried back in the pine needles, holding his sword up to his attackers. "If you're not going to help, *Your Highness,*" the soldier said to the prince, "at least climb the tree. I'd hate for you to be killed. Your death would secure my own."

Vrell's brows shot up at his snide tone. Prince Gidon only smirked. One of the poroo charged. The soldier waited until the last moment before dodging and swinging his blade into the creature's side. The soldier stiffened and the poroo fell at his feet.

Vrell felt his horror of having killed. He swallowed and exhaled before wrenching his blade free with a growl. His grey eyes flashed to the other two poroo. He steeled himself and stepped forward.

He could do this.

One of the poroo threw his spear. The soldier dodged it, and it sank into the soil near the prince's briarberry bush. The soldier advanced on the weaponless man and swung into his side, severing the man's arm above the elbow and cleaving into his torso. The soldier screamed as loud as the dying man. His eyes were wide, as if he hadn't expected that to happen.

The other poroo, a quite tall one, darted forward and jabbed his spear at the soldier, who jerked his blade free from the dying man and spun around. With a quick swing of his sword, the soldier cracked the spear. The poroo broke it fully over his knee and held up the shortened version.

An arrow thwacked into Vrell's tree. She jumped back. Two more arrows sank into the soil near Prince Gidon's briarberry bush sanctuary.

Three poroo approached from behind the prince, forcing him out into the open. Vrell hoped he would be killed so someone else would be king. Then she thought better of such treasonous hope, especially if the soldier would be punished for failing to protect his future king.

She concentrated. *The prince needs help.*

The soldier's head jerked to the side, taking note of how Prince Gidon skirted the bushes and the poroo chased him. The soldier, still fighting his poroo, couldn't get away to help. He swung a few times at his tall opponent, but the man dodged every strike—until an arrow pierced him through the back. The poroo stood still for a moment, then dropped his half-spear and collapsed.

The soldier grabbed the broken weapon and sprinted for the prince, bounding over dead bodies and ignoring the arrows raining through the mist.

"Your Highness!" The soldier tossed the half-spear to the prince and attacked a poroo with his sword.

"Typical insolence." Prince Gidon stabbed one poroo in the chest and kicked him into the other poroo attacking him. They fell. "Give your king a broken spear when you wield a sword." He crouched and jerked the spear free, then stabbed the second poroo in the neck.

Vrell looked away.

Where were the arrows being shot from? She crouched to peer through the trees, but she could not see any archers. In fact, there were no more Kingsguards fighting in this area of the forest, though there were quite a few bodies. She could see movement in the distant east. She could hear battle cries. But where were these poroo coming from?

The answer came as she turned back to the soldier's battle. The poroo were coming from the west. From Darkness.

The soldier dodged the thrust of his poroo attacker's spear. He grabbed the shaft with one hand and jerked it forward. The poroo man stumbled, and the soldier cut him down.

Prince Gidon pulled the bloody spear free from his second victim and waved the weapon about. "I'll tell you who I'd like to stab."

Two more poroo closed in on the soldier and he raised his sword. "I'm sure you'll get your chance." The soldier moved with incredible speed, and he quickly overcame all his attackers. He swiped the back of his hand across his forehead and flinched at an arrow sailing past his shoulder. "Will you get in the tree, now?"

Prince Gidon pointed the spear at the young soldier. "If you were to die by this spear, everyone would think it was at the hand of the enemy."

The soldier wiped each side of his blade on his trousers and sheathed it. "For Cetheria's hand, get in the tree."

The prince scowled. "But if I stabbed you, they might declare you a hero." He threw the spear down. "And I cannot have you exalted in death."

"Please, Your Highness." The soldier grabbed the prince's elbow and pulled him toward an allown tree with low branches.

"Don't touch me, stray!"

Vrell frowned. Stray?

The soldier released the prince. "Please. Climb up."

"I will not hide in a tree like a coward."

"Yet you hid in the briarberry bush moments ago," the soldier said.

Vrell smiled.

So did Prince Gidon. "I was hoping to see you killed. Alas, the gods have been thwarting my entertainment dreams of late."

The soldier continued, "It's my duty to protec—" He screamed.

Hot pain shot through Vrell's lower leg. She pulled away from the soldier's mind.

He spun around to the arrow protruding from his lower left calf. He grabbed the shaft, yanked it out with a grunt, and pitched it aside.

Vrell fortified her mind, shocked to have shared his pain so vividly.

The soldier pushed Prince Gidon toward the tree, gently at first, then harder, limping a bit. He growled through clenched teeth. "Now, Your Highness, I beg you!"

Prince Gidon pushed the soldier back. "Do not touch me!"

Arrows whooshed over the ridge and into the soil around them—they were coming from the trees!—and the soldier lost his patience. He punched Prince Gidon in the mouth, sending him stumbling back.

Vrell clamped a hand over her mouth to stifle a gasp.

The prince dabbed his lip. "You'll pay for that, dog!"

"Get. In. The. Tree!"

An arrow sliced across Prince Gidon's shoulder. He howled. "I've been hit!"

The soldier grabbed the prince's arm and inspected it, dragging him behind the allown tree in the process. "Just a scratch, Your Highness. Now, please. Get in the tree, or I'll hit you again!"

Prince Gidon glowered. "You're through, stray. I'll have you hanged!"

The soldier stood, a barrier between the prince and the mysterious arrows, while Prince Gidon clambered up.

An arrow plunged into the soldier's shoulder, jerking him forward. He stumbled and spun around, face white. He grabbed the branch with his good arm, but couldn't pull himself up. He hung swinging by one arm, trying to hook a leg over the branch.

Prince Gidon offered no assistance, the snake.

Vrell held her breath and watched from her hiding spot, fury pounding through her veins. She sought out Jax, annoyed she had not thought to do so before now. She told him of their location, the prince's predicament, and the archers, then closed her mind before he could lecture her for disobeying.

The soldier dropped from the branch and crashed to the ground. He staggered back to his feet and toward the hedge of briarberry bushes. Before he reached the gnarly sanctuary, another arrow pierced him, this time in his lower back.

He screamed and crumpled to the ground. He writhed like an inchworm, struggled to his right hand and knee and tried to crawl, but the arrows rendered his left arm and leg useless. His body tipped over the ridge of the hill and slid away.

Vrell feared the prince seeing her and possibly recognizing her, but she had to act to save the soldier. She bolted from her hiding place to the ledge, still clutching her own spear. She brought her pouch of healing herbs around to her front.

She got to the ridge but could find no sign of the soldier. She inched down the incline, until she spotted him lying facedown in the pine needles a few paces from the stream, arrows sticking out of him like garden stakes.

She ran the rest of the way and slid to his side, praying he would live. He had fought so bravely to save his wretched prince. He was unconscious but breathing. She lifted her healing pouch from her shoulder and set it beside her spear on the ground. She thought back to Mitt's training and Jax's stories of the battlefield. She would need her yarrow salve, something for bandages, and water.

The gurgling stream volunteered its service. She grabbed the soldier's hands and tugged him toward the sound. He was heavy, and thankfully, she did not have to drag him far before one foot sank into cold, shallow water. He moaned softly but did not wake.

Vrell unfastened his damp cloak and pulled it from under his limp body. She sucked in a sharp breath. Blood matted his once-white shirt. Patchy, brownish stains gave evidence to previous wounds. His left sleeve clung stickily with half-dried blood. She inspected that wound first and found a swollen, infected cut he must have received earlier and not cared for. She huffed. Men.

"Lo! Boy! What are you doing?" Prince Gidon's haughty voice called from behind.

Vrell shivered, remembering the last time he had spoken to her, at the tournament in Nesos. At least his words and tone were only demanding today, lacking familiarity. He was such a fool. For all he knew she could be his enemy, and the simpleton risked himself to speak to her.

"Yes, my lord?" She searched the ground for one of the arrows she had seen shoot over the ridge. If she was going to treat these wounds, she needed to know what kind of arrowheads these were.

"I said, what are you doing to my squire? The battle is over. Leave him."

Vrell paused. She'd known this soldier was a stray—the prince had said as much. But since when could a stray be squire to a Crown Prince? Peculiar. "I am trying to save his life. He did save yours several times over."

Footsteps swished until a pair of gilded boots stopped beside Vrell. The battle must have ended.

The prince kicked the squire in the side. "Is he dead?"

Vrell kept her head down. "No, my lord."

"Pity." The prince kicked his squire again. No wonder he was so bruised. "He's such a briar in my boot. If he dies, I shall make it worth your while."

A hot rush of anger shot through Vrell. Prince Gidon wanted his squire—his hero and rescuer—dead? "He will not die because of me."

"Well, in case you didn't know, boy, I am the Crown Prince of Er'Rets. If you are a healer, I insist on being treated first."

"You are injured?"

Prince Gidon turned his shoulder toward her. "I took an arrow in my arm."

Vrell fought back a sigh. She gripped her knife and stood. Keeping her eyes down, she cut the red silk at the bicep and tore the sleeve off.

The prince twitched. "Was that necessary?"

"If you want me to care for it." She dropped the shirt sleeve and examined his wound. It was as his squire had said: only a scratch. She cleaned it with a bit of her drinking water, added some salve, and left it unbandaged. "You will live, Your Majesty." Unfortunately. "The air will be good for it."

Vrell had a thought. Maybe the prince could be of some use. She needed a way to get the squire to Mahaniam. "Do you have a cart I could use to transport this man?"

Prince Gidon raised a dark eyebrow then stalked away into the mist.

Vrell sighed and scanned the ground. She spotted an arrow a few feet away with a bodkin point: a four-sided spike designed to penetrate armor. Advanced for people as primitive as the poroo. Not at all like their crude spears. The same people could not have made both weapons.

The stream gurgled. A breeze whipped through the trees. She shivered as she scurried over to the closest fallen Kingsguard. The man had died from a spear to the chest. No good. She needed a clean shirt. She ran to the next body and flipped him over. Her breath caught. His skull had been bashed in by something immense, probably a battleaxe. But his shirt was unsoiled.

She crouched to unlace the neckties and spotted someone's travel pack under a briarberry bush. She abandoned the dead man and went to the pack. She found a clean shirt inside and beamed. Infection was her biggest concern. The cleaner her materials, the better his chances.

She hoisted the pack over one shoulder and ran back to the soldier's side. She placed her palm against his forehead. He already burned with fever, likely due to his arm wound. She ripped the shirt into strips, anxious to get this over with.

She still had to remove the arrows. At least bodkin arrowheads would be easier to remove than the barbed, broadhead kind.

She opened her satchel and used her small knife to cut his shirt down the center back. His bruised and scarred skin stole her breath. He'd been beaten, often. She invested her fury into cutting the shirt off. She sawed at the fabric around the arrow protruding from his lower back, then shifted to remove the material from around the arrow in his left shoulder.

When the cloth fell away, Vrell stopped as if Arman had frozen time. White, raised skin scarred an S onto the squire's upper left shoulder. The skin underneath was maroon, a birthmark of some kind that brought out the S even more. The brand was slightly distorted due to the arrow piercing him.

The mark of a stray.

She remembered that the prince had called him a stray. Why, then, did he wear a soldier's uniform and wield such a fine sword? Wasn't it against Council law to train strays for Kingsguard service? Prince Gidon had plenty of guards. Where were they? Where was the irritable Sir Kenton, the Shield?

Some Shield.

The wound in the squire's lower back oozed thick blood, so she started there. She placed her hand against his skin, then stopped. Where was her head? How would she pack the wounds? She crawled to the stream, dunked her hand into the water, and clutched a handful of grainy soil. It was too coarse. She needed mud. If she dug a bit to find softer soil, she could probably make some.

She gazed into the bubbling stream, deep in thought. What else could be used to pack wounds? She didn't have enough herbs or fabric to do the job. This particular forest seemed void of mosses. She jumped to her feet and ran to the nearest briarberry bush. Prying the branches aside revealed a thick, white web. Hopefully no one was home. Vrell hated spiders.

She ignored the shiver gripping her and tore the fine white web off the prickly branches. This would not be enough. She set about collecting fuzzy white sacs from every bush in the area until she had a handful. She set the webs on a strip of white cloth and scrubbed her hands in the creek with a bar of soap from her satchel.

Her heart throbbed when she looked at the arrow in his back.

Jax's teachings played in her mind. She gently worked the arrow back and forth, pulling carefully. It would not do to lose the arrowhead in his body. When the arrowhead was visible, she gripped it with her thumb and forefinger and slid it out.

The squire squirmed and moaned. Blood pooled over the top of the wound and trickled down his side in a thick stream. Vrell shrank back and dropped the arrow. She scrambled for her water skin. Trembling, she doused the wound, dabbed it with a strip of fabric, and poked a glob of spider webs into the hole to clot the blood. Then she packed it with yarrow and bandaged it. No easy task, wrapping strips of cloth around the torso of a man lying prostrate.

He'd ripped the arrow out of his leg during the battle, so Vrell rolled up his pant leg and tended that wound next. It wasn't as deep.

The arrow remaining in his shoulder bothered her. She needed to cut the shaft somehow. After much thought, she decided to drive it out the way it had entered. She rolled him onto his side and used her knife to saw the sinews that bound the arrowhead to the shaft. When the binding severed, she gently pulled the arrowhead off and gripped the fletchings at the end of the arrow. She slid the shaft out in one swift motion, hoping it left no wood shards in its wake.

To her surprise, the squire did not react. She glanced at his chest, confirmed it was still moving, and set to work, quickly washing both sides of the wound and packing them with webs and yarrow. Then she wrapped his shoulder in strips of cloth, wrinkling her nose at his odor. Handsome or not, he needed a bath.

The infected wound on his bicep required more materials than she had. She cleaned it thoroughly, packed a little yarrow in, and bandaged it. She pulled a wool blanket from the pack and spread it over the pine-needled ground. She rolled the soldier back onto his chest on the blanket and draped a cloak from the pack over his back.

Vrell drew her knees against her chest and wrapped her arms around them. It was darker now than it had been, though it was difficult to guess the hour in the Evenwall mist. The ache in her stomach told her it was well past time for a meal. The sounds of battle were no more. The only voices she heard spoke in the king's language. The poroo must have fled. And now the Kingsguards were regrouping.

She thanked Arman that the squire was alive and that she had known what to do. She suddenly felt traitorous. Her master, Macoun Hadar, wanted to take advantage of this young man. Vrell could warn him, but what good would that do? As soon as she found Sir Rigil or Prince Oren, she would be rescued. She had a way out. This stray likely wouldn't.

She felt drawn to help this heroic warrior who did not know how to use his bloodvoices. She needed to keep him away from her master. If she went for her horse now, she could ride north toward home. Yet the squire would not survive such a journey.

She bloodvoiced her mother, who confirmed their original plan: wait for Sir Rigil.

She hoped Jax would bring a cart soon. The squire's wounds should have stitches, but she was not capable of such surgery. Hopefully her work would do the trick for now, but if he tried to ride or walk his packed wounds could burst.

A bit of color caught her eye. Prince Gidon's shirt sleeve. The rich color brought a small growl to her lips. How many peasants did it take to make such a hue? Still . . . she thought of Maser Hadar's basket of trinkets and the cabochon buckle. She picked up the sleeve and tucked it into her satchel. It might come in useful.

She studied the squire's tanned and scruffy face. He needed a shave. His dark hair was long, tied at the back of his neck with a leather cord, though most of it had escaped in battle and now fell around his chin onto the dark blanket. She fought against the urge to fix it. She missed her long hair. She missed being a woman.

Being a boy had its advantages, though. Prince Gidon had not recognized her. Life as Vrell Sparrow would keep her safe until she found Sir Rigil. Besides, men had more freedom than women. She looked down at her patient. Well, maybe not all men. This squire was a stray. How much freedom could he have? She studied him again. If she really were a boy, she would want to look like him.

His eyes flashed open. Vrell noticed they were grey, but then she cowered as a force threatened to burst her skull.

Sir Gavin? the squire bloodvoiced.

Dozens of voices called out in a rush.

What's happened to you?

Ahhhh!

You are hurt. Tell me your location and I will send help.

Vrell whimpered and clutched her ears as if that might mute the sound. "Stop!" she screamed. "Block them!"

The squire lifted his head, tangled hair hanging over a furrowed brow. "Shut the door?"

"Yes!" she cried. "Please!"

Achan! Where are you, lad?

Close your mind, man! The pain is unbearable.

"Sir Gavin?" The squire bolted to his feet, only to stagger, groan, and fall to his knees.

"No!" Vrell picked up the cloak he had thrown off him. She crawled to him and clutched his arm, forcing herself to speak over the pain his mind caused. "You must not walk." She panted and draped the cloak around his shoulders. "Lie back. You are wounded."

He stared at her as if she had spoken a foreign language.

She pressed her fingers against her temples, against the pain. "Please!" She repeated his phrase. "Shut the door!"

He closed his eyes and the pressure faded. Vrell sighed, thankful it was over. But when she clutched his arm to pull him to the blanket, he jerked away and the pressure flared again.

"Sir Gavin! Where is Sir Gavin?"

Achan! Calm yourself. Where are you?

"Please." Vrell tugged his arm. "You must rest your mind and your body."

He blinked, eyelids heavy. "Why can't I—"

"You were injured," Vrell said. "You have lost much blood."

"Sir Gavin?" He bellowed into the thick forest. "Sir Gavin!"

"He's not here, you imbecile." Prince Gidon stood above them, hands on his hips.

Vrell tensed. Where had he come from?

The squire looked up, pupils thick in his grey eyes. "But I hear him. Can't you?"

Prince Gidon mumbled, "For the sake of the gods," and punched the squire in the temple.

Vrell's patient slumped to the ground, unconscious.

Prince Gidon turned and strode away. "I was sick of hearing him whine."

19

Where am I?

Achan blinked and took in the dark, stone chamber that smelled of mildew and urine. He blinked again. Were those bars on the door? He rose onto one elbow and winced. His body felt like someone had beaten it to a—wait. Images of Silvo's friends flashed in his mind. Someone *had* beaten him.

He lay on a deep, stone bench covered in loose straw. Pale stripes of torchlight lit the bottom of a wooden door and shone though a small, barred window on top. A small animal scurried across the dirt floor. Something else moved in the corner. Achan blinked rapidly, adjusting his eyes to the dim light. He sensed pain.

A scrawny, round-faced boy of thirteen or so stared at him under a mess of oily brown hair. *You are in the dungeon at Mahanaim.*

Achan twitched. His eyes went so wide, the dank air tickled and he had to blink. *Scratch?*

The boy stared, his eyes cat-like. "I do not— Um, I *don't* know why you call me that," he said out loud.

"Because your voice is scratchy, why else?" Achan struggled to sit. He sucked in a sharp breath at the knife in his lower back. At least that was what it felt like. His shirt and cape were gone. Strips of linen bandaged his stomach and shoulder. Proof of the nobles' assault appeared in dark blotches on his skin, but what were the bandages for? "Where are my clothes? My bag?" A rush of cold flashed over him. He swung his legs off the bed and jumped to his feet, only to cower into a crouch at the pain. "My sword?" he croaked. "Where is my sword?"

"Your clothes were ruined," the boy said. "These quarters are so unsanitary. I have washed your wounds three times a day to fend off infection. There is no point in a shirt until you are healed. I never saw you had a bag. And the guards locked your sword in the dungeon strongbox."

I'm in a dungeon? And the dungeon has a strongbox?

Mahanaim receives more than its share of diplomats, the boy thought to Achan. *This is actually one of the nicer cells.*

Achan growled. "Stop that!"

Scratch's eyes went wide, and he scooted back farther into the corner. "What's your name?" he asked aloud.

"Achan Cham." He limped to the door and rose on the toes of his right foot to see out the barred window of his cell. The stab in his lower back inhibited the movement of his left leg.

"So you *are* a stray?"

His cell appeared to be at the end of a deserted stone corridor. A single torch hung on the wall about five paces away. He could see the doors to four other cells before the corridor turned a corner. He gripped the bars on the window and gave them a good shake. His left arm didn't want to obey. He glanced at his bandaged shoulder, then to Scratch. "Did someone claim otherwise?"

"You saved the prince. I saw you."

Saved the prince? Ah. The procession had been close to Mahanaim when the poroo had attacked. Achan had done what he could to aid that pompous . . . He stretched his good arm up over his head. His muscles were tight, everything ached, and he really needed to use that privy bucket in the corner. "He's alive?"

"Completely unharmed."

Achan sighed and nodded. "Then I'm not a complete failure."

"You are not a failure at all."

Achan huffed. "I'm sure Prince Gidon disagrees. Who are you?"

Vrell Sparrow.

Achan's eyebrows sank. "Sparrow? You don't wear the clothing of a stray."

My master dislikes the orange tunic. Where is yours?

The boy's voice in his head angered Achan. "How is it you speak without moving your lips? Are you a sorcerer or a demon that you enter my thoughts?"

The boy whimpered, as if somehow injured. *I am an herbalist sent to heal you.*

"A barber?"

"An *herbalist.*"

"What's the difference?"

Sparrow rolled his eyes. "Instead of a knife, I use herbs to make healing teas, salves, and tonics."

"I hate tonics." Achan paced the tiny cell, limping over the cool, clay floor. "How many days have I been here?"

"Four. Your arm wound gave you a fever. I gave you hops tea to sleep it off."

"*Four days*?" Achan sat on the stone bed and stared at the boy. "Do you know what happened? I mean . . . the bruises I remember, and fighting the poroo, but . . . " He fingered the bandage on his lower back. "How did I get here?"

"Poroo attacked your procession. Sir Kenton Garesh was knocked out by a rock that was thrown down from a treetop. The Kingsguard knights went to battle, and you led the prince to safety in the Evenwall. More poroo attacked and you fought them off alone. You were struck by three arrows as you fought to protect the prince. You are a hero."

Achan smirked. "What are you, some kind of minstrel?"

Sparrow lowered his head and his cheeks darkened.

Not meaning to embarrass the boy, Achan clapped his hands together and rubbed them. "I'm a hero, you say? Well, this is some hero's welcome, don't you think? I particularly enjoy the platters of meat and dancing girls."

Sparrow shot him a smirk. "I shall ask them to bring you something to eat. I can do no more than that, I'm afraid."

"You'll ask who?"

But Sparrow had closed his eyes. He still sat in the corner, knees pulled up to his chin.

Achan stretched his legs out in front. He could never sit as . . . small as the boy did. He stood again and hobbled to the door. He wanted out. The tiny space made him feel trapped, which was probably the point, seeing as this was a dungeon. Still.

Flashes of the battle suddenly came to mind. His stomach churned. He'd killed seven or eight poroo. They'd struck first. They were ugly to look at, but they were people. Achan shivered at the ache in chest. Sir Gavin had warned him that a knight would have to kill. But that didn't ease his memories.

Sparrow's soft voice in his mind interrupted his penitence. *They are bringing you food.*

Achan wheeled around. He focused hard on the allown tree, trying to find the place where his mind would be closed.

Sparrow seemed to notice. He sank into the corner and croaked, "Sorry."

Two burly guards with thick beards and black cloaks approached the door. A thin valet with carrot-orange hair stood behind them holding a tray.

"Back up against the wall," one of the guards ordered.

Achan turned to Sparrow. "How did you know they were coming?"

"I called them."

The guard kicked the door of the cell. "Against the wall!"

Achan obeyed and the door opened. The valet entered and set the tray on the stone bed. It held a hunk of bread, a wedge of hard cheese, and a mug of red liquid.

Achan pointed at the mug, knowing, but wanting to ask anyway. "What's that?"

"A tonic to give you strength," the valet said.

Achan forced a grin. "And I'll wager it's refreshing too." He offered the mug to the valet. "Would you like some?"

The valet stepped back.

A hot current shot through Achan's nerves. This would end, now. He threw the mug, shattering the pottery against the stone wall. The red liquid splattered like blood. Sparrow yelped.

One of the guards swung his thick fist. Achan ducked, bashed his elbow into the guard's back, and kneed the other guard in the stomach.

He fled the cell, his lower back screaming with each step.

The greystone halls were a maze that smelled of urine, torch smoke, and mildew. He ran past the occasional torch and barred wooden door. Inside each cell, chain scraped against stone or someone moaned. He met a dead end and backtracked until he found a stairwell leading up.

He made it halfway to the top when four guards started down. He turned back, only to see the two guards from his cell climbing up.

"Pig snout."

He awoke back in his cell with fresh bruises and no lunch. Sparrow still occupied the corner.

Achan sat up, his wounded body punishing him for the effort. "Aren't you uncomfortable?"

"Aren't you hungry?" Sparrow reached into his lap and held up a bread roll.

"Where'd you get that?"

The boy tossed it to Achan. "Took it off your tray when you ran. You cannot escape from here, you know. At least, I do not think you can."

Achan's mouth was too full of bread to comment on the wimpy scholar's lecture. He finished his bite. "How would you feel if you were me?"

Sparrow looked at the light streaming through the bars on the door. "Trapped. Alone. Like I have no control over my life."

Achan had forgotten the boy was a stray. Maybe he'd had a rough time of it too. "So, what am I thinking now?"

"That I am a scrawny runt who could be bested by a one-armed hag."

One side of Achan's mouth turned up in a smirk. "You *are* a sorcerer!"

Sparrow huffed and turned away, though Achan could swear the boy blushed again.

He wanted to continue the discussion he'd been having with Scratch—who was now Sparrow—to find out what the boy knew about bloodvoices. But Achan seemed incapable of admitting his bloodvoicing ability out loud and in person. Somehow that would make it all the more a reality. "Aw, Sparrow, don't be mad! Tell me—why am I in the dungeon?"

"You are being charged with attempting to murder the Crown Prince."

Achan burst into laughter. It jarred his wounds so he stopped. "But you said I saved him."

"I am sorry."

"Well, did I or didn't I save him?"

"You did."

"But I'm still being charged?"

"Yes."

Achan looked at the stone ceiling. "This reeks of Prince Gidon."

The guards and valet approached the door again. The valet held a corked vial. The guards drew their swords, apparently wary of another escape attempt.

Achan groaned.

This time Sparrow hopped to his feet and strode forward. He was short with skinny limbs but a bit pudgy around the middle. At least someone was getting his fill in Mahanaim.

"Who are you and what is this potion you carry?" Sparrow asked in a commanding voice that raised Achan's brows.

"No potion, boy," the valet said. "A tonic for the prisoner."

"Why does he need this tonic?"

"I don't know. But without it, my master assures me he'll die."

"I am an herbalist." Sparrow glanced at Achan. "He looks healthy to me, despite his wounds. Who is your master?"

"Lord Nathak."

"He is not," Achan said. "I've never seen him before."

"His Lordship retained my services upon his arrival this morning," the valet said.

Achan lowered his head. Lord Nathak was here? Pig snout.

Sparrow held up a silencing hand. "What does Lord Nathak want with a stray?"

"This stray belongs to his lordship."

The valet pushed the door open an inch, but Sparrow put his foot against it. The valet slid his fingers into the crack, and the boy shoved the door closed on them. The valet cried out. Sparrow pried the vial from his grip and loosened the cork with his teeth.

He smelled it and pulled back with a pinched face. "This poisons my patient! He will not take it." Sparrow slung the vial in the privy bucket.

The valet cursed. "You'll pay if I'm punished." He spun around and departed.

The guards stared at Sparrow as if not knowing what to do. Finally, the one holding the keys locked the door, and they lumbered away, sheathing their swords. Sparrow returned to his corner and sank against the wall.

Maybe Achan should talk with the boy. He seemed to know about the tonic. "You're really an herbalist?"

"I apprenticed for an apothecary before the Kingsguard knights brought me here."

"They brought you here for that? You must be a talented apothecary."

"No. They took me because I could bloodvoice."

A chill shook Achan. "And they knew that . . . how?"

"My master sensed my ability and sent the knights to fetch me. On the journey here, I sensed you. We all did."

Oh, this was rich. Achan didn't bother to hide his grin. "And you sensed what about me?"

Sparrow shook his head. "I barely understood my own gift at the time, so when I first heard you it was very . . . confusing . . . and scary. The voices frightened you, I heard that much loud and clear. I sensed a great orange light and blood. Lots of blood . . . on your arm." Sparrow reached up and touched his own left shoulder, his gaze downcast as if rehashing the memory. He looked up. "I thought you were injured at first. Other bloodvoicers wanted to know your name and where you lived."

Achan stared at Sparrow, speechless. The boy *had* been in his head that night, had seen the sun and felt the blood from the doe. Still . . . "Bloodvoices are a myth."

Sparrow huffed. "How can you say that when you and I have used it many times to speak to each other?"

"You want to know what's in my head? An ache. A massive headache. Got any *herbs* for that?"

"Of course. I could bring you some chamomile tea, but that's not what's causing your pain. The only thing that lessens the pressure of bloodvoicing is practice. I can tell you what I have learned. But I should warn you," Sparrow said, glancing at the cell door, "Master Hadar wants to use you."

"You work for the prince?"

The boy shook his head. "Master Hadar is a very old and distant relative to Prince Gidon Hadar. He lives in this manor, on the eighth floor."

Achan rubbed his hands over his face, overwhelmed by this boy's excessive information. Maybe if he played along, the know-it-all would explain how to reach Sir Gavin. "The tonic?"

"It is made from the âleh flower. It quiets the bloodvoices."

Which Lord Nathak had been doing for years. Did he know about them then? "But even when I've taken it, I can still sense things. Intentions."

"Can you? You must be very strong to still have some ability through that tonic."

"I don't know what you mean by 'strong.' Right now I'm feeling anything but."

"Your gift is so potent you hurt my head when your mind is not closed off," Sparrow said. "That is how so many can sense you. Your thoughts bleed over into every gifted mind, probably in all Er'Rets."

Achan's eyebrows shot up. "I hurt you?"

"You are doing it now. You cause so much pressure. You need to learn how to *shut the door*, as you put it, better than you do. And so people cannot find you. When your mind is open like that, if they are trying, they can find you anywhere."

"You think someone is looking for me?"

"I told you, my master is. With a power as great as yours, yes, some will seek to exploit it."

Achan couldn't process this. "Wouldn't Lord Nathak want to use it, then? He clearly knows I have this . . . thing. Why else would he make me drink the tonic all these years?"

Sparrow was silent for a long moment. "I *hate* Lord Nathak."

"Do you?" Achan grinned. "Then we have three things in common, Sparrow: hating Lord Nathak, strays who've lost their orange tunics, and this crazy bloodvoice business."

Sparrow straightened, eyes wide.

"What's wrong?" Achan asked.

"My master comes."

"Is that bad?"

"Close your mind—focus hard on it—and deny you know anything about bloodvoices." Sparrow stood and walked to the door just as the guards entered with an ancient-looking bald man in a thick grey cloak. Lord Nathak's new valet followed close with yet another vial.

The room seemed to grow colder. Achan lay back on his stone bed, closed his eyes, and pictured the allown tree on the edge of the Sideros River. In his mind, the wind blew the leaves about. He saw Gren's chestnut hair billowing around her rosy face.

Gren.

The valet's voice jerked Achan away from his longing. "He. Him. There."

Achan opened his eyes to see the carrot-topped valet pointing at Sparrow.

"He's the one who shut my hand in the door!" the valet whined.

"Did you, Vrell?" the old man's voice hummed as if each word he spoke tasted delicious. Achan had heard his voice before. In his mind.

The man looked twice as old as Poril. He had the same spotted skin, but he was thinner and shorter and had bulging eyes like Jaira's little dog. A thick grey cloak billowed around him. Now that was the kind of cloak Gren needed.

"Aye, master," Sparrow said. "He tried to give a tonic to the prisoner, but I think it is poisonous. If the valet would like to bring the ingredients down and prepare the brew in my presence, I could confirm whether it is safe."

The old man held out a claw-like hand and the valet handed him the vial.

"The prisoner is ill," the valet said. "He must take his tonic daily and has missed four doses in this mishap. If my master's orders continue to be ignored, I fear for the prisoner's life."

The old man pried the cork free. He stuck his pinky finger inside and touched it to his tongue. His face wrinkled, and he spat on the floor three times. "This is no regular tonic," he hissed. "Why does the prisoner take this?"

The valet shrugged. "He's ill."

"On whose authority?"

"Lord Nathak's, sir."

The old man yelled, "Out!"

"Lord Nathak shall hear of this," the valet said before scurrying away.

"See that he does," the old man said to himself.

"What is it, master?" Sparrow asked.

"Silencer." The old man turned toward Achan. His cadaverous, ashen eyes drilled into him.

The coldness penetrated Achan's mind. He glanced away and shivered.

The old man mumbled, "Lord Nathak has gone to a great deal of trouble to hide this young man's gift. I must discover why." He worked the cork back into the vial and turned to the guards. "Let no one inside—Lord Nathak, especially."

The old man and the guards left.

After a while, Sparrow said, as if to himself, "I shall try to follow. My master is too strong to enter, but I might be able to jump through him."

The boy may as well have been speaking Poroo. "What are you talking about?"

Sparrow ignored him and pulled something small out of his pocket.

"What you got there?" Achan asked.

Sparrow held up a scrap of cloth. "It is easier to connect with someone if you have something personal."

"And you collect fabric scraps?"

"I cut it from my master's pillow."

Well, that made perfect sense. Achan jerked his thumb over his shoulder. "I'm gonna use the bucket."

Sparrow flushed. He turned to face the corner, clutching the fabric against his chest.

Strange boy, Vrell Sparrow.

Achan made good time with the bucket and perched on the bed to watch Sparrow's performance. He toyed with the idea of trying to hear Sparrow's thoughts but decided against it. He didn't want to mess up whatever the boy was trying to do.

But Sparrow just sat there, boring Achan into a stupor. So Achan crouched behind him on the floor and placed one finger on the hem of his silky grey tunic. Cloth apparently formed some kind of connection. If so, and if what Sparrow said was true—that Achan was strong—maybe he could hear Sparrow's thoughts.

Achan closed his eyes and pictured Sparrow. Short Sparrow, with a gut like an old man. Blushing Sparrow, who'd blend in better wearing a skirt. Greasy-haired Sparrow, who bossed about guards and valets, despite his lowly station. Achan liked this boy. He pictured himself tiptoeing into Sparrow's head and looking under a pile of brains.

Then Achan was walking down a corridor, his back stiff and hunched. He pushed open a heavy door and entered a room filled with warm sunlight. Lord Nathak sat at a desk in front of a large window. Goosebumps raised on Achan's arms as he reveled in the room's heat.

Lord Nathak spoke without looking up. "Why have you kept my valet from the squire?"

Achan's arm held up the vial and spoke in the old man's voice. "He tries to poison the boy."

Achan held his breath. He was the old man. Amazing!

Lord Nathak sighed. "You and I both know what you hold in your hand is not poison."

"Then tell me what game you play, Lord Nathak. His gift is the strongest I've ever felt. Why do you wish it hidden? If you want my help, you must convince me of the cause I aid."

Lord Nathak tugged at the ties of his mask where they ran under his chin. "He disturbs the prince. His bloodvoice is untamable."

"I can tame anyone—given the chance."

"The prince despises him and does not wish him trained."

"Then why make him a squire? It's against Council law anyway, so why do it?"

"I did not make him a squire. Sir Gavin Lukos did. I merely made use of his training."

"If the prince despises him, why not have him killed?"

"I am not a murderer."

Achan heard Master Hadar snort. "I sense a different truth from you, Lord Nathak. You may be able to close your mind, but you cannot hide everything." The old man hummed. "Is he who I think he is?"

Lord Nathak leaned back in his chair. "What he *is* is my property. Prince Gidon has ordered him punished. I will not have him calling out for a rescue."

"Does he even know how to—"

Sparrow's voice seemed to scream in Achan's head. "What are you doing?"

Achan wheezed as if coming out of the water after nearly drowning. He blinked rapidly until Sparrow's round face came into focus. He shuddered. "That was incredible!"

Sparrow's forehead wrinkled. "What was?"

Achan rubbed the chill from his arms. The warmth of Lord Nathak's chamber had vanished. "They're going to beat me." He grinned. "Shocking, isn't it?"

Sparrow set the back of his hand against Achan's forehead.

Achan batted it away and clambered to his feet. "You didn't see? Or hear?"

"Hear what?"

"I followed you. I touched your tunic and concentrated and, bam!" Achan slapped his hands together. "I was the old man in Lord Nathak's chamber. A warm and spacious chamber, I might add. Do you think I'll ever get a warm and spacious chamber?"

Sparrow's eyes popped wide. "You jumped?"

Achan shrugged and sat down on his bed.

"I could see nothing. What did they say?"

Achan repeated the conversation.

Sparrow got to his feet. "This is astonishing. I have never been able to enter my master's mind, yet you used my connection for yourself and got further than I ever have. I did not sense you at all. Are you weary?"

"Should I be?"

Sparrow sat next to Achan on the stone bed. "Oh, Achan. No wonder they all want you. The power you have is magnificent . . . and dangerous. You must be careful."

Achan smirked. "Sparrow . . . "

"Do you not see? I cannot enter my master's mind, but you did. And through a jumped connection at that! Achan, you could enter any mind in Er'Rets."

Achan didn't know why he'd want to do that, but he was glad he wasn't afraid of the bloodvoices anymore. They had suddenly become a new plaything.

"Have you ever heard a different kind of voice?" he asked. "One that warms you from the inside and seems to know exactly what is happening in every moment of your life?"

Sparrow frowned, then opened his mouth to speak, but the door burst open and the two guards stormed inside. One carried a whip and a set of iron shackles.

Achan didn't like the looks of either. He stood and tried to look threatening. "You could have knocked first."

Sparrow scrambled into the corner.

The guards seized Achan by his arms. Pain shot through his injured shoulder. Goosebumps rose on his arms at the sudden chill that wafted though his cell.

"What are you doing?" Sparrow asked.

"This one tried to kill the prince," a guard said, clamping an iron cuff to Achan's wrist.

Sparrow wedged between the guards. "That is ridiculous. He *saved* the prince. I saw it happen."

"You know not what you say, Vrell." The old man stepped into the cell again, with Lord Nathak and the valet at his heels.

"Lord Nathak." Achan panted slightly as he waved his good arm around to keep the guard from securing the second cuff. He was finished with trying to get on anyone's good side. "I was just noticing how something smelled, and here you are."

Lord Nathak sighed. "The older you grow, the bolder you become. It does not suit a stray who hopes for a secure future."

"I hadn't realized there was such a thing in your service, my lord."

Sparrow spoke. "Master, he should be allowed to appear before the Council, where I will testify as a witness to his heroism. I saw him save the prince, when all his other protectors were gone."

The guards forced Achan onto the stone bed. The loose straw poked and scratched, and he arched his back to keep his wounds from being aggravated. Lord Nathak stepped forward holding a ceramic funnel and a large wooden mug. One of the guards squeezed Achan's cheeks until his jaw opened.

Pig snout.

Sparrow's sorrowful voice pleaded, "Master, please. This is barbaric."

Lord Nathak wedged the funnel between Achan's teeth and dumped the mug's contents.

Achan gagged but had no choice but to swallow the bitter goo. His teeth grated against the funnel, his eyes watered, and a tear ran down his cheek.

The valet handed Lord Nathak another mug, and he poured it into the funnel. Achan tried to swallow quickly this time, but the overwhelming mentha taste tingled his throat. He coughed, which only made swallowing harder.

The liquids trickled into Achan's stomach, and a fog drifted over his mind. He was both outraged and relieved. He'd finally accepted the voices as his, but they had nearly driven him mad. He lost control of trying to close off his mind. The voices screamed now, as if they had been waiting for an opportunity to speak and could feel the tonic pushing them out.

Do not go!

Who are you?

Come back!

Achan, wait! Sir Gavin said. *Stay open!*

Before Achan could reply to Sir Gavin, Lord Nathak removed the funnel and the guards yanked Achan to his feet. They looped the chains in his shackles through two iron rings high on the dank, mildewed wall.

Achan ran his tongue over his teeth, seeking to clear his mouth of all flavor. His mind felt numbed, but he wasn't bereft of his senses. "What exactly have I done to deserve this, my lord?"

"You led the Crown Prince into the Evenwall," Lord Nathak said, tapping his fingernails against the ceramic funnel, "thus endangering his life. Yet you were sworn to protect him. You will receive ten lashes for this blunder."

Achan stood facing the stone wall, the shackles holding him in place. "Ten? Oh, that's not so bad. You do realize my taking him into the Evenwall saved his life? And, in case you missed it, I took *three* arrows for His Royal Plague. The one in my back is particularly painf—Aagh!"

Achan screamed as a guard jerked the chains up the wall, raising his arms above his head and stretching his sore shoulder. His chest slammed against cold, slimy stone. Achan shivered and glanced at the beefy guard who held the chains. "Do you mind? I'm trying to have a conversation."

Lord Nathak motioned to the other guard. "Only ten. And go easy."

Go easy?

The other guard stepped forward clutching the whip.

20

"Hold still," Vrell scolded. The spicy smell of cloves mixed with calendula numbed her sinuses—a blessing in Achan's rank cell.

Achan lay prostrate on his horrible stone bed, his face buried in the crook of his arm, straw poking out from under him. "It hurts!"

"I can see that." Vrell scooped ointment with two fingers and ran it over a lesion on Achan's back. His muscles tensed, but the ointment had already made a difference in the newest wounds on his back. She still couldn't believe how scarred it was. She could not imagine Achan committing a crime that deserved such punishment.

It's cold, Achan bloodvoiced.

Sorry. She scooped up another glob of ointment and rubbed it between her hands before tending the next gash. She gasped. "You can hear my thoughts, now? Despite the tonic?"

"Aye. Your little fruit did the trick."

Vrell smiled. She had remembered Jax's advice and had taken a sack of karpos fruit from the kitchens and given it to Achan when he'd awakened after the scourging.

"What now?" Achan asked, his voice muffled by the fact that his face was buried in the inside of his elbow. "Teach me something."

Vrell twisted her lips. "Well, I am best at blocking. That would be a good thing for you to master. You must concentrate. It is like having drapes in your mind to draw closed around your thoughts. Once you learn, you can practice letting in only what, and who, you want."

Vrell rubbed more salve over the arrow wound on Achan's left shoulder, then traced along one shoulder blade to the other, smearing ointment into his skin as she went. With wounds like his, infection could kill, especially in this disgusting cell where rats flourished. So she added more ointment.

Achan's head popped up. "Did you hear that?"

"No. Did someone bloodvoice you?"

"He said, 'Gavin's coming.' But I didn't recognize his— Um, Sparrow?"

"Yes?"

"You've put on enough gunk now, don't you think? Or must you rub me raw?"

"Yes—uh, no." Vrell jerked back her hand and stood. Heat flooded her cheeks. "I believe that is plenty for now. Does it feel better?"

"Like new." He sat up and rolled his injured shoulder. "Think you can find me a shirt?"

"I should be able to."

"I had a spare, in my bag." Achan stared ahead as if remembering something sad.

Vrell didn't know what that sad thought might be. But judging from those scars on his back and the fact that he'd spent any time at all subject to Prince Gidon, his past was likely riddled with anguish.

Perhaps when Vrell was home, she could convince her mother to speak to the Council about strays. It was senseless to treat a man like an animal. They were all the same inside, physically anyway. Plus, both Achan and Prince Gidon were dark-haired, tall, and strong. But where the prince was cruel, Achan was knightly. The way he'd fought to protect a man who wanted to kill him . . .

Vrell shook her thoughts away, picked up the jar of ointment, and walked to the door. "Guard!" She turned back to Achan. "I shall try to bring more food as well."

He yawned and rubbed his droopy eyes. "While you're at it, how 'bout finding me a feather mattress and some furs to sleep on? This straw is like twigs. Oh, and I wouldn't mind a bath. But not from you. I'll do it myself, thanks. Just bring me one of those big steaming tubs like Gidon uses. And some oatmeal soap. I don't like that flowery rosewater stuff."

She smiled and slipped out. The guard locked the door behind her.

"And some apples. Crunchy ones!"

Vrell jogged up the dank stairwell to the first underground level. The Mahanaim dungeons—a labyrinth of stone hallways and barred doors—were located on the three levels below the stronghold's surface. Achan's cell was on the lowest level. Vrell climbed to the first level. As she neared the guards' station, the raised voices of two men grew louder.

"But it's only clothing." It was the voice of a young man. A very familiar voice. It slowed her steps shy of the corner.

"The prisoner's not to be seen or receive anything," the guard snapped. "No exceptions!"

"You still haven't told me his crime. He did his duty. This I know as fact."

Vrell rounded the corner to see the back of the burly guard standing at the gate shaking his head. The man he was talking to was hidden behind the guard's body. "I don't put 'em here, I just keep 'em here. Take it up with Lord Levy if you like."

The visitor sidestepped as if preparing to leave, and locked eyes with Vrell. His head cocked to the side, and he looked her up and down.

Bran.

She sucked in a silent breath and held it. Her pulse rose. Oh, she hadn't spoken to him since his proposal. It would be so wonderful if he recognized her—but the guard would report it to Master Hadar and all manner of unpleasantness would ensue. Mahanaim was not friendly territory these days. She doubted they would escape without being questioned.

No. Now was a bad time to make herself known. She needed to find Sir Rigil first as Mother had suggested. But if Bran was here, so was the knight he served. She noted that Bran's nose and face were peeling from sunburn. She had a salve that would help . . .

Instead, Vrell held her breath, lowered her gaze, and wove between Bran and the guard, slouching and bobbing in her best boy walk, praying he would not recognize her. As she placed one foot on the bottom step, Bran spoke.

"You there. Can you tell me anything about Achan Cham?"

Vrell froze, cheeks burning. How did Bran know Achan, and why did his question bring waves of guilt? She had done nothing wrong. She turned. Keeping her head down and her posture slumped, she gave her best stray boy accent. "What you wanna know?"

Bran strode forward, clutching a dirty linen sack in his hand. "These are his things. The guard won't let me take them to him. I'd like to see him."

Vrell shook her head. "I'm sorry, sir. No one's to see him."

"But you've seen him?"

"I'm tending his wounds."

Bran's sweet, sunburned face lit up, and he held out the sack. "Then you could take him this. Please. It's only clothing. I just . . . I think he'd want it."

Vrell accepted the grimy sack. Bran had come all this way to bring Achan his laundry? Why? "I'll take it to him, sir."

Bran bowed to her, bestowing a great honor to a stray boy like Vrell. Oh, he was such a good man. His poor nose. She yearned to rub some aloe salve on it.

"I thank you." Bran strode toward the stairwell leading out, then turned back. "Would you give him a message as well?"

Vrell nodded.

"Tell him, the offer's still good."

Vrell flushed. Oh, no, of course not. Bran was giving a message to Achan, not renewing his proposal. She swallowed her disappointment. "Will do, sir."

Bran bowed again and smiled at the burly guard. "I thank you."

When he was gone, Vrell trudged up to her room, leaking tears and wondering with each step where Bran was staying. It had felt strange to see him after so long. He looked different, but the same. Maybe even taller. She had wanted him to recognize her, sweep her off her feet, and take her home. At the same time, she'd hesitated. She furrowed her brow. She wanted to go home, did she not?

Of course she did, but first she had to help Achan.

She stopped on the landing halfway between the third and fourth floor. Why did she care about Achan, anyway? He did not have manners like Bran. He was rude and teased too much. But he was innocent and she'd seen him fight heroically to save a prince who despised him. Plus, he was injured. Without her help, his wounds could still become infected. And they had bloodvoices in common. There was something about him that drew her interest like moth to torch. What was it?

She carried Achan's sack to her room, which, as always, was dark and cold. She did not rank highly enough to have a fireplace in her chambers. She left the door open until she lit a candle. Then she dumped out the contents of Achan's sack.

A rock-hard bread roll tumbled across the floor, along with a few moldy meat pies, some clothing, a rolled up grey blanket, and a scrap of raw parchment that looked as if a child had made it. She wrinkled her nose at the smell of decayed food. What had Bran been thinking? There was no treasure here worth saving.

She picked up a brown linen shirt and lifted it to her nose. It smelled stale like the bread, but looked clean. Achan would appreciate it. She draped it over one arm and reached down for the other garment: a soft, doeskin doublet. She ran the suede against her cheek and smiled. This was quite nice. She folded the clothing and set it, and the bundled blanket, on the edge of her bed.

She lifted the parchment and unrolled it. The handwriting and spelling were atrocious.

Akan,

i cannat stand wuts to com. but i no what u did and i thank u for it. u ar mi best frend. u ar a tru keengsgard nite. my keengsgard nite. i dont want to mary Riga. id rathr mary u.

Vrell flushed and set the parchment on top of the clothing. She had no business reading such a letter.

She scurried to her sideboard and checked the new batch of ointment she was making for Achan. Poor, sweet, abused Achan. He had a woman who loved him. What had happened? Vrell sighed deeply and frowned as she stirred the mixture. Must all love in Er'Rets be thwarted or manipulated? Vrell masqueraded as a boy to dodge marriage, and here someone loved Achan but was apparently being forced to marry this Riga person.

Vrell stomped about the room, gathering the moldy and stale food from the floor. She set it outside the door for the chambermaid, then went back to her bed. She needed to go to the kitchens before taking these things to Achan. Maybe Mags could help her find some nice, crunchy apples.

She peered at the parchment out of the corner of her eye. There had only been a few more lines. She twisted her lips and snagged it.

prins gidon didint want me. he wantid to hert u. promis to get awey frum him. go to tafstown. wher yer nu cloths and be a nu man. i can nevr thank u fer saving me frum gidon. u wil alwas be mi hero. mi nite. i luv u.

gren

Vrell blinked back tears. Why did Prince Gidon insist on poisoning the lives of everyone? How she hated that venomous snake.

She ran to her sideboard and dug through her satchel until she found the prince's red silk sleeve, the one she had kept since that day on the battlefield. She could use it to see him in her mind, to know what he was up to. But how would that help Achan?

She left the sleeve and put the parchment and clothes back into the sack. She wandered down the stone steps, guilt flooding every thought.

Arman would not want her to carry so much hatred, she knew, even for a man as evil as Gidon Hadar. And was she any better? Reading Achan's private letter . . . lying to everyone about her identity . . . avoiding Bran when he could have taken her straight to Sir Rigil. Was this what Arman would have her become? Certainly not.

But Arman also would not want her to marry an abusive unbeliever. On that, she and her mother agreed wholeheartedly. There were few true believers in the Way in Er'Rets. Bran was one of them.

She groaned, not knowing how to make any of this right. When she reached the pillared foyer outside the chamber where the Council of Seven met, she turned and at the foot of the main staircase walked down the narrow corridor that led to the kitchens.

Vrell loved Bran. When all this was over, she was nearly certain Mother would permit them to marry. Mother had always said she wanted Vrell to be happy in marriage. Bran would be a good husband.

He might not make a good duke, though. Whoever Vrell married would inherit Mother's duchy. Bran was funny and kind and loyal, but he was no leader. He would need many advisors to run the duchy. Perhaps she should marry someone with experience with such things. If Bran were duke, Vrell would likely have to rule the duchy herself. But to be with Bran . . . it would be well worth it. She prayed Arman would forgive her until then.

Vrell entered the first kitchen and into a wall of heat. Along two walls were the hearths, only one of which was blazing. Vrell wondered how hot the room might be if all were lit. Six tables filled the center of the room. The cook, a plump woman with a stingy smile, stood at one, stuffing a chicken with bread crumbs and herbs. Three other servants were cleaning.

Vrell found the red-headed servant girl scrubbing dishes in a wooden tub. "Mags, think you could help me? I am gathering some things to take to the dungeon."

"To yer patient, the squire?" Mags pushed a strand of her red hair behind her ear, leaving a smudge of suds on her cheek. "I 'ear he's quite an Avinis."

Vrell rolled her eyes at the mention of the god of beauty. "I would not know about *that*."

Mags pinched Vrell's cheek with soapy fingers. "Oh, don't yeh sound so gloomy. Yeh'll grow into yer own, and all us maids will be crazy for yeh."

Vrell batted Mags's hand away. "Can you help or not?"

"Of course. What yeh want for 'im?"

Vrell rattled off the things she hoped for, and Mags came through on all accounts. Vrell trudged to the dungeon with Achan's sack, a jug of water, a wooden bowl, and her own lunch shoved into her pocket. The guard hassled her and searched the bag, but did not complain when Vrell reminded him that Master Hadar had assigned her to care for the squire.

Vrell didn't know why her master seemed to be going along with Lord Nathak, but she did know he still craved Achan's power. She guessed he would make a move to control Achan's fate soon. Vrell had claimed the squire was near death—fever from the lashings and all. Master Hadar had not questioned her time spent in the dungeons after that. He had suspended her lessons until the squire was healed. But she couldn't count on that ruse lasting too much longer.

The guard let Vrell into Achan's cell.

He was sitting on the floor in her corner, scratching at the dirt floor with a chicken bone. "Just wondered what's so great about this spot." His grey eyes sparkled in the torchlight.

Vrell set the bowl and the water jug on the hay-covered stone bed. "Are you leaning against the wall? Achan, your wounds will get dirty. Now I shall have to clean them again."

His gaze darted to the sack. "Is that mine?"

She sighed. "I met a squire who insisted you have it. The guards would not let him in to see you, but he gave me this, and a message."

Achan jumped up and took the sack. He peered inside. "What's the message?"

Vrell still was not used to him being so near her. Being so tall and . . . half dressed. She tried to act nonchalant, thankful he would be fully clothed soon. "He said to tell you, the offer is still good."

Achan met her eyes. "Bran was here?"

Vrell treaded carefully. "He did not give a name, sir. Only the message."

"No." Achan shook his head and grinned. "Don't call me 'sir.' Please don't. I'm no one's *sir*." He reached into the sack and pulled out the smaller linen bag that Vrell had brought from the kitchen.

Vrell's curiosity prompted her to snoop. "Is he a close friend, the squire?"

"Bran?" Achan sucked in a gasp as he discovered the contents of the small sack. "*Sparrow.*" He turned his wide smile to her—causing her stomach to boil with joy—and pulled out a fat, red apple. "Thank you." He sat on his bed, dropped the bag between his knees, and bit into the apple with a loud crunch. He tucked the bite into his cheek and pointed at the bowl and water jug. "What's all this?"

Vrell reached into her pocket and pulled out a half-used bar of soap. "It is unscented, all I could find. I figured you could use the bowl as a basin. The water will be cold, but . . . "

Achan slurped juice off his thumb. He took the soap and smelled it. "You sure know how to spoil a convict."

Heat flooded Vrell's cheeks, and she turned away, pretending to be looking for something on the ground. Was it foolish to be sweet to Achan? Would a boy do kind things for an innocent man? She settled in her corner and pulled the bread and figs from her pocket. She bowed her head and thanked Arman for His provisions.

"Why do you pray for food you already have?"

She glanced at Achan, whose eyes pierced through to her heart. She suspected that he, like most Er'Retians, believed in the host of false gods housed in ornate temples throughout the land. "I thank Arman for the blessing of having food to eat. I am not begging for more."

"Why thank Arman? He does not create plants or animals."

Vrell rolled her eyes. "There is only one God, Achan. His name is Arman. He creates everything. The other gods and goddesses are lies, devised to waste your days pining after false hope."

His forehead crinkled, and he looked at her as if she had sprouted a second head.

So she got back to her sleuthing. She took a bite of her bread and tried to appear disinterested. "Bran is your friend? Have you known him long?"

Achan pulled his blanket from the sack and spread it poorly with one hand over the bits of straw on the stone bed. "He journeyed with us from Sitna. Helped me out when Silvo and his friends made trouble. Even drew his sword for my sake."

Vrell grimaced. Silvo Hamartano. It figured. She pasted on an expression she hoped a boy might wear at the idea of a fight. "Tell me the story."

"Bah." Achan bit into the apple, held it in his teeth, and pulled the brown shirt over his head. His hair tousled as it poked through the neck opening. Vrell was glad he was finally clothed. Achan left the ties hanging loose and took the apple away from his mouth with a large bite. "It's not much of a story."

"Will you tell it? Please?"

Achan shrugged and took the suede jerkin into his lap, rubbing one finger over the nap. "Well, only if you don't think less of me. I'm not as obedient as most strays."

Vrell grinned and pulled her knees up to her chest. "This is going to be good."

Achan started the story by telling about Sir Gavin Lukos. Vrell had never met the Great Whitewolf, but had heard tales of his campaigns on behalf of King Axel. He had been the former king's closest advisor. Achan told how Sir Gavin had taken him as an apprentice in secret until he had killed the deer.

"That's the blood you sensed when you first heard me," he said. "I was carrying her back to Sitna Manor."

Then he told about the tournament where he had met Silvo, Silvo's sister—Lady Jaira—and Lady Tara Livna. Tara was Vrell's cousin and dear friend. She loved Tara, but she bristled when Achan went on longer than necessary about Lady Tara's kiss. Tara was stunning, with a voice like a lark. Vrell looked like a boy and sounded like a goose. A scratchy goose.

"She's the most beautiful woman I've ever seen, Sparrow. Well, next to Gren."

Vrell perked up at the name from the letter. "Who's Gren?"

Achan twisted the stem of the apple until it popped free from the core, then tossed both into the waste bucket. "A peasant girl I grew up with. She made me this shirt." He puffed out his chest. "Isn't it nice?"

Vrell nodded then pointed at the doublet. "And that?"

"Yeah." He beamed and pulled on the doublet, leaving it hang open like a vest. "She made this from the deer I killed. Clever, huh?"

Vrell should get back. Master Hadar would be waiting for an update. But she wanted to hear more. Achan told about serving wine to Silvo and Jaira at Prince Gidon's banquet, then lingered on another moment shared with Lady Tara. Vrell was not a bit surprised that Tara had been kind to Achan. Tsaftown did not keep slaves, and Achan was waggish and handsome. Still, it bothered Vrell how his face lit up when he spoke of Tara, beloved cousin or not.

Such thoughts! Vrell berated herself. She loved Bran, and he loved her. She had been gone from home too long. Life as an outcast was starting to take its toll.

Achan fiddled with the ties on his jerkin. "Lord Nathak discovered my training. After that, Sir Gavin left me. I still haven't learned why. And Gidon punished me for insulting Jaira, by making me his sparring partner. I think he wanted to *accidentally* kill me. Silvo and his demented cohorts ambushed me on the first night of the trip to Mahanaim, claiming to avenge Jaira's honor. As if she had any."

He smirked. "Anyway, you saw the bruises. Bran and Sir Rigil came to my aid. And that's that. To answer your question then: yes, Bran is a friend, if not for very long."

As Achan tucked the small bag of food into his sack he paused and pulled out the parchment. He held it in his lap, staring down at it, his face paling. Then he crumpled it into a little ball and tossed it into the privy bucket in the corner.

Vrell gasped and scrambled to her feet to retrieve it, but it had already soaked into the foul liquid. She spun back to Achan. "What did you do that for?"

"There's no reason for me to—" His eyes narrowed. "You little fox, you read it!"

Vrell straightened and turned up her nose. Hands on her hips, she stomped to the door. "Guard!"

Achan jumped up and grabbed her arm, dark brows furrowed, pupils swelling. "You had no right!"

"Back up!" the guard snarled.

Achan released his crushing grip, and Vrell slipped out, heart pounding. The guard slammed the door and clicked the bolts into place. Vrell glanced back to see Achan scowling through the black bars.

Maybe she should have denied his accusation.

Maybe she should not have read the parchment in the first place.

• • •

That evening, Master Hadar led Vrell to a lovely receiving chamber on the ninth floor and introduced her to the Levy family.

Vrell had been there years ago, and everything sat just as she remembered. Cream and indigo tapestries boxed in a spacious, warm expanse between two fireplaces, one on each end of the room. The family of five sat on carved couches that fanned out in a half circle around the fireplace nearest the door.

The valet announced, "Master Macoun Hadar and his apprentice, Vrell Sparrow," and led them before the family seated on the couches.

No one stood. Lord Levy nodded politely, an ivory pipe between his lips. His white hair and short, pointed beard made him look more snobbish than ever. She knew how Lord Levy felt about strays. As chairman of the Council of Seven, he had spearheaded the campaigns to brand strays and ban them from Kingsguard service.

Lord Levy's wife, Lady Fallina, sat near the hearth—elegance in human form. Her golden hair piled onto her head, held by a dozen sapphire clips. Gold embroidery embellished her cobalt silk gown, which draped over her body like a second skin. Her every movement captivated the eye. She smiled and said, "Welcome to Mahanaim." Even her voice was musical.

"Thank you," Vrell said with a bow.

Lady Fallina's charm had not been passed on to her daughters. Vrell had met the girls on several occasions, but thankfully they did not recognize her nor give her more than a fleeting glance.

The eldest, Jacqueline, was Vrell's age. She looked like her mother, but whined like a mule. She too wore a gown of cobalt silk, but hers hung on her bony body like a tent. Her younger sister, Marietta, at fourteen, was blessed with her mother's figure and smile, and, had she been less chatty, might have been a real contender for queen. But everyone knew that Prince Gidon despised what he considered insipid women and would certainly never choose one as his queen.

Reggio, a scrawny twelve-year-old and an even more stuck-up version of Lord Levy, said, "Really, Father, another stray?" He glared at Vrell, then Master Hadar. "They're not staying for dinner, are they? I'm certain Prince Gidon would not appreciate their presence."

Vrell shot Reggio her nastiest glare. She had heard he was a squire now. She pitied the knight who had taken him on. Whoever it was had most likely been pressured or paid, or both, by Lord Levy. She would have to ask Achan if he knew.

If he would still speak to her.

Marietta stood from the couch and skipped up to Vrell. She took her hand and twirled underneath Vrell's arm. "Can I borrow him, Father? He's ever so polite and not too tall."

Lord Levy looked up from his pipe. "Borrow him for what?"

"To practice dancing. My chambermaid doesn't do the boy part very well, and I want to be the best dancer at Prince Gidon's wedding."

"He's announced a bride?" Jacqueline clutched Lord Levy's arm, jerking the pipe from his lips. "Father?"

Lord Levy sighed and moved his pipe to his other hand. "Nothing has been formally announced, but it appears the match will be made with Mandzee Hamartano."

Jacqueline shrieked. “Mandzee! Oh, Mother! How will I tolerate her as queen? It’s not fair. Am I not pretty enough?”

Vrell stood silently beside Master Hadar, glad to have been momentarily forgotten.

“Oh, Jacqueline,” Lord Levy said, “you’re a jewel. You must understand that this marriage is more for the political match than the prince’s fancy. That I know from Lord Nathak. Mandzee Hamartano is from Jaelport, a strong city far south and in Darkness. An alliance with them will fortify the area for the kingdom.”

“It will fortify my forever being subject to Mandzee’s scorn,” Jacqueline said. “She’ll never let me forget this.”

“Then you shouldn’t have told her he’d pick you,” Marietta said.

Jacqueline stuck out her tongue at Marietta.

Vrell worked to keep her reaction internal. If Mandzee Hamartano really was to be queen, Vrell would have to consider moving across the sea. Jaelportian women had an eerily persuasive way about them. It was little wonder how she was chosen as Prince Gidon’s bride. She had simply worked her magic, whatever it was.

Reggio sighed dramatically. “Who cares about queens and weddings?” He turned to Lord Levy. “Has the stray that attacked the prince been sentenced?”

“Sentenced? A stray has no right to trial, as far as I’m concerned,” Lord Levy said. “I believe Lord Nathak is keeping him in our dungeons for now.”

“Why not execute him?” Reggio said. “I could do it, if you’d let me use an executioner’s axe.”

Lady Fallina sucked in a sharp breath. “Reggio! For shame, to think of such things.”

"Your mother is right," Lord Levy said. "That's no job for a young lord. Besides, a slow death is more appropriate for a man who attacks the future king."

Vrell glared at Master Hadar, but he avoided her gaze. They remained silent until the valet announced dinner. Master Hadar excused them, and he and Vrell walked back to his chambers.

Vrell could scarcely hold her tongue. "Forgive me, Master, but will you allow the squire to die? Did you not want him as a second apprentice?"

Master Hadar hummed. "I do, but there are things you don't understand, boy. First, many consider *me* a stray."

"You, Master?" No wonder he despised the orange tunic.

"Yes, Lord Levy seeks to be rid of me. But I've lived here since before he was born and have made myself indispensable. Still, I haven't the rank to make demands of noblemen."

Something was odd about such a confession. Vrell needed to contact Mother to see if Uncle Livna had information on who Macoun Hadar really was.

Master Hadar went on. "Prince Gidon is about to take his throne, but the Council has ruled for thirteen years. They do not relish the thought of giving up control completely. Lord Levy knows of my arrangement with Lord Nathak to use my gifts to watch over the prince. Despite his feelings toward me, Lord Levy is willing to give me a seat on the New Council if I keep him apprised of the king's plans. For that I need your help."

They reached the staircase and Master Hadar paused. "The problem is, watching weakens you. The squire, then, is the perfect solution. But Lord Nathak refuses to give him to me. And I need Lord Nathak's alliance to watch the prince's mind, or he'll tell the prince to block me. Prince Gidon cannot bloodvoice, but he knows how to block against those who seek to penetrate his thoughts. So you see, I have no remedy at present."

Vrell stared at her master's sunken eyes. She had heard the Council was corrupt, but this was lunacy. If Master Hadar reported every move and thought of Prince—no: *King*—Gidon, the king would have no control. The Council had been meant to disband once the king was in place, had it not? They should be seeking less control over the future king, not more.

And what was this talk of a *New Council*? Did Mother know of it? Would any one individual rule Er'Rets, or would it be run by everyone? With mini agendas and political coups, factions would rise up. Er'Rets would be at war with itself. And since everyone hated Gidon as prince, *King* Gidon would fall. Then what?

Master Hadar left her on the eighth floor, and Vrell continued on to the third floor. It was late. The torches on the stairwell had burned low. She lit a candle in her room and scraped her teeth, washed her face, and combed out her tangled hair. She climbed under her thin wool blanket and blew out the light. She did not like the blackness that shrouded her when the candle was out. With so much stone, the smallest sound in the fortress magnified as if it were inches away.

She lay awake praying Arman might show her what to do. Vrell wanted to help Er'Rets but could see no way to make a difference. She set her mind on finding Sir Rigil and freeing Achan before he was made to become Master Hadar's pawn—or was killed for a crime he didn't commit.

She tried bloodvoicing Achan, but she could find no sense of him despite holding the lock of hair she had cut from his head when he had been out with fever. Either he had run out of karpos fruit or he had perfected blocking.

There had to be someone who would help Achan. Perhaps Sir Rigil would. Achan had said that he'd come to his aid once before, and Bran seemed to like Achan as well. Yes. Vrell would find Sir Rigil. He would keep her safe and help Achan. It was a perfect plan. But what if she couldn't find Sir Rigil? Mags might know. If only there were someone else who could help Achan, then Vrell could focus on her own problems.

Suddenly she knew. She crept down into the massive foyer of the Mahanaim stronghold, wove between the columns, and stood before the entrance to the Council's meeting chamber. She snuck past the golden doors and examined the displays along the entry corridor.

Every five steps on both sides of the wall, little alcoves jutted off displaying tributes to the great Kingsguard commanders of old. She passed a bronze bust of Moul Rog the Great, the Kingsguard commander during King Trevyn the Explorer's reign. Pittan Remy, a native of Carmine, served during King Johan's time. There was a full body statue of him.

She stopped before a fluted pillar that held a limestone bust of a man with long hair and a braided beard. A cracked shield hung on the wall behind it. Vrell stepped around the bust, laid her hand on the shield, and, with her mind, sought out the face of the person it depicted.

The Great Whitewolf.

21

Vrell Sparrow.

Achan lay on his stone bed, staring at the cobwebs hanging down from the ceiling and trying to ignore Sparrow. The runt was sitting outside his cell, picking at his mind with some strange trick that penetrated his walls and drew a headache.

He was still mad at the boy. Bran had asked him to deliver Achan's stuff, not ransack it. The whelp had no business snooping. Achan sighed. He should've read Gren's letter.

He lifted his head and thunked it down gently on the hay-strewn stone bed again and again. Everything looked the same in his cell, no matter the hour. He had no idea what time it was. Late. Sparrow had brought him dinner hours ago. The prisoner down the hall had stopped moaning.

So many times since leaving Sitna, he'd meant to read Gren's letter. He didn't want to admit he hadn't done so because he was afraid of what it might say—but what else had stopped him? He'd likely never see Gren again. Probably he didn't read it because her words would've felt so final. Like she'd died somehow. In a way, Achan guessed she had.

Still, that Sparrow read Gren's words when Achan had not . . . It was like the runt held a secret that wasn't his. Something about that bristled the hair on his arms. Now he wanted to know more than ever what Gren had—

A crash in the corridor outside Achan's cell shot him to his feet. He darted to the door and peered outside. A man with shaggy, blond hair and a black cloak bent over an unconscious guard and pulled the keys from his belt. Achan flattened against the wall behind the door and waited. The bolts on the lock clicked, the door swung open, and the man stepped inside Achan's cell.

Sparrow's voice broke the silence. "What are you doing?"

"Where is the squire?"

"Who are you?" Sparrow asked.

Then came a scuffle, and the lad screamed like a girl.

Achan jumped out from behind the door. The man had pinned Sparrow to the floor. "Hey!" Achan kicked him in the side. "You looking for me?"

The man sprang up and elbowed Achan in the temple.

Achan went down, head throbbing. He rolled, trying to stand. He could hear Sparrow struggling and whimpering, but everything blurred before his eyes. He focused on his breathing, trying to clear his head.

The man's blurry form leaned over him. A finger wormed between Achan's lips and a woodsy liquid dribbled into his mouth.

Achan tried to spit the substance out, but a hand covered his mouth and held him down until he stilled, his eyes drooping. The man hoisted Achan off the floor and slung him over his shoulder. The door slammed shut and the lock clicked into place.

"No!" Sparrow's voice. Pounding on the door. "Guards! Help!"

Where were the guards?

Achan's captor ran through the maze of dark corridors and down a flight of stairs, making Achan's head bounce with each step. Achan wanted to protest, but words wouldn't come. Blackness shrouded his vision.

The bouncing stopped. "Inko!" his captor said. "Help me."

Achan felt his body lowered onto an unstable surface. Pale, yellow light danced over a dark, craggy ceiling. A cave?

"Did you be giving him the soporific?" a low, raspy voice asked in a jilted accent.

"Aye," his captor said.

Achan felt like he was falling. He gripped the wooden edge of something, which caused the bed he lay in to rock. A boat! He was in a boat in some underground canal. The motion made him queasy, and he focused again on his breathing until the pale light faded to black.

Over the next period of time—minutes? days?—he jerked in and out of consciousness, only to feel lost in a dream. Had he been taken into Darkness? Had they crossed over to the other side of the Evenwall?

Eventually they stopped. Someone lifted him out of the boat and tried to help him stand, but Achan's legs were as faulty as his vision. Cool air gripped his pores. Water sloshed against a wall of some sort. A single torch burned to his left but did not shed enough light to help his cause. Footsteps clunked over hollow-sounding wood. A drawbridge? A dock?

Again he was tossed over someone's shoulder and carried up several flights of stairs. A door creaked open. His captor brought him inside and lowered him onto a firm surface. Achan wanted to wake and see where he was, but sleep won out before he could focus.

Achan awoke on a straw bed. He swung his legs off the side and managed to sit.

He first noticed a small fire burning in a smoke-stained hearth. It brought the only light to a small room. He blinked. Bare walls, the ceiling dripping with cobwebs. A scuffed wooden floor. Achan turned to the other side of the room and jumped.

A man with grey skin stared at him. He sat in one of two mismatched chairs at a battered table on the other side of Achan's bed. His white hair grew straight up off his head like a round hedge. Like his abductor, this man wore a black cape.

"Who are you?" Achan asked.

"You may be calling me Inko." The man nodded, eyes fixed past Achan's shoulder. "He is being named Sir Caleb."

Sir? Achan swiveled his head back past the fireplace. His wild-eyed kidnapper sat on the wooden floor beside his bed, leaning against the bare wall. His chin-length blond hair was frizzy. He looked to be middle-aged. The firelight darkened the weathered lines on his cheeks and forehead. "You're a knight?"

"Aye. We both are." Sir Caleb smirked. "Or were."

Were? "What do you want with me?"

"Only to hold you until our master arrives."

Dizziness washed over Achan. He propped a hand on the bed to steady himself. "Who is your master?" Achan blinked fast to regain focus. His voice sounded far away and hollow. "And what does he want with me?"

"All in good time." Sir Caleb stood and pushed Achan back down to lie on the bed.

Sleep, lad. Sleep.

Achan's eyes fluttered closed, then snapped open. He bashed a fist into Sir Caleb's jaw, hopped off the bed, and managed to run to the door before crumpling to the floor in a haze.

Inko swept him up and tossed him back on the bed. Sir Caleb grimaced and massaged his jaw.

Achan glared. "Don't play with my mind!" He tried to focus on the allown tree, but his head merely throbbed.

Sir Caleb's wild eyes grew wider. "It's true? You *can* bloodvoice, then?"

Achan feigned ignorance and scooted back on the bed until his back touched the wall. "I don't know what you mean."

"Those who can sense it have the power to do it themselves."

Achan remembered Sparrow's warning that some would seek to abuse his power. Playing the fool was his best defense for now. "What power?"

"Bloodvoices."

Achan forced a cynical laugh. "You speak of kingly fables. No such ability exists in the real world of flesh and blood. Besides, I'm not a king."

Sir Caleb leaned over the bed, his shaggy hair framing his face like a sunflower. His bulging eyes glistened in the firelight. "The gift runs in royal blood. You do not have to be a king to have it, although you may be."

• • •

Vrell banged on the door of Achan's cell and called for help until she lost her voice. Finally, one of the guards regained consciousness enough to stagger to the door and let her out.

She ran to Master Hadar's chamber to report. She found him sitting at his desk, writing. She sucked in a long breath. "Someone has taken the prisoner, Achan. He's gone."

Master Hadar bolted to his feet. "Who?"

"I know not," Vrell said, her heart still beating wildly from her run up eight flights of stairs. "He locked me in. I—"

The door flew open and banged against the interior wall. Lord Nathak strode into the chamber. "You!" He pointed at Vrell. His eye was bloodshot and bulging. "You were left to watch him and warn your master of any complications. Where is the stray?"

Vrell shook at the volume of his voice. "I-I am sorry, my lord. I-I do not know."

Lord Nathak seized Vrell's shoulder and held a dagger up to her throat. "Where?"

Vrell choked back a sob. "Please, my lord! I-I do not know!"

Lord Nathak gripped the side of her face and stared into her eyes.

Master Hadar hurried over. "Lord Nathak, please allow me."

Lord Nathak released Vrell with a slight push and she stumbled.

Master Hadar's sunken eyes drilled into hers. "Tell me exactly what happened."

Vrell explained how the man with the wild hair had attacked her and carried Achan away.

"Can you sense the squire?" Master Hadar asked.

Vrell shook her head.

Lord Nathak pointed the dagger at her throat again. "Try."

"Seek him out, boy," Master Hadar said. "You've spent enough time with him. It shouldn't be difficult."

Vrell did not want to. If someone had rescued Achan, he was better off not being found. But if she did not try, she could face Lord Nathak's blade. Yet even if she reached out, Achan could block her. He had been blocking her all day. She was too good a teacher, it seemed.

Vrell closed her eyes. She cupped her hands over her face and breathed in the smell of the clove and calendula ointment that lingered on her hands. She thought about Achan's scruffy face, dark hair, and grey eyes.

Images of a dark chamber grew in her mind.

"He is close."

Vrell Sparrow.

Achan lifted his head off the straw mattress. *Sparrow?*

Are you safe?

He wasn't certain. He lay on his side on the straw mattress, hands bound behind his back, ankles bound too. But he sensed no hatred or hostility from his captors. Both men sat at the table mumbling to each other. He certainly didn't want to go back to Lord Nathak. *I don't know. They've bound me.*

Lord Nathak wants me to locate you.

"No!" Achan thought of the allown tree, and Sparrow faded away.

Sir Caleb was at his side in an instant. He sat on the bed beside Achan, a fresh bruise swelling on his jaw. "I'm sorry for the restraints. You left me little choice."

Achan's heart thundered in his chest. Who to trust? He sighed heavily. He'd take his chances with these men over any life with Lord Nathak. He decided to confide this truth. "Lord Nathak is looking for me."

"How do you know?" Sir Caleb asked.

"He's using Sparrow."

"A bird?"

"A boy. The old man's apprentice."

Inko jumped to his feet and bounded to the bed. "Be blocking it, quickly!"

"No. Let's see what they know." Sir Caleb nodded once. "Tread carefully."

Achan pictured Sparrow's small, ever-blushing, round face and narrow, green eyes. Voices from that targeted location flooded his mind, and he cringed as his head filled with pressure.

You must be patient, Lord Nathak, Hadar said. *The boy can do it.* The old man stood over Sparrow, sunken eyes like stone caverns. He wanted Sparrow's secret.

Achan frowned. What secret?

The boy is too slow, Hadar! Lord Nathak screamed, pushing the old man closer. *Do it yourself.*

I cannot, Hadar said. *I've spent no time at all with the squire. Leave it to Vrell.*

Vrell? Achan frowned. Oh, right. Vrell was Sparrow's first name.

Lord Nathak pushed the old man away and seized Sparrow by the hair. Something sharp bit into the boy's throat.

Coldness flashed over Achan. He clutched the stinging tickle at his neck but found no weapon. All he could feel were the prickles of his own need to shave. *Sparrow? I feel pain at my throat. What are they doing to you?*

Achan heard Sparrow speaking aloud to the men. He rambled, sobbing, hysterical. *He's in a dark room . . . Two men are with him . . . The one who attacked me is there. I cannot—* Sparrow sobbed, then quietly, like a whisper, *Achan, do you want to be found?*

Achan glanced at his captors. *No. I don't think so.*

I cannot see anything else, Sparrow said aloud to Lord Nathak.

Lord Nathak slapped Sparrow with the back of his hand then pressed the blade to the boy's throat again. *Find him! Your life depends on it.*

No, Lord Nathak, Hadar said. *You must let me do this.*

Sparrow gasped and broke into a long sob. The boy's pain and regret seeped into Achan, bringing tears to his own eyes. He could hear Sparrow's feelings.

It is too difficult to keep up this charade, the boy thought. *I cannot pretend any longer. I want to go home to be with—*

Sparrow let out a high-pitched scream. Achan winced as an icy vise gripped his head. Only it was Sparrow's head that was hurting. Sparrow's ears that were tingling.

Sparrow?

Hello, young man, Hadar's cold voice rang loud between Achan's ears. *Vrell is helping me to reach you. Aren't you, Vrell?*

Achan heard Sparrow whimper.

What have you done to him? Achan asked.

He'll be fine. A little weak, perhaps, but he'll recover. Lord Nathak cannot hear us, gifted one. So listen carefully. I have a proposition for you that does not involve him.

I'm not interested in your propositions.

Is not Vrell your friend?

Achan paused, thinking of how Sparrow had taken care of him, maybe saved his life. But the little snoop had read his letter. *That's debatable.*

Sir Caleb prodded Achan's shoulder. "What do you hear?"

Achan ignored him. He needed to know what Hadar wanted.

Your bloodvoice is very strong, Achan. I can mold you into a powerful man. Meet me at dawn tomorrow behind the tavern called Mig's Pit.

Why should I?

I hold Vrell's life in my hands.

There was a long silence and the pressure from the old man's mind lessened its hold on Sparrow. Achan heard the old man speak aloud. *I can see no more than Vrell, Lord Nathak. A dark bedchamber and two men. I don't recognize either, and now the squire has—*

Achan regretfully pulled back and closed his mind. Goosebumps broke out on his arms at the sudden warmth. Or was that the lack of coldness? The gods had truly forsaken him, if there were any gods. The moment he was free of one crazy, manipulative master, he was forced into the service of another.

He looked at Sir Caleb, who was staring intently at him. "What do you want? Do you want to teach me too?"

"Teach you what?"

"How to use my oh-so-powerful gift?"

"I don't give a pig's eye about your gift." Sir Caleb got up and stoked the fire. "I just do as I'm told. What did you hear?"

But Achan wasn't sure he trusted these men any more than Nathak or Hadar. His wrists chafed against the rope that bound him. He inched around until he was on his side and could see Sir Caleb. "What's so great about bloodvoicing anyway?"

"Well, for me and Inko, bloodvoicing is one of the reasons for our recruitment and quick promotion in the Kingsguard. The ability makes us better soldiers."

"You're both Kingsguards?"

"Old Kingsguards, in case you were not noticing," Inko said.

"At least I still have color in my hair," Sir Caleb said.

Inko snorted. "Very little of it."

Achan lifted his head. "You're Old Kingsguards? Do you know Sir Gavin?"

Sir Caleb smirked. "Aye. The name sounds familiar."

Achan's head turned between the two knights, studying their expressions. "Well, why should Lord Nathak care so much about me?" Achan asked. "I'm nothing to anyone."

Sir Caleb blinked his wide eyes. "The question itself should lead you to some conclusions."

"It does not."

A pounding rattled the door. Achan pushed himself into a sitting position, hoping this might be his chance to escape. Though how far he could get with his ankles bound, he didn't know.

Inko's eyes glazed slightly and he broke into a narrow smile. "What has been taking you so long?" He unlocked the door and pulled it open.

Sir Gavin bounded into the chamber.

Achan broke into the first true smile in days. His stomach filled with light, joyous air.

Sir Gavin was a mess. He looked like a hunchback with his red cape jutting out over a massive backpack. The cape was soiled with dirt and as wrinkled as his forehead. His beard braid frizzed out so much that Achan almost couldn't see the braid.

"Did you come on foot?" Sir Caleb asked.

"The forest is vast, my friends. Still, I made a two-weeks' journey from Tsaftown in five days. Was that not fast enough for you?" Sir Gavin looked to Achan and bared his wolfish teeth in a wide smile. "Hello, Achan." Then he frowned at Inko and Caleb. "Was it necessary to bind him?"

"Yes." Inko shut the door and settled back in his chair. "He is otherwise being a handful of ants."

Sir Gavin dropped his pack and crossed to the bed.

"Careful," Sir Caleb said. "He's gifted strong. He comes into you with massive force."

Sir Gavin smiled and winked his brown eye. "Aye, he does." He sat on the bed and loosened the bonds on Achan's wrists. "I'd expect nothing less from this one."

"You sent them to free me?" Achan rubbed his wrist, then the other. "Why didn't they just say they were with you?"

Sir Gavin shrugged and looked to Sir Caleb. "Why didn't you just say so, Caleb?"

"I barely understand this mission, Gavin. You expect me to spill my guts to a stranger? I left the business of talking to you. He has been bloodvoicing with a boy in Lord Levy's manor. Lord Nathak seeks him." Sir Caleb sat on Achan's other side and put his elbows on his knees. "Tell us, boy, what did you discover?"

Sir Gavin looked at Achan, his mustache curling up in another smile. "You've learned to bloodvoice?"

"Sort of. Sparrow taught me some." Achan paused, feeling somewhat embarrassed. "He says I'm strong, and his master wants to take me as an apprentice."

"Wait." Sir Gavin put a hand on Achan's shoulder. "Who's this Sparrow?"

"Lad who was with him in the dungeon," Sir Caleb said. "Pudgy little thing. Screams like an old hag."

"A criminal?"

"Macoun Hadar's apprentice," Achan said. "Sparrow took care of my wounds. Used to apprentice for an apothecary before the Kingsguards took him."

"*He's* the one who called out to me then!" Sir Gavin reached down and untied Achan's ankles.

Achan's eyes widened. "Sparrow called out to you? When?"

"Two nights ago. He said your life was in danger and gave me the location of your cell. Freeing you couldn't wait until I arrived, so I sent Inko and Sir Caleb."

Sparrow had called Sir Gavin? Then he had saved him. And now he was suffering at the hands of Nathak and Hadar. He had to try to help his fellow stray, this Vrell Sparrow.

Sir Gavin tugged on his beard braid. "You say the boy is Macoun Hadar's apprentice?"

Achan nodded. "Who is Macoun Hadar, anyway? Some royal cousin?"

"He's King Johan's illegitimate son." Sir Gavin slipped off his boots and stretched his legs out. "Which makes him King Axel's uncle, of sorts. He's not to be trusted, Achan. Macoun Hadar operates on his own agenda. And his age drives him to desperation."

"What do you mean?"

"He goes through several apprentices a year, uses them to do what he cannot. He spies on people. Knows more secrets than Arman himself."

Achan smirked. "Can't be that bad, then. Arman knows nothing compared to Isemios."

Inko sat straight up in his chair. "What? Isemios? The boy is not already believing in the Way?"

"Why would he?" Sir Gavin said. "Who in Sitna would have taught him right? They worship Cetheria there."

Inko shook his head. "I am being much hesitant, Gavin. Are you having certainty about this—absolute certainty?"

Sir Gavin yawned. "I am, old friend. But even if I'm wrong, his character speaks for itself. And anything would be better than what we have now."

Achan kept trying to follow, but he could not understand this thread of conversation.

"But there is Prince Oren," Sir Caleb said. "He is a believer, at least."

Sir Gavin folded his arms. "We shall take it before the Council and see if the truth will set us all free."

"Wait!" Achan yelled. "What are you talking about?"

Sir Gavin patted Achan's shoulder. "Nothing to worry yourself with today, lad. Did you learn anything from this Sparrow?"

Achan reluctantly let his confusion go. "He could sense this room, but not its location. He sensed two men with me. Then Hadar used Sparrow to speak with me."

Inko sucked in a sharp breath.

Sir Gavin's eyes zeroed in on Achan's. "What did he say?"

"He wants me as his apprentice. He said he has a proposal for me that doesn't involve Lord Nathak. And he said if I don't meet him at dawn, Sparrow will die."

"Fire and ash!" Inko jumped from his chair and paced to the door. "I am telling you, we should not be mingling with this man."

Sir Gavin turned to Inko. "We're not mingling with him. We're avoiding him."

"But he will be sitting there to be hearing it all. To be knowing our plans." Inko motioned to Achan. "It could be that he is listening right now."

Achan scowled. "I know how to block." Thanks to Sparrow.

"Don't worry," Sir Gavin said. "He'd find out soon enough regardless. It's in Arman's hands. He'll see justice done."

Achan grew ill of this coded banter. "What of Sparrow? Can't we help him? He's a smart little twig. And he's helped me more than once. Maybe you could use a healer like him on your assignments."

"We don't get assignments anymore," Sir Caleb said. "We've been banished."

"By who?"

"The Council of Seven," Sir Gavin said. "I'm the only one who still gets to serve, though even I am not considered an active Kingsguard. I don't know how much longer they'll use me at all. Over the past few years, Lord Nathak has corrupted several Council members. As have Macoun Hadar, Lord Levy, and a dozen others. They all seek to fulfill personal agendas."

Sir Gavin sighed. "When Prince Gidon takes the throne, the downward spiral will happen quickly. All who seek truth are being banished or killed. Their false gods have corrupted their minds. They've all lost their way and will drag Er'Rets into chaos and war if something isn't done."

War? A chill ran over Achan. "What can be done?"

"You'll soon see." Sir Gavin twisted his beard. "Now, tell us where you're to meet Macoun Hadar, and we shall try to save your little friend."

22

Vrell woke on the floor in front of the fireplace in Master Hadar's bedchamber. She focused in on a kettle hanging above the flames. Her head throbbed as if someone had taken an axe to it.

Then she remembered: Master Hadar had used her to speak to Achan. What had they discussed? Why had it hurt so? Because she had not invited him in? Or had he used her physical strength to compensate for his own?

She struggled to her feet, thankful Lord Nathak was gone. Master Hadar sat writing at his desk. She glanced at the windows and saw that it was dark outside. Still night.

Master Hadar rose from his desk. "Good. You're awake." He walked to his sideboard. "Sit, sit. I'll tend your wound."

Vrell lifted her fingers to her throat and released a trembling breath. The crusty scratch stung at her touch, but it could not be bad if the blood had dried. Why had Master Hadar not cleaned it already? She shakily lowered herself onto the stool at the table by his bed and fought back tears. What would Bran say if he knew Vrell had been threatened at knifepoint twice since leaving home? Not only threatened, but also cut by deranged men?

She needed to find Sir Rigil. The sooner the better. Hope welled inside. With Achan safe, she could now leave here without any worries. And she would. As soon as Master Hadar dismissed her.

Master Hadar offered a wet towel. "It's only a scratch. I doubt you'll even need a salve."

"Thank you." Vrell pressed the cool cloth to her neck.

Master Hadar hurried to the fireplace and carried the steaming kettle to the sideboard. "Some tea will calm you. Lord Nathak's temper sometimes causes accidents."

Vrell watched him fiddle with different canisters. Why was he being so nice? Never had he offered her tea. Rarely had she seen him so much as move, yet now he flitted about his chamber like a firefly.

He carried a mug of tea and a slice of bread to the table and set it before her. A blue vein pulsed on his forehead. "There now. That should help you feel better."

Vrell lifted the tea to her lips and sipped. A familiar bitterness flooded her mouth. The âleh flower! Master Hadar had doused the tea with honey, but its flavor could not be masked. Was he wanting to silence her bloodvoice—or open her mind to his probing?

She pretended to sip and nibbled the bread until the tea cooled. Master Hadar sat at his desk, eyes closed. Was he speaking to someone or spying?

Vrell took her chance. She lowered the cup to her side and drained it into her right boot. The tepid, slimy liquid doused her foot, but it was better than the alternative. Plus, if Master Hadar thought she was immune to the effects of the âleh flower, perhaps he would not try to sneak the tonic on her again. Before she could finish her bread, someone knocked on the door.

Master Hadar said, “Enter,” without opening his eyes.

Jax ducked through the doorway, followed by Khai. The men were dressed in their Kingsguard uniforms.

Vrell smiled, glad to see her giant friend. “Hello, Jax.”

“How are you, young Vrell? Faring well in your apprenticeship, I hope?”

Vrell nodded.

Jax’s gaze lost focus, as did Khai’s.

Vrell looked to Master Hadar, wondering what he was voicing to them. She tried to hear, but their connection was secure. A sudden notion grew deep within her. What if Master Hadar had discovered she was a woman? She had no memory of what he had said to Achan when he had jumped though her. Maybe he had discovered the truth while he was in her head.

Then why give her the silencer?

Khai’s eyes snapped open. He sneered and stepped toward Vrell. She shuddered as if millions of ants crawled over her skin. They knew! Jax also walked toward Vrell, although his expression was somber.

Arman save her, it was all over.

“Jax?” Vrell slipped off her stool and backed into the corner, hoping to appeal to the kinder man. The liquid in her right boot squished around her foot.

“It’ll be all right, lad,” he said. “Don’t fight, and you’ll be fine.”

Khai reached her first and snagged her by the hair. Vrell gasped.

Jax lunged forward and pulled Khai away. "If you're going to be cruel, I'll do it. He's just a boy."

Vrell froze, ignoring her stinging scalp. Boy? Praise Arman—they didn't know. But what were they doing, then?

Jax frowned and pulled a length of cord from his belt. "I need to tie your arms, Vrell. And your ankles. Would you like to sit first?"

Bind her? What was this madness? "Why?"

"No talking!" Master Hadar snapped.

Vrell's ears tingled.

Jax mi Katt.

Vrell opened her mind.

It's all right, Jax said. *I'll watch over you.*

Vrell offered her hands to the giant, thankful Arman had chosen him for this insane moment. Jax bound her wrists in front, then her ankles, and helped her sit in the corner.

"Master," Vrell said. "Why are you doing this? What have I done?"

Khai helped himself to Vrell's bread and stood over her, looking out the window. He chewed with his mouth open, a nasty combination of slurping and smacking.

"Please, Master. I promise to do better."

The old man ignored her. He just continued writing with his quill. Jax shot her several apologetic glances.

When Jax had finished binding her, she expected him to pick her up and carry her off somewhere. Perhaps on some new boat trip, or maybe to Achan's former cell in the dungeon. But Jax just backed away and sat against the hearth. Khai stood at the window. And Master Hadar dipped his quill into the ink and started in on a fresh scroll. So why had they bound her?

No one spoke for a long time. Vrell's ears tickled again and again with no declaration of who was knocking. Dozens of attempts to enter her mind failed. She glanced at Master Hadar. It had to be him. He thought she'd taken the âleh tonic and that her mind would now be easier to invade. Hopefully, all these failures would make him think she was immune to âleh.

She pressed her ear against the wall, attempting to ease the itch. The toes on her right foot felt cold and wet. A whisper and footsteps drew near. She closed her eyes. Someone nudged her side. Khai. She would recognize the point of his boot anywhere.

The weasel hissed, "He sleeps, Master."

"Very well. Come to the fire and we'll make our plan."

"Why not tell the boy?" Jax's low voice rumbled. "He's loyal. I'm sure he'd help."

"No," Master Hadar said. "Should something go wrong, I'll need to sacrifice him. And I doubt anyone is *that* loyal."

Vrell stiffened. Sacrifice?

Khai's steps faded with his voice. "He hides a secret, Master. Did you discover it?"

"No. Vrell's mind is a strongbox. Nothing I do can penetrate it. I forced myself into his mind to jump yesterday, but he managed to keep his walls up the whole time. Even now, after the âleh tea, I sense nothing. It's amazing. If only I could find such immunity for myself."

Vrell smiled in the darkness and wiggled the pruned toes in her right boot.

"What is your plan?" Jax asked.

"I seek a stronger mind," Master Hadar said.

Khai hummed. "The new one? I've sensed him."

"His power is amazing," Master Hadar said. "Yet he's not immune to âleh like Vrell. And I'll need your help to see I get to keep both prizes."

"I'll do all I can, Master," Khai said.

"What exactly do you want us to do?" Jax asked.

Their conversation ceased, but Vrell figured they were bloodvoicing. She drifted to sleep.

They left before dawn. Vrell sat in the bow of a boat, limbs still bound. Master Hadar and Khai sat together on the center bench. Jax sat at the stern of the boat, paddling down a wide canal that led away from the northern side of the stronghold. The putrid smell of the water seemed stronger in the dark.

Vrell's eyes drooped. The surrounding darkness gave her all the more reason to go back to sleep, though her mist-soaked tunic left her chilly and uncomfortable. She felt Master Hadar's eyes on her as the boat moved through the canal.

She still did not understand what had transpired between Achan and Master Hadar. Had they made some sort of deal? Was Achan so angry over Vrell reading his letter that he had agreed? Fear seized her heart. She should have gone to Bran when she'd had the chance.

They rowed for what seemed hours. Dawn broke and lit their surroundings to a slate murkiness. Every so often, orange torchlight blared through the thick Evenwall fog. Jax stopped the boat along a dock skirting a two-story redstone building on the corner of intersecting canals. A sign above the door read *Mig's Pit.* It looked like a tavern, though the place was silent. She guessed even the reveling patrons were not up at this hour.

Master Hadar pointed to the back door of the tavern. "Sit him there."

Jax lifted Vrell out of the boat and set her on the dock. Her wrists ached from being bound for so long.

Sparrow?

Vrell jumped. It unnerved her how Achan could penetrate her mind without any warning or knock. She scanned the canal and surrounding docks, but she could see very little through the thick fog. The stone buildings on the four corners of the intersection loomed above, looking dark and deserted. She did not see Achan.

She focused, closing out everything else before answering. *I am here.*

We've got a little surprise for your friends.

Please do not hurt the giant. He is kind.

For Lightness sake, Sparrow. How are we supposed to—

Achan, hush! a deep, harsh voice said. *Anyone with a bloodvoice can hear you, lad. You need more practice, and this is not the time for it.*

Vrell looked to where Khai and Master Hadar stood whispering. She hoped Achan had not spoiled the plan. Her heart thumped fast under her chubby disguise. Finally some knightly heroes. It had been two months since she'd left Walden's Watch. She had nearly given up hope that anyone good still existed in this cursed land.

"Hello?" A wooden dory emerged from the mist. She saw Achan rowing alone down the same wide canal that led from the Mahanaim stronghold.

"Ah!" Master Hadar rubbed his wrinkled hands together. "This way, young man." He waved Achan toward the dock, then leaned toward Khai. "When he arrives," he whispered,

"I want him bound. Be careful. I hear he knows how to use a sword."

"But his sword is still locked up in the dungeon, Master," Vrell said. She did not want Khai to be too prepared. Let the weasel think it was no contest.

Worry crept over her hope as she imagined how the scene might play out. Khai likely had more experience with a sword. He'd massacred all those ebens in a breath. What if he hurt Achan?

Nonsense! Achan had the Great Whitewolf on his side.

Plus, Arman would not let Vrell get this far only to perish, would He?

The boat glided nearer, parting the layer of slime like film on pea soup that had sat out too long. Achan looked well. He wore the same clothing he had been wearing when he had been taken from the dungeon: the doeskin vest and brown shirt from his girl.

The men stared, waiting. Vrell prayed fervently. Finally Achan's boat scraped against the dock right behind Master Hadar's boat. Jax stepped forward to help him out.

How was this a good plan? Where was Sir Gavin?

Master Hadar wrapped his cloak tightly around him and said to Achan, "As soon as you're bound, we'll lower the boy into the boat."

Bound? Achan was trading himself for her? Even if Achan did have some kind of trick planned, why would he be willing to give himself up for her? Didn't he hate her for reading his letter?

"No," Achan said. "Sparrow gets into the boat now, then you can bind me."

Khai drew his massive sword. "You'll follow the master's rules, lad."

"Whoa." Achan stepped back and raised his hands.

Why hadn't he brought a sword? What was he thinking?

Vrell caught sight of a grey-skinned man on a roof across the canal. He was gathering a rope, which slowly lifted out of the water, dripping with slime. As he pulled the rope, Achan's boat tugged away from the dock. No one else noticed. Something creaked overhead. Vrell looked up to see another rope being lowered over the side of the building, right above her head.

A ping thronged in Vrell's temples. *Sir Gavin Lukos.*

She opened to him.

Sir Gavin's voice boomed, *Grab on.*

The knotted end of the rope fell into her lap. She carefully tucked the knot between her legs so she could sit on it like a rope swing. Achan and Khai were still arguing when Vrell's body lifted silently off the dock. She twisted slightly and planted her feet to keep herself steady as long as possible. It was hard to hold on with her wrists bound.

Are you secure? Sir Gavin asked.

Yes, sir.

The rope suddenly jerked up two feet, then another two. Vrell's feet left the dock and she twisted, banging against the stone wall of the building. She tried to keep herself from spinning, but only managed to swing from side to side—over the dock, over the canal, over the dock, over the canal.

"Master!" Khai yelled, turning. "The boy!"

Vrell prayed Sir Gavin would pull quicker. She was no higher than Achan's head. Khai's boots thudded across the dock. Achan ran at his heels.

A flaming arrow shot out of the darkness and thunked into Master Hadar's boat. On the roof of the building diagonally across the intersecting canals, the grey-skinned man ran down a flight of stairs, a bow looped over one arm.

Master Hadar yelled, "Put out the fire!"

Jax crouched over the side of the dock and splashed water onto the boat, but the flame only increased. Khai threaded his way around Jax and drew his sword, narrow eyes on Vrell above him.

Achan kicked him in the rear. Khai spun around, sword ready, and Achan hit the dock on his belly. The weasel turned back and swung at Vrell instead.

The sword cut the rope and Vrell fell.

Her hip scraped on the dock, and she splashed into the canal. She writhed in the tepid water, but with her wrists and ankles bound, she could not swim. *Mother!*

Vrell?

Mother! Mother, I'm drowning!

A hand gripped her arm and pulled.

Averella! What's happening?

Khai's voice boomed in her consciousness. *Averella? That's a woman's name!*

No! She drew her mind closed and jerked back, but it was too late. Khai's grip on her arm remained firm. He groped along her undergarment for confirmation. She thrashed, kicked, and tried to bang her head into his, but he was too strong. She needed air. If she could push off the bottom, perhaps she could surface for a breath.

Something crashed against her back. A hand clawed and pounded at Khai until his hold vanished. A strong arm closed around Vrell's waist and she was hoisted up. She choked, sucking in a gulp of thick, tepid, water that tasted like mud.

Her head burst through the surface. She gasped and sputtered until her throat stung.

Everything was in shadow. She and her rescuer were under the dock. She looked at who held her. It was Achan. He held the back of her tunic in one hand, swimming silently. His hair was matted to his scalp like black syrup. A glob of green slime clung to his cheek. He put one finger to his lips.

"Khai!" she heard Master Hadar call from the planks above. "Khai!"

"He's there," Jax said.

Vrell turned in the water until she spotted Khai surface in the middle of the canal. Had he already bloodvoiced her gender to Jax and Master Hadar? How had he heard her words to Mother?

Achan reached up and grabbed onto a wooden beam. "Sparrow," he whispered. "Loop your arms over my neck."

Vrell nodded and lifted her bound wrists out of the water. A thick glob of scum dripped off her right elbow with a loud plop. She shuddered and, through an open knot in the wooden dock, met Jax's eyes.

She tensed, a wave of fire shooting through every nerve. Her ears tingled and she let him in.

Be safe, Vrell, Jax bloodvoiced.

She shuddered a sigh. *Thank you, Jax.*

Vrell looped her wrists over Achan's neck, and he twisted around until she hung off him like a backpack. One arm at a time, Achan pulled them along the beam under the dock, down the narrow canal, and away from Master Hadar and Jax and Khai.

A boat waited around the corner of the next intersecting canals. Sir Gavin Whitewolf and the grey-skinned man sat inside it. Sir Gavin's hair and beard were long and white. Inko's grey skin marked him as being of Otherling descent. The men pulled Vrell into the boat and sat her in the center.

Was she truly free? Free of Master Hadar and Lord Nathak and cruel Khai? She felt like weeping for joy.

Sir Gavin and the grey-skinned man hoisted Achan aboard next. Achan sat beside Vrell. Water ran off their clothing and pooled at their feet.

"Thank you, Inko," Achan said.

The grey-skinned man nodded from the back of the boat. He picked up the oar and rowed away with more precision and speed than Jax ever had.

Achan wiped the gunk from his face and spit into the canal. "That water's vile."

Vrell smiled and thanked Arman for her rescue. Achan untied her wrists. Her wet clothing clung to her and she shivered.

Sir Gavin sat in the bow. He turned to look at Vrell. "We need to get Achan's sword, Vrell. We will not have time later. Can you help us?"

Go back? Vrell had no desire to set foot in the Mahanaim stronghold again, especially now that Khai knew her identity. But she could not very well tell her rescuers no. "Um, there are two guards at the dungeon gate. One holds the key to the strongbox."

Inko steered the boat through the canals. Vrell untied her ankles, glad to have the use of her limbs again. The craft sailed toward a decaying yellowstone building too fast for Vrell's comfort. They were aimed for a hole in the stone wall that didn't quite look big enough to fit though.

"Watch your heads." Sir Gavin put out a hand and helped guide the boat through the opening.

Darkness swept over them as they entered the building. Vrell blinked to adjust her eyes, but there was no light. What if they crashed?

As if in answer to her fears, a torch whooshed to flame in the bow of the boat. It cast an orange glow over Sir Gavin's head. Inko paddled though a series of openings in stone walls. They were going under the buildings.

"Is this the way you took me out?" Achan asked.

"It is," Inko said.

The boat entered a cavern. Legions of dripstones hung from the ceiling, but they did not rain perspiration as they had in the Xulon hot springs. Vrell thought of Peripaso's underground home. Oh, to be there instead of heading back toward the place where people knew her secret!

Inko stopped the boat at a stone ledge. They climbed out, and Sir Gavin led the way through a gaping crack in the cavern wall.

The smell of minerals was strong as Vrell zigzagged with the men through dark tunnels lit only by Sir Gavin's torch. They climbed a crude staircase that had been chiseled out of the rock. At the top, the stone closed in so that Vrell's shoulders brushed each side. The men, with their broad shoulders, had to walk sideways.

Sir Gavin stopped and wedged his torch in a crack in the rock wall. "We'll leave this here," he whispered.

Vrell followed the men away from the light. Blackness surrounded them again, and Vrell bumped into Achan's back. The men had stopped. A dull orange glow filled a narrow slit between two rocks. Vrell peered through the opening into a corridor and saw that this tunnel had brought her to a place between the first and second dungeon levels. There *had* been a way to escape.

"Gavin and I will be getting the sword," Inko said in his strange accent. "Be waiting here."

Sir Gavin and Inko slipped out into the corridor.

Vrell wrung her hands together. She could only see a sliver of Achan's face in the dim light penetrating the crack. "Why do they want to get your sword so badly?"

The one eye of his that was visible flicked to hers. "Don't really know. Sir Gavin gave it to me. Said it belonged to a friend."

It must have special meaning then, for Sir Gavin to come back for it.

Achan's gaze was intense. "What did the letter say?"

A sudden warmth washed over Vrell at the thought of Achan's letter. Maybe he wanted to make peace. He had gone to great lengths to rescue her, after all. Should she apologize? Perhaps Achan hadn't read it because he could not read. Typical then, that he'd thrown the letter out before asking for help. Men were stubborn about such things. "You never read it?"

His voice sounded strained. "I meant to, but I didn't want Gidon to catch me."

Vrell loved how Achan called the prince Gidon, like he was no better than anyone else. "I cannot remember it word for word, but—"

"She can't spell."

"I noticed."

He sucked in a deep breath. "Tell me."

Vrell was glad for the dark. The whole thing was desperately awkward. "Well, she said you were her true Kingsguard knight. She wanted you to run away from the prince. She wanted to marry you and not . . . Riga, was it? She loves you."

He blew out a sigh. "Figured it was something like that."

"Why did you throw it away?"

His feet shuffled. "Because it didn't matter what she wrote. It changes nothing."

Vrell's stomach tightened. "How can you say that? It must have broken her heart to write those words. You should have cherished it."

He scoffed. "So I can read it again and again, dragging myself through the memories? That would be torture. Sparrow, you should have been born a woman."

Vrell bit her lip, then shoved Achan, figuring that was what a boy would do when called a woman. She chose her next words carefully. "What's wrong with remembering?"

"It hurts, that's what. And I want to forget. That's why I tossed it."

"Could you go back for her?"

His tone grew sharp. "I thought you said you read it. Look. I was just curious. I don't want to discuss this. Ever again. She married someone else. End of story."

"Well," Vrell said, feeling irked, "it is a terrible story."

Achan sighed bitterly. "Welcome to my life. Seriously, is there somewhere we can drop you off? Because I attract trouble. You do know *achan* means 'trouble' in the ancient tongue? That's me in a nutshell. The gods—or *God*, if you must—never let up with the trouble in my life. Something big and bad is probably about to happen any moment. Just you wait."

But nothing happened. After another ten minutes Sir Gavin and Inko returned with Achan's sword. They went back to the boat, and Inko paddled them through the darkness to a different yellowstone building, five floors high.

They went to a room on the third floor. The small space was the same one Vrell had seen through Achan's mind when he had been taken.

The shaggy kidnapper who had broken Achan out of the dungeon was waiting for them, a pile of clothing heaped on the bed beside him. His nose wrinkled. "What happened? Did you swim in the canal?"

"We've no time, Caleb," Sir Gavin said. "The Council of Seven convenes in an hour to decide Prince Gidon's fate. We need to be there and be presentable, especially Achan."

Achan's eyebrows sank. "Why me?"

No one answered. The shaggy Sir Caleb grumbled under his breath and dug through the clothing. He tossed a blue bundle to Vrell. She caught it and stood awkwardly hugging the garments to her chest. Sir Caleb steered Achan before the fireplace and unlaced his doublet. Inko poured water from a kettle into a basin.

Sir Caleb peeled Achan's doublet over his shoulders and tossed the soppy doeskin in the corner. Then he jerked Achan's shirt up his chest. "Arms up, make it quick."

Achan groaned and lifted his arms.

Vrell swallowed. Would they unclothe him fully? Worse, was someone going to help her change too? "Is there a privy? I need to—"

"You will be finding it on the left down the corridor," Inko said. "Be knocking seven times to be coming back inside here."

Vrell fled. She found the privy straight away. The smell struck her like a slap to the face. Nothing inside but a jagged hole cut in a wooden ledge. Vrell took a deep breath and stepped inside. The room was so small she whacked her hand on the wall as she turned. There was no water basin.

She peeled off her black leggings and grey tunic and dropped them down the hole. Good riddance. She loosened her undergarment and let herself breathe a moment. The smell of mildew and body odor of her undergarment rose over the stench of the privy. Where would she clean it now? Would she smell like the Mahanaim canals until she was safely home? Would she ever get home, now that someone knew her secret?

Home. Mother. Vrell sat over the hole and closed her eyes. She thought of home, the vineyards, the manor, her mother's auburn hair. Weeping, she sent a knock. *Mother?*

Mother's fearful voice came strong. *My darling, are you all right?*

Tears poured down Vrell's cheeks as she told her mother all that had happened.

I cannot understand how he overheard me. No one has overheard me all this time. Why him? Why now?

You were panicked and he was touching you. Both are reason enough for a trained man to break though someone's defenses.

What now, Mother? We are going back to the Council. Sir Gavin plans something. I do not want to go back.

Yet it is the only way for you to locate Sir Rigil or Prince Oren. Averella, you must. Stay by Sir Gavin's side, and no harm will come to you, I am sure. He is a good man. But do not reveal your true self until you hear from me. Stay with Sir Gavin and away from Macoun Hadar.

But Mother, the Council is convening and you are not here. What has happened?

In his latest attempt to win my hand, Lord Nathak has destroyed most of our wells and cut off our route to the Sideros River. We are making do with help from the north, but I did not dare travel now. He has posted sentries around the perimeter of the manor. Anillo has my proxy. All should be well.

Vrell processed this. Lord Nathak was a horrible fool. Did he truly think he could imprison and blackmail Mother into his good favor? Or do so by Vrell's marriage to the prince? *Will this never end, Mother? Is there no one who will help us?*

Arman will help us, dearest.

This is the last place I'd ever thought I'd be. In the room when they vote for Prince Gidon to be king. What if I am discovered? Khai could have told the whole stronghold by now. What if the prince should still claim me?

Stay close to Sir Gavin. I will watch through you. Do not try to speak to me or see me, for someone may be watching you and my connection could make you weak. Keep your wits about—

Vrell waited a moment. *Mother?* She sensed no connection, so she concentrated and called out again. *Mother?*

The privy's stink suddenly seemed overwhelming. She coughed and tucked her nose into her elbow. *Mother!*

Vrell prayed and prayed and called for her mother again and again, but there was no answer. Had something happened? Vrell didn't want to fret unnecessarily, but Mother had said that Lord Nathak's men were all around the stronghold. What if they had done something to Mother?

Through heavy tears, Vrell changed into the blue tunic and black trousers Sir Caleb had provided, both of which were far too big for her. She tucked the pant legs into her wet boots and cinched the rope belt tight around her waist. She hoped she had taken long enough that the men would be properly clothed. They would just have to deal with the canal water smell that clung to her corset and hair. She would not be having a bath in their presence.

Sure enough, when Inko opened the door, she found Achan cleanshaven and dressed for court. Her stomach somersaulted at the sight. They had dressed him in a blue shirt as deep as Lady Fallina's cobalt gown. A black leather doublet fit snugly around his torso. He wore his sword with the beautiful crossguard, black trousers, and a pair of shiny black boots. His hair was wet and shaggy around his face. Clearly they were not finished.

Still . . .

"You, uh, look nice," Vrell said. She couldn't help but notice that they matched. She was dressed as Achan's page.

Achan scowled. "I smell like *rosewater.*"

"No." Sir Caleb tugged a comb through Achan's hair. "You smell like canal water, despite my best efforts. I didn't know I'd need to prepare a bath."

"Sparrow's sorry for falling into the canal. Aren't you, Sparrow?" Achan grinned, then grimaced as Sir Caleb tugged a knot out of his hair. "Must you do that? Am I going to tournament?"

"Worse. You're going before the Council."

Sir Gavin and Inko sat down at a small table on the opposite side of the room. Vrell stood by the door, unsure what to do.

"But why take me to the Council?" Achan asked. "They want to kill me, remember? Why rescue me only to take me back?"

"He's such a whining squire, Gavin," Sir Caleb said, yanking the comb through another tangle. "How ever did you put up with him?"

"It's time." Sir Gavin stood. "Finish his hair in the boat." He glanced at Vrell appraisingly. "Good enough. Let's go."

They traipsed back down to the dory. Vrell sat on the center bench beside Achan, her heart stampeding in her chest. Sir Gavin sat in the front. Sir Caleb sat in the back with Inko, who paddled the boat from the yellowstone building down wider, more-traveled canals, heading toward the front entrance of the Mahanaim stronghold. Sir Caleb braided Achan's hair into a tail as they drew near.

Inko rowed until they came to the northern curtain wall. Then, instead of entering there, he turned left and paddled along the wall. Suddenly, bright, warm sunlight washed over them. Vrell shielded her eyes and twisted around to see the Evenwall mist fading away. The air was still muggy, but a warm breeze tightened the pores on her face. Judging from the position of the sun, she determined it to be near lunchtime.

Vrell studied Achan, seeing him for the first time in full daylight. When she'd first met his eyes in the Evenwall, she'd thought they were grey. But the mist, and later the dungeons, had made everything dim. Here in the morning sun, she saw that his eyes were the brightest blue she had ever seen. He was clearly of kinsman descent. Looking at him in such light, there was something almost familiar about him.

They turned at the gatehouse entrance and glided under the open portcullis. Dozens of empty boats lined the edges of the canal along the same stone ledge where Jax had first brought Vrell, only today they were coming from the opposite direction. Many had come to Council today. For locals, the vote for Prince Gidon was something not to miss. Goose pimples freckled Vrell's arms, and she sucked in a deep breath of humid air. She did not want to be here.

Achan asked the question that Vrell already knew the answer to. "What is happening in the Council today that we need to be there?"

"Gidon will be presented," Sir Gavin said. "He'll announce his intended bride, thus clearing the way for him to take the throne. The Council will vote on whether or not he is ready to be king."

Inko's voice came from behind. "And whom will he be marrying?"

Vrell tensed and watched Sir Gavin with interest.

"I know not," Sir Gavin said, stroking his beard. "Nor can I imagine any lady who would willingly have him, even for the title of queen. He's such a pestilence."

Inko chuckled. "Those are treasonous words you are speaking, my friend."

Vrell smirked, then remembered Lady Jacqueline's jealousy of Lady Mandzee. There were plenty of ladies willing to sink that low.

Inko steered their boat up to the ledge, and it knocked against the empty crafts on either side.

Sir Gavin tied the boat to a peg. "When he is king, Gidon may hang me. Until then . . . "

Vrell offered up her knowledge as they climbed out of the dory. "I believe, sir, that the prince has settled on Lady Mandzee Hamartano of Jaelport. I heard Lord Levy say as much to his daughter."

Vrell prayed that it would go as Lord Levy had suggested. That the prince would have finally chosen another. That he and Lord Nathak would have given up on trying to control the north. Though if her recent conversations with her mother were any indication, that was not the case. She only hoped Gidon would have at least chosen another bride.

Inko turned to Sir Gavin. "An alliance with Jaelport would be making the south quite strong."

"Better for us than his having control of the north," Sir Gavin said.

The group climbed the narrow stairs and walked across the cobblestone courtyard to the entrance of the Mahanaim fortress. There were no throngs of people as Vrell expected. Probably because Vrell's group was late. She had hoped to blend in with the crowd. What madness was Sir Gavin plotting? The entrance to the chambers was at the front of the room. If they walked in while the Council was already in session, they would draw the notice of everyone in the room.

Vrell dwelled on this fear as she followed Sir Gavin through the spacious but empty foyer. The golden doors to the Council auditorium were propped open. Sir Gavin led them single file along the entry corridor, past his own limestone bust and broken shield, to the inner doors. Vrell tensed, her pulse pounding in her temples. Sir Gavin pushed the doors open with a bang and strode inside, his boots clicking over the white and black speckled marble floor.

Vrell cringed. So much for staying out of sight.

They entered the packed auditorium. A raised platform stretched along the front wall. The seven Council members, a ruling lord from each duchy in Er'Rets, sat at a high table in ornate chairs. They each wore long black robes. Lord Levy sat in the center of the high table and wore a tall drum-like hat to signify his position as chairman over the proceeding.

Grandstands rose three stories high in a half circle around the high table. In the center front of the grandstands, Prince Gidon sat on a throne, facing the high table. A small wooden platform enclosed with half walls sat off to the right of the high table. Here, men and women were called to testify in a trial. New Kingsguardsmen lined the wall behind the witness platform. Three more stood just inside the entrance, only feet from where Vrell stood. Vrell scanned the guards for Jax or Khai but did not see either.

Hundreds of spectators filled the stands. Nobles and wealthy merchants occupied the lower seats. Peasants and slaves sat near the stone ceiling. Several nobles in front directed their attention to Sir Gavin as he barreled into the chambers. She caught sight of Bran and Sir Rigil sitting in the fifth row from the floor. Her heart fluttered. She only needed to get a moment to speak with them in private.

Vrell studied the faces of the Council leaders. She saw Prince Oren Hadar, Sir Dovev Falkson, Duke of Berland, Sir Yagil Hamartano, Duke of— Wait. Her mother was absent, yet seven seats were filled. Who had taken Mother's seat? She had expected to see Anillo, the advisor Mother had sent with her proxy, but that was not him in her spot.

The Council session had already begun. The crowd was unnaturally silent. Lord Levy, who was chairman of the Council of Seven, was moderating in an appropriately bored voice.

"We accept the report from the steward from Hamonah." Lord Levy looked up from his notes and turned to the door where Sir Gavin, Vrell, Achan, Inko, and Sir Caleb had entered. Lord Levy frowned. "What's this? Sir Gavin?"

Sir Gavin paced into the center of the room and shouted, "I've come to make a claim before Arman and this Council."

A murmur rose from the stands. Vrell heard Sir Gavin's name. Some pointed at him.

Just then, Vrell spotted the impostor on the Council. Lord Nathak squirmed in Mother's seat at the end of the platform, his eye flickering over Sir Gavin's group. Vrell scowled. Who had given the seat to Lord Nathak? Certainly not Mother. And no one else had authority to do so. Where was Anillo?

"I'm sorry, Sir Gavin," Lord Levy said, "but the time for new business is over. You will have to wait until next month."

"The business I bring cannot wait. It must be dealt with today." Sir Gavin strode to the center of the room and stood facing Lord Levy. "I've come before this Council to shed light on the truth." Sir Gavin pointed to Lord Nathak. "This man, Sir Luas Nathak, has deceived us all."

A hush fell over the crowd. Vrell's arms prickled. What was this? Did Sir Gavin have some way of incriminating Lord Nathak? Perhaps he knew of how he had been pressuring Mother.

Lord Levy leaned forward, scowling. "See here, Sir Gavin. You cannot storm into my Council room and make such a claim. Explain yourself."

Sir Gavin turned to face the audience. "All these years Lord Nathak has foisted a deception upon us all. We know the story. Good Lord Nathak discovers young Gidon Hadar in a field near Allowntown at age three. The boy's parents tragically murdered. Good Lord Nathak takes him in to raise as his own and to prepare him to take the throne. But that man—" Sir Gavin pointed to Prince Gidon, who sat on a throne-like chair, looking slightly bored—"is not Gidon Hadar."

The crowd burst into rattling chatter. Vrell stared at Prince Gidon. Could it be? Was the pig not really the prince after all? Maybe this would end well. If the man was not a prince, he could not force her to marry him, even if she should be discovered.

Lord Levy banged his gavel again and again. "Silence. I will have order in my Council chambers."

But before the voices quieted, Lord Nathak stood so quickly, his chair fell behind him. "I contest!" He glared at Sir Gavin. "How dare you interrupt this Council with such an accusation. Do you have proof?"

"My proof lies in the truth," Sir Gavin said dramatically. "Chairman Levy, I beg you to call Lord Nathak to testify—before the bloodvoice mediators."

A collective gasp filled the auditorium, and the crowd began to talk again.

Lord Nathak slammed his palms on the table. "This is an outrage!"

Lord Levy banged his gavel. "Silence! Sit down, Lord Nathak. Silence in this chamber!" When the chatter stopped, Lord Levy looked down on the Great Whitewolf. "Sir Gavin, make your claim. What is it you seek to prove?"

Sir Gavin approached the end of the table where Lord Nathak stood. The knight lifted a steady arm and pointed at the Lord of Sitna Manor. "I charge that Sir Luas Nathak did indeed find the child Gidon Hadar, the true heir to the throne. Yet before returning him to this council, he substituted his own son in his place."

Vrell jerked her gaze to Sir Gavin, mouth gaping. Could this be true?

The crowd erupted in reaction, gasping, crying out, and shouting all manner of comments.

Prince Gidon had straightened, sitting tall and stiff on his throne. His brow crinkled, he stared at Sir Gavin as if willing the man to burst into flame.

"Preposterous!" Lord Nathak yelled, his voice shrill.

"Calm yourself, Nathak," Levy said. He turned to Sir Gavin. "Then what, pray tell, did Lord Nathak do with the real Prince Gidon?"

"He branded him a stray and forced him to work in the kitchens of Sitna Manor." Sir Gavin turned and pointed at Achan. "Here he is."

23

Had Sir Gavin lost his mind?

Achan dug a finger inside the neck of his blue shirt and tugged. It was too tight. He couldn't breathe. Every eye in the huge room was on him. He wanted to melt into the floor. Was the knight hoping to convince these people he was royalty? Absurd.

The crowd had gone wild, so loud that Achan could not hear any one conversation with clarity.

Lord Levy banged the gavel so hard it offset his round, bucket-like black hat. "Silence! I will have silence in this chamber!" The noise quelled to whispers. He turned his pointed, white beard to the knight. "Sir Gavin. I will not have this Council in an uproar. If you have no evidence for this wild claim, I shall have the guards escort you and your party out. Really, the idea of a stray being royal!"

"I do have evidence."

Achan's eyes went wide. What new strategy was this? Surely this was some game Sir Gavin was playing. Achan couldn't be the—what would this make him?—the true prince of Er'Rets? Impossible. No, it had to be a ploy. Perhaps Sir Gavin was acting to disrupt Prince Gidon's accession. But why? Could this be a part of the resistance Sir Rigil and Bran were a part of? Men loyal to Prince Oren?

"Then I shall hear this evidence first," Lord Levy said. He stood. "Sir Gavin, join me in my chamber."

Sir Gavin followed the chairman into a room on the far wall. Lord Nathak scurried there as well.

Lord Levy turned to face him before they entered the room. "No, Lord Nathak. You will wait at your seat while I decide if this claim is of merit."

"I would like to hear the details of this outrageous claim myself," Lord Nathak said.

"If it is warranted, you will," Lord Levy said. "Now take your seat. Or do you need Kingsguard assistance to find it?"

Lord Nathak stormed back to the high table. He righted his chair and fell into it.

Lord Levy and Sir Gavin entered the room on the far wall. A guard shut the door, and the audience burst into talk.

Achan stood in the center of the room with Inko, Sir Caleb, and Sparrow. The Council members at the high table stared, some puzzled, some scowling. Achan purposely avoided eye contact with Lord Nathak but caught Prince Oren's gaze. The man smiled and winked. Achan couldn't look at him after that.

Prince Gidon sat on his throne looking as if he were being burned on the inside. Curious, Achan opened his mind to try to hear his thoughts. Instead, dozens flooded his mind at once.

A stray, our king? Never!

I knew the son of Axel and Dara would never be so cruel.

For Lightness sake! Who would have thought?

Gods help us all! We'll have a stray as king!

But how could we not have known? How could we have missed such treason?

How could they have? It must be a mistake. Achan closed his eyes and concentrated on the allown tree, Gren, and the Sideros River.

A peaceful silence settled over him.

Sometime later, someone grabbed his elbow. He turned to find Sparrow looking up at him with wide, green eyes.

"Sir Caleb and Inko have sat down," Sparrow said. "Are you well?"

His lips parted, but no words came out. He allowed Sparrow to guide him to a bench on the far right wall and settled between Sir Caleb and Sparrow. Surely this was some trick of Sir Gavin's. It couldn't be true. Achan wasn't a prince. He had no parents.

Sparrow's scratchy voice filled his head. *Neither does the prince have parents, Achan.*

"That doesn't mean Prince Gidon is not who he claims to be," Achan said. "Or that I am who Sir Gavin claims I am."

Sir Caleb leaned close. "Use your head, boy. Gidon had whiskers at twelve. He must be nearly twenty. He cannot bloodvoice, as both King Axel and Queen Dara could. Nay. He's Lord Nathak's puppet. Besides, Gavin would know Axel's child at a glance. He and the child had a bond."

Achan stiffened. He remembered the day he'd first seen Sir Gavin watching him from the armory. Was this why Sir Gavin had made him a squire? No. It had to be a mistake. "Just because Gidon cannot bloodvoice doesn't mean he's not the prince," Achan said. "Not all royals are born with it, right?"

"But Gidon Hadar was," Sir Caleb said. "His bloodvoice was the strongest I'd ever felt in an infant."

"For me as well," Inko said.

Achan sighed.

"It's true," Sparrow said. "I remember rumors of the scandal. It was said his skill faded away. Many thought it would return when he got older, but it never did. Prince Gidon—or whoever it is sitting in that throne like a mule—does not have the gift, not even in the slightest measure."

The door to the side chamber opened, and Lord Levy took his place at the high table. Sir Gavin returned to the center of the room, a bushy white eyebrow raised at Achan.

Achan could only stare. Would it have been too difficult for Sir Gavin to share his little plan before they had come in? A little warning would have been nice.

Lord Levy struck with his gavel. "The Council will hear evidence from Sir Gavin Lukos on the matter of the true identity of Prince Gidon Hadar."

The audience burst into debate.

An icy chill wrapped around him. This could not be. What could Sir Gavin possibly have said to convince the chairman of this charade?

Lord Nathak leaped again from his seat at the high table. "This is outrageous. I demand to put this matter aside until I can see this evidence myself."

"We shall all see this evidence now, Lord Nathak," the chairman snapped. "Sit down."

Lord Nathak lowered himself into his chair and glared at Achan, his eye smoldering.

Lord Levy lifted his chin. "The Council recognizes Sir Gavin Lukos."

Sir Gavin stepped forward. "Greetings, honorable Council members and citizens of Er'Rets. In the past few months I've stumbled onto a conspiracy. As most of you know, this Council sent me to Sitna to observe Prince Gidon. I was to ascertain his level of knowledge and skill in a variety of subjects and to report back as to whether I thought him ready to take the throne.

"The prince avoided me in Sitna, helped by Lord Nathak. When cornered, the prince barely acknowledged my presence. I thought this very strange, given the powerful connection the true prince and I had had when the lad was an infant. One morning in Sitna, I sensed something familiar. When I saw the face of this stray," he waved Achan forward, "I was drawn to him."

Achan somehow moved to Sir Gavin's side. Had he floated? Was he dreaming? He glanced at the Council. The scrutiny in their gaze brought a wave of heat. From then on, he kept his gaze fixed on the marble floor, inspecting the flecks of black.

The knight put his hand on Achan's shoulder and turned Achan to face the grandstands. "I served King Axel all my life. He was my friend and confidant. I served with him through many campaigns and joys." Sir Gavin patted Achan's shoulder. "This boy was the mirror image of the prince I squired for in my youth! Not only that, but I sensed his ability to bloodvoice.

"I bided my time in Sitna training this lad as my squire. I discovered not only that he's left-handed, like his father, but that he'd been forced to take âleh tonic each morning of his life, by order of Lord Nathak."

Whispers tore through the crowd.

Achan felt sick. He ran his left fingers over his sword's crossguard. Things that had always puzzled him were starting to make sense. But he couldn't accept this twist of fate. It had to be a cruel prank. He stared at his new, polished boots. They stood firmly on the bright marble floor, despite the sensation that he was falling, tumbling, spinning down into a pit of shadow.

"One morning this boy managed to not have the tonic in his system. Without the âleh silencing him, suddenly those of us gifted in bloodvoices heard his discovery, sensed his power. Even from half the kingdom away." Sir Gavin walked to the center of the high table and turned back to the audience. "This boy's bloodvoice is so strong because he is King Axel's son! And as such, he—and only he—is capable of bringing truth to Er'Rets and pushing back Darkness."

Achan winced at the level of noise from the crowd. Women shrieked. Feet stomped on the wooden grandstands creating the effect of a stampede. Applause. Boos. Three young pages scurried down the stands and out the door, as if running off to report this news to someone too busy to be here.

Achan gulped, his mind spinning with questions. Pushing back Darkness? What did that mean? He couldn't even imagine such a thing.

When the crowd's reaction died down, Sir Gavin continued. "I entered him in Prince Gidon's coming-of-age tournament to see how he'd fare in battle. When Lord Nathak discovered this, he not only sent this boy—named Achan Cham—back to the kitchens and forbade him to compete further, but he banished me as well. His words were, 'The Council no longer requires your service.'"

Lord Levy glared at Lord Nathak, who leaned back in his chair, the visible half of his face slack.

"I knew then my suspicions were valid." Sir Gavin reached into the neckline of his tunic and drew out a swatch of grey wool on a cord around his neck. "I cut this from Achan's blanket. Over the next few weeks, I kept an eye on him through bloodvoicing."

Achan stared at the snip of cloth. Sir Gavin had been the one to cut from his blanket under the ale casks in Poril's cellar. Achan turned to Sparrow, the fabric collector. The boy offered a loopy grin.

Sir Gavin went on. "This Council has not heard the true story of Prince Gidon's ambush two weeks ago. Achan has been charged with attempting to murder the Crown Prince. He was thrown into the Mahanaim dungeons. But this was more deception from Prince Gidon and Lord Nathak.

"The truth of it? Achan rescued Prince Gidon, almost single-handedly, from more than twenty poroo attackers. Through my bloodvoicing I was with him, encouraging him. I saw him save this false prince's life and nearly lose his own. Yet Lord Nathak pressed charges. Accused him of attempted murder! When I got word of Achan's arrest, I broke him out of the dungeons, and upon dressing him for court today—"

"Sir Gavin," Lord Levy said. "This court does not condone breaking into our dungeons."

"—I was reminded of one last confirmation of his true identity." Sir Gavin strode back to Achan's side and circled behind him. "It was well documented the infant prince bore a birthmark on his left shoulder. Not only does Achan have this mark, he bears the brand of the stray over it—despite the rule that all stray brands be placed over the right shoulder. Clearly this *accident* was meant to further conceal the truth."

Achan reached over his shoulder to feel the mark. He'd always assumed he'd been branded on the left by mistake.

"He's a fake!" someone shouted from the crowd.

"Absurd," Lord Nathak yelled.

Lord Levy banged his gavel and stood. "I will have no more outbursts in this assembly. The next person to speak out of turn will be held in contempt."

The room went silent.

"Continue, Sir Gavin," Lord Levy said.

"If we compare the two young men," Sir Gavin said, glancing at Prince Gidon, "I assure you, the evidence is stacked against this impostor. He cannot bloodvoice. He bears no birthmark. And he looks little like King Axel. Whereas this boy," he said, turning to Achan, "can bloodvoice, does bear the mark, and looks exactly like the King Axel I knew since boyhood." He pointed at Gidon. "This is a fake. An imposter. A puppet prince Lord Nathak substituted after finding King Axel's signet ring."

Achan's gut churned. He sucked in a long breath to settle his nerves and realized he hadn't been breathing much at all.

Someone called out from the crowd. "Let us see the birthmark!"

"Yes! Let us see for ourselves!"

Lord Levy banged his gavel. "We will examine both men for the birthmark. Step forward."

Achan was already standing before the high table, so he continued to stare at the floor, unsure of what was to happen next.

"Um . . . Prince Gidon," Lord Levy said. "We will need your participation in this matter, as well."

Achan turned to see the prince gripping the arms of his throne. "And if I refuse?"

The chairman nodded to a burly Kingsguard knight standing at the end of the high table. The knight stalked across the room toward Prince Gidon, but the prince jumped up at the last possible second and strode forward.

He ripped open his black satin doublet and tossed it dramatically to the floor, then he pulled his red linen shirt over his head and threw it at Sir Gavin. Raising both hands above his head, he twirled in a slow circle for all to see.

He did indeed have a mark on his left shoulder. It was pink, but that was all Achan could see about it.

"You too," the chairman said to Achan. "I call Master Ricken to the floor. Are you in the stands today?"

"Aye!" a voice called from the grandstands. A short, bald man hurried down the steps.

"Master Ricken is a medical expert I have known for many years," Lord Levy said as a short, thin man approached Prince Gidon and Achan.

Achan unlaced his doublet and shrugged it off. He untied his shirt and pulled it over his head. He draped the fine clothing over one arm, then folded his arms together across his chest.

He didn't know what to do with himself. He didn't feel comfortable showing the audience whatever was on his back, so he faced away from them. His heart pounded in his chest and vibrated all the way to his head. He wanted a good long nap, free from whips, arrows, dungeons, Prince Gidon, Lord Nathak, bloodvoices, and standing half-naked in front of people. At that point, even his bed under the ale casks would've been welcome.

Master Ricken approached Gidon first. He stepped behind the prince and leaned close, humming to himself. He touched the prince's back and Gidon flinched.

"Show us the stray's mark," someone yelled.

Sir Gavin nudged Achan's elbow and nodded.

Achan gritted his teeth and turned.

The crowd gasped. A woman cried out. Achan squeezed his fists and closed his eyes, mortified to have the brutality of his life on display. He knew his back was scarred. Sir Gavin hadn't been the first person to comment on it.

Master Ricken stepped toward him and sucked in a sharp breath. His cold fingers trailed over Achan's shoulder and back.

Achan held his breath, not knowing what the man was looking for, not caring. He only wanted to be dismissed. He threw up a desperate prayer to Sparrow's god. The boy claimed there was only one god, and so did the voice. It was worth a try.

Arman, help me. Why is this happening?

A burning rose in Achan's chest like a flash of fear, but continued to swell until he felt like he'd stepped into a sauna.

For I have appointed you as king over this nation. There is no one like you among all the people.

Master Ricken jerked to the side and looked at his own hand.

Achan gasped as the heat subsided. He pressed a hand against his forehead and wiped away the sweat. He breathed deeply as his pounding heartbeat slowed, trembling at the meaning behind the words he'd just heard in his mind from that other, mighty voice. The one that had told him nothing but truth. Achan, appointed by the gods—*the* God?—as king over Er'Rets? A single tear fell down to his chin.

Master Ricken stepped to the high table and whispered to the chairman. He turned, glanced at Achan with bulging eyes, then walked between Achan and Gidon back into the grandstands. Achan pivoted to face the audience and hide his back. He kept his head down.

The chairman cleared his throat. "Master Ricken has served as healer to the Mahanaim stronghold the past twenty years. No one doubts the validity of his expertise in matters of health and healing. It is his professional opinion that this man, Achan, bears an oval birthmark on his left shoulder that was branded over with the mark of a stray. He claims the mark on Prince Gidon's shoulder is not a birthmark at all, but a scar from some kind of burn, likely one that was inflicted more than once."

Shouts rang out from all sides. Achan flinched.

The chairman pounded his gavel into the hardwood table again and again until the crowd silenced. "Thank you, Prince Gidon and Master Cham, for your willingness to submit to examination. You may both be seated."

Achan hurried to his seat on the far left of the room and sat beside Sparrow. His wooden scabbard knocked against the bench, but he hardly noticed the sound over all the talk in the auditorium. He pulled his clothing back on with shaking arms.

Sparrow's voice came in a gentle whisper. "It will be okay."

Achan closed his eyes. How could anything ever be okay again? His entire life had been a lie. He had no doubt now that it was Arman who had been speaking to him. And if Arman—said to be the one true God—was real, didn't that mean Cetheria and Isemios and the rest were false gods? But what was he to do about what Arman had said? He had no business being king. He knew nothing of ruling. He knew nothing of anything important. Peeling potatoes. Stoking a fire.

Sparrow slid his small, thin fingers into Achan's hand and squeezed. Achan stiffened and glanced at Sparrow without moving his head. The boy squeezed again, smiled, and let go. Achan drew his hand into a fist and pulled it to his lap.

"Sir Luas Nathak," Lord Levy said, "please take the stand."

Lord Nathak rose from his seat and stepped down off the platform. He climbed into the witness box at the end of the high table and sat. Two men dressed in black capes came out of the side chamber. They climbed onto the platform and sat on either side of Lord Nathak.

Achan stared at the bloodvoice mediators. What did they do exactly? Were they there merely to scare Lord Nathak into speaking the truth? Or could they force the truth from him?

The chairman began, "If it is lies you hope to spread, Lord Nathak, do not bother. These two men are bloodvoice mediators, as I'm sure you know. You are also aware how bloodvoice mediators work. They are trained to sense deceit *and* omission. Tell us the truth, and we will take your honesty into consideration in the end. Now, by the authority of this Council, I implore you to tell us your side of this tale."

Lord Nathak sat in silence for a long moment. "As you know," he finally said, "I found the prince child near Allowntown, just over thirteen years ago."

"Remind the court how you knew the child was Prince Gidon," Lord Levy said.

"He wore the king's signet ring on a chain 'round his neck. I took him home, uncertain of what to do at first. He was King Axel's son, and I sensed his father's weakness in him."

A murmur rose in the court. Achan's eyes widened. He'd never heard anyone claim King Axel had been weak.

Someone yelled, "Traitor!"

"Silence!" the chairman cried. "Lord Nathak, you will refrain from insulting our fallen king in this Council room."

Lord Nathak bowed his head. "My apologies, Chairman Levy."

"Continue."

"My own son, Esek, had just turned four. Prince Gidon, I guessed, was nearly three. I kept the prince for several weeks, praying to the gods for guidance. Despite the age difference, the boys looked like twins. As they played together, Esek pounded the prince daily. He knocked him down, took his food and playthings. The gods' message was clear. King Axel had ruled the same way: weak and apathetic."

Murmurs rose again, but Lord Nathak spoke over them. "He allowed neighboring peoples to pillage our lands, our foods, our gold. If I allowed this weak prince to take the throne, I would be responsible for another generation of the same in Er'Rets."

Fury rose in Achan's chest. Weak? He'd been merely a babe!

Then he shook his head, surprised at his own thoughts. So now he believed this incredible story?

"Nearly six months passed before I sent word that I'd found the boy," Lord Nathak said, with a glance at the mediators. "When I brought him to Mahanaim, I presented Esek, my son, as the prince, wearing Hadar's signet ring. Those closest to the king had died in the attack. No one suspected. The ring was all that mattered."

Achan glanced at Gidon, who sat with one leg casually thrown over the other as if this tale bored him. But his hands betrayed his true emotions. They gripped the sides of his throne, knuckles white.

He hadn't known the truth either.

The chairman asked, "What became of the real Prince Gidon?"

"My cook lost his wife and child in childbirth." Lord Nathak's voice softened, as if trying to convince the court he was kind and thoughtful. "I urged him to raise the boy as his own. In this, they would have each other, and I would be able to watch over the boy's safety."

Achan scoffed. Safe at the end of Poril's belt. Why hadn't Lord Nathak just drowned him? There had to be more to this story than Lord Nathak was revealing. Why keep him alive?

"And you branded him a stray to hide his birthmark?" the chairman asked.

"He had food and a place to sleep. Death would have been worse."

"And this is when you gave him the âleh tonic?"

"I have given him the âleh tonic since his first day in my household."

Achan squeezed his fists until the veins popped out on his inner wrists.

"Why did you do this?" Lord Levy asked.

"It was well known the prince had the gift. If my plan was to work, I couldn't have people sensing his ability."

Lord Levy folded his hands on the tabletop. "Remind the Council how you came to the responsibility of raising the prince. You found him, yes, and presented your son in his place. But the boy should've passed to Prince Oren. Remind us why he was given to you to raise."

"Nearly everyone who cared for the child had been killed along with the king and queen, or sent to Ice Island. Prince Oren took the boy in for a short period, but he sent him back."

"Because the prince knew the boy was a fake," Sir Gavin mumbled.

Achan looked to Prince Oren. The man sat silent, one hand gripping his chin.

Lord Nathak shrugged. "My son missed me and his mother. His silence and depression worried the advisors. With the king dead and the heir so young, this Council was formed to rule until the prince grew to manhood. This same Council granted my plea to raise the boy. I built the stronghold in Sitna to keep the child away from prying eyes. I have taught him how to be a great king. He is shrewd and wise and quick with a sword. We have negotiated his betrothal to Lady Averella Amal of Carmine, and, once wed, he will move to Armonguard to take the throne."

Sparrow squeaked and turned pink over this latest declaration.

What was wrong with him? Achan frowned at this latest information from Lord Nathak. The Duchess of Carm had a daughter? He did not recall ever seeing the lady visit Sitna. Bran was from Carmine. Achan wondered if Bran knew of her.

A murmur rose in the fifth row of the stands. There was Bran, on his feet, face redder than from sunburn alone. Sir Rigil, the young knight Bran served, stood beside him. He whispered and tugged Bran's elbow. Suddenly Achan could hear their conversation as if he were a fly on Bran's shoulder. Or maybe he was looking though Bran . . .

I will speak, but I will not make accusations, Sir Rigil said.

Then I will, Bran said. *Lord Nathak is a usurper and traitor. He holds the Duchess hostage! Her daughter has fled to avoid his son's hand. I will not stand here and let him claim he has obtained Averella's hand by her own choosing!*

This is not a battle for today. Sir Rigil pushed down on Bran's shoulder. *Sit yourself down or I shall be forced to drag you out.*

Bran fell into his chair and crossed his arms like a sullen child.

"Sir Rigil?" Lord Levy said.

Achan noticed that everyone in the chamber seemed to be watching Bran and Rigil. Even Lord Nathak had fallen silent to observe the knight and his squire.

Sir Rigil turned to the high table. "Yes, my lord chairman?"

"Have you something to add to our discussions?" Lord Levy asked.

Sir Rigil raised his voice. "I beg the Council's pardon. Duchess Amal spoke to me of this matter, this 'arrangement' for marriage, when I stopped in Carmine on my way to the tournament for the prince's coming-of-age celebration."

The chairman banged his gavel. "The Council recognizes Sir Rigil Barak of Zerah Rock. What do you know of this matter?"

"That she has consented to no such match."

Nor will she, Bran said at the exact moment that Achan heard Sparrow mumble it under his breath.

Sparrow glanced up at Achan and stammered. "I m-mean, she'd have to be crazy to marry him, right?"

Achan turned back to Bran. A familiar fury filled his friend's visage. So Gidon had tried to take the woman *he* loved also. Achan wished the lady well, wherever she had hidden herself.

Chairman Levy sighed. He turned to face the witness stand. "Bloodvoicers, what say you? Has this man been truthful?"

The men on either side of Lord Nathak stood. One said, "He has. Though I sense he is withholding something greater. We would need more time to discern what that might be."

"I agree," said the second bloodvoice mediator. "I request additional time to question him further."

Lord Levy nodded. "Very well. Lord Nathak, you are dismissed until further notice." He addressed the audience. "We shall postpone any marital arrangements until this matter of identity is settled. The Council must take time to deliberate. We will reconvene when we have a majority vote."

The chairman rose and left the platform, heading to the side chamber. The rest of the Council members went after him. Lord Nathak left the interrogation platform and followed the Council.

"Why does Lord Nathak go to consult?" Sparrow asked. "What part does he play in the Council of Seven?"

"He was being seated on the platform when we were arriving," Inko said. "Something is being amiss. I shall be discovering it." Inko slinked toward the grandstands.

Achan watched Sir Gavin. The knight stood against the wall, eyes half closed as if in a trance, despite the noise of the crowd. Achan recalled that day in the dungeon when he had "jumped" through Sparrow's mind and witnessed Hadar and Lord Nathak's discussion. Could he do the same now with Sir Gavin?

Achan walked to the knight's side and stood so their shoulders touched.

Sir Gavin stirred, reached up, and gripped Achan's shoulder. "All will be well, lad."

Achan nodded. When Sir Gavin's mind drifted again, Achan closed his eyes and reached.

It came easily this time. Instantly he was in a florid chamber. Carved bronze sconces pinned massive torches to the wall between vibrant tapestries. An equally impressive bronze chandelier hung above a circular table, its flickering candles illuminating the faces of the Council members. Sir Gavin was watching the Council's deliberations! Achan was not certain whose eyes he looked out from.

The men all spoke at once, but Chairman Levy silenced them. "I want to hear from you all, one at a time. What is your will?"

The man whose mind Achan and Sir Gavin shared spoke, and Prince Oren's voice came forth. "Esek is not the prince. He is false. He is not who we thought him to be and has no claim to the throne. He cannot rule. There is nothing to discuss."

"Agreed," Duke Pitney said.

Duke Pitney? Achan studied the bronze-skinned man with black hair and mustache, then glanced at each face around the table, suddenly aware of each man's name, their duchy, their manor. He seemed privy to Prince Oren's knowledge. How strange.

"Then we should elect you, Prince Oren?" Duke Hamartano said. Achan recognized Silvo's father—he looked like an older version of his sons. His black hair was slicked back over his olive skin and was tied back in a tail.

"Not I," Prince Oren said. "Our true king sits in the courtroom. He is a good, strong young man who only needs a bit of instruction."

Achan wanted to believe that about himself, but his doubt was stronger than his desire.

Lord Nathak banged a fist on the table. "Esek has been trained to rule his whole life. The stray knows nothing of being king."

"He is not a stray," Prince Oren said. "And I myself shall train the boy to rule rightly. Chairman Levy, why is Lord Nathak even here? His deceit should have banned him from this debate."

"I concur," Duke Pitney said.

"We've all seen his letter of proxy," Lord Levy said. "Duchess Amal has sent him as her emissary."

"Rubbish," Duke Pitney said.

Prince Oren persisted. "Shouldn't his deceit void such a letter? I was not aware the Council was so forgiving where treason was concerned."

"Treason!" Lord Nathak leaned past Duke Orson's hairy profile to glare at Prince Oren.

Duke Hamartano's voice came smooth. "Your brother's lax rule nearly destroyed Er'Rets, Prince Oren. The Council has only just managed to set a level of order."

"Do not confuse compassion with neglect, Duke Hamartano. My brother was loved by the people."

Grey-skinned Duke Falkson murmured, "Peasants and slaves."

"It was illegal to keep slaves when King Axel ruled," Prince Oren said.

"My point exactly," Duke Hamartano said. "King Axel was soft, and his son, raised as a stray, will have pity on every low-life in the land. It will be his father's reign, only worse."

Prince Oren folded his hands and stared at a mound of wax that had formed in the center of the table, having dripped from the candelabra above. "Chairman Levy," he glanced at the chairman, "the throne has never been open for debate. We must obey Arman in this matter. Achan is rightful king."

"Hang Arman and hang the stray!" Lord Nathak yelled. "It will take years to train that nitwit. You forget, I know the boy—he was *my* stray. He's stubborn, rude, thick-skulled, and temperamental. Esek is ready for the throne, and Er'Rets needs a king. Let the Council vote."

Duke Falkson grunted in agreement.

"The Council was only created to serve until the prince was of age," Prince Oren said. "He sits there, of age, ready to serve. There is nothing to vote on."

"He knows only the life of a stray!" Lord Nathak cried. "He's at best a cook's apprentice."

"He is a squire," Prince Oren said, "and a good one, trained by Sir Gavin Lukos. And very worthy of much more."

"And we are to trust Sir Gavin?" Lord Nathak threw up his hands. "King Axel was murdered on *his* watch. He is lucky not to live on Ice Island with his friends! Let us not repeat mistakes of the past by placing fools and sentimentals in positions of power."

Achan jerked loose and floated back into his own eyes. King Axel was murdered on Sir Gavin's watch? He stood in a daze, contemplating all he had heard, unhinged that a roomful of men debated his future.

"I shall tell you my side of it someday," Sir Gavin said.

Achan wrenched his gaze to Sir Gavin. He knew Achan had been jumping through him? They stared at each other a moment, neither speaking.

A crowd had gathered on the floor, milling about and staring at Achan. Sir Rigil and Bran dodged through the crowd to where Achan and Sir Gavin stood. Sir Caleb approached them from the bench.

"What news?" Sir Rigil asked. His short blond hair stuck out in all directions. If it were longer, he might look like a younger Sir Caleb.

Inko slid between Sir Rigil and Sir Gavin. "Lord Nathak is having a letter of proxy from the Duchess of Carm. He is sitting in her place today because of it."

"The letter is false," Sir Rigil said. "Lord Nathak holds the Duchess hostage in her home. I had hoped to raise a party of knights to run off Nathak's thugs, but it is still difficult to tell who serves who. Perhaps this vote will help define the sides."

Sir Gavin sighed, his two-colored eyes flashing with rage.

"Calm, Gavin," Sir Caleb said. "All is going according to plan, is it not? Isn't the Council siding with the truth?"

A sniffle turned Achan's gaze back to Sparrow who still sat on the bench. Was the runt crying?

Sir Gavin shook his head. "Prince Oren pleads well, but he's outnumbered by greedy men. The mere fact that they deliberate at all shows they never meant for the new king to have power. It matters not who takes the throne in their eyes. They'll choose the easiest to control. Some among them might think a boy raised as a kitchen stray would be easier to manipulate, but Achan's deeds have proven him too noble to be their puppet."

What deeds? Achan could recall having done nothing to gain any reputation at all. Except fall in the moat. He stepped to the bench and sat down beside Sir Caleb.

Achan's stomach growled. He hadn't eaten breakfast, and now he'd missed lunch. It had to be almost dinnertime. He glanced quickly over the crowd and saw that most were staring at him. Gidon's miniature throne was empty.

Sparrow slid up beside Sir Gavin. "It's true," he hissed in a strangely low voice. His face was white, but all signs of tears were gone. "I saw scrolls in Master Hadar's chamber, letters. And he told me himself that Lord Levy promised him a seat on a 'new council' if he would report the king's every move."

"Insolence!" Inko snarled.

"New council? When did he tell you this, lad?" Sir Gavin asked.

Sparrow wrinkled his tiny nose. "Four days ago, I believe."

"And what of the scrolls?" Sir Rigil asked.

"Correspondence between Lord Nathak and Master Hadar. They planned to meet here in Mahanaim to discuss their plans. Lord Nathak pays Master Hadar to watch Prince Gidon, to see that no one attempts assassination."

"So the old man is taking bribes from both sides, yet he is turning them to being against each other," Inko said. "We should be destroying him."

Prince Oren burst out of the side chamber, strode up to Achan, and drew his sword.

The crowd gasped.

Achan shrank back against the wall.

But instead of striking, Prince Oren knelt before Achan and offered the blade to him on his palms. "I swear fealty and service to the crown of Er'Rets, to ever give wise counsel, to uphold the laws and customs of our land, to serve where I might, according to my knowledge and ability. Thus swear I, Prince Oren Hadar, to you, my king."

A chill broke out over Achan's body. His heart rate thundered and his face flushed. He glanced at Sparrow, whose eyes were as wide as his, then to Sir Gavin. The Great Whitewolf nodded.

Achan didn't know what to do or say. With shaky hands, he took the impressive weapon from Prince Oren and set it on his knees. He glanced again to Sir Gavin, who only nodded again, eyebrows raised.

Sir Caleb leaned close and his thoughts flooded Achan's mind. *Say, "Thank you."*

Achan licked his lips. "Thank you."

Sir Caleb. *You accept.*

"I accept."

Sir Caleb nudged Achan's elbow. *Now give it back.*

Achan turned the weapon, hilt out, and Prince Oren accepted it. He bowed low until his head disappeared below Achan's knees, then stood and walked back to his seat at the high table.

"This does not bode well," Sir Caleb said.

Sir Gavin sighed. "No. If Prince Oren left the chamber already, he's unhappy with the turn the discussion has taken."

Sir Rigil stepped forward and went to his knees before Achan. "Prince Oren declares you the rightful heir. That is more than enough for me. My sword is yours, my king, however you see fit to use it."

Achan repeated the awkward procedure with Sir Rigil. When the knight sheathed his blade, Bran jumped forward and fell onto his knees.

Achan tensed again. "Oh, no. Bran, please don't."

Do not insult him by making light of his oath, Sir Caleb warned.

Bran removed his sword and swore fealty to Achan as Sir Rigil and Prince Oren had done. Achan went through the motions quicker this time, feeling like he was playing a game with a bunch of friends. He tried to act solemn, but it was fear, not pride that heated his cheeks. The crowd had arranged itself in a semicircle around the impromptu fealty ceremony, and when Bran stood, a nobleman and his wife knelt down in his place.

Achan's chest tightened. He'd never seen people bow before Prince Gidon in such a way. With Gidon, they knelt out of fear. They cowered. These people beamed with hope. They wanted a real king to lead them. Achan couldn't do that or be that. He didn't know how.

Regardless, he forced himself to smile and spit out every phrase Sir Caleb sent to his mind. He couldn't help but wonder, *Who is the puppet prince now*?

After twenty minutes of this, during which everyone who desired to swear fealty to Achan had done so, the doors to the side chamber grated open, and the Council members came out. The people scurried back to their seats to hear the verdict.

Achan didn't want to know what the Council would say. Either way, life as he knew it would never be the same.

The prince came back and sat on his throne, accompanied by his Shield, Sir Kenton. The Kingsguard stood beside the throne and blocked Achan's view of Gidon.

When all the Council members were in their places at the high table, the chairman spoke. "We have verified the validity of Sir Gavin's claim. Master Achan Cham is the true son of King Axel Hadar."

Much of the audience broke out in applause. Some heckled. With Sir Kenton in the way, Achan could only see Gidon's ear, which was glowing red.

Lord Levy pounded his gavel, and the crowd quieted. "We are now ready to take a vote as to whom this Council feels would better serve Er'Rets as king."

Sir Gavin stood and clutched the shoulder of Achan's shirt. "Be ready to go. They will vote for Nathak's son.

They can better control him. And then we had better not be around."

Achan pulled his doublet on and fastened the laces with shaky fingers. At least it gave him something to do.

"Where will you go?" Sir Rigil asked.

"Into hiding for now," Sir Gavin said. "We need time to develop a plan."

"You will keep in touch with Prince Oren?"

"Aye."

Sir Rigil nodded. "We will stay with him then, and serve you however we can, though we must do our part to free the Duchess of Carm from her invaders."

Sir Gavin raised a bushy eyebrow at Achan and jerked his head toward Sir Rigil.

Achan realized Sir Rigil had been speaking to *him* when he'd said "serve you." He croaked, "Thanks."

Sir Caleb groaned softly. *You need much training in diplomacy. Tell him you wish we could be of assistance in that matter. That your prayers go with them.*

Achan regurgitated Sir Caleb's words. Sir Rigil thanked him. Bran bowed, face beaming with admiration. Achan caught Sparrow's glowing smile from behind Inko.

The chairman spoke. "Prince Oren Hadar of Arman. How do you cast your vote?"

"I vote for the true king, my nephew, the real Gidon Hadar, who is also known as Master Achan Cham."

Several people in the crowd cheered wildly. Tears threatened Achan's eyes. He blinked them back and berated himself for the weakness. What a great way to show what a kitten he was.

The chairman continued, "Sir Choresh Orson, Duke of Therion."

The hairy man said, "Master Achan Cham."

The crowd cheered again.

"Sir Dovev Falkson, Duke of Barth. How do you vote?"

"I vote in favor of Prince Gidon, the old one, that one." The grey-skinned man pointed to Prince Gidon, who sat sneering with folded arms.

The audience gave sporadic applause, though someone hissed. Gidon glared at Achan. If the people were this divided, what would that mean for the Council's authority? Or a king's reign? Would there be civil war?

"Silence!" the chairman banged his gavel, his black hat falling off his head. "I will have silence! To avoid confusion, from this point on, we will refer to the two men by their given names, Esek Nathak and Gidon Hadar."

Achan's eyes bulged. Well *that* wouldn't be at all awkward. Now he was Gidon?

The chairman replaced his drum-like hat. "Sir Herut Pitney, Duke of Nahar. How do you cast your vote?"

"Gidon Hadar."

The crowd clapped awkwardly, as if they too, were uncertain who that was.

"Sir Yagil Hamartano, Duke of Cela. How do you vote?"

No doubts there. Silvo's papa would certainly have heard of his son's humiliation at the hands of the stray squire.

"Esek Nathak."

Sparrow leaned to Achan's ear. "That these dukes would actually choose such a snake as their king . . . I cannot wrap my mind around this foolishness."

Achan huffed a laugh. "Am I so much better?"

Sparrow grinned. "You are one hundred leagues better. You must know that."

"I know nothing of the sort."

The chairman straightened in his chair. "I, Sir Abidan Levy, Duke of Allown and chairman to this proceeding, do vote for Esek Nathak."

Sparrow groaned.

The chairman said, "The vote is three to three. Lady Nitsa Amal, Duchess of Carm is not present. Lord Nathak is serving as her proxy as per Lady Nitsa's personal message."

Sparrow stood and strode toward the high table. "Lies!"

Achan straightened. What was the fool up to now?

"A forgery!" someone yelled.

"Nathak favors the pretender," someone else called. "He should get no vote!"

Sir Gavin stepped forward and addressed the chairman. "My Lord Chairman, certainly Lady Nitsa could not have known of this matter. Her proxy might not be given so surely in light of the deceit Lord Nathak has wielded all these years."

Lord Levy sighed. "Yet I see no other way. We cannot wait on this matter to send a messenger. Carmine is more than a week's journey."

"Surely you do not forget Lady Nitsa's bloodvoice ability? Why not ask your mediators to contact her?"

Lord Levy's chest swelled. "Surely *you* do not think me such a poor chairman to this Council, Sir Gavin. A page arrived with her letter of proxy before this meeting began. We have verified the signature as hers. We tried to bloodvoice Lady Nitsa for confirmation but she has not answered. I have no choice but to—"

"Is that not a sign of foul play? Lord Nathak has surely done something—"

"I have no choice but to accept the proxy at this time. I will send a Kingsguard squadron to Carmine after this proceeding to investigate. Today, however, my hands are bound. I must move on."

"My Lord Chairman, if I might speak?" Sparrow now stood before the high table, head held high as if he were the prince himself.

Sir Caleb leaned against Achan and whispered, "What's the lad up to?"

Achan shook his head.

Lord Levy raised his hand toward Sparrow, as if to say, "Why not?"

Sparrow cleared his throat. "Chairman Levy, my lord. I have information invaluable to this proceeding. I beg a private audience to discuss the matter."

Sir Gavin turned to Achan, bushy white eyebrows raised in question.

Achan shrugged. He had no idea what Sparrow was doing. Maybe he had more information about Lord Nathak's dealings with Macoun Hadar.

Lord Levy leaned forward to peer over the edge of the table. "What's this?"

"Please, my lord," Sparrow said. "A moment of your time to refute this . . . proxy."

24

Vrell lifted her chin. This was the only way. If she did not reveal herself now, they would vote for Lord Nathak's son. If the impostor were to take the throne, he might still seek Vrell's hand. She shivered. All along, the man who had sought her hand had been a fraud. Thank Arman he had been exposed. She would do her part to see the impostor fail.

"Apologies, my lord!" a wheezy voice said from the grandstands.

Vrell turned to see an old man creeping closer. It was Master Hadar!

"My apprentice vanished this morning," Master Hadar said. "I've been looking everywhere. Would someone please apprehend the runaway?"

Two Kingsguards rushed forward and seized Vrell's arms.

"No!" She twisted back to Lord Levy. "My lord, I beg you! Do not believe his lies. I am not what he claims. I—"

One of the guards clamped a hand over Vrell's mouth.

Master Hadar swept up beside her, Khai at his side. "Forgive me, my lord. This young stray is here without my consent. With your permission, I'll remove him."

Vrell thrashed and bit the hand covering her mouth. The guard did not flinch.

Lord Levy waved his hand in dismissal and banged his gavel. "Order please, and we will continue our vote."

The men dragged Vrell toward the door, and she squirmed to look over her shoulder. *Achan! Do not let them take me!*

Achan stared, mouth gaping. *What are you doing, Sparrow? Are you mad?*

I must confess. I am not who you think I—

Lord Levy's voice rang out in the chamber. "Lord Nathak, how do you vote?"

Vrell held her breath.

"I vote Esek Nathak the rightful king."

The crowd erupted in a divided chorus of cheering and booing.

The guards dragged Vrell through the door, past the tributes to great warriors, across the great foyer, and into a small chamber on the first floor. It looked just like Master Hadar's bloodvoicing room, empty but for a single wooden chair. They forced her to sit and bound her wrists and ankles with thin hemp twine.

She tried again, concentrating with all her strength. *Mother?*

There was still no answer.

She forced herself not to think about what might have happened to her mother and let her fear turn to anger.

"Untie me at once!" Vrell yelled. "How dare you treat me this way!"

Master Hadar looked down his pointed nose. "A stray mustn't speak to his master in such a manner, *boy*. Whatever are you thinking?" He motioned to Khai.

The weasel darted forward and uncapped a vial.

Vrell clamped her lips closed.

Master Hadar chuckled. "It's not what you think, my dear. I know the âleh flower has no effect on your mind. This is something more . . . basic."

Khai and the guard with the massive hands forced the liquid into her mouth. It was thin and tasted like bark. She tried not to swallow, but the guard covered her mouth and pinched her nose closed. She held off as long as possible, but as she ran out of air, she finally swallowed. The guard released her, and she sucked in a deep breath.

Vrell looked to her lap. Tears rained down on her tunic. She breathed in and out, calming herself, wondering what they had given her. She could not guess the ingredients from the taste. Her head spun, but that might be from the loss of air. She met Master Hadar's gaze. "Why are you doing this?" She glared at Khai. "What did he tell you?"

"More importantly, my dear child, is what he told our newly elected king."

Vrell looked from Khai to Master Hadar. Their faces blurred. "And what was that?"

"That he'd found His Majesty's elusive love. We've made a negotiation. You for Achan. The prince was all too willing. It seems he was going to get rid of his *squire* anyway."

Vrell wept from the injustice and from knowing she was about to pass out. They had given her some soporific. Her limbs tingled from its effect. "You cannot . . . Achan is . . . rightful . . . You cannot . . . locked up . . . serve your . . . ambitions." Her eyes drooped.

"Oh, but I can. Rightful king or not, Achan will soon be mine." Master Hadar leaned close, his face a beige blur. "Life isn't always fair, my dear, as I'm sure you know."

Achan. Vrell's head fell forward, eyes closed. *You must flee. Now!*

Sparrow? Sparrow!

Achan's sense of the boy vanished. He inched along the wall of the audience chamber behind Sir Gavin, heading toward the exit. Now was not the time to speak.

"Chairman Levy," Lord Nathak said at the high table. "What shall become of Achan? Of Gidon Hadar?"

Achan kept moving, but listened for the answer with trembling steps.

"I imagine he shall go to Armonguard and serve however our new king sees fit," the chairman said. "He is now second in line to the throne and must be available should anything—"

"You cannot suggest these two serve side by side?" Lord Nathak snapped. "It would be an assassination waiting to happen!"

Which was why Achan was enacting the exit-and-flee plan.

"The Council leaves that to the king and his many advisors. I trust it will not be long before Esek takes the throne."

Esek?

Sir Caleb reached the door first and pushed it open. It squeaked horribly. A guard outside the door raised his eyebrows.

"Sir Gavin leaves!" someone shouted from the stands.

Sir Caleb drew his sword. "Let's be quick about this, shall we?"

Inko and Sir Gavin ran past Sir Caleb, who knocked out the guard with the pommel of his sword. Achan quickly passed the old knights, mainly because their running was more like jogging. The group fled through the massive foyer, dodging around the yellow pillars, but New Kingsguard knights swarmed the entrance to the stronghold.

Sir Gavin and Inko drew their swords. Sir Gavin looked back, his gaze focused over Achan's shoulder. Achan turned to see Sir Caleb shove a display sword—ribbons and all—through the Council Chamber's door handles, locking it from the outside.

"Caleb," Sir Gavin said, "take Achan out the back. Hurry! We'll meet you there."

Sir Caleb sprinted deeper into the stronghold, dodging around pillars that reached above like redpines. He yelled over his shoulder, "Try to keep up, Your Highness."

Achan flinched at the title and ran after the knight. "Where are we going?"

Downstairs, Sir Caleb said to Achan's mind. *Sir Gavin will meet us with the boat.*

Achan concentrated on Sir Caleb's back, his blond hair, his wild eyes. *The dungeons, then?*

Sir Caleb slowed and grabbed Achan's shoulder. "My apologies, Your Highness. But no bloodvoicing for you until you are better trained. You've just announced our plans to anyone who can hear."

The blood drained from Achan's face.

"'Twas my fault. Best hurry, then." Sir Caleb sprinted around the rest of the pillars toward the grand staircase. He ran around to the back and started downstairs. Two flights down, he stopped on the landing and turned. "Change of plans. Back up the stairs. Quickly!"

Achan could see black Kingsguard cloaks approaching from the lower levels. He swiveled around and ran up the stairs and back into the foyer. Three Kingsguards approached from the entrance.

"This way." Sir Caleb ran to the far left of the foyer and sprinted into a corridor that stretched the length of the stronghold.

They made it halfway down before two Kingsguard knights stepped into the hallway from the other end. Sir Caleb spun and darted back to the foyer. Six guards spread out in an arc, inching toward them. Four more guards descended the stairs, boots pattering like rainfall as they spilled out onto the mosaic tile floor.

Sir Caleb pointed at Eagan's Elk. "Know how to use that?"

Achan drew the weapon, his hands trembling. "Aye."

Sir Caleb drew his own sword. Back to back, they inched into the center of the foyer as the black-cloaked Kingsguards circled around. The pillars acted as bars, further hemming them in. This didn't look like a battle they could win.

"Think positive, Your Highness," Sir Caleb muttered. "And please close your mind."

"Seize them!" Esek's voice rang out across the vast foyer.

Achan took quick, short breaths. Close his mind. Fight a battle of two against twenty. Answer to *Your Highness.* He'd had quite enough of this day. Regardless, he concentrated on the allown tree and raised his weapon to middle guard.

Behind him, someone clashed swords with Sir Caleb. Before Achan could turn to offer aid, a Kingsguard swung at him.

Achan stifled the blow with the flat of his blade and pushed off. Another guard struck. Achan ducked, and the guard's sword cracked against a pillar, sending bits of plaster over Achan's hair. He kicked the guard's knee in, and the man went down howling.

Achan sprinted left, desperately needing more space to work with. He turned abruptly, swinging Eagan's Elk at the soldier on his heels. His blade cut into the man's arm.

Achan winced but didn't have time to feel sorry. He jerked his blade free in time to parry a strike from another guard. Sir Caleb's shaggy blond mane twirled in his peripheral vision, then the knight collapsed. Achan screamed, but didn't have time to stop as he deflected blow after blow.

A shrill, familiar voice screamed, "Guards! Back away from the stray."

Achan's opponents drew back. Achan lowered his weapon and panted. He scanned the floor. Sir Caleb lay on his stomach, pinned by two guards, his face maroon with fury. Achan breathed a relieved sigh to find him alive. He quickly counted six bodies on the floor that were not.

Esek, the former Prince Gidon, raised a hand above his head and snapped. "Sir Kenton."

The Shield advanced from behind a pillar, gripping a thick sword in his hand. His steps on the mosaic tile were like the chop of an axe.

Achan lifted Eagan's Elk with his weary arms.

Forget his size and identity, Your Highness, Sir Caleb said to his mind. *He is just a man. Hold on until Sir Gavin and Inko get here. They are coming. Just hold on.*

Sir Kenton raised his weapon and paused.

Achan coached himself. If he could beat this man, he could go free. One man. That was all. One more win. Just one. And he didn't even have to beat him. He only needed to stall long enough until help arrived.

Sir Kenton finally lunged forward and swung for Achan's head. Achan waited, hands shaking, ready to block, and sure enough, Sir Kenton arched his sword the other way toward Achan's legs. Achan stepped back and parried.

Sir Kenton quickly worked Achan back against the wall. Achan barely managed to block the forceful cuts Sir Kenton delivered and, with each near miss, grew more uncertain of his ability to win. He didn't want to die, but how could he possibly defeat this adversary?

Where was his help? Achan opened his mind. *Sir Gavin?*

Hundreds of voices flooded into his mind at once. He quickly fortified his mind, but there were still so many voices. He turned to parry a strike and saw why.

A crowd had formed. The audience was pouring through the golden doors that led to the auditorium. Help was coming. Many of these people had cheered for him before. Surely someone in the crowd would step in. But the Kingsguard soldiers formed a wall, pushing the crowd back from where Achan and Sir Kenton fought until Achan could no longer see them.

Sir Kenton drove Achan back behind the staircase to the corridor. The Shield swung for Achan's neck. Achan blocked it, and the knight reversed his swing. Achan jumped back. He met the strike to his legs, but his sword slipped in his weakening hands. He fumbled for the briefest moment, and Sir Kenton batted it to the ground.

Achan slid back against the wall, his eyes glued to Sir Kenton's.

Esek clapped. "Well done, Sir Kenton, well done."

The knight lifted his sword to Achan's chest, then seized Achan's throat in his massive hand and squeezed.

Esek strutted forward and wove around Sir Kenton to stand at Achan's ear. He spoke softly. "You were a pitiful squire. Do you wish to take my throne?"

Airless, Achan croaked, "I . . . can't . . . "

"Oh, let him go, Sir Kenton."

Sir Kenton released his hold on Achan's neck but did not lower his sword.

Esek winkled his nose as if smelling something rank. "You may be the son of a *dead* king, but that does not make you king. The Council voted in favor of me."

Sir Caleb spoke from the floor. "Only because you're so weak they know they can control you."

Esek slowly turned to glare at Sir Caleb. "The gods have spoken, traitor. *I* am king. Nothing can change that now."

"You're mistaken," Sir Caleb said. "Arman will—"

"Save your breath, Sir Caleb," Achan said. "I don't want to be king."

Esek smirked. "I believe you. A stray could never handle the pressure of ruling a nation. And that's what you are. Whatever royal heritage you may have had is long gone. Back away, Sir Kenton."

Sir Kenton stepped aside but kept his sword out, as if daring Achan to move.

Achan stood still, eyes downcast. He was tired of fighting. He simply wanted to sit with Gren under the allown tree or listen to Minstrel Harp sing in the Corner.

Esek drew Ôwr from its scabbard and poised it over Achan's heart. "For some reason," Esek said, "Lord Nathak doesn't want you hurt. That, I never understood, even less so now that your true identity is revealed. If he wanted me to be king, why not kill you and be done with it?"

Achan couldn't help but wonder that himself. Or what was keeping Sir Gavin and Inko.

"So I ask myself, am I king?" Esek's eyes went wide, and he flashed a wicked smile. "What a coincidence. The Council says I am. Why, then, should I not have my way?" He traced an X over Achan's chest, Ôwr's tip scraping over the black leather doublet. "This was your father's sword. Did you know that? Soon you shall die by it."

"No!" Lord Nathak ran up behind Esek with Chora and a squadron of Kingsguards at his heels. "You must not do this."

Esek raised the weapon's tip to Achan's throat. "I've wanted to kill him ever since his ratty boot first stepped on my fine rug. Give me one reason—one real reason— why I shouldn't."

Lord Nathak said, "Because . . . "

"Why are you protecting him?"

Lord Nathak stuttered.

"I AM KING!" Esek screamed. "TELL ME THE TRUTH! NOW!"

Achan flinched as the sound resonated against the high ceiling.

Lord Nathak laid a hand on Esek's shoulder. "I will tell you, my son, I promise. But not here."

Esek shrugged Lord Nathak's hand off. "I am *not* your son." Esek remained still for a long moment, his face twitching with horrible expressions.

Lord Nathak glanced at Achan with his one eye then back to his son. "You may deny the truth all you want, Esek, but I did what I hoped was best for us all."

Achan stood motionless against the stone wall. Esek raised Ôwr's tip to Achan's ear and drew its edge down one cheek. Achan flinched at the sting. Then the other cheek. Achan closed his eyes and gritted his teeth. He could feel the blood ooze down both cheeks, tickling as it went.

Then Esek withdrew his sword and held it out to the side as if finished with it. Chora scurried forward and accepted the weapon.

Esek raised his voice in proclamation. "I shall kill you slowly, one nick at a time. But first a trade. My bride is being held hostage nearby and, for whatever reason, you are the price. I must deliver you unharmed if I am to secure her." He sighed dramatically. "But do not garner hope, stray. If you think I will not seize you back and kill you as soon as I have Averella by my side, you are a fool."

Esek turned to Lord Nathak. "Be careful where you place your loyalties, Lord Nathak, or your flesh too will sharpen my sword." Esek lifted his arm and snapped his fingers. "Chora, we depart for Armonguard shortly. Guards, secure my prize." Esek strode away, parting the Kingsguard squadron like a flame in parchment.

Lord Nathak glared at Achan. He turned and stalked after his son, his black Council cloak billowing behind.

Two Kingsguard knights approached Achan. One clamped irons onto his wrists. Achan sucked a sharp breath in through his teeth at his stinging cheeks. He kept his eyes shut, hoping that by not seeing what was happening he'd not fall further into despair. For there was truly no hope for him now. The guards jerked his arms and pulled him away.

25

Jax mi Katt.

Vrell took a deep breath and groaned. She did not want to wake.

Jax mi Katt.

Vrell opened her eyes. Her temples ached and her ears tingled. Someone was knocking in her mind. At the sight of the dark room, reality came rushing back. Khai and Macoun Hadar. They were going to hand her over to Prince Gidon. But he was not the real prince. He had always been an impostor. Achan was the real prince. Kind, sweet Achan.

Jax mi Katt.

Vrell opened her mind to the giant. *Jax?*

Vrell! Are you okay? Where have they taken you?

I . . . um . . . She looked around the barren chamber. A single torch, burned down to a stump, hung in a loop by the wooden door. *I am in a small chamber off the first-floor corridor. A servant's quarters, I think. It was the . . . third door on the right, I believe.*

How many are with you?

Vrell blinked. Where had all her captors gone? *I am alone.*

Good. I am coming for you. Hold tight.

A shiver ran up Vrell's arms. Could Jax help her before it was too late? And where were her captors? She was still bound to the chair. She twisted and pulled, but the ropes held tight.

What had happened to Achan? With Lord Nathak's illegal vote, the Council had elected the impostor. Would they let Achan go free? She doubted it. She closed her eyes and reached for him.

She sensed movement . . . pain. His surroundings came into focus. The main staircase off the foyer, going down. Achan's wrists were shackled and his face throbbed. Vrell winced. Had someone struck him?

The sound of stone grating on stone jerked Vrell away from Achan's plight. She looked over her shoulder. Mags, the serving girl from the kitchen, stood in a dark opening in the wall, holding a torch.

Mags scurried to Vrell's chair. "Yeh poor thing. What've they done to yeh? And all 'cause yeh don't want to 'prentice fer that creepy, ol' fool." Mags laid the torch aside carefully and untied Vrell's wrists. "Well, I say yer a smart boy fer wantin' to get away from 'Master' Hadar."

All Vrell could say was, "Thank you."

Mags untied Vrell's ankles and motioned toward the stone door. "Go on in. 'Tis a secret passage. I know it's a bit creepy at first, but it's the best way to move through the castle without being seen."

Vrell stepped through the dark doorway and into a cool, stone passageway. The flickering torch in Mags's hand cast a circle of yellow light in her immediate position, but Vrell could see only blackness beyond the torchlight in either direction.

Mags stepped in after her and pulled the stone door closed. It swung with a grating sound that raised goose pimples on Vrell's arms. When it was closed, Mags lifted the torch and led Vrell down the dark, narrow passage that smelled of mildew.

"Jax said to get yeh to the kitchens. He'd of come hisself, but he's too tall for this route." Mags giggled.

Vrell nodded and scurried along behind Mags, praising Arman every step of the way.

"Hold."

The guards jerked Achan to a stop on the landing between the first and second lower levels.

The guard who had been leading them whirled around with his sword in hand.

Achan's heart thudded. What was this?

They stood on the far side of the landing between the two floors. A lone torch burned from an iron loop on the wall.

"Trizo," said the guard on Achan's right. "What are you doing?"

"The keys, Jarek," the guard with the sword said.

Jarek reached to his belt and drew his sword instead. The third guard followed suit. "You cannot beat us both," Jarek said.

A wide smile stretched across Trizo's face. "I don't have to."

Footsteps pattered on the stairs below. Sir Rigil and Bran stepped into view on the landing, swords drawn.

Bran flashed a wide smile. "Hello, Achan."

"Bran!" Sir Rigil snapped.

Bran's pink face darkened a shade. "Sorry. Hello, Your Highness."

Achan managed a nervous laugh. "That's really not necessary."

Trizo lifted his weapon. "The key?"

Jarek lowered his sword and held out a single key on a scrap of leather. "You'll hang."

Trizo snagged the key from Jarek. "Not when *he* takes the throne," he said, nodding at Achan. "And he will. Let go of him, now, and back away, both of you."

The guards released Achan's arms and stepped back.

Trizo waved him over. "This way, Your Highness."

Achan stepped to Trizo's side in a daze, shocked at his good fortune.

The third guard spoke. "You know we'll report you as soon as we walk away."

Sir Rigil drew his sword and jutted his head at the guards. "Which is why you won't walk away." Sir Rigil jerked his sword up the stairs. "Up you go, quickly now."

The guards turned and climbed the stairs.

Bran followed and spoke over his shoulder: "See you later, *Your Highness*."

Achan smiled in spite of himself.

Trizo led Achan down the stairs to the bottommost level. There they followed a long corridor that stretched out the length of the stronghold just like the one on the entry level had. Trizo tapped his fingers lightly on each door they passed, as if counting. He stopped in front of a battered narrow door. He knocked three times, coughed, then knocked twice again. The door swung open to a servant's chamber decorated with a rough-hewn table and sleeping pad. They entered and the door swished shut behind them.

Achan turned to see Prince Oren twist the lock on the door. The prince, in his fine clothes, looked very out of place in the shabby room.

Prince Oren's taut lips stretched into a wide smile. "Achan, my boy. It's good to see you! What happened to your face?"

"Gidon—er, Esek." Achan shook his head.

Prince Oren took Achan's chin in thumb and two fingers and turned it from side to side. "He did this, but did not kill you?"

Achan swallowed, shaken by Prince Oren's intense scrutiny. "He said he needed to trade me for his bride first. Said someone holds the lady hostage and wants to exchange her for me."

"Lady Mandzee?"

"No. Lady Averella Amal."

Prince Oren's brows sank and he gripped Achan's shoulder. "Truly? I had heard she was safely hidden. This is most distressing. I hope the poor child is all right. Should Esek get hold of her, Nitsa will never forgive me." He patted Achan's shoulder. "Your wounds need tending, but there is nothing I can do here. They are not life-threatening, and my priority is to see you safely out of this castle."

"Will you be taking me out?"

Prince Oren gave a tight smile. "I'm afraid that would be unwise. The knights can get you out unseen."

"You really believe I'm . . . who they . . . Your . . . "

"Aye, I do."

"Why?"

"Because I know Esek is false, and I know Arman has not spoken to me as king."

Achan tilted his head at Prince Oren. "You as king?"

"I am King Axel's brother, as you know. But if Arman had chosen me to serve as king, He would be speaking to me, preparing me, guiding me." Prince Oren sat back on the mattress. "Has he spoken to you, Achan?"

Achan opened his mouth to explain about the voice he'd heard in the Council chambers and elsewhere, but a noise outside stopped him.

Three knocks, a cough, and two more knocks sent Trizo to the door. He opened it, and Sir Rigil and Bran slipped inside. They appeared out of breath but exhilarated.

Bran wiped his hands on his doublet. "Two enemy guards are taken care of, Your Highness—Highnesses."

Achan chuckled despite the pain in his cheeks.

"Shall we leave, then?" Sir Rigil asked.

"Aye." Prince Oren removed a ring from his pinky finger. He took Achan's hand and set the ring on it. "You are also a mirror image of my big brother when he was your age. We share the same blood, you and I. On that you can take my word. This ring will bring you help if shown to the right people. Sir Gavin will know who to trust. Stay with him, Sir Inko, or Sir Caleb at all costs. Obey them, for they know best how to make things right."

Prince Oren walked to the door. "You and I have much to discuss, Achan. When you are safe and have learned the basics, bloodvoice me. Hold the ring when you do, and it will be easier. Until then, my nephew, I bid thee well."

Achan glanced at the ring. At the top of the wide circle of gold, the shape of a castle was engraved with the letters OAH. He blinked rapidly to deflect the mist wetting his eyes. He gazed at Prince Oren, at his blue eyes and the thin crown of gold nestled into his black hair. This man was truly his family—his blood uncle. He was no longer a stray. He had family. Perhaps he was no longer even *Achan*. He stifled a shaky breath and stuffed the ring on his middle finger.

Prince Oren drew him into a quick embrace and patted him on the back. "Go."

Achan followed Sir Rigil to the door.

"Wait, men," Prince Oren said. "I've had news of Lady Averella."

Bran straightened. "What news?"

"Achan tells me Esek planned to trade him for her. That someone is holding her captive."

"How could that be?" Bran's eyes darted wildly around the room, as if this girl might jump out from under a rug. "I was told she was in hiding."

"I do not know. I just wanted you to be aware of the situation. Once Achan is safe, I will do all I can to help you find her."

Sir Rigil gripped Bran's shoulder. "And I."

Achan looked at the floor. He shouldn't feel guilty about this situation. He'd never once laid eyes on Lady Averella of Carmine, after all. Yet he felt responsible for her somehow. Esek had agreed to trade her for him. What would become of her when Achan didn't show? "Maybe if I went along with the exchange, and you were watching, you could get the lady to safety, then come for me later."

Bran's lips curved in a small smile. "I thank you, Your Highness, but no. It's too risky. Plus, Averella would maim me if she found out I had risked the true king 'just' to help her. She hates Prince Gidon—forgive me: *Esek*—more than anything."

Achan grinned. "A sign of her good taste."

"And we have no proof anyone truly holds her captive," Prince Oren said. "This is not your worry, Achan. We will see to Lady Averella once you are safe."

Achan nodded, and Sir Rigil led him into the hallway. Bran and Trizo followed. The men went slowly back down the corridor toward the stairs, watching for guards as they went.

Mags slid open a wooden screen and peered through a tiny hole in the wall. "All clear." She pushed the wall, and it swung open like a door, scraping the floor lightly. Light flooded through the opening, revealing a cellar the size of Vrell's chambers upstairs. "Jax said he'd meet yeh here."

"Thank you, Mags."

"Aw, 'twas nothin'."

Vrell hugged the serving girl and stepped into the cellar. The room overflowed with baskets, barrels, and sacks of food. Mags pulled the door closed, which turned out to be a shelf stocked with flour.

More than one set of footsteps sent Vrell ducking behind a barrel of pickles. She held her breath, hoping she would not be caught so soon after having escaped.

She heard Sir Rigil's voice. "Sir Caleb was supposed to meet us here."

Then came a voice as familiar as a dream. Bran's voice. "I hope he wasn't caught again."

Vrell tingled with joy and indecision. What should she do? Should she reveal herself? This was her best chance to speak with Sir Rigil. And there was no time to spare. If Lord Nathak's men had done something to her mother, she needed to get home right away.

"Bran," Sir Rigil said, "run up and see if Prince Oren can make contact with Sir Caleb. Have him find out where he is."

"Aye, sir."

Vrell heard the slapping of boots on stone. And just like that, Bran was gone.

Sir Rigil spoke to someone else. "Are you sure you're all right? Those cuts look nasty."

"I'm fine."

Vrell peeked over the pickle barrel. She spotted Achan, his face covered in blood. He leaned back against the wall and slid down to a sitting position, straightening his legs out in front.

Tears flooded Vrell's eyes and she stood. "Achan! What's happened?"

Sir Rigil drew his sword, and Achan dove away from the wall.

Vrell flinched and met Achan's eyes. His head cocked to the side. He huffed and leaned back against the wall. "You. Sparrow, where did you come from? And what's with you today? What was that stunt you pulled at the Council meeting?"

Vrell ran to him and crouched at his side. The cuts on his cheeks were not so deep, but they needed to be tended or they would scar terribly. "How did this happen?"

"Just *Esek* venting a little steam."

"Oh, Achan." She stood and her foot caught on something. She looked down. His scabbard was empty. "Where is your sword?"

Achan's expression drooped. "Lost. I dropped it when Sir Kenton bested me. The guards took me away, and I don't know if anyone picked it up."

"I am so sorry. What a terrible loss."

Vrell took in the shelves that filled the wall behind Sir Rigil. They were stocked with baskets of apples, pears, onions, and turnips. A shelf of hard bread lined the next wall. Vrell took a deep breath and her stomach pinged at the scents of food.

Sir Rigil sheathed his weapon. "You're Hadar's apprentice. The one they dragged out of the Council chambers." He turned to Achan. "You sure you trust this lad?"

Achan sighed. "I don't know who to trust anymore. Every time I think I'm on the right track, something happens to prove me wrong."

Vrell opened her mouth to speak, to reveal to Sir Rigil who she really was and perhaps hasten the rescue of her mother. But no words came. How embarrassing to admit such deceit in front of Achan—her king—especially when he felt he could trust no one. Maybe she could wait until he was away. Then he never need know.

Her ears tingled.

Jax mi Katt.

Vrell let him in. *Jax?*

Are you safe now?

Yes. Thank you.

I have your sword. I ran into a blacksmith's apprentice, who mentioned you had it commissioned. I paid the balance. Would you like it before you go?

Vrell clapped her hands. "Yes!" *Oh, Jax, thank you!*

"Are you talking to someone, Sparrow?" Achan asked.

"Yes. Just a minute. Achan, this is a cellar. Grab a sack and collect some food for your journey. If you are to go with Sir Gavin, he might not have had time to gather supplies."

Sir Rigil's jaw dropped like a drawbridge.

Achan held up his hands. "Hey! Who's the king? You or me?" But he smirked at Sir Rigil and clambered to his feet. "As if I don't know what a kitchen cellar looks like. I only slept in one all my life."

Sir Rigil glared at Vrell. He dumped out a sack of potatoes and started filling it with chunks of bread from the back shelf.

Jax voiced to Vrell. *You deserve proper training to go with this weapon. Perhaps our new king can teach you.*

You will not serve Esek?

I never really did. I am a Mârad spy, Vrell. I served Prince Oren Hadar until he swore fealty to the true king. Now I serve that king myself. Can I do anything else for him or you?

Vrell looked at Achan, who cradled a pile of green apples in his arms, holding the top one under his chin. A thick stripe of blood dripped down his cheeks, off his jaw, and onto the apples.

Vrell wrinkled her nose. *I need the satchel from my room. It is my healing kit. The king was wounded.*

I shall bring it right away. You are in the cellar?

Vrell paused a long moment. She trusted Jax, but if she was wrong, it would be a terrible mistake. *The first kitchen.*

I'll be there soon.

Vrell turned to Achan. "Someone is coming with my healing kit so I can tend to your wounds. I suggest you stay here in case he turns out to be against you. I do not think he is, but it is best not to risk it."

Sir Rigil gave the bag of bread a spin. "Who is this person?"

"His name is Jax mi Katt. He is a Kingsguard giant from—"

"I know him," Sir Rigil said. "He's on our side. Still, it's best he doesn't see us. That way, if he's interrogated he won't know anything. Let us hide ourselves, Your Highness."

"Fine." Achan bit into an apple, then froze, eyes narrowed, jaw stiff. "That hurts."

"Then do not eat," Vrell said.

He pouted. "But I'm hungry. In case you forgot, we didn't have breakfast or lunch."

"Then eat bread or something soft."

Achan dug his thumbnail into his apple, ripped out a chunk, and slid it into his mouth.

Vrell rolled her eyes.

Jax's voice came like a whisper, *Vrell?*

"He is coming," Vrell said. "Go."

The corner of Achan's mouth curved up. "As you wish, Your Highness."

Vrell sneered as Sir Rigil ushered Achan to the shelves filled with flour sacks. She had had her fill of his teasing. It would be nice to be a woman again and spend time in the company of people with manners. In Bran's company, especially.

Vrell hurried out into the first kitchen and made her way past cooks and servants bustling between the tables and hearths. The smells of fresh bread, pheasant, and mince pies set Vrell's stomach to growling. She had not eaten a bite all day, either.

A massive shadow spilled through the doorway and over the stone floor. Jax ducked inside. He smiled down, eyes twinkling, and held up a steel sword and her satchel.

"Afternoon, Mr. Jax," a serving girl said. "You hungry?"

"Not now, thanks. I've just come to see Master Sparrow."

The serving girl smiled and went back to her kettle.

Vrell led Jax to the far corner of the kitchen, where they would be out of the way. She took the satchel and draped its strap over her head and one arm. "Thank you, Jax, so much."

He shook the sword. "You know how to wear one of these?"

"I am certain I can manage."

He lowered his bulk onto his knees and waved her over. Vrell stepped toward him. He drew a metal ring out of his pocket. "Untie your belt." Vrell did and Jax took it from her. He looped the cord through the metal ring, securing it with a knot so it wouldn't slip. Then he handed it back. "You need this to hold your weapon, since you have no scabbard or sheath."

Vrell retied the belt over her tunic so the ring sat over her left hip. Jax handed her the sword and she threaded the point through the loop. The metal hung at her side, resting against her leg. She beamed. Now she could protect herself on the journey home, though traveling with Sir Rigil and Bran, she would surely have no need.

"Don't go using that without training. You can get yourself killed in a wink."

"I shall be careful."

Vrell? Jax voiced.

"Yes?"

Are you truly all right going with the men?

She had no plans to go with Achan once she revealed her identity to Sir Rigil. Still, it might be better if Jax thought she had. Then, if rumors spread, Esek and Master Hadar would not look for her in the castle. She didn't know how long it would take Sir Rigil to sneak her to a safe place. *Of course,* she thought to Jax. *I am getting away from those who seek to exploit my skill. I will be with the true king and Sir Gavin. I will be fine.*

Aye. But they are men, and you are not.

The blood drained from Vrell's face. Had Khai confided his discovery to Jax? She studied the giant's soft and caring expression. *How long have you known?*

Since I first saw you. He smirked. *You do not smell like a man.*

Vrell's eyes went wide, then she laughed. "I am so happy you were on my side."

"As am I, Vrell."

She said farewell—in case she never saw him again—with a big hug, then hurried back through the second kitchen to the cellar.

The room appeared empty. "Hello? Sir Rigil?"

A hand popped out from behind the shelf stocked with flour sacks. "In here."

The secret passage. Vrell found the crack and squeezed through.

On the other side of the door, everything went dark. She bet this tunnel continued on to the canals. She felt along the wall. "Sir Rigil?"

"He's left." Achan's voice came from very near Vrell's right shoulder. It made her jump. "It's just us," he said.

"And we should have left by now." Sir Caleb spoke from near Achan. "Have you got what you need to mend Achan's wounds?"

Vrell shuddered, tears stinging her eyes. No Sir Rigil? No Bran? They must have left when Vrell had been speaking with Jax. If only she had stayed in the cellar. "But where are they? Won't they be joining us?"

"No. They've gone back to assist Prince Oren," Achan said.

"Boy?" Sir Caleb said. "Have you got it?"

"Uh . . . y-yes. Yes, I have it."

"Good. Let's go then. The sooner we get Achan out of here the better for everyone."

But Vrell wanted to stay. She wanted to be with Bran. She needed to go home. A heavy tear fell down her cheek. She *could* reveal herself now, but . . .

A flame whooshed to life and Achan and Sir Caleb's faces appeared in the darkness. They looked orange and shadowed. Sir Gavin carried the torch down the tunnel. Achan shot Vrell a crooked grin, then touched his cheek as if the smile had been painful. He stumbled after Sir Gavin.

He needed her help. How awful for her to even consider deserting her king. Poor Achan. He had had the most terrible day. Vrell had forgotten that this morning Achan had been a stray and now he was king of Er'Rets. She could serve her king a while longer, could she not?

She sniffled and scurried to keep up with the men's long strides.

Achan sat in the center of a small boat, clutching two moist handkerchiefs to his face, at Sparrow's insistence. The boy had said they had some kind of healing ointment on them.

Inko paddled the boat through the mist. The water smelled rank and slapped against the sides of their boat, no doubt leaving a line of green slime. The Evenwall muted the afternoon sun, and the damp air clung to Achan's face like sweat. Or was that blood? Achan could only see a foot or two of the scummy water on any side of the boat.

Sparrow and Sir Caleb sat in the bow. Sir Gavin and Inko sat in the back. The two knights had rescued Sir Caleb when Sir Rigil and Bran had rescued Achan. They had been waiting in the cave when Achan, Sir Caleb, and Sparrow had arrived.

Achan looked the boy over. Sparrow sat on the front bench facing him, mixing something gooey in a jar with a stick. The boy's eyes were puffy as if he'd spent the day bawling. He still hadn't explained his behavior in the Council chambers that morning. Achan didn't entirely trust the little fox. His eyes caught sight of a sword hanging from Sparrow's belt.

"Where'd you get the blade?"

Sparrow's wide eyes darted to his. "I bought it. Jax delivered it with my satchel." He glanced down. "Where did you get yours? I thought you lost it."

"He did. Twice," Sir Caleb said. "And twice we've rescued it for him."

Achan looked at his boots. He was so thankful Sir Caleb had found Eagan's Elk. If only he could learn to use it as well as Sir Kenton used his. He sighed. He couldn't believe the incredible turn his life had taken. He didn't want to think about it, which wasn't difficult, considering their destination. They would soon enter Darkness, a place Achan didn't want to go.

He turned to Sir Gavin. "I thought you said never go into Darkness."

"Aye, that I did."

"And yet toward it we go?"

Sir Gavin glanced at a sign on a building that they were gliding past. It read: Tanner. "Aye, that we do."

"Won't we all go crazy in there?"

"Not if we stay together. And right now we need a place to hide."

Great. Achan had gone from an invisible nothing to a hunted king. Way back in that barn in Sitna, when he'd rescued Mox from Riga and Harnu, when he'd longed to change his station, he'd simply wanted a cottage of his own and the right to wear whatever color pleased him. Now look at him. "Do you have a plan?"

Sir Gavin chuckled. "Of course I have a plan. We head for Tsaftown."

"Lady Tara lives in Tsaftown." Achan's heartbeat upped a notch at the idea of seeing her again. Would their meeting be different with his new identity? He couldn't help but grin. "How long will it take to get there?"

Sparrow clunked the jar down on the bench and ripped the handkerchief away from Achan's right cheek.

"Ow! Take it easy, will you?"

"Sorry," Sparrow mumbled.

It was not yet dark in the Evenwall, though it had to be nearing dusk. Few boats were out on the narrow canal they traveled. Inko wanted to steer clear of the main waterways, for fear that they were being watched.

"Tsaftown is a very long journey," Sir Gavin said. "Much longer in Darkness. And we are without horses. We could have Sir Rigil bring our horses to Allowntown, but it will take us almost a week on foot to reach them."

"So, maybe a month to reach Tsaftown?" Achan asked as Sparrow swabbed his cheek with something cool.

"Or more."

Achan sighed. A long time, but at least seeing Lady Tara was something to look forward to. He did not relish entering

Darkness, nor did he look forward to upcoming arguments in which Sir Gavin would try to turn him into a king. At least now he understood why Sir Gavin had never accepted the service he'd tried to give him as a squire.

Sparrow spread more gunk from his jar over Achan's cheek. It seeped into his cuts and burned. "Ow!"

"Oh, stop being such a girl," Sparrow said.

Achan tried to block out the pain. "What do we seek in Tsaftown?"

"Not Tsaftown, exactly," Sir Gavin said. "Ice Island."

"Ice Island?" Sparrow cried.

Achan wondered too what they sought in the biggest prison in Er'Rets.

"We have friends to set free there," Sir Gavin said. "Friends wrongly imprisoned. That's where I went when Lord Nathak banished me. I was hoping to raise an army and come back for you. I ran out of time."

"What friends?" Achan asked.

"Old Kingsguard friends."

Sparrow looked terrified. Then his lips curved in a goofy grin and his cheeks flushed. "I am going to do the other side now."

Achan raised his eyebrows and turned his head. "Thanks for the warning."

Sparrow gently pulled the handkerchief away and swabbed Achan's cheek. He slathered gunk on, then froze, his fingers pressed against Achan's wound, and looked up.

The light faded, and Sparrow's face vanished before Achan's eyes.

They had entered Darkness.

NOT THE END

This is the end of the book 1 of the *Blood of Kings* series. Book 2 continues the adventures of Vrell and Achan as they flee into Darkness to avoid Esek's wrath. Sign up for newsletters from Marcher Lord Press or Jill Williamson's Web site to get updates on the status of *To Darkness Fled: Blood of Kings, Book 2.*

A Note from the Author

Thanks for reading *By Darkness Hid*, the first installment in the Blood of Kings series.

I'd like to hear from you. E-mail me with your thoughts on the book and sign up for my free mailing list to get updates on the next book and my upcoming events. If you'd like to help make this book a success, tell people about it, loan your copy to a friend, or ask your library or bookstore to order it. If you want to do more, check out the other ways you can help on my Web site under: Be an Influencer.

If you post a review of my book on Amazon.com and/or BarnesandNoble.com and e-mail me the link, I will enter you in a monthly drawing to win some great prizes. Check my Web site to see what the prize is for the current month.

My e-mail is: info@jillwilliamson.com.

If you'd like to download discussion questions, see the book trailer, or explore Er'Rets a bit more with my interactive map, check out my Web site: www.jillwilliamson.com.

Acknowledgments

Writing a book is as much of an adventure as reading one. There have been many who've joined me on my quest to write this story.

I am so thankful to God, that He's allowed this little desire of my heart to come to pass. Thank You, Yahweh. You are so very good to me.

Brad Williamson is amazing for putting up with this time-consuming activity of mine. I have the world's best husband. Without his listening ear, I'd have to talk to myself, which I have been known to do, but . . . yeah. A huge thanks to my B-radley. I'm so thankful God put us together for life.

Luke and Kaitlyn Williamson, my fabulous children, allowed Momma to sit at that computer again and again! My kids are so wonderful, and they love to read. Luke is working on his own science fiction stories now. Keep your eyes out for *Eukeylukey Goes to Mars.* It's a real page-turner.

Pastor Joe encouraged me to write, even when I doubted. He read my first chapter, went with me to my first writer's conference, joined my first "critique" group when everyone else's was full, and told me to write something else when my first book was driving me insane. He specifically said to write a breakout novel, so let's not let him down, okay? He's a super smart guy. That's why he's my new apprentice.

I'm thankful that Jeff Gerke likes what I write and published my story. This has been lots of fun, and it wouldn't have happened without Jeff and Marcher Lord Press.

To the members of the Christian Young Adult Writers and Readers critique group—specifically Andrea, Debbie, Diana, Elizabeth, Gretchen, Mary, Sarah, Shelley, Stephanie, and Vernona—they are all so amazing. I have never known a more dedicated and hardworking group of people. Thanks to all of them for their edits and feedback. This book would not be the same without them. I'm honored to write with them.

A special thanks to Diana Sharples, who started the critique group. She is an answer to prayer in so many ways. Not only did she provide a place for us young adult writers to connect, but she also gave wonderful insight on my book and bought me the Medieval Swordsmanship (Paladin Press) book that was filled with invaluable research.

Which leads me to mention John Clements, author of Medieval Swordsmanship, for writing such an honest, detailed, and fascinating book on this subject. He really helped me understand what the sword was all about.

Peter J. Grant, member of ACFW, answered my plea for a medieval doctor. His assistance brainstorming how one might treat arrow wounds was excellent. All credit goes to Peter for the spider webs!

And last, but never least, Christopher Burke, my very first reader for this book. His words of encouragement made me so excited to write more.

And so now I write the next one. What fun!